MATCHED *by* MISTAKE

Three cases of mistaken identity spark some unexpected matches.

Case #1: An arrogant millionaire mistakes his beautiful new employee for a woman who wronged his family...and he seeks a shocking revenge.

Case #2: A lonely bachelor thinks he telephoned his sister, but his conversation with a sultry-voiced stranger leads to a very unusual long-distance romance....

Case #3: A powerful and handsome Englishman unwittingly kisses his fiancée's exact double, then falls in love with *her* instead!

MATCHED *by* MISTAKE

Or a match made in heaven?

Relive the romance...

Three complete novels by your favorite authors!

About the Authors

Penny Jordan—Born in Preston, Lancashire, England, Penny Jordan now lives with her husband in a beautiful fourteenth-century house in rural Cheshire. Penny has been writing for over ten years and, with over thirty million copies of her books in print, she is one of the most well-known names in contemporary romance.

Gina Wilkins—Gina Wilkins had her first novel published in 1987 and, since then, has written more than thirty books, which have been sold in over one hundred countries. Gina consistently appears on bestseller lists and has received numerous awards. A native of central Arkansas, she still resides there with her husband and three children.

Carole Mortimer—Carole Mortimer grew up the youngest of three children in a small Bedfordshire village. She still loves nothing more than going "home" to visit her family. In her mid-thirties, Carole has three very active sons, four cats—and very little time for hobbies! She is a successful and talented author of over eighty romance novels.

MATCHED by MISTAKE

Penny Jordan
Gina Wilkins
Carole Mortimer

Harlequin Books

TORONTO • NEW YORK • LONDON
AMSTERDAM • PARIS • SYDNEY • HAMBURG
STOCKHOLM • ATHENS • TOKYO • MILAN
MADRID • WARSAW • BUDAPEST • AUCKLAND

HARLEQUIN BOOKS

by Request—Matched by Mistake

Copyright © 1996 by Harlequin Books S.A.

ISBN 0-373-20123-0

The publisher acknowledges the copyright holders
of the individual works as follows:
PASSIONATE PROTECTION
Copyright © 1983 by Penny Jordan
HOTLINE
Copyright © 1991 by Gina Wilkins
FORBIDDEN SURRENDER
Copyright © 1982 by Carole Mortimer

CONTENTS

Two reluctant enemies in
a love-hate relationship!

PASSIONATE PROTECTION

Penny Jordan

CHAPTER ONE

'HONESTLY, JESS, I don't know what that family of yours would do without you,' Colin Weaver told his assistant with a wry smile. 'Well, what is it this time? Has your aunt locked herself out again, or your uncle forgotten to collect his new cheque book?'

'Neither,' Jessica Forbes told him, hiding her own smile. It was true that her aunt and uncle did tend to ring her at work for assistance every time there was a family crisis, but they weren't really used to the hectic pace of the modern-day commercial world—Uncle Frank, for instance, still lived in a pre-war daydream fostered by the leisurely pace of life in the small market town legal practice he had inherited from his father, and Aunt Alice wasn't much better; nervous, dithery, she was given to complaining in bewilderment that life had changed so much, she barely recognised it anymore, and as for Isabel! Jessica sighed; the problems dumped on her by her eighteen-year-old cousin made those of her aunt and uncle seem mere nothings.

'Okay, okay, I'm sorry for criticising your beloved family,' Colin apologised with a wry smile. 'I suppose I'm just jealous really,' he admitted plaintively. 'Would you drop everything and come running for me if I locked myself out?'

'It wouldn't do any good if I did,' Jessica pointed out with a grin. 'You live in a penthouse apartment, my aunt and uncle live in a rambling old vicarage with a pantry window that simply won't close, but which neither of them can fit through, whereas yours truly...'

'Umm, I'm beginning to get the point,' Colin agreed, glancing appreciatively over her slender five-foot-eight frame, 'but that doesn't stop me from wishing they would stop depriving me of your valuable assistance.'

'I have to go this time—it's Isabel.' Jessica frowned, chewing the soft fullness of her bottom lip, dark eyebrows drawn together in a worried frown. The problem was that her aunt and uncle had been slipping gently into middle age when Isabel had arrived unexpectedly on the scene and neither of them had ever totally recovered from the shock.

'Oh, Isabel,' Colin said grimly. 'That girl's lethal,' he added with a grimace. 'I remember when you brought her here...'

'Here' was his exclusive London salon where he showed the alluring ranges of separates that bore his name. Jessica had worked for him ever since she left art school. She loved her job as his assistant, and if he needed mollycoddling occasionally, he more than made up for his lapses when they were over. In Jessica's view there was no one to match him in the design of separates. His secret, he had told her on more than one occasion, lay as much in the careful choice of fabric as the style the materials were eventually made up in. 'Couture Classics' were how *Vogue* described them, and Jessica reckoned there could be few wealthy women in Britain aspiring to the well-dressed lists who didn't have something of his in their wardrobe. For some clients he designed individual ranges, but it was, as Jessica knew, his great dream to take his designs and elegance into the high streets at prices every woman could afford.

'She is a little immature,' Jessica agreed, repressing a sigh at the thought of her cousin—pretty, headstrong Isabel, who reminded her of a frisky lamb, throwing herself headlong into whatever came her way on a momentary whim.

'She's exactly two years younger than you were when you first came to work for me,' Colin reminded her a little grimly. 'You all keep that girl wrapped up in too much cotton wool, Jess, you spoil her, and she laps it up. What were you doing at eighteen? I bet you weren't still living at home, financed by Mummy and Daddy?'

'No,' Jessica agreed sombrely. Her parents had died three months before her eighteenth birthday. They had been killed in a car crash on their way home from visiting friends. She could still remember Uncle Frank trying to break the news; Aunt Alice's white face. They had offered her a home, of course, but by then she had her career planned, first art school and then, she hoped, a job in fashion design, and so instead she had used some of the money left to her by her parents and had bought herself a small flat in London, but she had stayed in close contact with her aunt and uncle; after all, they were the only family she had left, and as she grew older the ties between them had strengthened. Family came to mean a lot when there was so little of it left.

Isabel had been a little girl of ten at the time of the accident, too young to remember very much about Jessica's parents, and somehow Jessica had found that as the years went by she was called upon to mediate between impatient youth and dismayed late middle age in the storms that swept the household as Isabel grew into her teens, Isabel urging her to support her on the one hand, while her parents were pleading with Jessica to 'make Isabel realise' on the other.

The plan was that Isabel would go on to university after leaving school, but in the sixth form she had suddenly decided that she was tired of studying, that she didn't want a career at all, and so at eighteen she was working in her father's office, and complaining bitterly to Jessica about it whenever they met.

'I wanted to talk to you about our visit to Spain as well,' Colin said sulkily, interrupting her train of thought. Jessica gave him a teasing smile. At forty-eight he could sometimes display all the very worst characteristics of a little boy in the middle of a tantrum, and he was not above doing so to make her feel guilty or get her attention when he felt the need arise. Jessica excused him on the grounds that he was a first-rate designer and an excellent employer, flexible and with sufficient faith in her ability to make her job interesting. The Fabric Fair was something he had been dangling in front of her for several months. Initially he had planned to go alone, and then he had suggested that she should go with him. He heard by word of mouth about a Spanish firm who had discovered a series of new dyes for natural fibres, and that the results were stunningly spectacular. Their fabrics were sold only to the most exclusive firms, and Jessica knew that Colin was angling for an introduction to their Managing Director.

'I don't know whether I'll be able to go,' Jessica frowned, hiding a sudden shaft of amusement as his manner changed from smug satisfaction to anxious concern.

'Not that damn family of yours again!' he protested. 'This time you'll have to tell them to do without you. I need you, Jess,' he told her plaintively.

'Very well, but no more unkind comments about Isabel,' she reprimanded him severely. 'I know she's a little headstrong . . .'

'Headstrong! Stubborn as a mule would be a better description, but I can see nothing I have to say is going to have any effect on you, so you may as well finish early tonight.'

COLIN REALLY was a love, Jessica reflected fondly an hour later, opening the door to her flat. They had an excellent working relationship, and if she sometimes chafed against his avuncular manner it was a small price to pay for working with such a talented and experienced man. There was no one to follow him in the business, and he had already mentioned that he might be prepared to offer her a partnership if things went well. They would make a good team, he had told her, and Jessica agreed. In spite of his experience, he would always listen to her suggestions, and often adopted them.

She grimaced at her reflection as she caught sight of it in the mirror. She had hurried away from the office without combing her hair or renewing her lipstick, and both looked untidy; her lipstick because she constantly nibbled on her lower lip, and her hair from running impatient fingers through its sable length.

Without doubt her hair was her greatest asset, in her eyes; long, thick and glossy, it fell smoothly past her shoulders in a gentle bell. Sometimes she twisted it into an elegant chignon, on those days when Colin wanted her to meet clients and she wanted to create the right impression. One of the bonuses of working for a well-known designer was the fact that she got most of her clothes at cost; another was that her lissom shape and long legs were ideally suited to the subtle tweeds, silks and linens Colin preferred to use.

'I do love seeing my clothes on a real woman,' he had told her once, appreciatively. 'Models are caricatures of the female species, clothes-horses, the complete antitheses of the heavy county types who buy from me, but you… You might have been made for them,' he had told her.

Isabel laughed about her cousin's employer. 'An old woman' was how she referred to him, and while it had traces of truth, Jessica chided her. Colin was shrewd and extremely talented, and while he might not be as charismatic as many of the men Jessica came into contact with, he was genuine, with a genuine love for his chosen career.

Another thing Isabel derided was Jessica's own fastidious reluctance to indulge in what she was pleased to term 'fun'.

'Fun' to Isabel encompassed a wholly idealistic impression of what it was like living alone in London. In Jessica's place there was no end to the 'fun' she might have, but unlike Jessica, who was footloose and fancy-free, she was tied to the boring old parents, and dull Merton with its farmers and relaxed pace of life.

After one or two attempts to correct her misapprehensions Jessica had acknowledged that her cousin had no intention of letting herself be disillusioned, and besides Jessica's 'freedom' was a useful tool to wield against her parents when rebellion stirred. It had struck Jessica more than once lately that her aunt and uncle were beginning to look tired. Uncle Frank was talking about retiring, and Jessica sensed that in some ways it would be a relief to them when Isabel eventually married and someone else took on the responsibility of their rebellious daughter. But so far Isabel had shown no signs of wanting to marry, and why should she? Jessica reflected. In her opinion eighteen was far too young—or perhaps that was just one of the penalties of still being single at twenty-six; one became supercautious of marriage, of the risks and dangers involved in making such an enormous commitment to another human being, and demanding so much from them in return.

Jessica was aware that Isabel had a far lighter approach to life than she did herself and would consequently probably have a much easier ride through life. She sighed, and chided herself for getting old and cynical as she showered quickly, barely sparing the briefest glance at the slender length of her body before draping it in a towel and padding into her bedroom.

Jeans and a T-shirt would suffice for the drive down to her aunt and uncle's, and she pulled them on quickly, zipping up the jeans before brushing her hair with a swift economy of movement. Her skin was good, thank goodness, and she rarely used much make-up; less when she was 'off duty'. Her eyes were a tawny gold—an unusual combination with the satin sable hair, oval and faintly Oriental, even if she did lack Isabel's pretty pouting beauty.

It was just after eight-thirty when she turned her small car into the familiar road leading to the Vicarage. She frowned as she remembered her aunt's tearful telephone call. What on earth had Isabel done this time?

Silence greeted her as she stopped the car and climbed out. Nine o'clock was normally supper time, so she walked round to the back of the house, knowing she would find her aunt in the kitchen.

Alice James gave a small start, followed by a relieved smile as she saw her niece, enveloping her in a warm hug.

'Jess! You made it—oh, I hoped you would! We've been so worried!'

'Is Belle here?' Jessica asked her, pulling a stool out from under the kitchen table and perching comfortably on it. She knew from old how long it took to drag a story out of her aunt.

'No. She's out, with ... with John Wellington, he's the young partner your uncle's taken on. Belle seems pretty keen on him.'

'And that's a problem?' Jessica enquired humorously, correctly reading the note of doubt in her aunt's voice. 'I thought this was what you'd been praying for for the last couple of years—that she'd find someone safe and steady and settle down.' She was still at a loss to understand the reason for her aunt's concern. 'Isn't that what you've always wanted for her? A nice safe marriage?' she prompted again.

'Everything we wanted for her,' her aunt confirmed. 'And now it's all going to be spoiled, because of that wretched holiday!'

'Holiday? What holiday?' Jessica asked, a frown creasing her forehead.

'Oh, it was several weeks ago. She wanted to go to Spain with a girlfriend. John didn't want her to go—he's quite jealous—but you know what she's like. The very fact that he didn't only seemed to make her keener. Anyway, she went, and it was while she was there that it happened.'

'What happened?' Jessica asked patiently, quelling her rising dismay, her mind alive to all the fates that could befall a girl like her cousin, bent only on 'having a good time'.

'She got herself engaged—well, almost,' her aunt amended. 'To some Spanish boy she met over there. They've been writing to one another—none of us knew a thing about it, until she showed me his last letter. Jessica, what on earth are we going to do? She's as good as promised to marry John, and if he finds out about this ...'

'Why should he?' Jessica asked practically, mentally cursing Isabel. Trust her to have two men dangling; she was all for the competitive spirit, Jessica acknowledged wryly. 'All she has to do is to write to this Spanish boy and simply tell him that it's over.' Privately she was surprised that Isabel's Spaniard had bothered to write; most of them made a hobby out of 'falling in love' with pretty tourists.

'She daren't. She's terrified that he'll come over here to find out what's happening, and then what on earth will she tell John?'

If Isabel didn't feel able to tell John the plain truth now, it didn't bode well for their marriage, was Jessica's private opinion, but she refrained from voicing it, practically deciding that her aunt's obvious distress was what needed her attention right now.

'Don't worry about it,' she soothed her. 'It will all be all right.'

'Oh, Jess, I knew you'd be able to sort it all out,' her aunt confided, promptly bursting into tears. 'I told Isabel you'd help.'

Jessica spread her hands ruefully. 'Of course, but I don't see what I can do...'

'Why, go to Spain, of course,' her aunt announced as though she were talking about a trip to the nearest town. 'You must go and see him, Jess, and explain that Isabel can't marry him.'

'Go to Spain?' Jessica stared at her. 'But, Aunt...'

'You were going anyway,' her aunt said hurriedly, avoiding her eyes, 'and you can speak Spanish, Jessica, you can explain to him in his own tongue, soften the blow a little. Think what it would do to Isabel if he were to come here. She genuinely cares for John, and I think he has the strength she needs.' She sighed. 'I sometimes think your uncle and I should have been stricter with her, but...' she broke off as the kitchen door suddenly burst open and a small, fair-haired girl hurried in. She stopped dead as she reached the table.

'Jess!' she exclaimed joyfully. 'Oh, you've come—thank goodness! Has Mum told you...'

'That you're being pursued by an ardent suitor? Yes,' Jessica told her cousin dryly. 'Honestly, Belle...'

'I really thought I loved him,' Isabel began defensively. 'He was so different from John, and it was all so romantic... Oh, there's no need to look like that!' She stamped her foot as Jessica raised her eyes heavenwards. 'It's different for you, Jess, you'd never get involved in anything like that, you're so sensible, so unromantic, but me...'

Jessica winced a little as her cousin's unthinking comment found its mark. How often had she heard that comment 'You're so unromantic'? Every time she refused to go to bed with her escort? Every time she refused to get involved? And yet she had always thought secretly that she was too romantic; that her ideals were too high.

'You're really sure then about John?' Jessica questioned her cousin later in the evening when they were both preparing for bed.

'As sure as I'm ever likely to be,' Isabel told her with a rare flash of honesty. 'But it will spoil everything if Jorge decides to come over here to find out why I've stopped writing to him. You will go and see him, won't you, Jess?' she appealed. 'I don't think I could bear it if I lost John!'

There were tears in her eyes, and unwillingly Jessica felt herself giving way. She supposed it wouldn't hurt to try and see this boy while she was in Spain; even perhaps add a few days to the trip to make sure she did see him, although she was quite convinced that it was highly unlikely that he would turn up in England.

'But you don't understand,' Isabel wailed when she pointed this out to her. 'We were practically engaged. He will come over, Jess, I know he will!' She practically wrung her hands together in her fear, and Jessica, feeling immeasurably more than only eight years her senior, sighed.

'Well, I'll go and see him then, but honestly, Belle, I'm sure you're worrying unnecessarily.'

'YOU MEAN to tell me you actually agreed to go and see this impetuous Romeo on your cousin's behalf?' Colin expostulated three days later when she explained to him that she would like to add a couple of extra days' holiday to their trip to Spain. 'Can't she do her own dirty work?'

'Not in this case,' Jessica assured him, quickly outlining the facts. 'And of course, I do speak Spanish.'

In actual fact she spoke several foreign languages. They were her hobby and she seemed to have a flair for them.

'Well, I can see that nothing I can say is going to cure you of this protective attitude towards your family,' Colin admitted. 'All I can say is—thank goodness I don't have one!'

'And my extra days' holiday?'

'They're yours,' he agreed. 'Although I'd much rather see you spend them on yourself than squander them on young Isabel. She's a leech, Jess, and she'll suck you dry if you let her. You must see that, so why?'

'She's family,' Jessica said simply. 'She and my aunt and uncle are all I have left.'

Often she had wondered after her parents' shocking deaths if the accident had somehow not only robbed her of her mother and father, but her ability to love as well, because ever since then she had held the world at a distance, almost as though she was afraid of letting people get too close to her; afraid that she might come to depend on them and that she would ultimately lose them.

SEVILLE WAS a city that appealed strongly to the senses. Jessica fell in love with it almost from the moment she stepped off the plane into the benevolent spring sunshine. Madrid was more properly the home of Spanish commerce, and Jessica had been there on several previous occasions, but Seville was new territory to her.

Initially she had been surprised when Isabel told her that Jorge lived in Seville; she had expected to find him somewhere on the Costa Brava, but Isabel had told her that Jorge had been holidaying like herself at the time they met.

Colin, running true to form, had insisted on her staying at the hotel the extra few days at his expense, and although Jessica had demurred, he had insisted, and in the end she had given way. Knowing Colin, the hotel he would have chosen would be far more luxurious than anything she could have afforded, and this supposition was proved correct when her taxi drew up outside an impressive Baroque building.

Her fluent Spanish brought a swift smile to the face of the girl behind the reception desk, and in no time at all she was stepping out of the lift behind the porter carrying her case and waiting while he unlocked the door to her room.

The hotel had obviously once been a huge private house, and had been converted tastefully and carefully. Jessica's room had views over the city; the furniture, although reproduction, was beautifully made and totally in keeping with the age and character of the room. There was a bathroom off it, rather more opulent than she would have expected in the hotel's British equivalent, a swift reminder that this part of the world had once been ruled by the Moors, who had left behind them a love of luxury and a sensuality that had been passed down through the generations.

Once she had unpacked Jessica went down to the foyer, where she had seen some guidebooks and maps on sale. The evening meal, as she was already aware, was the all-important meal in the Spanish home, and she wanted to make sure that her visit to Jorge did not clash with this.

As she had suspected, the receptionist was able to confirm that in Seville it was the general rule to eat later in the evening—normally about ten o'clock—which gave her the remainder of the afternoon and the early evening to make her visit, Jessica decided.

She had already formulated a plan of action. First she intended to discover if Jorge's family were listed in the telephone directory. If they were she would telephone and ask when she might call, if not she would simply have to call unannounced.

She lunched lightly in the hotel's restaurant—soup, followed by prawn salad, and then went up to her room to study the telephone directory. There were several Calvadores listed in the book, but none under Jorge's address, and Jessica was forced to the reluctant conclusion that she would simply have to call unannounced.

A call to the reception desk organised a taxi to take her to her destination. She showered and changed into soft jade green silk separates, from Colin's new range; a pleated skirt that swirled softly round her legs and a blouson top with full sleeves caught up in tight cuffs. The colour suited her, Jessica knew, and to complement it she brushed toning jade eye shadow over her lids, thickening and darkening her lashes discreetly with mascara.

Soft kid sandals of jade, blue and cerise completed her outfit. It was warm enough for her to be able to dispense with a jacket, and she was just flicking a comb through the silken length of her hair when her phone buzzed and the receptionist announced that her taxi had arrived.

Because she spoke Spanish so well, Jessica had no qualms about giving the driver instructions herself, but she began to wonder if, after all, she had made some mistake, when they drove into what was obviously a very luxurious and exclusive part of the city. Imposing buildings lined the streets, here and there an iron grille giving a tantalising view of the gardens beyond. Fretworked balconies and shutters lured the eye, but Jessica was left with an overall impression of solitude and privacy strictly guarded, so that it was almost as though the buildings themselves seemed to resent her intrusion.

At last the taxi stopped, and rather hesitantly she asked him if he could return for her in half an hour. That surely would give her sufficient time to explain the situation to Jorge? She only prayed that he was in!

Quickly checking the address Isabel had written down on the scrap of paper she had given her, she climbed unsteadily out of the car and glanced hesitantly at the imposing frontage of the building. There was no need for her to feel nervous, she reassured herself; the building, impressive though its outward appearance was, probably housed dozens of small apartments. However, when she reached the top of the small flight of stone steps there was simply one bell. She pressed it and heard the faint ringing somewhere deep in the recesses of the building. An aeon seemed to pass before she heard sounds of movement behind the large studded door.

Honestly, it was almost like something out of a horror movie! she reflected as the door swung back, creaking on its hinges.

The man who stood there had 'upper-class servant' stamped all over his impassive countenance. He looked disapprovingly at Jessica for several seconds and appeared to be on the point of closing the door in her face when she babbled quickly, 'My name is Jessica James and I've come to see Señor Calvadores. Is he at home?'

The man seemed to consider her for an age before grudgingly opening the door wide enough for her to step into a hallway large enough to hold her entire flat. The floor was tiled with the famous *azulejo* tiles, so beautiful that she almost caught her breath in pleasure. If only Colin could see these! The colours were fantastic, shading from softest blue to a rich deep azure.

'If the *señorita* will please wait,' the manservant murmured, opening another door and indicating that Jessica was to precede him into the room. Like the hall, it was enormous, furnished in what she felt sure must be priceless antiques. Whoever Jorge was, he quite obviously was not a poor man, she reflected, gazing in awe at her surroundings.

'Señorita James?' he repeated slowly. 'I will see if *el Señor Conde* can see you.'

'*El Señor Conde!*' Jessica stared after his departing back. Isabel had said nothing to her about a title. What was the matter with her? she asked herself sardonically several seconds later; surely she wasn't impressed by something as outmoded as an inherited title? She, who had always despised those who fawned on the county and titled set, because of who they were rather than what they were!

She was lost in a deep study of a portrait above the fireplace—a Spanish don of the seventeenth century if she was any judge, formidable and with a magnetism that refused to be confined to the canvas—when she heard footsteps outside the door, firmer and far more decisive than the manservant's. She felt herself tense. Now that the moment was almost upon her she felt ridiculously nervous. What on earth was she going to say? How could she simply say baldly that Isabel no longer wanted him; and that in fact he was an embarrassment to her, now that she was on the verge of becoming engaged to another man.

The door opened and the man who stood there took her breath away. Her first impression was that he was impossibly arrogant, standing there staring down the length of his aristocratic nose at her, his lean jaw tensing, as though he was controlling a fierce anger. Ice-cold grey eyes flicked disparagingly over her, the aquiline profile inclining slightly in an acknowledgement of her presence, which was more of an insult than a courtesy.

He was tall, far taller than she had expected, his hair dark, sleek as ravens' feathers, and worn slightly long, curling over the pure silk collar of a shirt she was sure had been handmade especially for him.

Everything about this man whispered discreetly of wealth and prestige, and never in a million years could Jessica imagine him holidaying on the Costa Brava and indulging in a holiday romance with her cousin.

For one thing, he must be almost twice Isabel's age—certainly in his early thirties—and nothing about him suggested the type of man who needed the admiration of a very young girl to boost his ego. This man did not need any woman; his very stance suggested an arrogant pride which would never admit to any need of any kind. He was the result of centuries of wealth and breeding of a type found almost exclusively in the great Spanish families, and Jessica felt her blood run cold at the thought of telling him that her cousin had decided she preferred someone else.

'Señorita James?'

He spoke perfect accentless English, his voice clipped and cool, and yet despite his outward control, Jessica sensed that beneath the ice-cold surface raged a molten torrent of barely held in rage. But why? Or had he guessed her purpose in coming? This man was no fool, surely he must have realised from the recent tone of Isabel's letters how the land lay?

'Señor Calvadores?'

Her voice was no way as controlled as his, and she had the dismal conviction that he knew he had unnerved her and that he deliberately intended to.

It was obvious that he didn't intend to make things easy for her. So much for Spanish hospitality! Jessica thought indignantly. He hadn't even offered her so much as a cup of coffee. Well, there was nothing for it but to plunge in; there was no easy way to say what had to be said, and all she wanted to do now was to say her piece and make her escape. His attitude and hauteur had killed all the sympathy she had initially felt towards him. Never in a thousand years could she imagine her flighty young cousin holding her own against this man whose very stance exuded an arrogant contempt that filled the air around them.

'I've come to see you about . . .'

'I know what you've come to see me about, Miss James,' he cut in brutally, not allowing her to finish, 'and no doubt you want me to make things easy for you. No doubt you hoped to sway me with your large, worried eyes, no doubt you've been led to believe that I can be persuaded to give way. Unfortunately—for you—that is not to be. To put it in its simplest form, Miss James, and having seen you for myself, having had confirmed every one of my very worst fears—that is to say, having seen for myself that you are a young woman who likes expensive clothes, and doubtless everything that goes with them; that you are at a guess somewhere in your mid-twenties; that you are bold enough to come here demanding to see me; there is simply no way I shall allow you to ruin my brother's life by trapping him into marriage simply because of an affair you had with him several months ago!'

Jessica was totally lost for words. His brother, he had said. That meant he wasn't—couldn't be Jorge de Calvadores, but he obviously thought she was Isabel. She was on the verge of correcting him when she realised what else he had said. 'An affair'. Isabel had given her the distinct impression that Jorge was the one pressing her into an unwanted engagement, whereas his brother seemed to think the boot was very much on the other foot. Clearly there were some misunderstandings to be sorted out!

CHAPTER TWO

SHE TOOK A deep breath, wondering where to begin. Perhaps if she were to explain to him first that she wasn't Isabel. How contemptuous he had been about her cousin! He really was insufferably proud and arrogant; she didn't like him at all, she decided, eyeing him militantly.

She opened her mouth to explain, but was stunned into silence by the cynical way he was looking at her; a way no man had ever looked at her before, she realised, feeling the heat rising through her body. His study was an openly sexual one, and not merely sexual but contemptuous. Good heavens, it could have been Isabel exposed to that merciless scrutiny that made no allowance for feminine modesty or embarrassment! And she had thought Spaniards were supposed to be reticent, cultured and, above all, respectful to women!

'You don't understand,' she began shakily when she had recovered her composure, anger fanned into tiny, darting flames by the look she had seen in his eyes.

'On the contrary, I understand all too well,' came the crisp response. '*Diós,* do you not think I know what goes on at these holiday resorts?' His finely cut mouth curled sneeringly downwards. 'You must have thought yourself extremely fortunate to meet a young man as wealthy and unworldly as my young brother, but unfortunately for you, Jorge does not come into his inheritance for half a dozen more years, when he reaches his twenty-fifth birthday.

Until then I stand guardian to him, and you may take it that I shall do everything in my power to free him from your clutches. I must say I am surprised at your coming here,' he added. 'I thought Jorge had already made it clear to you that the affair was over. You should have persuaded him to pay for his pleasure at the time, Miss James,' he told her contemptuously. 'Now it is too late; now he sees you for what you really are.' His lip curled, and Jessica went hot and cold to think of Isabel being forced to stand here and listen to these insults.

'Your brother loved m-my... me,' she corrected herself hurriedly. 'He...'

'—Desired your body,' she was told flatly, 'and in his innocence mistook such desire for a far different emotion—a fact which you used to your advantage, using his lust for you to force him...'

'Just a moment!' she inserted, with a sudden resurgence of her normal coolness. 'If you are implying that Jorge was forced into...'

'Oh, I am aware that there was no question of "force" as such,' the icy voice agreed. 'Bemused, dazzled, dragged out of his depth—these would perhaps be better descriptions. You are an attractive woman,' he told her, openly assessing the shape of her body beneath the thin silk, 'not perhaps in Jorge's usual style, but no matter... Of course I realise why you are here. I suppose you thought that a personal appearance might be just the goad he needed. Absence makes the heart grow fonder—of someone else, is that it?'

Matters had gone far enough. There was a limit to the amount of time she intended to simply stand there and allow him to insult her.

'Before we go any further, I ought to tell you that I have
no desire at all to become engaged to your brother,' Jessica told him truthfully, 'In fact . . .'

'Oh, come, you cannot expect me to believe that?' he
said softly. 'Perhaps I should refresh your memory. I have
here your last letter to Jorge. He brought it to me in a very
troubled frame of mind. It seems that while he enjoyed
your...company, the constant pressure you put on him to
announce your engagement has panicked him into confiding in me.'

'You having considerable experience of ridding yourself of unwanted women, I suppose?' Jessica supplied
sweetly. 'One of the penalties of being wealthy!'

The dark flush of colour beneath his skin brought her a
fierce sense of satisfaction. He hadn't liked her implication that women would only find him attractive for his
wealth, and she knew it wasn't true. He was too intensely
male for that. She found herself wondering if he was married, and then squashed the thought as being of no concern to her.

'You must accept that Jorge no longer wishes to have
anything to do with you,' she was told implacably, 'and
even if he did, I would do everything in my power to dissuade him from marrying a woman like you. What attracted you to him the most? Or can I guess?'

'If you did you'd be wrong,' Jessica told him in a
clipped voice. 'As I've already said, I have no desire to
marry your brother.'

'No?' With a swift movement he reached inside his
jacket and removed a folded piece of paper. 'Read this—
perhaps it will help you remember,' he said contemptuously.

Unwillingly Jessica took the letter, her fingertips brushing him as she did, strange quivers of sensation running up her arm as she recoiled from the brief contact.

Matters had gone far enough. She would have to tell him the truth. She opened the letter, and her heart dropped. She had barely done more than read the first couple of lines, skimming quickly over them, but it was enough to bring a burning colour to her face. Isabel and Jorge had been lovers—that much was obvious; as was Isabel's impassioned plea for Jorge to marry her. What on earth had possessed her cousin to write a letter like this? Jessica felt sick at the thought of her aunt and uncle reading it; and what about John? Why on earth hadn't Isabel warned her? And why had she been so convinced that Jorge intended to come to England? To judge from his brother, the young Spaniard wanted to escape from the relationship just as much as Isabel herself.

'Edifying, is it not?' her persecutor drawled insultingly. 'And I understand from Jorge—although he was reluctant to admit it—that he was far from being your first lover.'

Jessica's eyes widened, mirroring her shock. Was it true?

'So, obviously realising that your letter had failed, you decided to come in person. Why, I wonder? It must surely be obvious to you by now that Jorge does not wish to marry you.'

What on earth had Isabel got her into?

For a moment she contemplated telling the truth, but to do so meant betraying her cousin. She had protected Isabel for too long to stop now.

'Perhaps, failing marriage, you had something else in mind?' The soft suggestion held a trace of bitter contempt. 'I know Jorge has told you of the marriage his family had hoped might take place between him and the daughter of a close friend of ours—a marriage, I might add, which would stand a far greater chance of success than the one you proposed. Perhaps you hoped to turn this fact to your advantage. Barbara's family are very old-fashioned. They would be intolerant of any folly on Jorge's part.'

Jessica went white, reaching out blindly to grasp the back of a chair for support as the meaning of his words sank in.

'You thought I'd use blackmail!' she whispered disbelievingly. 'You thought I came here to... to...'

'Very affecting,' the cool voice mocked. 'But I am not Jorge, to be easily impressed by a pair of huge amber eyes that plead with me to believe in an innocence I know they cannot possess. You are several years older than my brother; you used his inexperience and calf love for you to further your own ends. You must have known that his family would never tolerate such an alliance—so, Miss James, let us get down to business, shall we?'

'If by business you mean you'll pay me to forget any claims I might have on your brother, you're wasting your time!' Jessica told him furiously, too angry to care about the danger emanating from him as she pushed bitterly past him, blinking away tears of rage as she wrestled with the huge front door. She could hear him behind her, and the terrible fear that he would never allow her to leave made the blood pound in her head, her fingers trembling as she tugged at the door.

He swore harshly and she felt his hand on her shoulder, sobbing with relief as the door yielded and she half stumbled into the street. Her taxi was waiting and she flung herself into it without a backward glance, not caring what conclusions her driver might be drawing. The first thing she intended to do when she got back to the hotel was to put a call through to her cousin and find out exactly what was going on.

Fortunately, it was her aunt and uncle's bridge night, and Isabel answered the phone, her pleasure turning to petulance as she recognised the anger in Jessica's voice.

'You saw Sebastian?' she exclaimed nervously. 'Oh, no, Jess, what did he say?'

She had a good mind to tell her, Jessica thought wrathfully. So Sebastian was his name; it suited him somehow.

'Nothing flattering,' she told Isabel grimly. 'In fact he seemed to think I was you. Oh, Belle,' she exclaimed as the scene in the vast and opulent drawing room flashed quickly through her mind, 'you should have warned me, told me the truth. Why on earth did you want me to come here? Sebastian told me that Jorge had no desire to become engaged to you, he even showed me your letter.'

She knew from the sudden catch in her breath that Isabel hadn't expected that, and yet true to form her cousin, even now, seemed to be trying to turn the situation to her own advantage.

'You didn't tell him he was wrong, did you?' she asked quickly, 'about us, I mean, Jess?'

'I wasn't given the opportunity,' Jessica told her dryly. It hadn't been pleasant listening to what the arrogant Conde had to say, and some of his more stinging barbs still hurt.

'He mustn't know,' Isabel was saying positively. 'Oh, Jess, try to understand—when I wrote that letter to Jorge, I was desperate—I thought I might be pregnant... Jess... Jess, are you still there?'

Trying not to betray her shock, Jessica murmured an assent. 'Oh, you don't understand at all,' she heard Isabel saying crossly, obviously correctly interpreting her silence. 'Honestly, Jess, you're so old-fashioned it just isn't true! Living like a frigid spinster might suit you, but it doesn't suit me,' she told her frankly, 'and why shouldn't I have fun if I want to?'

'Was it fun, thinking you might be pregnant and un-married?' Jessica asked her bluntly. Isabel was still very much a spoiled child, and it did neither of them any good thinking now that she should have been treated far more firmly as a child—the damage was done, and Isabel seemed to think she had a God-given right to indulge her-self in whatever she chose.

'No,' she heard Isabel admit sulkily. 'But what else could I do? I had to write to him—he was as responsible as me.'

'Go on,' Jessica told her briefly. The more she heard, the less able she felt to defend her cousin—but then there were her aunt and uncle to think of. Both of them would be un-bearably shocked if they heard the truth.

'Oh, nothing.' She could almost see Isabel's petulant shrug. 'I discovered it was a false alarm, by that time I had met John, and so...'

'So you asked me to come here to see someone I thought you were on the verge of becoming engaged to. I don't understand, Belle. There must be something more to it.'

There was a long silence during which mingled exasper-ation and fear gripped her, and then at last Isabel admit-ted sulkily.

'Oh, all right then, when I wrote to Jorge he didn't write back, but his brother did. Jorge had shown him my letter, he said, and he wanted to know what proof there was that any child I might have was Jorge's—beast!' she added vi-triolically. 'It was a hateful letter, Jess, and I was scared—Jorge had told me about him, that he was his guardian and that he was very strict. I was terrified he might come over here—come and see me because of what I'd written—so I panicked. I thought if you could see Jorge and tell him that I didn't want him anymore then he would tell Sebastian and . . .'

And she would have been safe, without having to endure the unpleasantness of an interview with either Jorge or Sebastian, Jessica reflected bitterly. Trust Isabel to want to wriggle out of the situation with the minimum amount of discomfort to herself!

'You do understand, don't you, Jess?' Isabel pleaded. 'I couldn't run the risk of Sebastian coming over here. If the parents or John had seen him . . .'

'So you sent me into the lion's den instead,' Jessica supplied dryly. 'Thanks!'

'I didn't know that you'd see Sebastian or that he'd mistake you for me,' Isabel defended herself, 'but perhaps it's all worked out for the best,' she added with what to Jessica was colossal selfishness. 'Now he's seen you and you've told him that you don't want Jorge, he won't bother us again. What was he like?' she asked curiously. 'To hear Jorge talk about him anyone would think he was God!' She giggled. 'I quite fancied meeting him; Jorge said all the women were after him. He's immensely wealthy, and the title goes back to the days of Ferdinand and Isabella. He sounded fearfully haughty and proud.'

It was becoming obvious that Isabel knew far more about the Calvadores family than she had told her, Jessica realised. She was furious with her cousin, but as she knew from past experience, it was pointless getting angry with Isabel. Even if she were to drag her out here and make her face Sebastian and Calvadores herself, what possible good could it do? Isabel was probably right, it had all turned out for the best, although Jessica doubted that he would ever have felt sufficient concern about her hold over his brother to go the lengths of seeking her out in England.

'He sent me the most hateful letter,' Isabel was saying, her voice quivering slightly. 'He said that he didn't believe I might be pregnant and that it was just a trick to get Jorge to marry me. At least it's all over with now, Jess,' she added on a happier note, 'I'm so relieved. By the way,' she added coquettishly, 'John proposed last night and I've accepted him—the parents are over the moon!'

Privately Isabel thought her cousin far too young to be thinking of marriage. It was plain that Isabel was far from mature, and she doubted that John was the right husband for her, but she knew better than to interfere.

'When will you be back?' Isabel demanded. 'We're having a proper engagement party, and I want you to be there, of course.'

A sop to ease her conscience, Jessica thought wryly. She had done the dirty deed for her and now she was to be rewarded; Isabel couldn't get engaged without her. Had her cousin the slightest idea of what it had felt like to have to stand there and listen to Sebastian de Calvadores's insults? To be told that her morals were questionable, that she was motivated by financial greed—no, she thought grimly, Isabel didn't have the slightest conception.

Since she had allowed herself two days to sort out Isabel's romantic problems, Jessica found herself with a day on her hands. She wasn't going to waste it, she decided as she breakfasted in her room on warm rolls and fresh honey. She would explore Seville.

She already knew a little about it; that it had once been ruled by the Moors who had ruled all this part of Spain; that during the Middle Ages it had had a fine reputation as a centre of medical learning. Once Colin arrived there would be scant time for sight-seeing, which in any case did not interest him, so after checking the time of his flight, which was due in early in the evening, Jessica collected her guide books and set out to explore the city.

But as she wandered the Moorish Alcazar, instead of simply being able to drink in its beauty, at almost every turn she was forcibly reminded of Sebastian de Calvadores; it was from the men who had built the civilisation from which this beauty had sprung that he drew his arrogance, she thought as she looked around her. There was Moorish blood running in his veins, underlining and emphasising his total masculinity. She shivered, suddenly feeling cold, glad to step out into the warmth of the sunshine. Forget him, she told herself, why worry about what had happened? She knew that he had been totally mistaken about it, and that should have been enough. But somehow it wasn't. She could forget the contempt in his eyes, the explicitly sexual way they had moved over her body and yet at the same time had remained so cold, as though he had been saying, see, I know everything there is to know about you as a woman and it does nothing for me, nothing at all.

If it wasn't for the fact that by doing so she would betray Isabel she would have gone back and told him how wrong he was about her; then it would be his turn to feel her contempt, her condemnation.

Seville was a beautiful city, but she wasn't in the mood to enjoy it. Almost everywhere she looked she was reminded of Sebastian de Calvadores; Moorish faces, sternly oppressive, stared back at her from paintings; Moorish men who had guarded their women like precious jewels in rare caskets and who would never in a million years permit them the kind of freedom Isabel enjoyed.

Chastity and desire burned strongly in twin flames in these people; either saints or sinners, but knowing no middle road; their history was a proud one and there could be few natives of Seville who did not boast some Moorish blood, some fierce elemental strain they had inherited from their forebears. They had been a race who, even while they tasted the cup of pleasure to the full, always remained a little aloof, knowing that where there was pleasure there was pain. A cynical, sophisticated race who had kept their women closeted away from the world to be enjoyed by them alone.

Jessica was glad when the time came to go and meet Colin's plane. He seemed so solid and safe somehow as he came towards her, carrying his briefcase, frowning uncertainly until he saw her.

'Jessica!' His hug was affectionately warm. 'Everything sorted out?' he asked her as they got into their taxi, his tone implying that he wouldn't be surprised to find that Isabel in her tiresomeness had allowed her problems to overflow into Jessica's working life.

'I think so.'

His relief made her laugh. 'Thank goodness for that! I was terrified that we'd have a tearful besotted Latin lover on our hands!'

Just for a moment Jessica compared this image to the reality of Sebastian, and wondered if Jorge was anything like his formidable brother. Probably not. She couldn't see Sebastian allowing himself to be manipulated in the way she was coming to suspect that Isabel had manipulated Jorge. No, when it came to the woman in his life, Sebastian would be totally in control. Was he married?

'Jess?'

Stop thinking about him, she chided herself, giving her attention to Colin. She was in Seville to work, not concern herself with the private life of a man who was virtually a stranger. Stranger or not, for those first few pulsating seconds when she had seen Sebastian she had been aware of him in a way that still had the power to shock her. For all his repressive arrogance there was a sensuality about him, a total maleness and a dangerous allure, reminiscent of that of a jungle cat for its prey.

Colin was tired after his flight and it was decided that he would dine in his room and have an early night.

'Have you been to the exhibition centre yet?' he asked Jessica. She shook her head. 'Well, the exhibition doesn't open until tomorrow. We've got an appointment with Calvortex after lunch. Keep your fingers crossed, won't you?' he asked her. 'I've done all next season's designs with their fabrics in mind. If they're anything like last season's we'll be on to a real winner—especially if he gives us the exclusive use of his stuff for the U.K.'

'How much do you know about them?' Jessica asked him as they stepped into the hotel foyer.

'Very little, and most of that word of mouth. The Chairman of the company handpicks his clients, from what I've been told. The company is a small family-run business; apart from that I know nothing, except that they produce the sort of fabrics that fill the dreams of every designer worth his or her salt. I'm relieved to hear you've sorted out all that business with Isabel,' he added as they headed for the lift. 'Tiresome girl! Why should you run round after her?'

'Well, I won't have to much longer,' Jessica told him. 'She's got herself engaged.'

'God help the man!' was Colin's pious comment as the lift stopped at their floor.

Their rooms were not adjacent and outside the lift they went their separate ways.

In her own room, Jessica tried to concentrate on the morning and the textile show, but somehow Sebastian de

Calvadores's aquiline features kept coming between her and her work. A hard man and a proud one, and her face burned with colour as she remembered the way he had looked at her, the insulting remarks he had made to her.

She went to bed early, and was just on the point of falling asleep when she heard someone knocking on the door.

'Jess, are you awake?' she heard Colin mutter outside. 'I've got the most dreadful indigestion, do you have anything I can take?'

Sighing, she went to her suitcase and found some tablets. If Colin had one fault it was that he was a hopeless hypochondriac and that he refused absolutely to carry even aspirins about with him, preferring instead to play the martyr for the uninitiated. Jessica had got wise to this within her first few months of working for him, and had grown used to carrying what amounted almost to a small pharmacy around with her whenever she travelled with him.

She opened her door and handed him the small packet.

'You're an angel!'

Colin bent forward, kissing her cheek lightly, and as he did so out of the corner of her eye Jessica glimpsed the couple walking down the corridor towards them; the woman small and petite with smoothly coiled dark hair and an expensive couture evening gown, her escort tall, with raven's-wing dark hair and a profile that made Jessica's heart turn over thuddingly as she stared at him.

Sebastian de Calvadores! What was he doing here, and who was he with?

Her face paled as he stared contemptuously at her, suddenly acutely aware of her thin silk nightgown and tousled hair, Colin's hand on her arm, his lips brushing her cheek. Her face flamed as she realised what interpretation Sebastian de Calvadores would be placing on their intimacy, and then berated herself for her embarrassment. Why should she care if he thought she and Colin were lovers? What possible business was it of his? And yet his steely glance seemed to say that he knew everything there was to know about her, and that he doubted that her motives for being with Colin were any less altruistic than those he had accredited her with in his brother's case.

'Jess, is something wrong?' Colin asked her with a frown, sensing her lack of attention. 'You've seemed strangely on edge ever since I arrived. It's that damned cousin of yours, I suppose.'

'Nothing's wrong, I'm just a little tired,' she lied huskily, glad when Sebastian and his companion turned the corner of the corridor. 'I'll be fine in the morning.'

CHAPTER THREE

As a PREDICTION it wasn't entirely true; Jessica felt
strangely on edge and tense, her muscles clenching every
time someone walked into the dining room where they were
having breakfast.

She would be glad to get back home, she thought wryly
as her nerves jumped for the third time in succession at the
sight of a dark-haired man. Arrogant brute! He hadn't
even given her an opportunity to explain, denouncing her
as though she were some female predator and his brother
her completely innocent victim. She thought about what
she had learned from Isabel and grimaced slightly. How
could her cousin have behaved in such an unprincipled
way? She had always had a streak of wildness, a tendency
to ignore any attempts to curb her headstrong nature, but
to actually try and force Jorge into marriage . . . And that
was what she had done, no matter how one tried to wrap
up the truth, Jessica admitted unhappily. Even so, that was
no reason for Sebastian de Calvadores to speak to *her* in
the way he had.

'Time to leave for the exhibition,' Colin reminded her,
dragging her mind back to the real purpose of her visit to
Seville.

Half an hour later they were there, both of them lost in
admiration of the fabrics on display.

'Just feel this suede,' Colin murmured to her. 'It's as
supple as silk. It makes my fingers itch to use it!'

'And these tweeds!' Jessica exclaimed. 'The wool comes from South America, I believe?'

'Many Spaniards have family connections in South America,' Colin reminded her, 'and I suppose it's only natural that they should turn those connections to commercial advantage, in this case by importing the wool in its raw state, and dying and weaving it here in Spain.'

He drew Jessica's attention to the display belonging to the company they were to see. 'In a class of its own, isn't it?' he asked, watching the way she handled the supple fabric. 'And those colours!'

'They're incredibly subtle,' Jessica agreed with a touch of envy.

On leaving college her first intention had been to find a job in a design capacity with one of the large manufacturers, but such jobs were hard to come by—even harder with the downturn in the textile industry in Britain, and although her languages had stood her in good stead, she had found that without exception the Continental firms preferred to take on their own young graduates. Now working with cloth in its raw stages was only a pipe dream.

There was quite a busy throng around the Calvortex display and it was several minutes before Colin could talk to one of the young men in charge. He explained his purpose in Seville, producing the letters of recommendation he had brought with him, while Jessica swiftly translated.

'Unfortunately I am merely a member of the staff,' the young man exclaimed regretfully to Jessica, 'but I will certainly mention this matter to my superiors. If we have a telephone number where we can reach you?'

Handing him both his card and their telephone number at the hotel, Colin announced that they had done enough for one morning and that it was time for lunch. Typically he decided that they would lunch, not at the restaurant within the exhibition, but at another one, far more expensive and exclusive, as Jessica could tell at a glance when their taxi stopped outside it.

She was wearing another of his outfits, and attracted several admiring looks from the other diners as they were shown to their table, Colin beaming delightedly at the attention they were receiving.

Over lunch though he was more serious. 'I hope I do manage to get to some arrangement with Calvortex,' he confided.

Jessica, sensitive to his mood, picked up the tone of worry in his voice.

'It would be very pleasant,' she agreed, 'their fabrics are fantastic, but it won't be the end of the world if we don't, will it?'

'It could be,' Colin told her gravely. 'Things haven't been going too well this last couple of years. The people with money to spend on haute couture are getting fewer and fewer, and we don't exactly produce high-fashion stuff. Calvortex fabrics have a worldwide reputation, if we could use them for our clothes I'm convinced it would help boost sales—I've already had one approach from the Americans, with the proviso that we use Calvortex. Somehow they got to hear that we hoped to do so, and they've suggested an excellent contract. There'd be enough profit in it for us to start a cheaper line—bread and butter money coming in with the designer collections as the icing.'

What he said made sense, and Jessica knew enough about the fashion world to know he wasn't exaggerating. Several of the larger fashion houses were cutting back; designers came, were acclaimed for a couple of seasons, and then simply disappeared, but it was like chilly fingers playing down her spine to realise that Colin might be in financial difficulties.

'Well,' Colin told her when they had finished eating, 'let's get back to the exhibition and see if we can find something to fall back on if we don't get anywhere with Calvortex, although I'm afraid if we don't we'll lose the American contract—and one can see why. The texture and colour of those tweeds they were showing...'

'Mmm,' Jessica agreed, 'they were marvellous. I wonder how they manage to get such subtle colours?'

'I don't know. I've heard it's a closely guarded secret. Their Chairman is also their main designer and colour expert. It's quite a small concern really, but as I said before, extremely exclusive.'

The rest of the exhibition, while interesting, fell very far short of the standard of the Calvortex display, although Jessica did think that some of the supple leathers and suedes might prove useful to them. For some time she had been trying to persuade Colin to try a younger, more fashionable line, and she could just see those suedes, in pewters, steel blues and soft greens, in flaring culottes and swirling skirts, topped with chunky hand knits.

It was shortly after dinner that Colin received a message from reception to say that there had been a call from Calvortex.

'Stage one completed successfully at least!' he announced to Jessica when he returned to the bar, faintly flushed and obviously excited. 'I've spoken to the Chairman and he's agreed to see me tomorrow. I've explained to him that I've got my assistant with me, so he's arranged for us to tour the factory, and afterwards we can talk.'

She wouldn't be included in the talks, of course, Jessica reflected, but it wouldn't be too difficult a task to occupy

herself for a couple of hours—in fact she would enjoy
seeing how such beautiful fabrics were made.

Although Colin had not suggested that she do so, she
dressed with particular care for the visit—an outfit chosen from their new season's designs, a cream silk blouse
and a russet velvet suit with a tiny boxy jacket with narrow puffed sleeves and scrolls of self-coloured embroidery down the front. The skirt fell smoothly in soft loose
pleats from the narrow waistband, and it was an outfit that
Jessica knew suited her.

Colin obviously thought so too, because he beamed with
approval when he saw her.

'Very apt,' he approved as he looked at her. 'The jacket
has a certain matador air, very much suited to this part of
the world, and I must say I'm very pleased with the way
that embroidery has worked out. The colour suits you as
well.'

'I thought about the tweed,' Jessica told him, referring
to a tweed suit which was also part of the new collection,
'but as it doesn't compare favourably with their fabrics, I
thought...'

'Quite right,' he approved. 'Now, I've ordered a taxi for
us, we've just about got time for a cup of coffee before it
arrives.'

He looked more like an Old Etonian than a famous designer, Jessica reflected, eyeing his sober Savile Row suit
and immaculate silk shirt. Colin belonged to an older
generation that believed in dressing correctly and that one
could always tell a gentleman by his clothes—Turnbull &
Asser shirts and handmade shoes.

The factory was situated just outside Seville, surprisingly modern and with access to the river and the port. It
was, as Colin pointed out, very well planned, close to main
roads and other facilities, and when he gave in their names

at the gates they swung open to allow their vehicle to enter.

They were met in the foyer by a smiling dark-haired young man, dressed formally in a dark suit, his glance for them both extremely respectful, although there was a gleam of male interest in the dark eyes as they discreetly examined Jessica.

Having introduced himself as Ramón Ferres, he told them that he was to escort them round the factory.

'Unfortunately the Conde cannot show you round himself,' he explained in the sibilant, liquid English of the Spaniard, 'but he will be free to have lunch with you as arranged,' he informed Colin. 'Forgive me if I stare,' he added to Jessica, 'but we did not realise when Señor Weaver mentioned an assistant that he was talking of a woman. I'm afraid you might find the chemical processes of the factory a little boring . . .'

'Never,' Colin interrupted with a chuckle, while Jessica suppressed a tiny flare of anger at their escort's chauvinistic remark. Of course in Spain things were different. On the whole women were content to take a back seat to live their own lives, especially in the more wealthy families. No doubt someone such as Sebastian de Calvadores's wife, if indeed he had one, would never dream of interfering in her husband's life, or of questioning him about it. That was how they were brought up; to be docile and biddable, content with their families and their homes.

'You'll find that Jessica is far more knowledgeable about the manufacturing process than I am,' Colin added to their guide. 'In fact I suspect she prefers designing fabrics to designing clothes, if the truth were known.'

'Both fascinate me,' Jessica said truthfully.

The next couple of hours flew past. There was so much to see, so much to learn. The factory was the most up-to-

date she had ever seen, the equipment of such a sophisticated and superior type that she could only marvel at the
technological advances made since she had left college.

They were shown the dyeing vats, but prudently Ramón Ferres said nothing about how they managed to produce their delicate, subtle colours. All he would say in
answer to Jessica's questions was that in the main they used
natural and vegetable dyes.

'But surely there's always a problem in stabilising such
colours?' she pressed him.

He smiled and shrugged slim shoulders. 'This is so,' he
agreed, 'but we have been lucky enough to discover a way
of stabilising them—I cannot tell you how, you understand, but be assured that we have done so.'

'And next season's range?' Jessica queried. 'Could
we...'

Again Ramón Ferres shook his head. 'That is for the
Conde to decide,' he explained. He glanced at his watch.
'I will escort you back to the foyer, it is almost time for
lunch.' He glanced at Jessica. 'Originally it was intended
that we should lunch together, but as I explained, we had
expected Señor Weaver's assistant to be a man.'

It was plain that he had expected Colin's assistant to
want to talk shop over lunch, and it exasperated Jessica
that he should think that simply because she was a woman
she was merely paying lip service to appearing interested.

'I should love to have lunch with you,' she said firmly.
'There are several points I should like to clarify regarding
the manufacturing processes; problems you might have in
maintaining the quality of your wool, for instance...'

They were back in the foyer, and an elegant, dark-haired
secretary came to conduct Colin into the Chairman's private sanctum, leaving Jessica with Ramón Ferres.

A little to her surprise he guided her out to a car, explaining that although the factory had a restaurant, they operated a scheme similar to that adopted by the Japanese, in that all the staff dined together.

'While the food is excellent, the atmosphere is not conducive to a serious discussion. However, there is a restaurant not far from here.'

'And the Chairman?' Jessica asked curiously, visions of Colin in his Savile Row suit sitting down to eat with several hundred noisy Spaniards.

'He has a private dining room in his suite which he uses for business entertaining.'

As Ramón Ferres had said, the restaurant was not very far away. It had once been the shipping office of a wine exporter, he explained when Jessica expressed interest, but had now been converted into a restaurant.

As they walked inside the unusual barrel-vaulted ceiling caught Jessica's attention, and as they were shown to their table Ramón told her that there were very deep cellars beneath the ground.

'Almost every house in Seville has its cellars—a legacy from the times of the Moors—places of sanctuary and safety.'

'And sometimes prisons,' said Jessica, shivering a little. Like most people she found something distinctly frightening about the thought of being imprisoned underground.

'That too,' he agreed. 'The thought distresses you? There are not many of our leading families in Seville who have not had recourse to their cellars, for one reason or another, at some time in their history.'

'This is a very fascinating part of Spain,' Jessica commented as they were served with chilled *gazpacho*. 'A true mingling of East and West.'

'Not always with happy results,' Ramón told her. 'The Moorish character is a proud one, sombre too, and those in Seville who can trace their line back to the Moors are inordinately proud of their bloodlines. It has not always been so, of course. There was a time, during the Inquisition in particular, when to own to Moorish blood was to sign one's own death warrant.'

'Do you have Moorish ancestors?' Jessica asked him, genuinely interested.

He shook his head ruefully. 'No, my family was originally from the north, but the Conde can trace his family back to a knight attached to the Court of Pedro the Cruel. It is said that he ravished away the daughter of his archenemy, although there is a legend in the Conde's family that this was not so; that the girl was seduced by her cousin and in fear of her father she laid the blame at the door of his most bitter enemy. The Conde's ancestor was a proud man, and rather than endure the slur on his good name he offered to marry the girl—that is the story passed down through the Conde's family.'

And it bore a sombre echo of truth, Jessica thought wryly. She could well imagine a man who could not be moved by any other emotion being moved by pride; pride in his name and his race. She could almost see the dark flash of bitter eyes as he was faced with his crime... She shook herself mentally; what was the matter with her? For a moment in her mind's eye she had mentally imagined Sebastian de Calvadores as that accused ravisher. She would really have to stop thinking about the man. What was the matter with her? She was behaving like a teenager! If she felt anything for him it could only be contempt—and yet when he had stood there saying those dreadful things to her she had longed to tell him the truth, to see him smile instead of frown.

It was Jessica's turn to frown now. Why should she care whether Sebastian de Calvadores frowned or smiled? It was immaterial to her; not that she was ever likely to see him again anyway!

Ramón Ferres was an entertaining companion, and although Jessica suspected that he did not entirely approve of a woman in what he plainly considered to be a man's world, he answered all her questions as pleasantly and fully as he could.

'Much of this you will have to ask the Conde,' he told her with another of his shrugs, when she had asked several highly technical questions. 'I'm afraid I am employed more as a public relations manager than a technical expert. The Conde, on the other hand, knows everything there is to know about the manufacturing process. The whole thing was his brainchild; he conceived the idea when he was in South America working on the *rancho* of his godfather—it is from there that he gets the wool; it is of the highest quality and the partnership is a good one. It is said that Señor Cusuivas would like it to be even closer—he has a daughter who would make the Conde an excellent wife. Forgive me,' he added hastily, 'I should not have said that. The Conde . . .'

'I've forgotten it already,' Jessica assured him, amused that he had so far forgotten himself to gossip a little with her. As he had said himself, he was not from Southern Spain, and perhaps a little homesick here among the more taciturn, secretive people of Seville, who had lived too long in the shadow of death and danger not to weigh their words carefully. Centuries of bloodshed had stained this soil, leaving the inhabitants a legacy of caution—deep-seated and ineradicable.

'I shall have to leave you in the foyer for a few minutes,' Ramón apologised to her when they got back to the factory. 'Señor Weaver should not be long, and I'm afraid I have some business to attend to, but I shall leave you in Constancia's capable hands.'

Constancia was the secretary. She gave Jessica a brief smile, and offered a cup of coffee. Jessica accepted; the wine with their lunch had left her feeling thirsty.

The girl had been gone about five minutes when the door behind her desk was suddenly thrust open.

'Constancia . . .'

Jessica felt her heart lurch in recognition of the voice, less grim than when she had heard it last, but recognisable all the same. She was halfway out of her seat, the blood draining from her face, when Sebastian de Calvadores turned and saw her, frowning in disbelief. *'Dios!'* he swore angrily. 'You would pursue me even here? Have you no pride, no natural feminine reticence? I have told you as plainly as I can, *señorita,* that my brother has no interest in you. And nor will you find him here. He is away from home at the moment, visiting the family of his *novia*-to-be,' he added cruelly, 'a young girl of excellent family who would rather die than tell a man to whom she was not married that she was to bear his child.'

This last gibe brought the hot colour back to Jessica's face.

'Did you send your brother away so that he couldn't see . . . me?' she asked heatedly.

'Hardly. I had no prior warning of your arrival. However, I am sure that had we done so, Jorge would have thanked me for saving him from an unpleasant confrontation. What did you hope for by coming here? To browbeat him into changing his mind and offering you the protection of his name—our name?' he added proudly.

Before Jessica could retaliate the door opened again and Colin came out, beaming as he caught sight of her.

'Ah, Jessica my dear, you're back. Conde,' he smiled, turning to Sebastian de Calvadores and astounding Jessica, 'allow me to introduce my assistant to you. Jessica—the Conde de Calvadores, Chairman of Calvortex!'

'This is your assistant of whom you have spoken so highly to me?' Just for a moment Jessica saw that Sebastian was practically dumbfounded, although he managed to conceal his shock faster than she could hers.

He was the Chairman of Calvortex! He was the person on whom the future success of Colin's business depended. Her heart sank. She couldn't see him agreeing to anything that involved her, no matter how remotely.

'Yes, this is Jessica,' Colin was agreeing happily, plainly unaware of any undercurrents. 'Like Señor Ferres, the Conde expected my assistant to be a man,' he added to Jessica.

'Perhaps because I'm a woman he would prefer to see me shut away behind a locked gate—or better still, in one of Seville's many dungeons,' Jessica said lightly, and although Colin laughed, she knew from the tiny muscle clenching in the Conde's lean jaw that he had not missed her point.

'The Conde has invited me to join him for dinner this evening,' Colin told her. 'We have still not discussed everything.'

Jessica's heart pounded. Was the discovery that she was Colin's assistant going to affect his decision adversely? Surely as a businessman Sebastian de Calvadores would make his final judgment on commercial grounds only, and yet she couldn't help remembering what Ramón Ferres had said about his family and how it tied in with her own impression that he was an inordinately proud man. Would he turn Colin's suggestions down simply because Colin employed her?

Constancia returned with her cup of coffee and Jessica took it, grateful for an excuse to turn away from Sebastian de Calvadores's bitter eyes.

What an appalling coincidence! She had never imagined for one moment that Jorge's arrogant brother and the head of Calvortex would be one and the same man.

'. . . and of course, Jessica is of particular help to me because she speaks several languages fluently,' she suddenly heard Colin saying, and her fingers trembled as they curled round the coffee cup and she realised that the two men were discussing her.

'Most fortuitous,' she heard Sebastian de Calvadores replying, cynicism underlining the words, and bringing a faint flush to her pale skin. 'I believe you told me that she was also fully qualified in textile design and processing?'

'Oh yes,' Colin beamed. 'In fact that's really her first love, but as I'm sure you know, we have nothing in England to rival anything such as Calvortex.'

'I believe you mentioned that you would like to use the telephone,' Jessica heard Sebastian murmuring to Colin. 'If you would care to go with my secretary, she will help you with your calls.'

As Colin followed Constancia into her office, Jessica had a cowardly impulse to beg him not to leave her alone with Sebastian de Calvadores.

'Quite a coincidence,' he observed coldly when they were alone, 'and one that makes me even more suspicious of your motives. You knew, of course, when you first met Jorge of his connection with Calvortex and from that doubtless deduced that he was a comparatively wealthy young man. For all your much vaunted feminism and independence I find you are very little different from our own women in that you are looking for a man who will support you and ease your way through life, although unlike them you do not have the honesty to admit it, nor the accomplishments to make the bait tempting, especially not to a Spaniard, who expects to find his bride pure and innocent. No wonder you went for a boy like Jorge! He is still young enough to find a certain charm in experience—of course it is expected that young men will…experiment, but you are singularly foolish if you honestly believe that Jorge would marry a woman such as yourself.'

Jessica's hand snaked out—she couldn't help it—anything to destroy that cynical, infuriating smile. But the instant her palm made contact with the lean tanned cheek, a sick wave of self-disgust swept over her. What on earth was happening to her? She had never struck anyone in anger before, no matter how much she had been provoked.

And it seemed that Sebastian de Calvadores shared her shock. His fingers touched the faintly reddening flesh, his eyes darkening rapidly to a fury that scorched and terrified her, but Jessica refused to be cowed. No matter how much she was trembling inwardly, he would never be allowed to know of it!

'*Dios*, vixen!' The words were breathed harshly, fastidious disgust etched in every line of the aristocratic features. 'Nobody strikes a Calvadores and is allowed to escape without retribution!'

He moved, silent and agile as a cougar, grasping her wrists and pinioning them with hard fingers that locked on to her tender flesh. She tried to pull away, infuriated by her sudden imprisonment, and with a speed that left her startled and breathless she was jerked forward, the fingers that had held her wrists, grasping onto her shoulders, the dark grey eyes smouldering with an anger that touched off something elemental deep within her own body, mutual antagonism crackling between them.

'*Cristos!*'

She heard Sebastian swear and then his mouth was on hers, angry and hatefully contemptuous—the very worst kind of punishment, letting her know that she was less than the dust beneath his feet, her breasts were crushed against the fine wool of his suit and it appalled her that such a bitter and punishing embrace should still have the power to ignite a powerful sexual chemistry so that she was aware of Sebastian de Calvadores as a man in a way that she could never remember being aware of any man before. The expensive suit and silk shirt were simply the trappings of civilisation masking the true nature of a man who was still every bit as much a conqueror as his ancestors had been. He was enjoying using his body to punish her—she could sense it, feel it in the hard arrogance of his flesh against hers, forcing her to submit.

Against her will her lips softened, trembling slightly beneath the determined assault. Almost instantly Sebastian drew away.

'I am not my brother, Señorita James,' he told her sardonically. 'The warmth of your mouth trembling beneath mine leaves me cold—especially when I know that I am far from being the first man to have tasted its sweetness.'

'How hypocritical of you!' Jessica flashed back, walking unsteadily away from him. 'You obviously expect your wife, when you eventually marry, to be as pure as the driven snow, but you, I feel sure, can make no such claims!'

'Would you give a Stradivarius violin or a Bechstein piano to a mere beginner?' he mocked back, astounding her with his cynicism. 'And I think you need not concern yourself with the views of the woman who will be my wife, Señorita James. You and she will be worlds apart in your views on life.'

'Just like me and the girl Jorge is to marry,' Jessica stormed at him, irrationally hurt by his comment. 'How do I know Jorge really wants to marry this girl? How do I know it's not simply your idea?'

'Jesu Maria!' Sebastian breathed, as though imploring the heavens for patience. 'Jorge has told you himself!'

'Perhaps because you insisted,' Jessica told him doggedly, not sure why she was needling him like this, except that it had something to do with the contempt in his eyes when he had released her after kissing her. 'Perhaps I should get in touch with Jorge myself, talk to him...'

'Never! I will not allow it!'

He looked so grimly implacable that Jessica felt a tiny frisson of fear. Why on earth had she goaded him like that? She knew she had no intention of saying anything to Jorge! And yet something seemed to drive her on, so that she shrugged and said nonchalantly:

'You couldn't stop me.'

She almost flinched when she saw the look of utter fury in his eyes; eyes that had darkened almost to black, only the pale grey rim shimmering with barely suppressed rage as he stared at her.

'You dare to challenge me?' he demanded with awesome control. 'You are not only venal, you are a fool as well!' he told her softly.

CHAPTER FOUR

'YOU'RE QUITE SURE you'll be all right?' Colin asked her fussily for the fourth time.

Jessica sighed. 'You're going out for the evening, not leaving me on the steps of the workhouse,' she reminded him dryly. 'Of course I'll be all right, what on earth could possibly happen to me?'

It was eight-thirty before Colin left for his dinner engagement with Sebastian de Calvadores, and after he had gone Jessica leaned back in her chair in the bar and tried to relax.

Her nerves had been like coiled springs ever since they left the factory. She had alternated between longing to confide in Colin and a firm determination not to involve him in her private affairs.

Sebastian de Calvadores couldn't possibly deprive Colin of the contract simply because he employed her, surely? And yet there had been a look in his eyes just before Colin had rejoined them which suggested that he would be perfectly willing to journey to hell and back again if he thought that by doing so he could punish her.

And what better way of punishing her could there be than putting Colin's business at risk? It wasn't inconceivable if things didn't improve that Colin would be forced to let her go, and she had no delusions about herself. In spite of her qualifications and experience she would find it extremely difficult to get a job of equivalent standing.

Against her will she found herself remembering Sebastian's kiss—in no way meant to be an affectionate embrace, but rather a gesture of disdain and condemnation— her memory lingering on the hard length of his body against hers, disturbingly male.

She went up to her room before Colin returned, mentally crossing her fingers that all would go well. He had been full of optimism when he set out, and she only hoped that it was well founded.

'SO HOW DID things go last night?'

Colin looked up from his breakfast, and it seemed to Jessica that he avoided her eyes as he answered, 'Quite well. The Conde seemed very interested in my proposals.'

'Did he agree to them, then?' Jessica pressed, for some reason alarmed by Colin's hesitancy.

'In a manner of speaking, although there were certain conditions...'

'Only to be expected in view of his company's reputation,' Jessica agreed, her spirits lightening. 'What were they?'

For a moment Colin didn't speak, and several seconds later when Jessica replaced her coffee cup she found him regarding her with an expression compounded of uncertainty and appeal. Suspicion sharpened her gaze, fear sending the blood pounding through her veins. Sebastian had told him he would only give him the contract if Colin got rid of her!

'He wants you to fire me, doesn't he?' she said calmly. 'Oh, I...'

'No, no, Jessica, it's not that,' Colin quickly reassured her. 'Quite the contrary. It seems that they're having problems with the designs for their next collection of fabrics. The Conde works on them himself with the help of another designer, whom he has recently lost to a rival organisation. As you can imagine, the Conde is most anxious to complete the work on the season's designs, and he's asked me if I would be agreeable to you working for him until this is done.'

Whatever Jessica expected to hear it was not this! For a few minutes she was too astounded to say anything.

'You see, you were quite wrong in thinking he disapproved of you,' Colin told her. 'He seemed most impressed when I told him about your qualifications. Over dinner tonight he questioned me in detail about you—where you'd trained, how long you'd worked for me. I must admit that I had no idea what he was leading up to, but it seems that Ramón Ferres had told him how interested you were in the manufacturing processes and how knowledgeable, and he confided to me the difficult situation he finds himself in.'

'But surely a firm such as Calvortex would have no trouble at all in finding a junior designer,' Jessica suggested, feeling a tinge of suspicion. Why did Sebastian want her to work for him? She couldn't understand it, especially when he had let her know how much he despised her and how determined he was to keep her away from his brother.

'Certainly,' Colin agreed, 'but it seems he's reluctant to take someone on on a permanent basis at this stage—employing someone on a temporary basis would suit him admirably, but as he admitted to me, it's very difficult to find an accomplished designer willing to be employed for a mere matter of weeks. It seems the Conde has a brother who may eventually take the place of the departed designer, but he needs a designer now to help him complete the new season's range of fabrics. It's quite an honour that he should ask for you,' he pointed out logically, 'and you've always said how much you'd like to work in textiles. It would only be for a few weeks—I should hold your job for you, of course—we can do nothing on next season's designs in any case until we know what fabrics Calvortex will produce.'

'Is your contract dependent on my agreeing to work for the Conde?' Jessica asked, frowning. She could not understand why the Conde would make such a stipulation, but if he had it could not be for any reason that would benefit her.

'Not in so many words,' Colin told her wryly, 'but I suspect if you did refuse . . .'

He left the sentence unfinished, but Jessica felt she knew enough about the Conde to guess at the pressure he would bring to bear on her employer. Despite her love of textiles she had not the slightest desire to work for Sebastian de Calvadores. But if she refused Colin's company might well fold. What should she do? Not for the first time she found herself wishing there was someone she could turn to for advice, instead of always being the giver of advice to others.

'What's wrong?' Colin asked her hesitantly. 'I thought you'd jump at the chance.'

'It's such a surprise,' Jessica told him, not untruthfully. 'How long would it mean staying in Spain?'

'I'm not sure. The details would have to be arranged with the Conde. Initially he is merely enquiring if I would be prepared to let you go on a temporary basis, and if you would be prepared to work for Calvortex. One other thing . . .' he paused and glanced at her uncertainly. 'He did suggest that he would be prepared to pay you extremely well.'

He would, Jessica thought cynically, her fingers curling into her palms, an irate expression in her eyes, and for one heady moment she toyed with the idea of telling the Conde exactly what he could do with both his job and his money. And then common sense intruded, bringing her back down to earth. Colin was watching her with a heartrendingly pathetic expression, and she knew she simply hadn't the heart to tell him she was going to refuse. It was a golden opportunity, she told herself, trying to cheer herself up; she would undoubtedly learn a considerable amount, and in years to come it would stand her in good stead to say she had worked for Calvortex, no matter how briefly, if she wanted to obtain another job.

'You'll do it?' Colin asked eagerly, correctly interpreting her expression.

'I don't see that I've got much option,' she agreed dryly.

'Good! I'll telephone the Conde and give him the good news. Doubtless he'll want to talk to you to finalise all the arrangements.'

'Doubtless,' Jessica echoed ironically. She could well imagine the sneering expression and suffocating arrogance Sebastian would adopt when he knew that she had agreed to his suggestion.

A tiny seed of doubt had taken root in her subconscious, warning her that she would regret this weakness, but she couldn't see what Sebastian could possibly do to her other than attempt to make her life a misery with his cynical remarks and contemptuous eyes, and she would soon show him that she was completely impervious to both.

Jessica had just stepped into the shower when she heard someone knocking on her door. Thinking it must be the maid with the light meal she had ordered, she shrugged on her towelling robe and quickly opened the door.

To her consternation it was not a maid who stood there, but Sebastian de Calvadores, looking cynically urbane as he lounged carelessly against the open door, his eyes slowly appraising her.

'I thought you were room service,' she stammered, feeling as gauche as a raw teenager. 'I . . . what did you want?'

'To speak to you. Surely Colin has already apprised you of my suggestion?'

'You want to speak about that? But Colin said you were going to telephone . . . at least . . .' She couldn't remember now exactly what Colin *had* said; Sebastian's unexpected appearance had thrown her completely, her thoughts were a chaotic muddle.

'Are you going to invite me in, or shall we hold our discussion here in full view of the other guests? On balance I think we would be better inside,' he drawled, walking past her and calmly closing the door.

'But I'm not dressed . . .' Jessica protested, hot colour storming her face as he looked her over thoughtfully.

'An age-old ploy, but one that unfortunately does not work on me. I'm immune to women who use their bodies as you use yours.'

'And yet you still want me to work for you? I should have thought I would be the last person you would want in your employ.'

'Sometimes it is necessary to give way to expediency,' he told her crisply. 'Now, could I trouble you for your decision?'

He really was the most unbearably arrogant man she had ever met in her life! Jessica thought wrathfully. Anyone with the slightest pretensions to consideration would have suggested that they meet downstairs, or at least have given her an opportunity to dress, but not Sebastian de Calvadores. No doubt he enjoyed having her at a disadvantage!

'I can't believe you want me to work for you,' she protested, wishing he would not watch her so closely. She felt like a particularly obnoxious life form being viewed beneath a microscope.

'Come, I'm sure I do not need to boost your ego by paying you flattering compliments. I am assured by your employer that you are a first-rate designer. He is a man whose judgment I trust—I need a designer badly enough to be prepared to overlook certain aspects of your personality. It is as simple as that.'

'You must want me very badly if you were prepared to threaten Colin that you would withdraw the contract!'

'As I said before, it is a matter of expediency. I am already behind with work on next season's fabrics. There have been problems with some of the dyes. Primarily I am a chemist, not a designer, and the work I have had to do on this side of things has meant that there have been delays in the design end of things. Like any other manufacturer, I have deadlines to meet. My suggestion to Colin was based purely on commercial necessity. He understands this even if you don't. I am prepared to help him if he will help me, there is nothing out of the ordinary in that.'

Nothing at all, and yet still Jessica felt uneasy, as though there was something she wasn't being told; something hidden from her.

'And you will merely want me to work for you for a matter of a few weeks?' she pressed.

'Two months at the most. Señor Weaver has said he can spare you for this length of time—the rest is up to you.' He gave a comprehensive shrug. 'I doubt that I would ever be your choice of employer—Señor Weaver obviously has no idea of your true personality—but if you wish to save his business I am sure you will see the wisdom of agreeing.'

He must want a designer very badly, was Jessica's first thought, but then he had already admitted that he did. So why did she have this nagging feeling that there was something else?

'You...' she began.

'I have no time to waste in answering further arguments,' he interrupted her with an arrogance that had her spine prickling as defensively as a ruffled kitten's. 'Either you agree or you refuse, but if you refuse, be very sure at what cost.'

It really wasn't fair, Jessica thought, shivering a little, as she hugged her robe even more firmly around her slender body. What choice did she have?

'I...I agree,' she said huskily at last, the tiny thread of disquiet she had felt earlier exploding into full-blown fear as she saw the triumph glittering briefly in his eyes.

'Most wise. So...if you will be ready to leave in the morning, I shall collect you at nine, that will leave us enough time to...'

'Leave?'

'Ah, yes, didn't I tell you?' he drawled mockingly. 'I intend to spend the next two months working from my *hacienda*. I have...responsibilities there, and the peace and quiet of the *hacienda* is more conducive to design work than the factory. Besides, it is there that I have my laboratories where we experiment with the dyes.'

'I'm not going with you.'

'Oh, but I think you are,' came the silky response. 'Only five minutes ago you told me that you were prepared to work for me. Surely the mere fact that you have learned that you are to be a guest in my family home instead of living alone in a hotel cannot be the reason for this sudden turnaround. Think of Colin,' he told her hardily, 'think of your own future, just as I am thinking of my brother's.'

'Jorge?' Jessica looked bewildered. 'What does he have to do with this?'

'Everything,' he told her succinctly. 'Did you honestly think I would allow you to remain in Seville to further harass my poor brother upon his return, spreading the lord only knows what rumours about his relationship with you—rumours which could well reach the ears of his *novia?* Seville is a very enclosed society and a very rigid one. Barbara's father would never consider Jorge as a husband for his daughter if he were to learn of his relationship with you.'

'I should have thought it was Barbara's opinion that mattered, not her father's,' Jessica remarked sardonically, watching him look down the aquiline length of his nose at her, 'and besides, I had no intention of staying in Spain.'

'You tell me that now, but you cannot deny you came here initially with the express purpose of seeing my brother, when he had already written to you telling you that your association was at an end? No, even if you swore to me that you would never try to contact Jorge again I would not believe you. There is only one way to end your interference in our lives.''

'And what may that be?' Jessica asked tartly. 'Or does the mere fact that I'm in your employ mean that no one would ever believe a Calvadores guilty of demeaning himself by becoming involved with a mere wage slave?'

Her sarcasm brought a dark tinge of angry colour seeping beneath his tan, his eyes as cold as granite as he stared at her aloofly.

'By no means,' he said at last, 'but what they will think is that Jorge would never stoop to become involved with my mistress.'

'Your... You mean you'd let people think I was your mistress?' Jessica gasped. 'Oh, this is infamous! You wouldn't dare!'

A muscle clenched in his jaw, beating angrily against the taut skin, and her eyes were drawn betrayingly to it, as it echoed the uneven pounding of her own heart.

'I thought you might have learned by now not to challenge me,' he told her softly, and she knew that he did dare—anything—if he deemed it necessary.

Heavens, it was like a Restoration comedy! First of all he accused her of being his brother's mistress and now he was saying everyone would think she was his!

'You're exaggerating,' she said positively. 'No one would believe, because I was working for you, that I was your mistress.'

'Of course not,' he agreed smoothly, 'if we were working at the factory. But we shall be working at my home, and I shall take good care to make sure that our relationship is not merely that of employer and employee.'

'But this is all so unnecessary!' Jessica cried heatedly.

'To you perhaps, but not to me. The Calvadores name means a great deal to me, and I will not have it dragged in the mud because some greedy woman tries to blackmail my brother into marrying her.'

His last unforgivable words infuriated her. By what right did he presume to stand in judgment of her?

'Well, if you expect to stop me by dragging me off to your *hacienda,* you're in for a big disappointment,' she told him coldly, 'because I'm not coming with you, and there's no way short of using physical force that you can make me.'

'You've already agreed to work for me,' he pointed out icily, '—of your own free will. If you don't...'

'I know,' Jessica agreed wearily. 'Colin will lose the contract.'

'No doubt he will understand—when you explain to him your reasons for refusing,' he told her smoothly, and a sick dismay filled her. Of course she could not explain to Colin why she had refused, it was all far too complicated now and he would probably simply tell her to tell the truth. How could she do that now? How could she expose Isabel to his wrath? For one thing, she would not put it past him to go to England and terrorise Isabel into doing something foolish. And what about John? How would he react to the news that his fiancée had been having a brief fling in Spain when she was supposed to be thinking over his proposal, and moreover that she had actually thought that she might be pregnant by her lover? No, she could not tell the truth, and the only alternatives were to either accept the proposition and everything that went with it, or refuse it and risk jeopardising Colin's business. Some alternative!

She knew she really had no choice, but it infuriated her to have to give in to such outrageously buccaneering tactics.

'I will come with you,' she said coolly at last, 'but if you attempt to give anyone the impression that we're anything other than business colleagues, I shall be forced to contradict you.'

'Who said anything about "telling" anyone?' he mocked her softly. 'There are other, more subtle ways— like this, for instance.'

Before she could stop him, he had jerked her against his body, his hands locking behind her, holding her against him. She could feel the steady thud of his heart, so much at variance with her own which was racing unsteadily, the breath constricted in her throat, her eyes on a level with the plain severity of his tie. Her heightened senses relayed to her the sharp, clean fragrance of his cologne, the pristine freshness of his shirt, and the smooth brown column of his throat. She lifted her eyes. There was a dark shadow along his jaw suggesting that he might find it necessary to shave night and morning, and she shivered at the thoughts the knowledge conjured up in her mind.

'Let me go!' Her voice was husky, edged with anger and pain. She saw the curling mockery of his smile, the darkness of the cold grey eyes, and knew there was about as much chance of her plea being answered as there was of a hawk dropping its prey.

'You are trembling.'

It was a statement that held an edge of surprise, accompanied by a quick frown. The hand that wasn't securing her body against the hard length of his moved to her shoulder, flicking aside the collar of her robe to reveal the silky paleness of her skin.

'You didn't do much sunbathing when you were on holiday, or is it simply that Jorge told you how much we Latin races admire a palely beautiful skin? Yours has the translucency of a pearl.'

His fingers stroked lightly across her exposed collarbone, tiny tendrils of fear curling insidiously through her lower stomach. Oh no, she thought achingly, what was he trying to do to her? What *was* he doing to her? She had been touched before, for heaven's sake—but never with such explicit sensuality; never as though the male fingers drifting against her skin were touching the softest silk.

'*Dios,*' she heard him murmur smokily, 'one would think you had never been touched by a man before. But we both know that is not true, don't we, *señorita?*'

And then, shockingly, his mouth was where his fingers had been, the eroticism of his touch sending tiny shivers of pleasure coursing through her body. Mindlessly Jessica allowed him to mould her body to his, her head falling back helplessly against his arm, his eyes darkening to obsidian as the neckline of her robe dipped, revealing the pale curves of her breasts.

'Like marble,' he murmured huskily, trailing his fingers seductively along the hollow between her breasts, ignoring her stifled gasp of shock, 'but unlike marble, your skin feels warm to my touch.' His fingers tightened ruthlessly on her hair, his voice hardening as he demanded savagely, 'Tell me now that someone walking in here would not immediately think that we were lovers!'

She shivered bitterly with reaction, hating herself for the way she had yielded so completely to his superior strength, hating her body's purely female response to his masculinity.

His sardonic, 'Perhaps you need further convincing,' made her stomach muscles coil tensely, her body stiffening as he grasped her chin, tilting it so that there was no way she could avoid the hard punishment of his lips, and yet even knowing that he was punishing her, something elemental and fierce sprang to life inside her the moment his mouth touched hers. Her robe was pushed aside, tanned fingers cupping the soft swell of one breast. Jessica shuddered uncontrollably and pushed frantically away, and by some miracle Sebastian released her, surveying her flushed cheeks and furious eyes with cynical amusement.

'What is wrong?' he drawled. 'Surely I took no liberties that have not been permitted to countless others?'

The truth of the matter was that he had; but Jessica wasn't going to admit as much.

'As you've pointed out,' she responded icily, '*they* were permitted them, you weren't.' Not even for Colin's sake could she agree to work with him now; she would never know a moment's peace, never be able to relax . . .

'I'm not going to work for you,' she told him quickly, huddling into the protection of her robe, and avoiding his eyes. 'I . . .'

'You are trying to tell me you won't work for me because of that?' He was openly incredulous and disbelieving. 'You are behaving like an affronted virgin; quite unnecessary, you cannot imagine you stand in any danger of receiving unwanted advances from me? If I haven't already made it clear, perhaps it's time I did,' he told her with deadly silky venom. 'I am not interested in other men's leavings—whether it is one man or a hundred. You are as safe with me as you would be locked up in a convent. Don't mistake a timely warning for any desire for you, and that was all that was—a warning. You will come with me,' he added softly, 'I promise you that. Be ready— I shall pick you up tomorrow morning at nine.'

IF SHE HAD any pride, she would be on a plane back home right now, not sitting staring at her suitcases and wondering if she was doing the right thing, Jessica decided as she glanced round the impersonal hotel bedroom. A glance at her watch showed that it was half past eight. Colin had already left for the airport, full of praise and gratitude—they had talked all evening, and she had tried on several occasions to tell him that there was simply no way she could work for Sebastian de Calvadores, but every time her nerve failed her.

A knock on her door startled her. The porter entered and picked up her cases. Nervous dread fluttering through her stomach, Jessica followed him to the lift.

To try and calm herself a little she ordered herself a cup of coffee, but when it came she felt totally unable to drink it. She hadn't had any breakfast either. Why, oh, why hadn't she left Spain with Colin? He would have understood if she had explained. But she hadn't been able to disappoint him, to know that she was destroying everything he had come to Spain to achieve. She was a coward, she berated herself. She should have told him, and if she had, she wouldn't be here now, waiting... her heart leapt into her throat as she saw the familiar tall figure striding towards her.

'Come!'

It was the first time she had seen him wearing anything other than a formal suit; the dark, narrow-fitting pants clinging to the taut muscles of his thighs, the thin silk shirt hinting at the shadow of hair across his chest. Her stomach muscles tensed protestingly, and she was vividly reminded of how she had felt when he touched her. A fine linen jacket emphasised the breadth of his shoulders, and Jessica suddenly felt acutely nervous. What did she know of this man, apart from the fact that he had an almost obsessive pride in the good name of his family? Nothing!

'You may cease looking at me as though I had suddenly grown two heads. I assure you, you are quite safe,' he told her urbanely. 'Just as long as you behave yourself.'

'And if I don't, you'll do what?' Jessica demanded huskily. 'Punish me as you did yesterday, by forcing yourself on me?'

'Be careful, Señorita James,' he warned her softly. 'You challenge me so recklessly that I wonder if you find the "punishment" as unpalatable as you claim. You have a saying, do you not, "Any port in a storm", but I will not be the port for your frustrated desires, no matter how much you goad me.'

Jessica stared at him fulminatingly. Did he dare to suggest that she actually wanted him to touch her? To...

'You're quite wrong,' she told him bitterly. 'I would rather endure the worst tempest that can rage than seek a haven in your arms!'

Just for a moment she thought she had disconcerted him. There was a brief flash of surprise in his eyes, but then it was gone, and he was ushering her through the foyer to the main entrance of the hotel. Outside, he guided her towards a gleaming Mercedes, while a porter brought out her luggage.

Jessica glanced at the car and shivered slightly. Once she was inside it there would be no going back, no chance to change her mind. She hesitated, torn between a longing to escape no matter what the cost, and a feeling that she owed it to Colin to stay.

'Do not do it,' a dulcet voice murmured in her ear. 'Where would you run to? Come,' Sebastian added, 'get in the car, and stop regarding me as though I were a convicted felon. I assure you I am quite harmless when I am treated with respect.'

Blindly Jessica groped for the rear door handle, but to her surprise, he opened the front passenger door.

'What's the matter?' she asked him bitterly as she climbed in. 'Surely you aren't afraid I'll try and escape?'

'We are supposed to be lovers,' he told her succinctly. 'That being the case, you would not sit alone in the rear of the car.'

'Certainly not,' Jessica agreed sarcastically. 'That, from what I recall of Spanish life, is a privilege accorded only to wives!'

They drove for several kilometres in silence, Jessica's nerves tensing every time Sebastian glanced at her. He was a fast but careful driver. She looked surreptitiously at him, flushing when she discovered that he was watching her.

'I have already told you,' he said harshly, 'you have nothing of a sexual nature to fear from me.'

'I don't,' Jessica told him, surprised by the anger in his eyes and the rigid line of his mouth.

'No? You are clutching the edge of your seat as though you expect an imminent assault on your virtue. Or are you simply trying for an effect? If so, it won't work,' he told her laconically. 'Even if I did not know all about you from Jorge, I could never believe that a Northern European woman in her twenties had retained the virginal innocence you are trying to portray.'

'Why not?' Jessica snapped at him. 'That comment has about as much basis for truth as saying that all Spanish girls are virgins when they marry—it simply doesn't hold water.'

'I shall not argue about it,' she was told evenly, 'but if I were you I would not tax my patience too greatly by trying to assimilate a personality we both know you do not possess!'

Jessica didn't know how long it would take them to reach the *hacienda,* but when eleven o'clock came and went and they were in the depths of the country she started to realise how difficult it might be for her to leave the *hacienda* if she wished.

'Not much farther now,' Sebastian told her. 'Another hour, perhaps.'

'How on earth can you work so far away from the factory?' Jessica asked him.

'There are such things as telephones,' he told her dryly. 'The *hacienda* has been in my family for many generations. We still grow the grapes that go to make one of our fine local sherries, although now this is not produced exclusively from Calvadores vines.'

Jessica had already noticed the vines growing in the fields, but pride had prevented her from asking too many questions—that and a growing nausea exacerbated by the fact that she had had no breakfast. In fact she was beginning to feel distinctly light-headed, but she forced herself to appear alert and interested as Sebastian told her about the local wines, and the art of making sherry.

It was almost exactly twelve o'clock when they turned off the main road, throwing up clouds of dust as they bumped down an unmade-up track. Vines covered the ground as far as the eye could see, and it was only when they crested a small incline that Jessica got her first glimpse of the *hacienda*.

For some reason she had expected a simple farmhouse-type building, and she caught her breath in awe as she stared down at the collection of Moorish-style buildings, shimmering whitely in the strong sunlight, the cupolas gilded by the sun, for all the world as though the entire complex had been wafted from ancient Baghdad on a magic carpet.

'The original building was constructed many centuries ago by an ancestor of mine,' Sebastian told her. 'He was given this land as part of his wife's dowry and on it he built the first house. Since then many generations have added to it, but always retaining the Moorish flavour—of course there have been times, for instance during the Inquisition, when it was not always wise for people to admit to their Moorish blood, when it has even perhaps been expedient to deny it.'

Looking at him, Jessica couldn't imagine that he would ever deny his heritage; indeed, she could far more easily see him condemning himself to the flames of the *auto da fé* than recanting his Moorish blood and his proud ancestors.

They drove under a white archway and into an outer courtyard, paved and cool. As Sebastian opened her door for her, Jessica was aware of movements, of a door opening and people hurrying towards them. A wave of dizziness struck her, and she clung hard to the nearest solid object, distracted to realise it was Sebastian's arm, and then, catching her completely off guard, Sebastian bent his head, coolly capturing her lips and plundering the unguarded sweetness of her mouth.

Just for a moment time seemed to stand still, crazily improbable emotions racing through her heart. What was happening to her that she should want to cling to those broad shoulders and go on clinging? And then her lips were released and Sebastian was saying lazily, in English, 'Ah, Tia Sofia, allow me to introduce Jessica.'

And Jessica was being scrutinised thoughtfully by a pair of snapping dark eyes, very much like Sebastian's, although in a feminine and less arrogant face.

'You are on time, Sebastian,' was all his aunt said. 'The little one is so excited I have had to tell her to go and lie down for a little while. It is always the same when she knows you are coming.'

'My aunt refers to my... ward,' Sebastian explained to Jessica. 'She lives here at the *hacienda* with my aunt and will do so until she is old enough to go to school.' His fingers rested lightly on her arm, and although she was looking discreetly away, Jessica knew that his aunt was aware of their intimacy.

'I have had Rosalinda's rooms prepared for your guest,' she was saying to Sebastian, glancing uncertainly at him.

'Rosalinda was the first Calvadores bride to occupy the *hacienda*,' Sebastian told Jessica. 'Her rooms are in one of the towers, quite secluded from the rest of the house with their own courtyard and stairs leading from it.'

Jessica's face flamed as the implication of his words sank in, and out of the corner of her eye she saw his aunt frown a little and glance at her uncertainly. There was no doubt at all in Jessica's mind that his aunt thought that they were lovers. Lovers! A sharp pain seemed to stab through her heart, her muscles tensing in protest at the images the word invoked. But she and Sebastian were not lovers, she reminded herself, nor ever likely to be. For one thing, he felt nothing but contempt for her, while she, of course, equally detested him . . . Just for a moment she remembered her mixed emotions when he had kissed her, quickly banishing the treacherous suggestion that there had been something infinitely pleasurable in the pressure of his mouth against hers. How could it have been remotely pleasurable? He had kissed her in punishment and she had loathed and resented it! Of course she had.

CHAPTER FIVE

IT WAS Sebastian's aunt who showed Jessica to Rosalinda's tower, much to her relief.

They approached the tower via a narrow, spiralling staircase, the smoothly plastered walls decorated with decorative frescoes and friezes in the Arabic style.

At the top of the stairs, Tia Sofia opened a door and gestured to Jessica to precede her. Once inside Jessica caught her breath on a gasp of pleasure. The room was large and octagonal in shape, an arched doorway leading to another room, and the view from the medieval slit windows stunned her with the magnificent panorama spread out below.

'This room is the highest in the house,' Sofia de Calvadores explained. 'Although latterly it has not been used— it is too impractical for a married couple, and there have been no daughters of the house to make it their own as was the custom in the past.'

'It's beautiful,' Jessica said reverently, gazing at her surroundings. The walls were hung with a soft apricot silk, matching rugs on the polished wood floor. This room was furnished as a small sitting room, and she guessed that beyond it lay the bedroom. Bookcases had been built to fit the octagonal walls; one of the larger window embrasures was fitted with a cushioned seat, and it wasn't hard to imagine a lovely Spanish girl sitting there perhaps playing her mandolin while she gazed through the window waiting for her husband to return home.

Her guide opened the communicating door to show Jessica the bedroom, once again decorated in the same soft apricot, the huge bed covered with a soft silk coverlet.

'There is a bathroom through there,' she told Jessica, indicating another door set into one of the walls. 'It is fortunate that when the idea of this octagonal room was conceived it was built within the existing square tower, so we have been able to make use of the space between the walls to install modern plumbing. I shall leave you now— Maria will come and unpack for you, and we normally have lunch at one.'

Taking the gentle hint, as soon as she was alone Jessica opened the bathroom door, gasping with fresh delight when she saw the sunken marble bath and mirrored walls of the room, reflecting images of her whichever way she turned, the mirrors possessing a greenish tinge, given off by the malachite.

She washed quickly, then changed into a linen skirt in a buttercup yellow shade that complemented her colouring, adding a delicate short-sleeved embroidered blouse. She was going to need more clothes if she was to stay here for the time stipulated. She would have to write to her aunt and ask her to arrange to send some of her things on.

She checked her makeup, renewing her lipstick, chagrined to see how little of it was left after Sebastian's kiss, and having brushed her hair she walked through the sitting room to the top of the stairs, conscious of a nervous butterfly sensation in her stomach, and something faintly akin to anticipation tingling along her spine, as she steeled herself to face her host and new employer.

Whatever his aunt might privately think of Jessica's presence, it was plain to Jessica that she was a Spanish woman of the old school, and that the will of the male members of her family was law. She greeted Jessica pleasantly when she reached the bottom of the stairs and explained that she was waiting to show her the rest of the house, 'Which is rather rambling,' she told her, 'so I will show you round so that you will not get lost.'

Jessica followed her into the main *sala*, furnished with rare antiques, and with a silkily beautiful and probably priceless Aubusson rug on the floor. Beyond the windows lay a courtyard similar in design to the one beneath Jessica's tower, only this one was larger, encompassing several formal beds of flowers, and whereas Jessica's boasted a fountain and a small pool, this one possessed a shimmeringly blue swimming pool and a terrace.

'This is the main courtyard,' Sofia de Calvadores told her. 'There are others, because the Calvadores are first and foremost a Moorish family and for many centuries strictly segregated the differing sections of the family; privacy becomes of prime importance when a house is shared by several generations, and while this *sala* and its courtyard has always been considered a gathering place, there are several small, secluded courtyards which in the past were the private domain of various family members.'

'Just as the tower belonged to Rosalinda,' Jessica suggested. 'It must be fascinating to be able to trace one's family history back so far,' she added genuinely, suddenly remembering what Ramón Ferres had told them about the first Calvadores bride.

'Sometimes—sometimes it is not so pleasant to have the world privy to all one's secrets.'

'But the first Calvadores was one of Pedro the Cruel's knights, wasn't he?'

'Ah, you have heard that story,' Sofia smiled. 'Yes, indeed, that was so. He married the daughter of a Christian knight and it was for her, Rosalinda, that the tower was built.'

Jessica longed to question her further, but refrained, not wanting to appear too curious. What was it Ramón Ferres had said about the girl? That she had claimed her father's enemy had ravished her, and that rather than endure the taint of such an accusation he had married her?

'There you are!' a tiny voice suddenly piped up childishly, from the back of the room. 'Tio Sebastian sent me to look for you.'

'Lisa!' Señora Calvadores' voice reproached. 'Please remember we have a guest.' Her face relaxed into a faint smile as she turned to Jessica and explained in English, 'She is a little unthinking at times, and as always is excited by Sebastian's arrival. Lisa, come and meet Miss James, who is to work with Sebastian.'

A small, dark-haired child, with unexpectedly shadowed brown eyes, stepped forward and gravely offered her hand. She was immaculately if somewhat impractically dressed in a flounced white dress, matching ribbons securing her long hair, gleaming white socks and little black patent shoes such as Jessica couldn't remember seeing a little girl wearing since she herself had been a child.

She regarded Jessica with anxious gravity for several seconds and then burst out impetuously, 'Tio Sebastian won't be working all the time, will he?'

'Not quite,' Sebastian announced, startling Jessica with his silent entrance. 'You were so long, *pequeña,* I thought I should come and look for you.'

'Then, if you are not to work all the time, this afternoon we may go for a ride?' Lisa suggested with innocent coquetry. 'Please, Tio Sebastian! No one else lets me ride as fast as you.'

'We shall see, after lunch,' he told her. 'First your aunt must tell me if you have been a good girl while I have been gone.'

The child ran across to him, clinging to his arm while she assured him that indeed she had, and Jessica was shocked by the sudden wave of longing she experienced to be part of that charmed circle, with Sebastian's free arm securely round her.

The feeling was gone almost immediately, superseded by the knowledge that she was indulging in a ridiculous daydream, probably brought on by the fact that she was virtually alone in an alien land, excluded from the intimate family scene being played in front of her.

'Sebastian spoils her,' Sofia Calvadores complained as she and Jessica followed them out of the room, 'but in the circumstances it is easy to understand why. She is the image of her mother and...' She broke off as though feeling that she had said too much, drawing Jessica's attention to the doors leading to some of the other rooms as they walked into the hall.

'This is Sebastian's study,' she told her, opening one door and giving Jessica a brief glimpse of highly polished heavy furniture and a stained wooden floor covered in rich animal skins. 'But of course he will show you that himself later.'

The dining room seemed huge, the glittering chandeliers and frank opulence of the heavy mahogany table, polished until one could see one's reflection in it, making Jessica blink a little in dismay. She had forgotten how formal life could still be in the great Spanish houses.

'First an aperitif,' Sebastian announced, pouring small measures of golden sherry into small glasses and handing first his aunt and then Jessica one. 'This is made with the produce from our vines,' he told Jessica as she sipped hesitantly at the amber liquid. She had had nothing to eat all day and was beginning to feel the effects. A glass of sherry on an empty stomach was the last thing she wanted, but rather than cause offence by refusing she sipped hesitantly at the rich liquid. It slid warmly down her throat, but any hopes she had had of simply sipping a little and leaving the rest were dashed when Sebastian said ominously, 'Perhaps it is not to your liking?'

As though she would dare not like it! she thought half hysterically, and quickly drank the rest, and wishing she hadn't when her head started to spin muzzily.

It was still spinning when Sebastian indicated that she should sit down at the table. A servant was holding her chair for her, and she walked hesitantly towards it, appalled to realise how disorientated the sherry had made her feel. Surely it was far more potent than anything she had drunk at home?

'Jessica!' Sebastian's voice cut sharply through her muddled thoughts.

'I...it's...I'm so sorry,' she managed to gasp as the world started whirling round dizzily and she reached for the first solid thing she could find, her fingers tightening convulsively on Sebastian's jacketed arm.

She heard him swear mildly, and then to her relief the mists started to clear.

'It was the sherry,' she managed to explain apologetically. 'I didn't have any breakfast, and...'

'It is very potent if you are not used to it,' Sebastian's aunt agreed. 'Sebastian,' she directed her nephew, 'it is your fault for insisting she drink it, but you will feel better directly, my dear,' she comforted Jessica.

What a terrible impression she must be creating, Jessica thought with burning cheeks, and she released Sebastian's arm as though it were live coals. She didn't miss the flash of sardonic comprehension in his eyes and shrank back when he bent his head and murmured softly, 'You cling to me as fiercely as a dove to the branch that gives it shelter, but I am not deceived by your air of helpless dismay. Jorge told me of the wild beach barbecues you both attended, when drinking raw Sangria was the order of the day, so please do not expect me to believe that one single glass of sherry could have such a calamitous effect.'

What was he trying to imply? That she might have some other motive for clinging to him? But what?

'If you are having second thoughts,' he added, supplying her with the answer, 'and thinking that any man in your bed is better than none, do not, I beg you, even think of nominating me for the role. As I have already said, I am particular about with whom I share the pleasures of the act of love.'

'Tio Sebastian, what are you saying to Miss James?' Lisa piped up curiously. 'She is looking all pink and funny!'

His aunt quickly shushed the child, but not before Jessica had pulled away and slid into her chair. What must his aunt think of her? she wondered bitterly; or was she inured to her nephew's habits? Did she perhaps simply ignore the real role in his life of the women whom he brought home? They would think they were lovers, he had told her, and she was forced to admit that he had been right, but how did one correct such insidious suggestions? By simply and frankly correcting them? How could she tell his aunt they were not lovers? It was impossible!

After lunch Sebastian suggested that he should show her round the laboratory.

'Can I come too, Tio?' Lisa pleaded. 'I promise I will be good.'

'If you have no objection?' he murmured enquiringly to Jessica.

She shook her head. In truth she would be glad of the little girl's company, because her excited chatter broke the constrained atmosphere that stretched between them.

The laboratory was situated at the back of the *hacienda,* in what had originally been an immense stable block but which Sebastian explained to Jessica had been converted into garages and his laboratory.

The door was padlocked and bolted, and he told her as he unlocked it that because of the dyes and processes used he allowed no one apart from himself to enter the building.

'At the moment we are working on a new generation of dyes, almost entirely based on natural substances, but there is still some problem with the stabilising agent, although that should not take too long to sort out.'

'You are the only company I know that uses only natural dyes,' Jessica mentioned. 'It's quite rare, but of course that's why no other concern can match you for delicacy of colour.'

'This is so,' Sebastian agreed, 'and that is why the exact blending and stabilising of the various agents is a closely guarded secret. Indeed, I am the only person in the company who possesses the complete formula—it is as valuable as that to us.'

Jessica could well understand why. The subtlety and delicacy of their colours was one of the things that helped to make their range of fabrics so successful.

The laboratory was well equipped, and she followed with interest Sebastian's description of the work he was carrying out, although her prime interest lay not so much in the dyeing of the fabric but in the design of it.

There was an office off the laboratory with a row of metal filing cabinets, and Sebastian unlocked one, producing some detailed sketches and swatches of fabric which he handed to her.

'These are the colours we are hoping to produce for next season's fabrics—as you know, the Colour Council normally decide a season's colours two or three years in advance. These are the colours suggested by the last Council meeting. What we have to do now is to incorporate them into the design of the fabric. What I should like you to do initially is to work on them and produce some suggestions for me.'

Jessica nodded, excitement stirring as, against her will, she became fascinated by the project ahead. She did know that the Colour Council worked two years ahead of the fashion designers, selecting the spectrum of colours for a particular season, and the swatches Sebastian had handed her made her mouth water in anticipation. They were autumn and winter colours; black, charcoal grey, softly muted heathers and a bright peacock blue shading to mauve.

'You can use the office here, or the sitting room in the tower, whichever you wish,' Sebastian told her carelessly, glancing down at Lisa as she tugged impatiently at his hand.

'You said we could go riding,' she reminded him, pouting a little. 'You promised!'

'You are forgetting that we have a guest,' Sebastian reminded her firmly. 'Would it not be polite also to ask Miss James if she would care to come with us?'

The question was for Lisa's benefit and not hers, Jessica acknowledged. Like other Latin races Spanish children were petted and indulged, but good manners were considered paramount. Hesitantly Lisa asked if she would like to join them, her relief patent and winning Jessica a wide relieved smile, when she gently refused.

'I'll take these up to the tower with me,' she told Sebastian, adding to Lisa, 'Enjoy your ride.'

She didn't go straight back to the tower, but found her way instead to the small enclosed courtyard she could see from her bedroom window. Jacaranda bloomed profusely against the walls, mingling with the bougainvillea, while two doves cooed melodiously on the rim of the pool. The courtyard had a secluded, mysterious air, as though it preferred moonlight and the seductive whispers of lovers to sunshine and birdsong. Had Rosalinda ever walked here with a lover—the husband who had married her so unwillingly, perhaps? Had they ever found love together?

When she returned to the house she met Sebastian's aunt in the hall. 'Lisa and Sebastian are going riding,' she told her, adding impulsively, 'Lisa is a delightful child.'

'Charming—when she wants to be,' Sofia Calvadores agreed dryly, 'but Sebastian spoils her. It is natural, I suppose. He is all she has.'

'Her parents are dead, then?' Jessica asked sympathetically.

Was it her imagination or did the Señora hesitate briefly before saying, 'Yes, I'm afraid so, she is Sebastian's ward. It could be difficult for her should Sebastian marry and have children of his own.'

'But surely, when he does, his wife will understand and accept that Lisa is bound to find it hard at first,' Jessica suggested.

Señora Calvadores smiled. 'One would hope so, but it would depend very much on the wife. Sebastian must marry, of course, to carry on the name. He was betrothed once, but his betrothed died—a tragic accident in a car.'

She sighed and shook her head. 'It was all a long time ago, and best forgotten now.'

It was late afternoon before Lisa and Sebastian returned to the *hacienda*. Jessica had been working in her sitting room when a maid had knocked and told her that it was the custom for the ladies of the household to drink sherry and eat almond pastries at this particular time of the day, adding that Señora Calvadores was waiting for her in the main courtyard.

She hadn't realised how cramped her limbs had become, and she was still a little stiff when she emerged into the sunshine to find that Lisa and Sebastian had returned and were sitting with the Señora.

Sebastian moved and Jessica realised there was someone else with them; a tall stately woman in her early thirties, her thick dark hair drawn back in a chignon, her cold dark eyes appraising Jessica as they moved over her.

Jessica recognised her from the hotel in Seville, and wondered who she was.

'Ah, Jessica, there you are. Allow me to introduce Miss James to you, *cara,*' he said to his companion. 'She has come here to work for me for several weeks.'

'I hope she realises her good fortune,' was the brunette's acid response.

'Jessica—Pilar Sanchez, a close friend and neighbour of ours.'

'Merely a close friend,' Pilar pouted, slanting Jessica another acid glance. 'Come, our relationship is stronger than that. If poor Manuela had lived we would have been brother and sister.' Scarlet-tipped fingers lay provocatively along Sebastian's forearm, the look in her eyes as she gazed up at him anything but sisterly. There was a strange aching sensation in Jessica's stomach. They could be lovers. *Were* they lovers? Surely not; Pilar obviously came from a family as exalted as Sebastian's own; her sister had obviously been engaged to him. If he needed a wife surely he need look no further than Pilar. Or was there perhaps some bar on such a marriage because of his relationship with her sister? Jessica wasn't sure about the Catholic church's ruling on such things.

She was brought back to her surroundings with a jolt as Pilar scolded sharply, temper flags flying scarlet in her cheeks, 'Lisa, your fingers—don't touch my dress, child, you will ruin it!'

The little girl's face crumpled. She looked uncertainly at Sebastian, who was frowning, and then towards his aunt, who said gently, 'Lisa, go and find Maria. It is time for you to rest.'

'Really, Sebastian, that child is growing impossible!' Pilar commented sharply when Lisa had gone. 'You should send her to a convent where she could learn obedience.'

'As Manuela did?' Sebastian drawled sardonically, but Jessica couldn't understand the expression in Sofia's eyes or the reason for his aunt's suddenly tense body.

Jessica had to wait until after dinner to show Sebastian the work she had done during the day. To her surprise he didn't criticise it as thoroughly as she had anticipated, instead showing her some work he had done himself.

'Initially I didn't want to give you any guidelines,' he told her, 'because it is important that we work on the same wavelength. What you have done shows me that you have a natural sympathy for our fabrics and what we hope to achieve with them. Tomorrow we shall spend an hour together in my study talking about what line the new range will take. You like the tower?' he asked her unexpectedly.

Caught off guard by the absence of his normal cynicism and contempt, Jessica replied enthusiastically, 'I love it, but I can't help wondering if Rosalinda was happy there. She occupied those rooms alone...'

'Instead of sharing those of her husband?' Sebastian interrupted. 'This is true, but it was only in the initial days that she occupied the tower. You have obviously heard the story and you must remember that she had accused her husband of seducing her, when in fact he knew he had not. He had married her to protect his good name, but he swore he would remain celibate rather than touch an unwilling woman who had already given herself to another. So matters might have continued if Rosalinda hadn't found the courage to go to him and confess that she had lied to her father, but not to conceal any affair with another man, simply because she had fallen desperately in love with Rodriguez, and wanted him for her husband, but she knew that because of the enmity that existed between him and her father she had no chance of marrying him. So she conceived her plan. She knew of the pride of both Rodriguez and her father and knew that if she were to accuse Rodriguez of dishonouring her he would be forced to make reparation. It was a bold step to take; she had to face dishonour herself—admit to her lack of chastity, perhaps endure the hatred of her husband forever, when he knew how he had been tricked.

'But Rosalinda was beautiful as well as bold. Rodriguez could not resist her tears of contrition for the trick she had played, and she told him that she was still a virgin. She did not spend many nights alone in her tower,' Sebastian added dryly.

'So she tricked him into marriage, just as you've accused me of trying to trick Jorge,' Jessica pointed out.

He looked at her angrily. 'The two cases are entirely different. She was motivated by love, which excuses much;

you are motivated by material greed, which is unforgivable.'

Why was it that no matter what subject they discussed they always ended up quarrelling? Jessica wondered tiredly as she gathered together her designs and the swatches of fabric.

'You are looking pale,' Sebastian confounded her by saying abruptly. 'My aunt tells me you worked all afternoon, and then into the evening.'

'You had a guest,' Jessica pointed out, without reminding him that Pilar had looked anything but pleased at his suggestion that she stay with them. 'And besides, I enjoyed it.'

'In future you will take proper exercise.' He frowned. 'Can you ride?' Jessica shook her head.

'A pity, you could have joined Lisa when she rides with me in the morning.'

He made her sound like another child to be humoured and scolded, Jessica thought wryly.

'I can walk, or swim,' she told him. 'And besides, the sooner the work is completed the sooner I can leave.'

For some reason his mouth compressed angrily at that statement, and with one of those quickly shifting moods she was coming to dread Jessica felt a frisson of awareness steal through her. He had discarded his jacket, and the breeze from the open windows flattened his shirt tautly to his body, moulding the muscled power of his torso. His shirt was open at the neck, the pale glimmer of the white fabric emphasising the darkness of his skin. A pulse beat steadily at the base of his throat, drawing her eyes, a curious sensual tension enveloping her. She moistened her lips and watched as he moved slowly towards her.

'Jessica . . .' He broke off as the *sala* door was suddenly thrust open and a tall young man with a shock of dark hair and a mobile mouth hurried in, coming to a standstill as he saw Jessica.

'Jorge!' Sebastian exclaimed in surprise. '*Dios!* What are you doing here?'

Jorge! Jessica stared in disbelief at the newcomer. This was Sebastian's brother?

It was plain that he was slightly taken aback by Sebastian's attitude. He glanced uncertainly first at his brother and then at Jessica.

'I wanted to see you,' he said in a puzzled voice. 'I had no idea you were planning to come here. You never mentioned it when we spoke on the telephone.'

'Perhaps because I had no idea you were intending your stay with the Reajons to be of such a short duration. It was, I believe, to be for one month.'

Jessica felt sorry for the younger man as he flushed and looked uncomfortable. 'That is one of the things I wanted to talk to you about, Sebastian. I . . .' He broke off and glanced hesitantly at Jessica, then turned to his brother, saying gallantly, 'But you have a guest—and a very beautiful one. Aren't you going to introduce me?'

To say that Sebastian looked stupefied was an overstatement, but there was a certain amount of shock as he registered the words. He too turned to look at Jessica, and she quailed beneath the message she read in his eyes.

'I thought Miss James was already known to you,' he said in icy tones. 'In fact to such an extent it is not so long ago that you were pleading with me to help you remove her from your life.'

Jessica felt sorry for the young man when he flushed again, but it was obvious to her that Sebastian intended to spare her nothing.

'I am Isabel's cousin,' she explained to Jorge, ignoring Sebastian. 'There's been a slight misunderstanding and your brother mistook me for Isabel. When I learned what he had to say to her I decided not to enlighten him. For all her faults, Isabel is acutely sensitive...'

She didn't need to say any more. Jorge looked appalled, and turned horrified eyes on his brother. 'Sebastian, you said nothing about speaking personally to Isabel! We were agreed that a letter...'

'So we were, but then I had no idea that she intended to come and plead her case personally—or so I thought. Naturally my first priority was to protect you.'

'Another misconception on your part,' Jessica told him bitterly. 'Isabel...didn't tell me the full facts. She was terrified that you intended to go to England to see her. She is now engaged to someone else...and quite naturally...' She was beginning to flounder, not wanting to betray Isabel's stupidity and lack of moral fibre, but Sebastian, it seemed, had no such qualms.

'What you are saying is that your cousin lied to you.'

'Not deliberately,' Jessica hastened to defend Isabel. 'She simply wanted to make sure there would be no repercussions from her letter to Jorge—written when she was feeling extremely worried and almost desperate. She wanted me to tell Jorge that she fully accepted that their liaison was at an end.'

It wasn't quite the truth, but it would suffice.

'You knew I had mistaken you for her, why did you not tell me the truth then?' Sebastian demanded, watching her with narrowed eyes.

'Because I didn't want to expose Isabel to the same sort of insults I had been forced to endure myself,' Jessica told him coolly. 'Just as you wanted to protect your brother, I wanted to protect my cousin!'

'We will speak of this later,' he told her silkily. 'For now...'

'You naturally want to be alone with your brother,' Jessica supplied dryly, not adding that she was more than happy to leave them alone together.

Jorge's unexpected arrival had given her a bad shock. Whereas she ought to be experiencing relief and satisfaction that Sebastian now knew the truth, all she could think was that he might now send her back to England, and for some reason she didn't wait to analyse too carefully, she didn't want to go!

CHAPTER SIX

'AH, THERE YOU ARE, I hope you will permit me to join
you?'

Jessica glanced at Jorge's concerned face and smiled.
She was sitting in her small courtyard, working on some of
the designs, and enjoying the sunshine.

'Sebastian is working in his laboratory,' Jorge informed her, needlessly, since Sebastian himself had told
her at breakfast that he could be found there should she
want him. There had also been a look in his eyes that told
her that there was still a reckoning to come, but that was
something she was refusing to think about!

'I must apologise, for my...for my brother's behaviour,' Jorge managed at last, flushing a little. 'It is unforgivable that he should have involved you in this affair.' He
bit his lip. 'He has given me the gist of what has happened
between you, although why, feeling as he does, he has
brought you here to the *hacienda* to work for him I do not
know!'

He looked perplexed and unhappy, but Jessica didn't
enlighten him. He might think Sebastian had told him the
truth, but she knew differently.

'I was speaking to my aunt this morning and she seems
to think...that is, Sebastian has given her the impression...that...that you are lovers,' he added uncomfortably, 'and yet plainly this is not so. I shall speak to him

about it on your behalf. Isabel talked of you to me, I know you are not . . . that you do not . . .'

'That I'm not promiscuous?' Jessica supplied dryly, privately suspecting that Isabel had been far more unflattering in her description of her, but Jorge seized on the expression gratefully.

'*Si,*' he agreed, 'this is so . . . Sebastian cannot appreciate what my aunt thinks, for he would never expose a young woman of unblemished reputation to such an insult.'

Heavens, he sounded like something out of a Victorian novel! Jessica thought to herself. Surely he couldn't be serious? But apparently he was.

'I shall speak to him about it,' he added again. 'It is not right.'

Right or wrong, she couldn't see Sebastian being easily influenced by his younger brother, Jessica reflected when Jorge had gone.

She had been on her own for about half an hour when she glanced up, hearing footsteps coming in her direction. To her surprise she saw Pilar coming towards her, the older woman's mouth grimly compressed, two bright coins of colour burning in her otherwise completely pale face.

'You are wasting your time!' she hissed to Jessica without preamble. 'Sebastian does not really want you. He has only ever loved one woman—my sister, and . . .'

Jessica tried to interrupt, to assure her companion that she had no romantic interest in Sebastian. Something about the way the older woman was watching her triggered alarm bells in her mind. It struck her that there was something driven, something almost bordering on hysteria, in Pilar's manner.

'He was obsessed by her,' Pilar continued almost as though Jessica wasn't there, 'but one day he will have to marry, if only in order to have sons, and who better than the sister of the woman he loved?'

'But surely...' Surely there is Jorge, Jessica had been about to say, but once again Pilar didn't give her the opportunity to finish.

'You are thinking of Lisa,' she said bitterly, 'but she is only a daughter. Sebastian needs sons.'

Lisa was Sebastian's daughter? Shock coursed through Jessica, stingingly, followed by a hot, molten anger. How dared he question her morals when he...

'You didn't know?' Pilar started to laugh wildly. 'Of course he wouldn't tell you. No one is supposed to know about it. My sister Manuela had been his *novia* for many months and the preparations for the wedding were all in hand when she suddenly became ill. It was the strain of preparing for the wedding, our doctor told my parents, and Manuela was sent to Argentina to stay with relatives there. When she returned it was obvious that there was to be a child—Sebastian's child. My parents were bitterly hurt and shocked. Sebastian whom they trusted and treated like a son had taken Manuela's innocence before they were married. Preparations for the ceremony were speeded up. My mother begged Manuela to tell her why she had not confided in her before her visit to Argentina. I myself was married then. I too was shocked by Sebastian's behaviour, but I knew how much he loved her. And then just two days before the ceremony Manuela asked me if she could borrow my car.' Pilar hesitated and for a moment there was a sly, almost gloating expression in her eyes.

'She was involved in an accident near Seville, and was taken immediately to the hospital. They were able to save the child, but by the time Sebastian reached the hospital Manuela was dead.'

Jessica couldn't conceal her shock and distaste. Poor Manuela! By all accounts she had been tragically innocent and young, and now she was dead and Sebastian was left only with memories of what might have been, and a child—his child! Why then had she been introduced as his 'ward'?

'Of course everything was hushed up,' Pilar continued. 'Only the closest members of the family know of the circumstances of Lisa's birth.' Her lips twisted, and Jessica was reminded of how much she seemed to dislike the little girl—a child who was after all her niece. 'Lisa is a constant reminder to Sebastian of my sister,' Pilar continued, and with a flash of insight Jessica realised that Pilar was jealous; jealous of her sister's child.

'It was a tragic year for our family,' she added. 'First Manuela and then my own husband and parents were killed when my husband was taking them to Minorca in his plane, but worst of all—Lisa.' She shuddered. 'It is just as well Manuela died. Had she lived she would have been shunned for her sin.

Jessica could hardly believe her ears. What Pilar was saying was positively feudal—and what of Sebastian, surely he was equally to blame, if indeed 'blame' was the word. And poor Lisa! She obviously didn't realise that Sebastian was her father. Jessica felt an upsurge of anger against him. How could he deny his daughter her right to her relationship with him? Pilar said he had loved Manuela, but in Jessica's opinion it was a poor sort of love that denied the human evidence of that love.

SHE WAS STILL TRYING to come to terms with what Pilar had told her after lunch, when Sebastian announced that he wanted to talk to Jorge in his study.

Lisa was at a loose end, and asked Jessica if she could sit with her. 'I will be very good,' she promised, 'but it is Tia Sofia's day for having her friends round, and it is very dull.'

Jessica was touched that the little girl should want her company. Her work on the designs was well advanced, and in fact she could do little until she had spoken to Sebastian, so she suggested instead that Lisa show her round the environs of the *hacienda*.

The little girl was an entertaining companion. Jessica had always liked children, and concealed her pity carefully when Lisa commented on how lonely she sometimes felt.

'Pilar wants to send me away,' she confided fearfully, 'but Tio Sebastian will not let her.'

How could Sebastian deny his relationship with his child?

It was late afternoon when they returned. Sebastian's aunt was in the *sala* with her friends, and Lisa politely listened to their questions, responding demurely, quite different from the exuberant child she had been when she had been with Jessica.

Jessica could tell that she herself was the subject of a good deal of discreet curiosity.

'Jessica is a particular friend of Sebastian's,' his aunt explained.

'But I understand from my niece that you were here primarily to work for him,' one formidable matron said icily.

Jessica wasn't surprised to discover that she was Pilar's aunt. 'And your family don't mind?' she asked, apparently unable to believe it when Jessica assured her that they didn't. 'In Spain no young woman of good family would be permitted to stay in the home of an unmarried man without a female relative with her.'

'I am here to work,' Jessica reminded her coolly, uneasily reminded of what Jorge had said. Did these women think she was Sebastian's mistress? What did it matter if they did? And yet it was an uncomfortable sensation to have them studying her, perhaps talking about her when she wasn't there.

After they left the *sala*, Jessica went upstairs to her tower, while Lisa was whisked away by her maid for a rest.

The household ran like clockwork, and yet apparently without any effort on the part of Sebastian's aunt, although Jessica had noticed that the staff consulted her every day just after breakfast. It must be an enormous responsibility caring for the valuable antiques and art treasures that filled the *hacienda,* and she reflected that it was impossible not to admire the selflessness of Spanish women when it came to devoting themselves to their homes.

She had wanted to see Sebastian about the designs she was working on and gathering up her work she went downstairs to his study. She could hear voices from inside, one of them recognisably Jorge's and bitterly defensive.

Now was obviously not the time to intrude, and she was just walking away when Rafael, the majordomo of the household, appeared.

'I was hoping to have a word with the Conde,' Jessica explained in response to his unspoken question, 'but...'

'I shall inform him when he is free,' Rafael assured her. 'Perhaps you would care for a tray of tea? In the past our English guests have often asked for tea at this time.'

It was six o'clock and as Jessica knew from experience, it would be several hours before they dined. Spaniards dined late, so she thanked Rafael and told him that tea would indeed be most welcome.

It arrived twenty minutes later—a bone china tea service and a plate of delicate almond cakes. Until she saw them Jessica hadn't realised how hungry she felt. She had just finished her second cup of tea when someone knocked briskly on the door. She knew without opening it, with some instinctive sixth sense, that it was Sebastian.

He looked preoccupied and bleakly angry, and her heart sank. Now was obviously not the time to discuss her ideas with him.

'Now,' he said, when he had closed the door with a precision that sent shivers of alarm feathering along her spine, 'perhaps you will be good enough to explain why you did not tell me the truth about your cousin?'

He was leaning against the door, arms folded across his chest, unconsciously straining the fabric, his eyes glinting metallic grey as they waited for her response.

'I've already told you,' Jessica said tightly. She had forgotten the implicit threat she had seen in his eyes when Jorge unwittingly revealed the truth, in the shock of listening to Pilar's disclosures.

'I wanted to protect Isabel . . .'

'Protect her, or her engagement?' he asked with devastating insight. 'Jorge has told me of this John—apparently she was contemplating becoming engaged to him when she met Jorge.'

'Jorge was simply a holiday romance,' Jessica told him firmly. 'Isabel is silly but not venal. I can assure you she had no mercenary interest in Jorge.'

'No? Then why did she threaten him with this child she says she conceived?'

'A mistake,' Jessica told him. 'Surely you can appreciate her position? She came back from holiday, and then discovered that she might be carrying Jorge's child, or so she thought, so she panicked . . .'

'And tried to force him into marrying her,' Sebastian concluded distastefully. 'And this is the innocent child you wished to protect? No, I cannot accept it.'

She wasn't going to tell him how Isabel had lied to her, Jessica decided angrily, her chin tilting defiantly as she stared up at him.

'It doesn't matter to me whether you do or not,' she told him unsteadily. 'All I want to do now is to put the entire incident behind me.'

It wasn't completely true—certain aspects of it would remain to haunt her always, and she was very much afraid that what she felt for Sebastian came dangerously close to love. Quite how or why it should have happened she didn't know, but these last few days had underlined, time and time again, that she was far from indifferent to him. She only had to register the way her pulses raced whenever he walked in a room to be aware of that! And yet he was the complete antithesis of all she admired in men. Arrogant, domineering and apparently incapable of facing up to his responsibilities.

'Easier said than done.' He frowned, unfolding his arms, and moved silently to the window. 'As Jorge has just been at considerable pains to point out to me, my aunt, and no doubt by this time, her cronies, all believe you to be my mistress.'

He seemed to be waiting for some response, and Jessica refused to acknowledge the hurting shaft of pain his indifference occasioned.

'We know differently,' she told him. 'And besides, the opinion of half a dozen or so people I've never set eyes on before and am not likely to see again doesn't trouble me.'

'I'm sure it doesn't,' Sebastian agreed grittily, 'but unfortunately, I do have to see them again and it does concern me, as everything touching upon the good name of our family must.'

It was on the tip of Jessica's tongue to tell him that this was something he should have thought of before, but instead she said unsteadily, 'Yes, I see that having a reputation such as yours must be a great burden to so proud a man.'

Instantly she realised she had gone too far. Fingers like talons gripped her wrist.

'Just what do you mean by that?' he demanded softly.

'I think you know,' Jessica managed bravely. 'There's Lisa, and people are not blind...'

'Ah, someone has told you about Manuela,' he said comprehensively, his mouth twisting in a cynically bitter smile. 'And of course you are quite right. There is endless gossip about Lisa, and her parenthood, and because of that I have to be extremely circumspect—for her sake as much as my own.'

'I can't see why you don't tell her the truth,' Jessica told him huskily. 'It's cruel not to do. She's bound to find out.'

'You are very concerned on her behalf.' Again the mockingly cynical smile.

'Because I happen to like her; and because also I know what it's like to lose both parents, and nothing, but nothing compensates for that loss. Any parent is better than none at all,' she told him fiercely, 'a ¹ you're depriving her of the right to that relationship.'

'Enough!' With a ferocity that jerked the breath from her lungs she was dragged towards him. 'I will not listen to any more. You will be silent!'

'How will you make me?' Jessica demanded breathlessly. 'By flinging me in your dungeons?'

'Oh no.' The soft way he spoke, and the insolently appraising look that accompanied the words, sent nervous tremors of warning chasing down her spine. 'Like this!'

He moved so suddenly that she couldn't evade him, hard fingers tangling in her hair and tugging painfully until she thought her spine would crack under the pressure. His eyes searched her vulnerable, exposed features in silence, while hers spat the defiance she now dared not voice.

'It is too late for obedience now,' he told her silkily. 'You must take your punishment.'

His mouth on hers was brutally chastising, his fingers forcefully gripping her waist, a savage anger that she had not seen before burning in the pressure of his mouth against hers.

She felt frozen and completely unable to feel, her eyes glazing as she tried not to mind that he was humiliating her like this, turning what should be a sensually exciting experience into a deeply humiliating one.

As though he sensed that somehow she had escaped his vengeance, the pressure of his mouth suddenly softened and then shockingly his lips left hers, his tongue slowly tracing their quivering outline, until she ached and yearned for the feel of his mouth. The anger had gone from his eyes, to be replaced by a slumbrous heat.

Her body seemed to melt against him entirely without her consent, her eyes closing as he feathered light kisses over the trembling lids.

'*Por Dios,*' he muttered hoarsely against her ear, 'there is a chemistry between us that refuses to be denied!'

Jessica knew she should make some protest, tell him to release her, but his fingers were stroking soothingly along her scalp, his mouth investigating the exposed vulnerability of her throat, releasing a fluttering fever of sensations that made her long only to cling to the breadth of his shoulders, and offer herself up to whatever he wanted from her.

Not even the heat of his fingers scorching the curves of her breasts had the power to alarm her. Instead she felt an elemental response to the caress, coupled with a primitive need to feel his touch against her skin without the constricting barrier of clothes. As though somehow her thoughts communicated themselves to him, Jessica heard him groan and saw with surprise the dark flush mantling his skin and the heated glitter of his gaze.

She made no attempt to stop him when he unbuttoned her blouse and slid it from her shoulders. Her lacy bra emphasised rather than concealed the curves of her breasts and her pulses seemed to quicken in elemental excitement as Sebastian's dark gaze lingered on the pale almost translucent skin.

'How much more attractive is this than the overexposed bronzed bodies that litter our beaches! This,' he added emotively, stroking a finger over the pale flesh, 'is an enticement to man to touch and taste. The very paleness of your skin hints at a chastity that arouses the hunter in man, no matter how false that impression might be.'

Jessica gasped as he released the catch of her bra, exposing her breasts fully to his gaze. She knew she should feel shame; yet what she did feel was a tremulous, aching excitement; a need to have him touch her. As though he guessed her thoughts his hands cupped her breasts, her nipples hardening devastatingly at his touch. The stroke of his thumbs over the sensitised and aroused flesh incited a need to writhe and press herself close to his body, the husky moan torn from her throat shocking her with its sensuality.

'Dios, I despise myself for it, but right now I want nothing as much as I want to take you to bed, to feel your

silkiness against my skin, like a soothing balm to over-heated flesh. I want to lose myself in your softness...
I... What is it about you that makes me forget what you are?' Sebastian muttered huskily, lifting her in his arms, his eyes moving from her face to the rosy peaks of her breasts and then back again.

She shouldn't be letting him do this, Jessica thought distractedly, but every nerve centre in her body was screaming for the satisfaction she knew only he could give. She felt the bed give under their combined weight, and all her muscles tightened in stunned protest as his mouth moved hungrily over the curve of one breast, the rough stroke of his tongue against the aching nipple causing her stomach muscles to lock in mute protest at the waves of pleasure crashing down on her, teaching her more about sensuality and her own body's response to it in two min-utes than she had learned in twenty-odd years.

'*Dios,* I want you!'

He was only echoing her own thoughts, her own need. She had never felt this overpowering desire to know a man's possession before, and it shocked her that she should now. But then she had never loved a man as she loved Sebastian.

Loved! With sickening certainty she knew that it was too late to banish the treacherous and insidious truth. She *did* love him.

'Jessica?'

He was watching her, studying the flushed contours of her face, the arousal she felt sure must be there. She longed to touch him as intimately as he was touching her, and she reached out tentatively towards him, her fingers trem-bling as they encountered the rigidity of his collarbone.

'*Dios,* I have hungered for your touch against my skin,' he told her huskily, burying his mouth in the curve of her shoulder, 'almost from the very first. It is true, is it not, that there was a vital chemistry between us—a desire that neither of us can deny.'

Jessica wanted to say that it was not purely desire that motivated her, but Sebastian was wrenching open his shirt and her eyes were drawn to the naked virility of his body. Without the trappings of civilisation, the expensive suit, and the silk shirt, his body was totally male, tautly muscled, his chest shadowed with dark body hair that tapered towards his waist.

'*Dios,* Sebastian, what is the meaning of this!'

They were so engrossed in one another that neither of them had heard the door open. Jessica's shocked eyes saw his aunt's disturbed face and behind her Pilar's glitteringly triumphant one.

'I told you you were wrong,' Pilar said triumphantly. 'I told you they were lovers!'

Sebastian was shielding Jessica with his body, but that didn't stop the shame coursing through her, burning into her soul as she realised how they must appear to their onlookers.

'Sebastian!' his aunt's voice was deeply reproachful. 'I am wounded beyond words that you would use your home as...'

'That is enough.' Quietly and calmly Sebastian silenced both women. 'If you will wait in the sitting room, there is something I must say to you both.'

He waited until they had gone and then quickly stood up, his back to Jessica.

'My apologies for that,' he told her curtly. 'I never imagined that...'

'That what? Jessica wondered. That he would allow his desire to overrule his dislike of her as a person?

'I must speak with my aunt.'

He was gone, closing the door behind him, leaving Jessica to bitterly regret giving in to the wild clamouring tide of desire he had aroused in her. How on earth could she face his aunt or Pilar again? She felt humiliated beyond bearing that they should have witnessed such intimacies. She had wanted to give herself in love, but somehow their interruption had reduced her to the status of a kept plaything, whose only role was to satisfy the needs of her master who might enjoy her body while openly despising her mind.

'Jessica, could you give us a moment?' The quiet voice suggested that if she didn't he would come in and get her.

What was he going to say to her? she wondered nervously, checking in the mirror that she was properly dressed, before screwing up her courage and walking nervously into the other room.

From Sebastian's aunt she received a kind if somewhat sorrowful look. From Pilar she received one of blazing hatred.

'You cannot mean this, Sebastian,' she was saying as Jessica walked into the room. 'It is total folly!'

'That is something only I can decide,' Sebastian replied with iron inflexibility. 'I have just told my aunt and Pilar that we are to be married,' he told Jessica coolly, his eyes warning her against saying anything to contradict his statement. 'As Pilar and Jorge have pointed out to me, I have already been responsible for the destruction of one girl's good name. I will not have the Calvadores name dragged in the mud a second time.'

'But, Sebastian, to go to these lengths!' Pilar protested, glaring at Jessica. 'It is not necessary. You have only to send the girl away. Nothing will be said.'

'No, Sebastian is right,' his aunt interrupted firmly. 'You must not try to dissuade him, Pilar. Jessica, I am pleased to welcome you to our family.' She walked across to Jessica, grasping her hands, kissing her gently on either cheek. 'Come Pilar, it is time we left. Sebastian, if you will tell me what arrangements I am to make...'

'If he does intend to marry her he will want it done as quietly and quickly as possible,' Pilar said spitefully. 'He will not want another bride giving birth before he can get her to the altar!'

'Enough!'

Jessica quailed at the fury in Sebastian's voice, but Pilar seemed not to mind, merely shrugging insolently as she looked at Jessica. 'He may marry you,' she told her, 'but always you will know why. Can you live with that?'

She was right, Jessica thought as they left the room and Sebastian closed the door. Of course she could not marry him. And yet he had admitted that he desired her, surely from that something might grow? His family was one that for generations had endured arranged marriages, marriages with far less hope of success than theirs, and surely she had enough love for them both?

All these were wild and foolish thoughts, she admitted as Sebastian turned and she saw the bleak anger in his eyes.

'We don't really have to get married,' she faltered. 'I can leave...'

'And have everyone know that once again a Calvadores has betrayed his name?' he said bitterly. 'Never! I cannot believe that marriage to me will be so abhorrent to you. Sexually we are compatible,' he gave her a thin smile. 'At least we will not be bored in bed, and as for the rest,' he shrugged, 'I shall have my work, and please God eventually you will have our children.'

Why, when he said it like that, did it sound such a barren existence, so different from the one she had visualised?

'I should have listened to Jorge and not given in to my need to feel the softness of your skin beneath my hands,' he added bitterly. 'We will be married just as quickly as it can be arranged, do you agree?'

Jessica wanted to say 'no'. She should say 'no', but it was a weak, hesitant 'yes' that finally left her lips, earning her a look of burning contempt.

'A wise decision. You will be the first Calvadores bride in nearly a thousand years of history who has not come to her marriage bed a virgin.'

'You once told me you would never marry a woman who had known other lovers,' Jessica reminded him with a dry throat, wondering if now he would change his mind.

'Circumstances sometimes dictate a lowering of one's standards. If I do not marry you now, doubtless I will be accused of despoiling two innocent young women.' His mouth twisted bitterly. 'I cannot allow that to happen, for the sake of my aunt and brother, if not for myself.'

'It's rather a high price to pay for family pride, isn't it?' Jessica queried numbly. Never in her wildest imaginings had she ever imagined herself in a situation such as this.

'For some things no price is too high,' he told her sombrely, 'and when we celebrate the birth of our first son perhaps I will be able to tell myself that there is after all some virtue in our marriage.'

She would never allow a child of hers to be brought up thinking that his whole life must be given over to upholding the pride of the Calvadores name, Jessica decided fiercely. Her child would not be sad and lonely like Lisa. Her child . . .

With a shock she realised that already she was thinking
about bearing Sebastian's child, and she knew then that
she would marry him, no matter how much common sense
warned her against it.

CHAPTER SEVEN

THREE DAYS LATER they were married in Seville. Sebastian had asked Jessica, with the same distant politeness he had adopted towards her ever since she had accepted his proposal, if there was anyone she wanted to invite to the ceremony.

She thought fleetingly of her aunt and uncle and Colin, and then regretfully shook her head. To invite them would lead to too many questions; too many doubts to add to those already crowding her mind. It would be far easier to simply tell them once it was over.

Over! She was viewing the thought of her marriage in much the same light as she would a trip to the dentist, and who was to blame? Ever since the afternoon she had agreed to marry Sebastian their marriage had been treated as though it were an unpleasant necessity. It was true that Lisa had greeted the news with unalloyed joy.

'I'm so glad you're going to marry Tio Sebastian,' she had confided Jessica only that morning. 'I would have hated it if he had married Pilar. She doesn't like me!'

But as far as the rest of the family were concerned, it had been all long faces and grave expressions.

Jorge had sought Jessica out and confided that he could not see what other course his brother could have taken.

'He should never have allowed you to become the object of Pilar's speculation in the first place,' he had told her. 'Sebastian knows how possessive Pilar is about him, how she would seek to discredit anyone who is close to him.'

Jessica scarcely felt that she came into that category, and if that had been the reason for Pilar bursting in on them in the manner she had, it had had completely the opposite effect from the one she had desired.

She glanced briefly at Sebastian, wondering what thoughts lay behind the shuttered face. They had been married this morning, she was now the Condesa de Calvadores. She touched the new band of gold on her finger, as though the touch of the shiny metal would make her new status more real.

A wedding breakfast had been arranged at the Calvadores town house. Fifty-odd guests had been invited—all close family, Sebastian's aunt had assured her, and all of whom would be bitterly resentful if they were not invited.

'They look upon Sebastian as the head of our family,' she had explained to Sebastian when she had protested. 'It will only cause problems later if they are not invited. There has already been so much turmoil in his life...'

She broke off, and Jessica sensed that she was thinking back to that other girl Sebastian should have married. In fact Sofia had done all she could to welcome Jessica into the family, her serene expression betraying no hint of the shocked reproach Jessica had glimpsed in her eyes in those few horrifying seconds when she had followed Pilar into the tower room.

Only this morning as Jessica was dressing for the service she had come into her room, proffering a pearl choker.

'You must wear them,' she had insisted. 'Every Calvadores bride does.'

'But I'm scarcely the bride you can have wanted for your nephew,' Jessica had protested miserably. Today of all days she longed to have her aunt with her, longed for the misty white dress she had always secretly dreamed of wearing, instead of the expensive silk separates she had bought hurriedly in Seville—extremely beautiful in their way, but scarcely bridelike.

'You love him,' Sofia had stunned Jessica by saying quietly, 'and that is enough for me. Above all else Sebastian is a man who needs a wife's love. I know he can sometimes seem hard, arrogant even,' a small smile lifted her mouth. 'My own husband was much the same, it is a Calvadores trait, unfortunately, but Sebastian has had to endure much in his life. The loss of his parents was a terrible blow to him. He had to assume the role of guardian and mentor to Jorge; and then there was poor Manuela. So much misery and pain! I have hoped for a long time to see him married. You will make a good wife, I know, because you love him.'

'But he doesn't love me!' Jessica hadn't been able to stem the anguished words.

'He desires you, who knows where that desire may lead?'

Who knew indeed? Jessica thought unhappily, glancing down the length of the table, listening halfheartedly to the hushed Spanish voices. She was a part of this family now, an important part, as one dowager had already reminded her, for she would be the mother of the next head of the family.

They were not having a honeymoon; Sebastian had deemed it unnecessary. They would return to the *hacienda,* at least for a few weeks, until he had completed his work on the designs, and then they would divide their time between the house in Seville and the *hacienda*.

Out of the corner of her eye she noticed Jorge. Sebastian was angry with him because Jorge had announced that he would not marry Barbara.

'Isn't it enough that one of us has married without love?' he had flung at Sebastian in the middle of their argument, and Jessica, who had been standing outside the study waiting to talk to Sebastian, had fled, just managing to reach the privacy of her room before she dissolved in tears.

What sort of marriage had she committed herself to? One where her husband took his pleasure of her body while ignoring her mind? Could she endure that?

The breakfast seemed unending, her head throbbing with the rich food and drink, her body aching with a bone-jarring tension that made her jerk away from Sebastian when he rose, to cup her elbow, when they eventually left.

'*Dios,*' he swore, his eyes darkening to graphite, 'why do you shrink from me like a petrified virgin?'

Because that's exactly what I am, Jessica longed to scream, but somehow the words wouldn't come. Why on earth had she allowed him to think otherwise for so long?

She had the long drive back to the *hacienda* to dwell on her folly. She had no illusions about the nature of their marriage. It would be for life and there would be nothing platonic about it. Sebastian wanted children, he had told her so, and so did she, but up until now she hadn't allowed herself to think any further than the fact that she loved him. Now she was forced to concede that he believed her to be a sexually experienced woman; while in fact...

The hum of the powerful air-conditioning was the only sound to disturb the heavy silence of the car. Sebastian was driving the Mercedes himself, and his glance flicked from the road to her pale face, with dispassionate scrutiny.

'You are very pale. Do you not feel well?'

'A headache,' she managed to whisper, through a throat suddenly painfully constricted.

'That is the excuse of the married woman, not the bride,' Sebastian told her curtly. 'You are my wife, Jessica, and I will not have you reneging on our marriage now. There is something more than a headache troubling you—what is it?'

Was this the moment to tell him the truth? She cleared her throat hesitantly, wishing he would stop the car and take her in his arms. Somehow then it would be much easier to tell him that she was still a virgin.

'Stop playing games!' he warned her irately, swearing angrily as a cyclist suddenly wobbled into the centre of the road and he had to take evasive action. '*Por Dios,* my patience is almost at an end!' he muttered savagely. 'I can only thank God that I am spared the necessity of initiating a virgin. We were interrupted at a singularly inappropriate moment by my aunt and Pilar, and my need for the satisfaction their appearance denied me has been an aching hunger in my body ever since. But it is one which will be fully appeased tonight,' he added grimly, shocking her with his frankness.

'My payment for the privilege of bearing your name?' Jessica said tautly.

'Payment?' He frowned. 'What rubbish are you talking now? Your desire was as great as mine—you admitted it.'

And so she had, but that desire had been aroused by her love for him, and had been totally obliterated by her fear. How could she tell him the truth now?

'The others are a long way behind,' she murmured nervously at one point, glancing over her shoulder at the dust-covered road.

'They are indeed,' Sebastian agreed dryly, 'a full twenty-four hours behind. Tonight we shall be completely alone—my aunt's suggestion, and one I could not argue against. As it is, she points out to me that many of the family find it strange that we are returning to the *hacienda*.'

'I'm sure Pilar will acquaint them with the truth,' Jessica heard herself saying bitterly. 'That I trapped you into this marriage, just as you once thought I was trying to trap Jorge.'

'Pilar will say nothing,' Sebastian assured her coldly. 'And you are becoming hysterical—I cannot conceive why.'

No, Jessica raged inwardly, you wouldn't, would you? You're totally unfeeling and blind. If you weren't you'd know that I'm not...

They turned into the drive leading to the house. Dusk had crept up on them as they drove, and the evening air was full of the scent of the flowers, the chirp of the crickets filling the silence.

As Sebastian had said, the house was completely and almost eerily empty. She felt his eyes on her back as she headed for the tower, freezing as he drawled mockingly,

'You are going the wrong way. From now on you will share my suite.'

His suite. His bed! Almost suffocating with the fear crawling through her body, Jessica allowed him to propel her towards another flight of stairs.

This was a part of the house she had not previously seen. A large but austere sitting room looked out onto a secluded, darkened courtyard. Lamps threw soft shadows across the room. It was decorated in soft mochas and creams; modern furniture that was entirely masculine. Expensive Italian units lined one wall, two dark brown velvet-covered settees placed opposite one another across an off-white expanse of carpet.

'The bedroom is through here.'

Jessica stared disbelievingly. Surely when he had talked about his desire he had not meant that he intended to satisfy it now?

She stared blankly at the door. It was barely seven o'clock, far too early to... A hundred confused thoughts jumbled through her mind. She had been hoping to find a way of telling him the truth; had hoped that during the course of the evening his manner might soften a little ...

'I'm hungry,' she lied wildly, 'I...'

'So am I,' Sebastian agreed obliquely, 'and I thought I had already warned you about playing games with me ... What are you trying to do,' he demanded brutally, 'drive me to the point where I'll commit rape? Does the thought of that turn you on, is that it?'

'No!' Jessica was totally revolted. 'I...' 'I'm not ready' was what she wanted to say, but how could she? 'I'd like to shower and change, if you don't mind,' she managed with pathetic dignity. 'It's been a long day, and ...'

'Of course I don't mind,' he said smoothly. 'The shower is through there.'

He indicated a door across the width of the bedroom. As she craned her neck to see it, Jessica was acutely aware of his proximity, of the maleness he exuded and her own tremulous reaction to it.

'If you'll just excuse me for a second,' he drawled mockingly, 'there's something I have to do.'

At least he was affording her some brief respite, Jessica thought thankfully as she saw the sitting room door close behind her. He probably realised she would prefer to prepare for what was to come in private. The bedroom was as masculine as the sitting room, echoing its colours, with sliding patio doors into the courtyard. She flicked the light switch and instantly the room was bathed in soft light.

What about her clothes? she wondered anxiously. She could scarcely put back on her silk suit. She had just reached the sitting room door and opened it when Sebastian seemed to materialise out of nowhere.

'Going somewhere?' he asked sardonically.

'Er... my clothes, I...'

'You will find them in one of the cupboards. The maids will have attended to it during the day.' He watched her lazily. 'Why so nervous? It cannot be the first time you have been in such a situation.'

'It's the first time I've been married, though,' Jessica managed tartly, almost instantly wishing she had been less aggressive when she saw the way his eyes darkened.

'Rafael has left us some chilled champagne. I shall go and pour some out, although I doubt that it will be consumed in the spirit he anticipates. He probably left it thinking that to drink it would help allay your maidenly qualms,' Sebastian explained succinctly when she glanced hesitantly at him.

At last he was gone, and Jessica searched feverishly through her clothes, finding clean underwear and a fresh dress. Luckily some of her clothes had arrived, and although there was nothing remotely bridal among them they brought a nostalgic touch of home.

The bathroom was luxuriously masculine; a deep dark red and cream, the bath enormous. After one brief glance at it, she opted for the shower, wishing fervently that the bathroom door had a lock, and then chiding herself for her lurid fears. She was behaving like a swooning Victorian heroine faced with her would-be ravisher. She loved Sebastian, she reminded herself.

But he didn't love her; and he didn't know that he would be her first lover.

The sting of the shower spray cooled her heated skin. Someone had placed her toiletries with Sebastian's and she used her perfumed shower gel to soap her body, enjoying the fragrance, but reminding herself that she mustn't linger. She was just about to turn on the water to wash off the soap when a deep voice murmured provocatively, 'You've missed a bit!'

Sebastian! She hadn't heard him enter the bathroom, and she turned quickly, reaching instinctively for a towel.

'Such modesty!' he mocked, twitching it away from her, 'and so unnecessary... hmm?'

'Sebastian, please!' Her voice was curiously husky, a strange deep heat pervading her body, her head oddly light.

'There is no need to beg me, *querida,*' he drawled huskily, deliberately misunderstanding the nature of her plea. 'You are a very desirable woman, a little slender perhaps,' he mocked, and Jessica wondered if he was thinking of Pilar's lusher charms, 'but very tantalising for all that. I like your perfume,' he added softly, his finger moving along the ridge of her spine.

Panic clamoured inside her, her body tensing under the explorative caress, but Sebastian appeared not to notice. His fingers moved rhythmically over her skin, and as though he sensed that she was about to protest, he said softly, 'Like I said, you've missed a bit. What's the matter?' he asked, frowning as he sensed her tension.

'I... I'd like to get dressed,' she muttered huskily. 'As I said before, I'm hungry, and...'

'Like I said, so am I... I hope you're not getting any foolish ideas about reneging on our marriage. I want you, Jessica,' he told her coolly, 'and I want you now... Perhaps you're right,' he added softly, 'and now is not the time to play games in the shower. Later—er—when we have more leisure for playing. Right now, all I want is the scented warmth of your body in my arms, your heart beating against mine...'

'No!'

Jessica managed a husky protest, but it was lost, smothered as he lifted her out of the shower, careless of the dampness of her naked body against his clothes, carrying her effortlessly into the bedroom and depositing her on the bed.

'Beautiful,' he murmured with pleasure as his fingers drifted exploratively across her skin. 'So soft and pale.'

Jessica looked imploringly at the lamps revealing her body in its most intimate detail.

'You want us to make love in the darkness?' Strangely the idea seemed to displease him. 'Why?' he demanded. 'So that you can pretend I am someone else? Oh no, querida,' he told her tightly, 'I want you to know who it is who possesses you, and besides, your body is so beautiful I want to enjoy it with my eyes as well as my hands and lips. Just as I want you to enjoy mine,' he added seductively. 'A pity you had decided to shower before I could join you. I would have enjoyed undressing you.'

'I'm a woman, not a doll!' Jessica protested fiercely, terrified by the images his words were conjuring, the pulsating sensations radiating to every part of her body.

'Tonight you are my wife, and no matter what has gone before, it shall be as it has been with no other man, so that by morning you will remember only the touch of my hands, my body...'

And Jessica remembered the Moorish blood in his veins, the blatant sensuality that would be part of his legacy from that blood, and every muscle in her body constricted in terrified dread. He expected her to be a sexually experienced woman, instead of which ...

She shivered, and he frowned, moving away from the bed, and returning with a glass of frothing liquid.

'Drink this,' he commanded. 'You are cold.'

The champagne bubbled in her throat, tickling her nose. She coughed, spilling some and feeling it splash down on her skin.

'*Dios,* but I want you,' Sebastian murmured throatily, then he bent his head, his tongue touching the spot where the champagne had fallen in the valley between her breasts. Tension coiled through her, a cramping sensation stirring in her stomach, weakness invading her muscles as his fingers gripped her hips and his mouth continued its subtle exploration of her breasts, first one and then the other— light, delicate caresses, the mere brush of his lips against her skin, tormenting her with the ache of unappeasement they left.

Her fear was forgotten. All she wanted was right here within reach. She groaned a half protest as Sebastian's lips continued their teasing assault, her fingers locking into his hair as she tried to silently convey her need for something more.

'You are too impatient,' he murmured against her skin. 'We have all night before us, your skin is as sweet and tender as a fresh peach, tempting to the tongue and firm to the touch.'

His hand left her hip to stroke wantonly across the soft tension of her stomach, his lips following a downward path.

'Sebastian ...'

'How sweetly you say my name,' he told her huskily, 'and how much sweeter it would be to feel your lips against my skin. Surely, *querida,* I don't have to tell you that?'

He moved, and Jessica was instantly aware of his arousal, but a languid yielding sensation was spreading through her, driving out fear. Her fingers trembled over the buttons of his shirt, exploring the moistness of the skin beneath. His skin was warm, silk shielding hard muscle and bone, and merely to let her fingers drift over the smooth muscles of his back provoked a racing excitement that seemed to invade every nerve. His skin burned against her palms, his husky moan inciting her to press quivering lips against the smooth column of his throat, tasting the salty male scent of him.

'*Dios,* Jessica,' he protested hoarsely as her tongue delicately probed the curve of his throat, her hands clinging to his shoulders, the soft movements of her body inviting his touch. His hand cupped her jaw, imprisoning her as his mouth possessed hers with hot urgency, forcing her lips to part, tasting the moist inner sweetness. His hands moved urgently over her body, desire burning hotly in his eyes as he urged her to help him with his pants. He had none of the self-consciousness she possessed, his body golden and taut in the light from the lamps as he stood up briefly, watching her eyes move wonderingly.

'You look at me as though you have never seen a man before, *querida,*' he told her softly. 'Such a look is a temptation to any man, and I am more than willing to be tempted.' He leaned over her, tanned fingers gently cupping first one breast and then the other as he bent his head, stroking the pulsating nipples lightly with his tongue, his mouth finally closing over the aching core, and waves of sensation beat through her as she gasped and trembled at the sensations he was arousing. A need to press wild, scattered kisses against his body seized her, his husky growl of pleasure reverberating along her spine.

His mouth left her breasts to stroke delicate kisses across her stomach, quivering with shock at the unaccustomed sensuality of his touch, but it seemed it wasn't enough simply for him to kiss her, she had to kiss him, and the feel of the tautly male flesh against her lips seemed only to increase the deep ache she could feel inside her. Then, as though he sensed her need and shared it, Sebastian parted her thighs, the heated masculinity of him unbearably arousing, as his tongue brushed softly over her lips, making her moan and cling desperately to his shoulders, mutely imploring him to cease tantalising her.

His mouth suddenly hardened on hers, his body taut with a need that communicated itself to every part of her. He moved, and suddenly, starkly, all her fear returned. There was pain and anger in his eyes, an anger which she had to blot out by closing hers, and weak tears seeped through as the sharp pain ended, taking with it her earlier euphoric pleasure.

'A virgin! You were a virgin,' Sebastian accused her. He was standing beside the bed wearing a dark silk robe, his hair tousled, and his expression bitter. 'Why didn't you tell me?'

'How could I?' Jessica muttered. 'I was going to when you started telling me how glad you were that I was a woman of experience ... Anyway, I don't see why you should complain,' she added acidly. 'It isn't many men who get to have two virgin brides ... Although, of course, in Manuela's case ...'

His jaw tightened in fury, all the muscles in his face tensing, and Jessica had the overwhelming suspicion that if she hadn't been a woman he would have hit her.

'You should be pleased,' she threw bitterly at him, refusing to give in to the tiny voice warning her not to go any further. 'I thought that was what all the Calvadores men expected in their brides—innocence, purity!'

'You should have told me,' he repeated icily.

'Why?' Tears weren't very far away, everything had gone disastrously wrong. In a corner of her heart Jessica had been hoping that somehow the discovery that she was a virgin might soften him towards her, but instead . . . 'So that you could have been less . . . excessive? Would it have made any difference? You would still have hurt me.'

It was a childish accusation, and her emotions were more bruised than her body, but his face closed up immediately, his expression grimly unreadable as he assured her curtly, 'In that case you may be sure that I will never . . . hurt you again. I want no unwilling sacrifice in my bed,' he added cruelly.

'And there is always Pilar, isn't there?' Jessica flung at him. 'She's no shrinking virgin, to be shocked and distressed by your . . . your demands!'

He laughed mirthlessly. 'My demands, as you call them, are no more than any sensual aroused male experiences. My mistake was in hoping to share them with you. Plainly you prefer to remain frigidly prudish. Then you may do so!'

CHAPTER EIGHT

IT HAD ALL gone disastrously wrong, Jessica thought numbly, listening to Tia Sofia while Lisa perched on her knee. The three of them were in the *sala* that Sofia had claimed as her own, drinking coffee and eating the cook's delicious almond biscuits.

Tia Sofia had been explaining to Jessica that they were expecting a visit from Sebastian's godfather and his daughter.

'*Querida,* are you not feeling well?' she broke off to ask Jessica with concern. 'You look pale—you have been in-doors too much working on Sebastian's wretched designs, you must go out more.'

'Yes, you promised you would go for a walk with me,' Lisa reminded her reproachfully.

Assuring them both that she was fine, Jessica forced a smile to lips that felt as though they would crack from the constant effort of having to smile when it was the last thing she wanted to do. How could two people live as intimately as she and Sebastian did and yet remain so far apart? Ini-tially she had expected him to suggest that they have sep-arate bedrooms—he could hardly want to share his with her now, but to her dismay he did no such thing. Perhaps the terrible pride of the Calvadores would not allow him to admit that he did not desire his wife. Whatever the rea-son, she was forced to endure the humiliation, night after night, of knowing that he was lying merely inches away

from her, but his attitude towards her was so cold and dis-
missive that they could have been separated by the Sierras.

And the strain was beginning to tell. More than once she
thought she had glimpsed sympathy in Sofia's eyes, and
she wondered if the older woman suspected the truth. She
roused herself when Lisa repeated insistently that she had
promised to go out with her.

The little girl was wearing another of her dainty dresses,
and while they looked enchanting, Jessica wished she could
see her in shorts and T-shirts, getting grubby; living a more
natural life.

'I wish Tio Sebastian was with us,' Lisa confided as they
walked through the courtyard and past the swimming pool
towards the outbuildings. 'When will he be back from Seville?'

'Tonight,' Jessica told her, trying not to admit to the
sinking sensation she experienced whenever she thought of
Sebastian. She had thought she had seen him angry before, but it was nothing compared with the icy hauteur
with which she was now treated. How foolish she had been
to think that her love was the key to his heart! He wanted
neither her love nor her body.

'I'm going to show you my secret place,' Lisa told her
importantly. 'No one knows about it but us... And Tio
Sebastian.'

Lisa took her hand and led her towards the stable block.
Her pony whinnied as they walked past, and they stopped
to stroke his nose and feed him carrots from the bucket by
the door.

'A long time ago this was where they made the wine,'
Lisa told her importantly, opening a door into what Jessica had thought must be part of the converted garages,
but which in fact she realised was a store place of some

description. There was an old-fashioned wine press which she recognised from pictures, several large vats and some decaying barrels. 'It's down here, come on!'

Urged on by Lisa, she followed her to a cobwebby corner of the building, startled when Lisa motioned to another door. Jessica opened it, almost overbalancing on the steep flight of steps leading down from the door. As she glanced down the narrow, dark steps she felt a shuddering reluctance to descend them. She had always loathed the thought of being underground, but Lisa displayed no such qualms.

'It's fun, isn't it?' she demanded, leading the way with an agility that suggested she knew every step by heart. Jessica had to duck quickly to avoid the low roof as the steps suddenly turned and then levelled out.

They were in a rectangular room, illuminated by one single bare bulb suspended from a wire which ran the length of the ceiling. The ceiling itself was arched and composed of crumbling bricks. Moisture streamed off the walls, and the air felt cold and damp. Lisa, completely oblivious to Jessica's dislike of her treasured hidey-hole, beamed up at her with evident pleasure.

'No one ever comes down here now,' she told her. 'They used to store the barrels here a long time ago.'

She was going to have a word with Sebastian about allowing Lisa to wander so freely somewhere so potentially dangerous, Jessica decided when the top of the stairs was gained and they had switched off the light. It made her blood run cold just thinking what might happen to her alone down there. For one thing, the ceiling hadn't looked too safe; there had been deep fissures in some of the bricks.

They were on the way back to the house when Jorge suddenly caught up with them. He had been out riding and his hair was tousled from the exercise. He was an attractive boy, Jessica reflected, smiling warmly at him, but he was not Sebastian.

'Tio Jorge, Tio Jorge, put me down!' Lisa squealed, laughing as he swung her up in his arms and whirled her round and round.

'Not until you give me a kiss,' he threatened teasingly.

Obligingly she did so, while Jessica laughed. 'So that's the secret of your great charm, is it?' she mocked. 'Kisses by threats!'

'Be careful I don't do the same thing to you,' Jorge told her mock-threateningly, while Lisa announced earnestly, 'You can't kiss Jessica, Jorge, because she's married to Tio Sebastian!'

'Out of the mouths of babes,' Jorge drawled, sliding Jessica a sideways dancing glance. 'Not that I wouldn't like to try. My brother is a very lucky man.'

They were still laughing when they reached the courtyard, Lisa in the crook of one of Jorge's arms, while the other rested lightly on the back of Jessica's waist in a gesture more protective than provocative.

But the laughter drained out of Jessica's face when she saw Sebastian's grimly angry face. He was sitting on the terrace with his aunt and Pilar, and all at once Jessica felt acutely aware of her untidy appearance, cobwebs no doubt clinging to her dress and hair, Jorge's arm on her waist.

'Jessica, had you forgotten Pilar was coming to see you this afternoon?'

Jessica shot a surprised glance at the Spanish woman's perfectly made-up and bland face. As far as she knew they had made no such arrangements, nor was there any reason why they should do so. She didn't like Pilar and she knew the feeling was reciprocated. For one thing, she disliked the way Pilar treated Lisa, who was, after all, her sister's child.

To save any argument she apologised lightly, and was about to excuse herself to run upstairs and tidy up, when Pilar astounded her by saying, 'That is perfectly all right, Jessica. I quite understand. When one has an attractive man as an escort one tends to overlook engagements with one's woman friends.'

Sebastian looked thunderously angry, and Jessica bit her lip. Surely he didn't think she had deliberately ignored an engagement with Pilar? And Jorge—why was he looking at his brother in that evasive fashion, not explaining that they had simply met at the stables and walked back together?

Lisa, sensing the tension in the atmosphere, reached imploring for Sebastian's hand, her voice uncertain, her small face anxiously puckered. She was stretching on tiptoe and suddenly she overbalanced, clutching the nearest thing to her for support, which happened to be Pilar's arm. The glass of *fino* Pilar was holding in her hand spilled down onto the cream silk dress she was wearing, and with a cry of rage she rounded on Lisa, taking her by the shoulders and shaking her furiously.

'This is too much, *querido!*' she complained to Sebastian. 'The child is uncontrollable and clumsy. I have told you before, she should be sent to a convent and taught how to conduct herself... What may be suitable behaviour in an English household does not commend itself to our people. Perhaps you should explain that to your wife, for it is obvious that she has been encouraging Lisa to run wild. Clumsy girl!' she told Lisa, now pale and trembling, her dark brown eyes huge in her small face. 'When I was a child, I would have been whipped and sent to my room for the rest of the day for such unmannerly behaviour!'

Jessica longed to intervene. Her blood boiled in answering fury. How could Pilar terrorise Lisa so? It had

been an accident; admittedly it was unfortunate that the
sherry should have been spilled, but Jessica doubted that
the cream silk was the only dress in Pilar's wardrobe, or
that she couldn't replace it quite easily.

'Perhaps you are right, *querida*,' she heard Sebastian
saying evenly. 'Lisa, you will apologise to your aunt, and
then I think you will go to your room . . .'

'It is probably more Jessica's fault than Lisa's,' Pilar
added maliciously. 'Have you seen how grubby the child
is? She is probably overexcited.'

'My wife does seem to have that effect on some people,' Sebastian agreed coldly. 'Lisa,' he commanded,
looking at the little girl, 'I have told you once to go to your
room, I will not do so again!'

Jessica saw his aunt check a response, her expression
unhappy, and all her own indignation boiled over.

'It was an accident,' she interrupted hotly. 'Poor Lisa is
no more to blame than . . . anyone else. Sebastian, I . . .'

'Be careful, Jessica,' Pilar mocked. 'Sebastian does not
like to have his decisions queried, do you, *querido?*'

Jessica ignored her. 'Come, Lisa, I'll take you upstairs,' she said softly, hating the hurt pain in the little girl's
eyes. She had just seen her god topple from his plinth,
Jessica suspected, still unable to understand why Sebastian had spoken so harshly.

Dinner was always a formal occasion in the Calvadores
household, but it had never been as silently tense as it was
tonight, Jessica thought to herself as she refused any car-
amel pudding in favour of a cup of coffee.

'Señor Alvarez and Luisa arrive tomorrow, will you
collect them from the airport?'

'I have some work to complete on the designs,' Sebastian said curtly. He had hardly spoken to any of them
during the meal, and Jessica thought she might be wrong,

but there was a controlled tension about him she had never noticed before. Was it because of their marriage? Was he, like her, wishing it had never taken place?

'I could go,' Jorge offered. 'I could take Jessica and Lisa with me.'

'I think not,' Sebastian cut in coldly. 'The car will be cramped with five of you, and besides, it is time that Lisa learned that good manners are something that cannot be discarded simply at whim. She will remain indoors to-morrow as a reminder.'

'Does that apply to me too?' Jessica demanded, temper flags flying in her cheeks. 'Am I to be "sent to my room", for forgetting Pilar's invitation?'

Sebastian's mouth compressed into a thin hard line. 'Lisa is at an age where her nature can still be moulded and formed. Regrettably, you are not. Now, if you will excuse me, I have work to do.'

'Phew!' Jorge grimaced when he had gone. 'He has a black monkey riding on his back tonight, hasn't he? Have you two had a quarrel?'

Quarrel! Jessica suppressed hysterical laughter. To have a quarrel they would need to talk, to share an emotion. They weren't close enough to quarrel.

'Sebastian is tired,' Tia Sofia palliated. 'He has been working too hard. I have warned him before . . .'

'I didn't know Pilar intended to visit me,' Jessica explained to his aunt, not wanting her too to think she had been remiss.

'Pilar tends to be a little possessive towards Sebastian,' Sofia said gently, 'and sometimes that prompts her into actions of impulse. I'm sure she did not mean to cause any friction between you.'

Jessica said nothing. She was pretty sure that was exactly what Pilar had wanted to do, but she had no intention of saying so to the others.

'Has Sebastian said anything to you about Barbara?' Jorge asked her half an hour later as they wandered through the courtyard.

'Nothing,' Jessica told him, without adding that it was hardly likely that he would do so.

'He is annoyed with me, I am afraid, but I cannot marry a girl I do not love.'

It was a sentiment Jessica wholly appreciated. 'Of course not,' she agreed sympathetically.

The courtyard was illuminated by a full moon, bathing everything in soft silver light. The air was warm, almost too warm, and curiously still.

'We could be in for a storm,' Jorge commented as they headed back to the house. 'We need rain badly. It has been a very dry spring.' His sleeve brushed against Jessica's bare arm and he stopped her suddenly, his hand on her shoulder as he turned her towards him.

'You are so very different from your cousin,' he said softly. 'She is a taker from others, while you are a giver, but be careful you don't give my brother too much. He has a devil riding him that cannot be exorcised. He has been this way since Manuela died.'

What was he trying to tell her? That Sebastian still loved Manuela? Tears strung her eyes and she lowered her head, taking momentary comfort from Jorge's presence before turning to return to the house.

As always, she felt a reluctance to go upstairs. Sebastian was never there. He always worked late—avoiding the awful moment when he must join her, Jessica thought bitterly. If she had hoped that somehow the fact of her virginity might incline him towards her she had been bitterly disappointed. And the mutual desire he had spoken of so freely before they were married might never have existed. Jessica didn't know what was responsible for the change in him—but she hated the long, empty nights when she lay sleepless at his side, knowing she had only to stretch out her hand to touch him, and knowing it was the one thing she must never do. And humiliatingly she still wanted to touch him; it was there like an alien growth inside her, this need to touch and know. She couldn't forget his final cruel words to her on the night of their wedding, and there was still an unappeased ache within her that throbbed like an exposed nerve whenever she thought about how it had felt to be in his arms.

She opened the bedroom door, stiffening with shock as she saw the moonlit figure by the patio door.

'So you have returned,' Sebastian's voice was flat and unemotional. 'I thought after what I just witnessed that you might have decided to spend the night with my brother.'

For a moment Jessica stared uncomprehendingly at him, and then enlightenment dawned.

'Jorge and I were simply talking,' she protested, silenced by the harsh sound of his laughter.

'The way you had been simply talking this afternoon, I suppose,' he said savagely.

It was useless to tell him that she had simply met Jorge on the way back from her outing with Lisa, but at the thought of the little girl, she remembered the tearstained face and trembling mouth when she had gone in to say good-night to her, and read her the story they were both enjoying.

'You were very unfair to Lisa this afternoon,' she told him angrily, able to defend his daughter if she couldn't defend herself. 'It was an unfortunate accident, but she

was in no way to blame. Pilar always contrives to upset
her. She adores you, Sebastian, and you were viciously
cruel to her. I can't understand why you turned on her like
that.'

'You can't? Perhaps it's because a wounded animal does
claw at other things in its agony; perhaps it's because I'm
going out of my mind with frustration,' he told her bluntly.
'When I married you it was not with the intention that our
marriage should be platonic.'

'I should have told you the truth,' Jessica admitted
huskily. 'I wanted to, but . . .'

'But you preferred to let me find out the hard way—for
us both—and then you turn to my brother for solace. Well,
you may not find solace in my arms, Jessica,' he told her
brutally, 'but I'm no saint to burn in the fires of hell when
the means of quenching them is at hand. You were prepared to give yourself to my brother, now you can give
yourself to me!'

Her panicky protest was lost against his mouth, storming her defences, sending waves of heat pulsating through
her body. Instantly everything was forgotten but the wild
clamouring in her blood, the need for his possession which
had been aching inside her ever since their wedding night,
although never fully acknowledged.

'I want you,' Sebastian muttered thickly against her
mouth, 'and when I take you, you will think only of me,
not my brother, not anyone but me. It will be my name you
cry out in the fiery midst of passion; my body that gives
yours the ultimate sweet pleasure.'

A shaft of moonlight illuminated his face, drawn and
shadowed, so that Jessica could almost deceive herself that
it was pain she saw in his eyes. Was he thinking of Manuela
when he spoke to her? A sharp stabbing pain shot through
her, her small moan of protest igniting a ferocity within

him that shocked and excited as he stripped her swiftly, his
face a mask of concentration, his hands only stilling when
he had removed everything but her minute briefs.

The knowledge that he wanted her trembled through her
on an exultant wave, and slowly she reached towards him,
unfastening the buttons of his shirt, sliding her hands
across the breadth of his chest and feeling it lift and tense
with the sudden urgency of his breathing. Her marauding
fingers were trapped and held against his heart as it
pounded into her palm, and a curious sensation of time-
lessness gripped her.

This time she felt no shyness at the sight of his naked
body, rather a desire to touch and know it, but his smothered groan as her fingertips stroked lightly against his thigh
warned her of the intensity of his need. His hands cupped
her breasts, his mouth following the line of her throat and
shoulders, before returning to fasten hungrily on hers. His
body burned and trembled against her, sweat beading his
forehead and dampening his skin.

On a swiftly rising spiral of excitement Jessica explored
the maleness of his body, feeling the increasing urgency
within him; the blind hunger that made him shudder under her touch, and she knew beyond any doubt that this
time nothing would appease the ache inside her but the
hard, demanding pressure she could feel building up inside him.

She wanted his possession of her body with a need that
went beyond anything she had ever experienced. Her hips
writhed and arched, and Sebastian groaned against her
throat, holding her, shaping her until she was formless and
malleable, her only purpose in life to fulfil the explosive
ache that possessed her every conscious thought and action.

'Sebastian...' She moaned his name under his caressing hands, trying to communicate her need, but instead of fulfilling her, he stilled. She opened desire-drugged eyes and stared at him uncomprehendingly, a tiny protest leaving her lips.

'Sebastian, please!' Her fingers curled into the smooth muscles of his back, her mind still shying away from actually telling him how much she needed him, while her body ached wantonly for her to do so, no matter what the cost.

'You want me.'

It was a statement rather than a question, but something forced her to respond to it, her nervous, husky, 'Very much,' making his eyes darken until they were almost black, his breathing suddenly altered and uneven. '*Dios*, Jessica,' he told her rawly, 'I want you, even though I know...'

She didn't want him to say more, to spoil what was between them with any words that might make her face up to the truth. Now lying in his arms, the full weight of his body pressed against hers, she could almost convince herself that he could love her, but if he spoke, if he said that word 'want' again when she wanted to hear him say 'love', it would burst her protective bubble, and that was something she didn't want. So in desperation she pressed her finger to his lips and then clasped her hands behind his neck drawing him down towards her, running her tongue softly over his lips, tracing the firm outline of them, until, suddenly, he muttered a husky protest, capturing her face with his hands and holding it still while his mouth moved hungrily over hers and the heated pressure of his thighs ignited a heat that spread swiftly through her body until it welcomed his shuddering thrust, rejoicing in the bittersweet mingling of pain and pleasure, knowing with some

prescient knowledge that this time he was tempering his
need so that she could share fully the pleasure of their entwined bodies.

And then all thought was superseded as swiftly urgent
pleasure contracted through her body and she was free-
soaring into realms of delight she had never dreamed existed.

WHEN SHE WOKE UP she was alone; there was a dent in the
pillow where Sebastian's head had lain, but no other traces
of his presence. Jessica swung her legs out of the bed, surprised to discover how lethargic and weak she felt. She
steadied herself as the room spun round, and faintness
overwhelmed her. Just for a moment she wished Sebastian was there, to take her in his arms, and kiss her with the
tenderness a man might reserve for the woman he had just
made wholly his, if he loved her, but then she banished the
thought. Perhaps last night would lead to other improve-
ments in their marriage. Perhaps his desire for her might
lead Sebastian to treat her with tenderness and affection.

She had forgotten that he had said he was going to Seville and was disappointed to get downstairs and find him
gone. Jorge was at the breakfast table, trying to cheer up
a tearful Lisa.

Jessica had started going with Tia Sofia when she discussed the day's menus and work plans with the staff. The
hacienda was enormous, with so many valuable antiques
and works of art that cleaning it had to be organised with
almost military precision. Many of the staff had inherited
their jobs from their mothers and fathers, and all were
devoted to the family. Jessica had found that they treated
her with respect and affection, and when she murmured to
Sofia that she was sure she would never be able to cope as
admirably as she did, the older woman had laughed.

'You will,' she had told her, 'and before very long as well. You have a natural flair with people.'

If she did, it didn't extend to include her husband, Jessica thought ruefully.

Lisa was so unhappy that Jessica spent a large part of the morning with her. Her part of the designing work was now almost complete until Sebastian came to a final decision. She had received a delighted letter from her aunt and uncle, full of exclamations and wishes that they had been able to attend her wedding.

'Isabel gets married in three months' time,' her aunt had written, 'and of course you must be there. She was going to ask you to be bridesmaid, but now it will have to be matron of honour. John's parents are holding the reception at their house—there's to be a marquee in the garden, and John's mother is a splendid organiser, so I won't have anything to worry about other than finding an outfit.'

As she folded the letter Jessica sighed. Would Isabel be any happier than she was? She certainly hoped so.

In an effort to try and cheer Lisa up, she taught her to play Snap with an old pack of cards she had found, and although she played dutifully, her eyes kept straying to the door. How could Sebastian have been so cruel to her? Jessica fumed. His own child, even if he did refuse to acknowledge her. This cruel streak in a man who was otherwise so strong was a weakness that caused her concern. His pride she could understand and even forgive, but his refusal to tell Lisa her true parentage was something that worried her.

'Will Tio Sebastian really send me away to a convent?' Lisa asked her at one point, her chin wobbling slightly.

'I'm sure he won't,' Jessica told her, trying to comfort her.

'But when you have babies, he won't want me,' Lisa appalled her by confiding. 'Pilar told me so.'

'Of course we'll still want you,' Jessica assured her, inwardly wondering how Pilar could be so deliberately malicious. 'What shall we do this afternoon?' she asked her, trying to redirect her thoughts. But Lisa refused to respond.

Jorge returned with the visitors from South America just after lunch. Señor Alvarez, Sebastian's godfather, turned out to be a genial, plump South American, who kissed both Jessica and Sofia enthusiastically, his eyes twinkling as he told Sofia that she didn't look a day older.

'Then you must need new glasses,' Sebastian's aunt told him practically, 'for it is over twenty years since we last met.'

'I remember it as though it were yesterday,' he assured her. 'You were then a bride of six months, and how I envied my cousin! Just as I'm sure many men must envy Sebastian,' he added gallantly, turning to Jessica. 'Jorge tells me that he has to work but that he will return in time for dinner. You must not let him work so hard—all work and no play, don't you English have a saying about that?'

'Sebastian has a black monkey on his back at the moment,' Jorge interrupted cheerfully. 'Poor Lisa felt the weight of his temper yesterday, and all because of that cat Pilar Sanchez.'

'Ah, Pilar!' Señor Alvarez grimaced. 'A very feline woman, is that one. I shall have to take care to guard my little Luisa from her claws!'

He drew his daughter forward to be introduced, and Jessica noticed the look in Jorge's eyes as they rested on her. Small and dainty, her glossy black hair was drawn back off her face, her huge pansy brown eyes were nervous and hesitant as they were introduced. She couldn't be more than eighteen, Jessica reflected, but already she had the ripeness, the innocent sensuality of Latin women.

At Jorge's suggestion she allowed herself to be detached from the others to explore the courtyards. The *hacienda* was so different from the style of architecture she was accustomed to that she was eager to explore.

'Your daughter is extremely lovely,' Jessica commented warmly when they had gone.

'She is a crimson velvet rose,' her father agreed poetically, 'but many men prefer the beauty of the golden rose that grows best in the cooler climes of the north.'

Señor Alvarez had come to Spain on business as well as pleasure, and when he discovered that Jessica had been helping Sebastian with his new designs he started to talk to her with great enthusiasm and interest about wool and South America. Jessica found it all fascinating; he was an entertaining companion; scholarly, and yet worldly enough to add a little salt to his speech, and like all Latins, he was an expert at turning a neat compliment. Sebastian had never complimented her, Jessica realised with a shock. He had never flirted with her either. The tiny cold lump of unhappiness she had felt on waking and discovering that he had gone grew and refused to be banished.

Sebastian eventually returned to the *hacienda* just before dinner. Pilar had been invited to join this celebratory meal, mainly because she knew the Alvarez family well, and as she was a widow, it was perfectly permissible for her to join a family party without a male escort.

She arrived just as they were sipping sherry in the *sala,* her black silk evening dress a perfect foil for her dark beauty and curvaceous figure. In comparison, Jessica felt pale and insignificant in her softly draped cream chiffon suit with its camisole top and loose jacket, even though she had loved it when she tried it on in the shop.

Luisa, as befitted a young girl, was wearing a plain dress in white, and pretty though it was, Jessica didn't think it did the younger girl's complexion justice.

Sebastian had been late joining them and had come into the room only minutes before Pilar, who, the moment she saw him, made a beeline for him, linking her arm with his in a very proprietorial manner, scarlet fingernails like drops of blood against the darkness of his jacket, as she laughed and joked with Señor Alvarez.

'Have you been in to see Lisa?' Jessica managed to ask Sebastian quietly before they went in to dinner. 'She's been moping all day because you were so cross with her.'

She didn't think anyone else had heard her until Pilar turned round suddenly, her eyes raking Jessica's face coldly, her voice falsely sweet as she said smoothly.

'I must go up and see her too before I go. Lisa is suddenly displaying a very naughty strain,' she added for Señor Alvarez' benefit. 'I'm afraid I had to be quite cross with her yesterday.'

Sebastian hadn't answered her question, and Jessica was afraid to ask it again. All her hopes that somehow last night might have had a softening effect on his attitude to her had been destroyed the moment he walked into the *sala*, his face grimly blank as he sought her out and with meticulous politeness enquired about her day. His very politeness seemed to hold her deliberately at a distance as though he wanted to warn her not to try to come too close. Had his love for Manuela been such that he could never love anyone else? Had her death frozen his emotions, making it impossible for him to feel anything other than desire for another woman?

Jessica sighed, reflecting that the evening ahead wasn't likely to be an easy one. Already she could see that Jorge was being more than simply politely attentive to Luisa and that she was responding with glowing eyes and happy smiles. Sebastian hadn't noticed yet, but when he did . . .

Jorge hadn't been forgiven for refusing to marry Barbara, although privately Jessica thought it was very wrong of Sebastian to attempt to dictate to his brother whom he should marry. But of course that was the Spanish way.

The night was hot and stuffy, thunder growling in the distance. Halfway through the meal Jessica was attacked by a wave of nausea and dizziness, which, fortunately, she managed to fight off. She didn't believe anyone had noticed, until she realised that Pilar was watching her with narrowed, assessing eyes. Trying to dislodge the cold feeling of disquiet she always felt when the other woman watched her, Jessica discreetly refrained from eating much more. Doubtless it was the overpowering heat and threatening storm that was making her feel so odd, and at least Sebastian seemed more relaxed, as he chatted to his godfather. She heard him mention her name and listened, wondering what was being said.

'Your husband has just been praising your ability as a designer,' Señor Alvarez told her, with a smile. 'He tells me that your ideas are nothing short of inspired.'

Again Jessica was conscious of Pilar's malevolent regard, but she tried to ignore it. Sebastian praising her! A tiny thrill of pleasure lightened the ice packed round her heart. Perhaps after all there might be some future for them; some basis on which they could build the foundations of a relationship.

CHAPTER NINE

'TIA SOFIA, have you seen Lisa?' Jessica had been looking for the little girl for half an hour, but no one had seen her since lunchtime. She glanced out of the window at the black sky and pounding rain. Surely Lisa wouldn't have ventured outside? The rain fell in sheets rather than drops, bouncing on the hard dry earth, and on the radio there had been flood warnings.

Sebastian had been concerned for the vines, although he explained that fortunately they were not at a stage in their development when too much damage would be done. The poorer growers might suffer some losses, Jorge had told Jessica later, but Sebastian, together with other wealthy landlords, had formed an association that could help the small growers through difficult patches.

'He takes his responsibilities as head of our family very seriously,' Jorge explained to her. 'Too seriously, I sometimes think, perhaps because he was so young when he had to take over from our father.'

And he had had to take over alone, Jessica reflected, without Manuela at his side.

'I'm getting worried about Lisa,' she confided in Sofia with a frown when no one could remember seeing the little girl. 'Where can she be?'

'She has been very upset recently,' Sofia agreed, echoing Jessica's concern. 'I told Sebastian he had been too harsh with her, but he seems to have devils of his own to fight at the moment.'

'I think I'll go upstairs and check again that she isn't in her room—she might just have slipped out,' Jessica commented.

'If you don't find her, we'll organise a search. Children get odd ideas into their head when they're upset—even the most sensible of them.'

Lisa wasn't in her room, but Jessica bumped into the girl Maria, who looked after her, as she came out. She looked worried and upset.

'Have you seen Lisa?' Jessica asked her. The girl shook her head.

'Not since morning,' she told Jessica. 'She was very upset, the little one. Last night...' she bit her lip, flushing and hesitating.

'Yes, go on,' Jessica urged her. 'Last night...?'

'Well, it is just that Señora Sanchez came up to see her. I had gone downstairs to get her some hot milk to help her sleep, and when I came back I could hear their voices. Señora Sanchez was very, very angry. I could hear her shouting, but I didn't go in. When she came out she didn't see me, and I went into the room and found Lisa crying. The Señora had told her that she was to be punished for being naughty and that the Conde was to send her away—to a school where they would be very strict with her—and that she would never be allowed to come back.'

Jessica was appalled and looked it. How could Pilar be so heartless, and why had Sebastian not confided his plans to *her*? Of course Pilar was Lisa's aunt, but surely he might have consulted her before deciding to send Lisa away to school? She had been intending to suggest that there might be a good school in Seville she could attend, and that during the week they could live in the house there to be with her. How could he treat his daughter so unkindly?

'I tried to comfort her,' Maria went on to say, 'but it was many hours before she went to sleep.'

'You should have come and told me,' Jessica said remorsefully, hating to think of Lisa lying awake and crying while they were dining downstairs unaware of her misery. 'Did she say anything this morning?' she probed.

Maria shook her head. 'Not a word. She was very subdued and quiet, but she said nothing.'

Feeling more apprehensive than she wanted to admit, Jessica hurried back downstairs to give Tia Sofia the news.

She too looked grave when Jessica had finished. 'You say Pilar told her that Sebastian was to send her to school? I cannot believe he would come to such a decision without telling us first. Do you think she could have exaggerated?'

It was a thought, but Jessica felt that not even Pilar would have dared to tell such a barefaced and hurtful lie without some justification.

Jorge was summoned and told of their fears, and Señor Alvarez, who had accompanied him, was quick to suggest that they each take portions of the house to search.

'Sebastian must be told,' he added firmly.

'I'll telephone him,' Jorge agreed. 'Unless, of course...' he glanced at Jessica, but she shook her head. She didn't trust herself to speak logically to Sebastian at the moment; she was too concerned about Lisa. She thought of the little girl's misery and was overwhelmed by a sensation of nauseous sickness. She had felt slightly unwell when she first woke up and had put it down to the richness of the food at dinner last night and the fact that her system had still not grown accustomed to eating so late.

'You are not well?' Señor Alvarez had seen her pale face and hurried to her side.

'It's nothing,' she assured him. 'I'm fine now.' She saw the glance he and Sofia exchanged and was puzzled by it, until she murmured discreetly to her,

'I have noticed on a few occasions recently that you have not seemed well. Could it be . . . ?'

It was a few minutes before Jessica realised what she meant. Could she be carrying Sebastian's child? Surely it was too soon to know, and besides, there had only been those two occasions . . .

One of which would have been more than enough, she reminded herself grimly, panic clawing through her at the implications. She wasn't ready yet for the responsibility of a child. Her relationship with Sebastian was too fraught with difficulties; they had no right to bring a child into such an insecure marriage. Children should be wanted, surrounded with love and care.

She was letting her imagination run away with her, she decided later, as she listened to Señor Alvarez speaking quickly to Sebastian. She probably wasn't pregnant at all.

'Sebastian is returning immediately,' he told them. 'Meanwhile we must do all we can to find her.'

Señor Alvarez quickly took command, much to Jessica's relief. They were each given different sections of the house to search, apart from Luisa, who elected to help Jorge with his.

Jessica walked with them to the top of the stairs, thinking it was a pity that if Sebastian had to arrange a marriage for his brother he didn't do so with pretty little Luisa, who plainly was quite ready to fall in love with him, just as he was with her.

She was halfway through her own part of the *hacienda* when suddenly a thought struck her. She hurried downstairs and out into the courtyard, ignoring the heavy rain as she dashed across to the stables. She had hoped to find

Enrico, who was in charge of the horses there, but he had obviously taken shelter somewhere, because the place was deserted. The first thing Jessica noticed as she approached the building Lisa had shown her was that the roof was dipping badly under a weight of water. Once inside she realised that it was also leaking because the floor was damp, but she didn't waste any time worrying about the dampness, hurrying instead across to the cellar door, wrenching it open and anxiously calling Lisa's name. The light was on, and she thought she heard a faint reply, when suddenly almost overhead there was a terrific clap of thunder. She eyed the steps uncertainly. Moisture trickled down the walls, the light was dull and pale, and she felt an increasing aversion to go down, but Lisa might be down there, hurt or frightened. She hesitated, wondering whether to dash back to the house, acknowledging that she should have gone to Señor Alvarez in the first place and told him of her fears. She was just about to go when she heard a sound. Straining her ears, she caught it again. Lisa! She was down there!

'Don't worry, Lisa,' she called out, 'I'm coming down!'

She had almost reached the bottom when she heard a sound, a dull heavy rumbling which she tried to tell herself was thunder, but which instinct told her was something much worse. The only sound she had ever heard to resemble it was avalanches witnessed on television, and there was certainly no snow on the *hacienda*. There was water, though, she reflected nervously, remembering the dilapidated roof, bowing under the weight of water. If that roof collapsed! She daren't allow herself to think about it. Terror clawed painfully at her stomach and she crossed her hands protectively over it, knowing in a blinding moment of realisation that she *did* want Sebastian's child.

Somehow the thought that she might already have conceived it made her feel all the more protective towards Lisa.
Half running, half stumbling, she hurried down the steep
steps, searching the cavern at the bottom with frantic intensity, until she saw the little girl at the farthest end, her
face tearstained.

'Oh, Lisa!'

'Jessica, I can't get up,' Lisa cried plaintively. 'I fell and
hurt my ankle. I thought I was going to be here forever!'

'Hush, darling, it's all right,' Jessica comforted her,
hurrying over and crouching on the floor beside her. 'Let
me look,' she said gently, running her fingers over the little girl's leg and anklebone. She thought it was more
sprained than broken, but she couldn't let Lisa risk putting any weight on it. She would have to carry her out.

'Put your arms round my neck,' she instructed, 'and
hold on tight. It might hurt a little bit, but just think of
how quickly we're going to be back in the house. You gave
us all a nasty fright, you know,' she went on, talking quietly as she tried to make Lisa as comfortable as she could.
'Tio Sebastian is coming back from Seville to help us look
for you.'

'But you found me,' Lisa protested drowsily, gasping as
Jessica tried to lift her. Dear God, what if she had banged
her head when she fell? She could have concussion—anything! Should she leave her and go and get help?

'Don't let Tio send me to school, will you?' Lisa begged
tearfully.

'Is that why you came down here, so you wouldn't have
to go to school?'

Lisa shook her head. 'I just wanted to think,' she said
simply, and they both winced as they heard a loud rumbling overhead.

'Only thunder,' Jessica said firmly. She glanced up-wards and stared in horror at the crack appearing in the arched ceiling. Dirt and rubble trickled down, spattering onto the floor, the light bulb swinging wildly before the cavern was suddenly plunged into darkness. With the light gone Jessica's ears became attuned to sounds she had not heard before—the steady trickling of moisture on the walls, the ominous rumblings from above them, and the slowly increasing dribble of debris through the now invis-ible crack in the ceiling.

She couldn't possible leave Lisa now, Jessica acknowl-edged. In fact neither of them could stay where they were for a moment longer than they had to.

'We've got to move,' she told the little girl, relieved when Lisa answered in a matter-of-fact if somewhat breathless voice,

'Yes, otherwise the roof might fall in on us, mightn't it?'

'Well, just hold on tight,' Jessica cautioned her.

Surely the best thing to do would be to feel her way along the wall. That way they were more likely to avoid any cave-in. It was a painfully laborious task inching her way along the wall, trying her best not to jar Lisa's ankle. She had no idea how far they had gone when they both heard the sudden crack above, and it was only blind instinct that sent her stumbling for the stairs, her head bent over Lisa's as they were showered with debris and the water that cas-caded through the hole in the ceiling.

She could have cried with relief when she felt the first step; she had been terrified that they were going to be trapped by the falling ceiling. Her body was trembling with tiredness and relief when they finally reached the top stair. She fumbled for the catch and pushed, but the door re-fused to open. She tried again, forcing her whole weight behind it, and still it refused to move.

'Something must have blocked it,' Lisa murmured apprehensively. 'What are we going to do?'

'We're going to sit here and wait for someone to come and unblock it,' Jessica told her, trying to appear calm.

'But no one knows we're here.'

It was all too dreadfully true. What could she say? Taking a deep breath, Jessica lied, 'Oh yes, they do—I told Jorge I thought you might be here, but I didn't say anything before, because I didn't think you'd want me to tell anyone else about your secret place.'

'Now four of us know,' Lisa replied drowsily. 'You, me, Tio Sebastian and Tio Jorge.'

Yes, Sebastian knew, but did he care enough about either of them to think of looking here? Eventually someone was bound to notice that the roof had caved in, but they might not realise that they had been trapped in the cellar.

Dreadful pictures flashed through her mind, stories of walled-up nuns and petrified skeletons tormenting her until she wanted to scream and beat on the door until it gave way, but if she did that it would only upset Lisa. She would perhaps never know whether she had been carrying Sebastian's child, and he would have lost another bride, although this time... She sighed and shivered as the cold sliced through to her bones.

Lisa's teeth were chattering; the little girl was only wearing a flimsy dress and Jessica pulled off her own knitted jacket, draping it round her shoulders and pulling her into the warmth of her own body.

Time dragged by. Jessica wasn't wearing a watch, and the only sounds to break the silence were their own voices and the ominous cracking sounds as more of the ceiling gave way.

Lisa started to cry. 'We'll be trapped in here forever,' she sobbed. 'We'll never get out!'

'Of course we will. Look, I'll tell you a story, shall I?'

She did her best, inventing impossible characters and situations, but she only had a tiny portion of Lisa's concentration.

'Stop!' she insisted at one point. 'Jessica, I thought I heard something.'

Her heartbeat almost drowning out her ability to say anything else, Jessica listened. There were sounds...faint, but clearly discernible from those of the falling ceiling.

'We must shout,' Lisa urged, 'so that they know we're here.'

'No, we'll tap on the door instead,' Jessica told her, terrified that if they shouted the reverberations might be enough to bring down what was left of the ceiling.

She tapped, and there was no response, and no matter how much she strained her ears she could hear nothing from the other side of the door. Perhaps they had simply imagined those sounds after all, perhaps there wasn't anyone there—or even worse, perhaps someone had been and gone.

'We must keep tapping,' she told Lisa doggedly, not wanting the little girl to lose heart.

Her wrist was aching with the effort of supporting Lisa and trying to tap on the door at the same time, when at last she heard a faint but unmistakable response. Just to be sure she tapped again—Morse code learned when she was a girl and only dimly remembered, the same definite pattern of sounds coming back to her.

Tears of relief poured down her face. Her chest felt tight with pain, and she could scarcely think for relief.

The sounds outside the door became louder and took on definite patterns; at the same time more of the roof came crashing down, bricks and rubble falling sharply onto the steps. It was a race between life and death, Jessica thought, shivering at the knowledge, and they were the prize.

A piece of brick fell on her foot, but she scarcely felt any pain. She was so cold her body was practically numb.

'How long do you think it will be?' Lisa asked huskily. 'I'm so cold, Jessica!'

'Not long now,' she comforted her. There was a splintering sound above them, followed by a high-pitched whine. In the darkness Jessica could see nothing, but she could feel a faint dust settling on her face. They must be cutting through the door. A tiny glimmer of light appeared, followed by a small hole.

'Jessica?' It was Sebastian's voice, crisp and sharp. 'Jessica, where are you?'

'We're here,' she told him tiredly, hugging Lisa. 'At the top of the steps.'

'Listen carefully, then. The roof has collapsed and the door is jammed. We're going to cut the top half away, but whatever you do, don't move from where you are. We think there's been some subsidence underneath and the shift of your weight might cause the steps to collapse.'

'Lisa's hurt her ankle,' she told him, 'but I think it's only sprained.'

There were sounds of further activity beyond the door. The thin beam of light grew and at last she could see Lisa's face. She could also see how precarious their position was. Where the cellar had been there was simply a mound of rubble, and she shuddered to think of their fate had they been trapped beneath it. Several of the lower steps were already cracked, and even as she watched the cracks deepened and spread. At last the buzzing of the saw ceased, and light flooded their prison. She looked up, joy and love flooding her eyes as she saw Sebastian looking down at them.

'Take Lisa first,' she told him, lifting the little girl. His face was smudged with dirt, his hair ruffled and untidy, a curiously bleak expression in his eyes.

'Sebastian, hurry, the whole thing's going to go at any minute!' she heard Jorge call behind him, and she realised that Sebastian was alone in the crumbling shell of the building.

She also realised that she couldn't scramble over the half door without some help and that she would have to stay here alone while he carried Lisa to safety. He seemed to hesitate as though he guessed her fear, but she forced a smile, and lifted Lisa towards him.

His arms closed round her and he turned. Watching his back disappear into the darkness was the most terrifying and lonely feeling Jessica had ever experienced. When he disappeared she wanted to claw and tear at the wood in panic, but no matter how much she stretched she couldn't get over the wooden barrier. Behind her she heard a dull crack, and gasped in horror as half the steps suddenly disappeared, leaving her clinging to the door.

'Jessica, Jessica, it's all right, I've got you!' Strong arms clamped round her body, lifting her upwards, as she clung unashamedly to their warm strength.

It was only as he lifted her over the door that Jessica realised the appalling risks Sebastian had run. The building was completely demolished, a yawning chasm gaped beneath them. As Sebastian carried her to safety she heard a dull rumble, and glanced over his shoulder just in time to see the ground sliding away, taking the remnants of the building with it.

'It's the rain,' Jorge muttered as Sebastian reached him. Señor Alvarez was with him, holding Lisa, and both men were soaked to the skin, their faces anxious and drawn. Jessica hadn't even realised it was still raining until that moment, and she felt she had never enjoyed anything quite as much as the rain against her skin, and the cold breeze blowing down from the Sierras. 'It eroded away the ground beneath and the sheer weight of the building caused it to collapse.'

'If Sebastian hadn't remembered Lisa's "secret place" we might never have found you,' Señor Alvarez said gravely as they hurried towards the house. 'It is a blessing that he reached you in time.'

It was indeed, Jessica reflected numbly, shivering with the cold that seemed to reach into her bones, despite the warmth of Sebastian's arms.

In the house Tia Sofia was waiting, fear etched deeply into her face until she saw the two burdens Sebastian and Jorge were carrying.

'Lisa has hurt her ankle,' Jorge told her quickly. 'Doctor...'

'I shall telephone him now...but first we must get them upstairs and out of those wet things. Tia, you help Lisa, I...'

Lisa murmured a protest and begged feverishly for her aunt Jessica. 'Go with Lisa, Tia Sofia,' Sebastian said quietly. 'I can help Jessica.'

Jessica wanted to protest, to tell him that she was too weak now to endure the touch of his hands on her body without betraying her love—a love he did not want. She knew that now. She had seen rejection in his eyes when he turned away from her by the cellar door when she had looked at him with her heart in hers.

He took her to a room she had never seen before, richly furnished in peaches and greens.

'You will want to be alone,' he told her almost curtly. 'This was my mother's room, it is part of the suite she shared with my father. I once said that when I married my wife would always share my bed, but there are times...' He paused by the door. 'I am sorry about the child. I did not intend that it should happen,' and then he was depositing her on the bed, ignoring the dark smudges she was making on the silk coverlet.

The child? Did he mean . . . ? But . . .

He disappeared into the bathroom, reemerging several seconds later with a sponge and towel.

'Tia Sofia told me,' he said quietly. 'She was concerned for you and wanted me to know.'

'She may be mistaken,' Jessica told him, as a terrible pain tore at her heart. He didn't want her and he didn't want their child.

'Perhaps.' He didn't sound convinced. 'Come, let me sponge your skin, and then I will leave you in peace. You will feel better directly.'

She would never feel better again, Jessica thought numbly as he sponged away the dirt and dust, treating her as though she were a child of Lisa's age. The warmth of the room was making her feel sleepy, soothing away the intense cold that had gripped her in the cellar.

Sebastian finished his self-imposed task and reached for the towel, and Jessica looked at him. His face seemed almost austere, and for the first time she could see the ascetic in him. 'You had a lucky escape.' He said it almost broodingly, and Jessica wondered bitterly if he had hoped that she wouldn't.

'It was lucky for us that you knew about Lisa's special place,' she told him.

His mouth tightened and he seemed about to say something, but instead he simply dried her body, then pushed back the covers. As he lifted her and slid her beneath the sheets, Jessica had a wild longing to reach up to him and beg him to stay with her, to take her in his arms and heal her aching body with the beneficence of his. But what was the point? He didn't want her; he didn't want their child. He probably wished he had never married her.

She was almost asleep when the doctor came, accompanied to her disappointment by Tia Sofia and not Sebastian. He examined her thoroughly, smiled at her and told her that she was a very brave young lady and that she had had a lucky escape.

'It is fortunate that your pregnancy is so little advanced,' he added calmly, 'otherwise . . .'

So it was true. She was carrying Sebastian's child. Tears stung her eyes and she longed for things to be different, for him to want their child as much as she did herself.

She thought later that she must have been given something to help her sleep, because she was suddenly aware of feeling oddly light-headed, with a longing to close her eyes. When she opened them again it was morning, and the sun was dancing on the ceiling of her bedroom.

Her bedroom! She felt like a small child banished for a sin it didn't know it had committed. Why had Sebastian put her in this room? Perhaps because he could no longer endure her presence in his room, in his bed. Perhaps the fact that she carried his child reminded him too much of the past, of Manuela who he had loved as he would never love her, but he had not kept faith with Manuela. He was denying their child. It was a strangely cowardly act for so brave a man. He hadn't hesitated to risk his own life to save both hers and Lisa's.

The day dragged. She was to stay in bed for several days, Tia Sofia told her when she came to see her. Lisa's ankle was merely sprained and she too was confined to bed. Jorge and Luisa wanted to come and see her.

'And Sebastian?' Jessica asked, dry-mouthed.

'He has had to go to Seville on business,' Sofia told her, avoiding her eyes. 'He will come and see you when he comes back.' There was pity in her eyes. 'Do not distress yourself, Jessica. Think of the child you carry and let that give you hope.'

Jessica was alone when the door opened later in the afternoon and Pilar came in. As always she was dressed impeccably and expensively, her face and nails fit to grace a *Vogue* cover.

'Ah, you are awake—that is excellent,' she purred with one of the coy smiles that Jessica dreaded. 'We can have a little talk.'

'What about?' Jessica asked wearily.

'Why, Sebastian, of course, and your folly in believing you could possibly hold him. He only married you out of pity and compunction because he thought he had wronged you. You must know that?'

She did, of course, but she realised that Sofia didn't like Pilar saying so. 'And now you carry his child and you believe, foolishly, that it will give you the key to his heart. It won't. His heart...'

'Belongs to your sister. Yes, I know,' Jessica agreed tiredly. 'But I am his wife, Pilar, and I am to have his child.'

'His wife, yet you have separate rooms,' Pilar pointed out maliciously. 'His child... Yes, but men can easily have children, you cannot hope to keep him because of that. You would do better to leave now, before he asks you to do so. It must be obvious to you that he doesn't want you; that your marriage was a mistake from the start. Sebastian doesn't want you—if he did why would he move you in here?' she asked scornfully. 'He is a deeply passionate and sensual man, not a man who would give his wife her own bedroom unless he was trying to tell her something. I shall leave you now,' she finished softly, sweeping towards the door, 'but think about what I have said and soon, I am sure, you will realise that I speak the truth.'

She was gone before Jessica could retaliate, leaving her with the sickening knowledge that what she had said was probably the truth. Sebastian didn't want her, and if she had any pride, any backbone, she would leave, just as soon as she was able to!

CHAPTER TEN

'JESSICA, HOW ARE YOU feeling now? Tia Sofia says that you are well enough to receive visitors, but that I am not to tire you out.'

Jessica smiled at Jorge. 'How is Lisa?' she asked. 'I haven't seen her yet.'

'Recuperating faster than you. Dr Bartolo told Sebastian that if you hadn't shielded her from the cold with your coat she might well have been much worse. She has a weak chest,' he explained, 'something she inherited from her mother, and if she had got badly cold it would be aggravated. On the other hand, our good doctor is very concerned about you. He says you are too pale and drawn. You do look pale.'

'I'm just a little tired. How is everyone else, Señor Alvarez and Luisa?'

'Very well, but soon their visit ends. Señor Alvarez has invited me to visit them in Argentina,' Jorge said carelessly. 'Of course, it all depends on whether Sebastian will let me go.'

'Have you told him how you feel about Luisa?' Jessica asked him.

Jorge shook his head. 'I've never known him so unapproachable,' he admitted. 'I just don't know what's got into him.'

She did, Jessica reflected. He was feeling the strain of being tied to a marriage he didn't want. Pilar was right; it would be best if she left.

Jorge was just confiding in her how much he wanted to go to Argentina, when the door opened and Sebastian walked in. Jessica's first thought was that he looked drained and tired; her second that he was furiously, bitterly angry.

'Er... I'll come back and chat to you later,' Jorge muttered to her, obviously also seeing the anger in his brother's eyes.

'What was he doing here?' Sebastian demanded angrily, when Jorge had gone. 'You are supposed to be resting!'

'He came to talk to me.'

'Just to talk?' His mouth twisted aggressively. 'Did he have to sit on your bed simply to talk to you?' Jessica couldn't understand his mood. He seemed bitterly antagonistic towards Jorge, for some unknown reason. 'And what was he talking about?'

'He was telling me that Señor Alvarez had invited him to visit Argentina, and how much he wanted to go. I suspect he thought I might be able to plead his cause with you,' Jessica added with wry self-mockery.

'Dr Bartolo tells me that you are not recovering as fast as he had hoped,' he told her with an abrupt change of front. 'He believes a change of scene might be beneficial to you. Perhaps a visit to your family.'

Jessica felt as though all the breath were being squeezed out of her lungs. It was true, he did want to get rid of her.

She turned away so that he wouldn't see the pain in her eyes. *'Por Dios,'* he muttered savagely, 'did you not think to tell someone where you were going? Did it not occur to you that no one knew where you were? If I hadn't thought on the long drive back from Seville of the *pequeña's* secret place, both of you could have died there!'

'Much you would have cared!' Jessica flung at him bitterly. 'Your own child, and you talk about sending her away to some convent—and not even to one of those close enough to her to soften the blow! You tell Pilar, who you must know hates her, even though she is her sister's child. Well, that isn't going to happen to my baby! Poor Lisa, she doesn't even know she is your child, but everyone else does; how can you keep the truth from her forever? Haven't you thought of her pain and disillusionment when she discovers the truth, possibly at a time when it can do her the most harm?'

'Lisa—my child?' He frowned down at her, making her feel conscious of her flushed cheeks and undoubtedly tousled hair. 'What are you talking about?' he grated. 'Lisa is not my child!'

'I know that's the polite fiction you would want to preserve, but I've been told differently. She's Manuela's child, conceived during the time of your betrothal.'

'Who told you this?'

Jessica trembled under the look of biting anger he gave her. 'I...'

'No matter... You believed it, whoever told you. You think I would actually dishonour the girl I was to have married? A virgin?'

There was so much horror in his voice that Jessica felt acute jealousy of Manuela.

'I am not talking about dishonour, Sebastian,' she said tiredly. 'You loved her and she loved you. What could be more natural...'

'*Dios,* you talk as though you were reading a fairy tale!' he snapped at her. 'And what you say contains about as much truth. Manuela did have a child out of wedlock and that child is Lisa, but she is not my child.' He saw her expression and smiled bitterly. 'You don't believe me? I assure you it is quite true, although no one knows the truth apart from myself and Pilar. Perhaps I had best tell you the whole and then there will be no more of these hysterical accusations about my lack of feelings towards my "child".

'Manuela's family and mine had always been close friends, through several generations. The idea of a marriage between us was first mooted when we were quite small, as is our custom, and both of us grew up knowing we were destined to marry, although we were more like brother and sister. The year Manuela was eighteen we were to marry. When she was seventeen we were formally betrothed; it was then that Manuela's father confided to me that he had been seriously worried by her suddenly changed behaviour. There were wild moods, fits of tears, terrible emotional storms that blew up out of nothing. It was decided that she would go to South America to spend some time with relatives over there. Her father felt that the change would do her good. We parted as the friends we were. If our relationship was not all that I could have hoped for from marriage, it was pleasant and undemanding. I would be free to make a life for myself as long as I was discreet. There would be children.' He broke off when he saw Jessica's expression.

'There is no need for your pity,' he told her brusquely. 'It is an accepted code of behaviour that harms no one. While Manuela was away I prepared for our wedding. She was to return two weeks before our wedding day. I have since learned from Pilar that her father feared if she returned any sooner her bouts of hysteria might overcome her. Pilar was already married at this time and had no idea how serious Manuela's condition had become.

'She had been away eight months, but I barely recognised her when she returned. I met her at the airport, and she was swathed in black garments, her face haggard and pale. She refused to see me when I called at the house. "Wedding nerves", her mother told me.

'A week before our marriage was due to take place I received a phone call from the hospital in Seville. Manuela had been involved in a car accident and was asking for me. They gave me no hint of whether she was injured or how badly, and it was only when I got there that they told me she was not likely to live. They also told me that she was seven months pregnant, and knowing of our betrothal they had imagined that the child was mine and had called me to ask my permission to try to save its life even though they couldn't save Manuela's.

'Of course I telephoned her parents, but they refused to come to the hospital, so great was their shame. How on earth they had expected her condition to go unnoticed at the ceremony I do not know, but it seems they believed by some miracle that once we were married, everything would be all right.

'I didn't know what to do, and then, briefly, Manuela regained consciousness. She told me her lover had been someone she had met in Argentina, someone she loved in a way that she could never love me. She knew she was going to die and begged my forgiveness, urging me to try to save the life of her child and look after it. I learned later from ... connections in South America that her lover had also been married, something he had obviously neglected to tell her, and in some ways I wonder if it was not kinder that she should have her brief moment of happiness and then oblivion before it was destroyed by the realisation that she had been deceived.

'I stayed with her until the end. She died just after Lisa was born, and I'll never forget the look on her face when she opened her eyes and saw her child. I vowed then that I would bring Lisa up as though she had been our child. I suppose it is inevitable that people should think she was mine.'

'I'm so sorry,' Jessica managed in a husky whisper. 'I should never... You must have loved Manuela dreadfully,' she added.

'Loved her?' He looked at her incredulously. 'As a brother, yes, but as a lover—no. One selfish part of me even rejoices that we did not marry. With the benefit of hindsight I can see that there was a weakness in her—not her fault, poor child, but the result of too much marrying among cousins, too much thinning of the blood. Her hysteria, and bouts of temper... But I am tiring you, and Dr Bartolo says that you are to rest.'

Jessica wanted to tell him that she wasn't tired. She wanted to beg him to stay, but she knew she wouldn't. Not once during their conversation had he said anything about their marriage, and she wondered if he was regretting it as much as Pilar had said.

Pilar had led her to believe that he still loved Manuela, she had lied about Lisa, while according to Sebastian... Was Pilar too tainted with her sister's weakness, was that perhaps why, in spite of the obvious suitability of it, he had not married her? She wanted him, Jessica knew that, and she would stop at nothing to get him, she acknowledged with a sudden flash of insight. Her possessiveness was almost maniacal.

TWO DAYS PASSED and Dr Bartolo pronounced that Jessica was well enough to get up. Sebastian as always was scrupulously polite when he saw her, which seemed to be more and more infrequently. When they did talk, it was about the factory, the designs—polite, distant conversation that tore at her heart, leaving it bruised and aching. She couldn't stay any longer, she admitted one afternoon after he had gone to inspect the vines, and she was alone in the house, Lisa and Tia Sofia were out visiting, and Jorge had taken Señor Alvarez and Luisa on a sight-seeing expedition.

Only that lunchtime Sebastian had mentioned in conversation that he had been making enquiries about a flight to England for her. His aunt had looked surprised when he mentioned that she might go for a visit, and Jessica had tried to hide the hurt in her eyes that he was so anxious to get rid of her.

And he never even mentioned their child. Dr Bartolo had confirmed that she was indeed pregnant, but Sebastian had simply compressed his mouth and looked grimly distant when, falteringly, she told him that her condition was confirmed.

Perhaps now was the time to leave, she thought miserably, before the decision was forced on her. Oh, she knew Sebastian would disguise it in the guise of sending her home for a 'holiday', but they both knew that she would not be coming back. There was simply no point.

Many of her things were still in Sebastian's room, and now would be a good time to retrieve them. She was busily engaged in removing clothes from cupboards and they were on the bed in neat piles when the door was suddenly flung open. She straightened, her heart pounding, half longing and half fearing to see Sebastian. Only it wasn't Sebastian, it was Pilar, her face contorted with a rage that made fear curl unpleasantly along Jessica's spine.

'You here!' she hissed malevolently. 'I thought I told you that Sebastian didn't want you, but then the maid tells me you are in his room!'

Jessica was just about to tell her that she was simply removing her clothes when a sudden spurt of anger—and the memory of what Sebastian had told her—moved her to say lightly, 'I am his wife, Pilar. I have a perfect right to share his room, if I want to.'

'He doesn't want you,' Pilar spat positively. 'Jesu Maria, you must know that! Sebastian is a man above all else, he would not deny himself your bed and body as he has been doing these last weeks if he desired you!'

Jessica knew that it was true, but something compelled her to stand her ground and say calmly, 'If Sebastian has been denying himself, it is for my sake, and the sake of our child,' she added softly. 'Sebastian knows that I have...'

'You are to have his child?'

The bitter hatred in Pilar's eyes appalled Jessica, who realised how unwise she had been to fan the flames of the other woman's resentment. Far better to have simply told the truth. Now she was alone in the room with what she was convinced was a badly deranged woman, who was advancing on her like a panther on its prey, scarlet-tipped fingers curled into talons, as though they would like to tear into her flesh and destroy the life growing within it.

'All these years I have waited for him to turn to me,' Pilar said softly, 'all these years of waiting and watching, knowing he must eventually marry for the sake of his name, and then, just when I think he will be mine, you come along... Well, he will be mine,' she snapped venomously. 'Manuela thought she could take him from me, and was punished for it, and I shall not let you and the brat you carry come between me and what is rightfully mine!'

She was mad—she had to be, Jessica thought shakily as she stared at the wild eyes and twisted features. But she was also dangerous, and Jessica could almost feel those fingers on her throat, gripping it, depriving her of breath.

She backed into the corner, realising too late that it was the wrong thing to do. Pilar was stalking her like a cat with its prey, a rictus smile twisting the full lips. She lunged, her hands reaching for Jessica's throat, her wildly exultant laughter filling the room.

The door was suddenly flung open and Sebastian was standing there, his jacket thrown carelessly over one shoulder, his shirt unbuttoned at the neck, tiredness lying in the shadows and hollows of his face. His expression changed as he took in the scene, alertness replacing his earlier exhaustion.

'Pilar—*Dios*, what are you about?' He gripped her arms, dragging her away from Jessica and opening the door, as he called to someone outside.

Dr Bartolo came hurrying in, his expression one of shock as he looked at Pilar and saw the murderous intent in her eyes.

'Allow me to deal with this, my friend,' he said sorrowfully to Sebastian. 'I have been afraid for a long time that...' He broke off as Jessica felt herself succumbing to the eddying whirls of blackness trying to suck her down.

'I'm all right,' Jessica managed to assure him. 'Just a little faint. I...'

'She wanted to take you from me, Sebastian!' Pilar cried bitterly. 'I told her you were mine. I...'

'Pilar, you must come with me,' Dr Bartolo said firmly. 'She needs specialised treatment,' he murmured in an aside to Sebastian. 'Her behaviour has troubled me for a long time, but there is a clinic I know of where they are used to cases of this kind. She has allowed her feelings for you to become obsessive.'

Pilar allowed herself to be led out of the room, and Jessica fought off the attack of faintness that had threatened her. Her legs felt weak and shaky, but when Sebastian moved towards her she fended him off, her expression unknowingly one of sharp horror.

'I am sorry about that,' he said flatly. He had his back to her, and walked across the door leading out into the courtyard. 'I should have warned you about Pilar, but she had seemed so much improved... She has already suffered two breakdowns; on each occasion she convinced herself that she was deeply in love with the victim of her obsession. I am sorry that you had to be involved.'

He turned round, his eyes going to the neat pile of clothes, his expression changing, darkening. 'What is this?'

'My clothes,' Jessica told him quietly. 'I was just getting them when Pilar came in. I suppose finding me here in your room was the last straw.'

'If you wish your clothes moved from my room to yours one of the maids can do it,' he told her brusquely. 'There is no need for you...'

'To invade your privacy?' Jessica suggested shakily. 'You needn't worry about it happening again. I'm removing my clothes, because I'm also removing myself from your life. I'm going home.'

'No!' The denial was grittily abrasive. *'Por Dios,'* Sebastian suddenly added hoarsely, crossing the room and taking her roughly in his arms. 'I can endure no more—I will not permit you to go! You are carrying my child, and I will not allow you to go.'

'But you wanted me to go,' Jessica reminded him

shakily, wondering if he could feel the unsteady thud of her heart, and the quick race of her pulse. His arms felt like a haven—heaven itself, and she never wanted to leave them. She could see the faint beginnings of a beard growing along his jaw, and wanted to touch it. He smelled of the outdoors and fresh sweat, and the combination was unbearably erotic to her heightened senses.

'Because I feared something like this would happen.'

Within the circle of his arms, she raised her hand to push her hair back off her forehead, the brief gesture emphasising the gentle thrust of her breasts. Sebastian's eyes flared hotly as he studied the soft mounds, then with a savage imprecation he drew her against the hard pulsating length of him, letting her feel his arousal, his mouth moving blindly over her skin, touching and tasting, until he buried it hotly in hers, kissing her with an intensity that sapped her willpower and made her cling helplessly to him, offering herself up to whatever it was he wanted from her.

'I won't let you leave me,' he muttered throatily against her skin. 'You are mine, Jessica, and mine alone. *Dios,* the torment I have suffered seeing you smile at my brother, my aunt—anyone but me! You cannot know how I have longed to see you look at me with love, how I have hungered for you to want me as I want you—not simply for the pleasure our bodies find in one another, but with your heart and soul!'

She was unbearably moved, unable to deny the conviction in his voice, the emotion in his eyes as they searched her face as though willing a response.

'You love me?' Jessica asked uncertainly, still not fully able to accept.

'Do you doubt it?' He smoothed her hair back off her forehead, and she could feel the heated shudder of his body as she touched him. 'I wanted you from the first,' he told her softly. 'I hated you at the same time because of what you were. Or what I thought you were.'

'I thought you despised me,' Jessica told him. 'You were so cold, so distant.'

'Because I daren't let myself be anything else. All the time I was giving myself reasons why I shouldn't, all I wanted to do was to take you in my arms and make you admit that no man could give you the pleasure I could. I hated Jorge because he had been your lover, and when you threatened to stay in Seville and see him. I couldn't understand why he had stopped wanting you. I thought if he saw you again, he would do...'

'And so you concocted that tale about needing a designer to save him from me,' Jessica supplied dryly.

Sebastian smiled grimly. 'Nearly right, only it was because I wanted to keep you away from him and with me,' he supplemented. 'And then he arrived and my whole world was turned upside down. You weren't the girl he had met, you were someone else; someone about whom I knew nothing. Someone who might have a lover or a boyfriend in the background whose claims on you I couldn't destroy. And then Jorge gave me the perfect weapon. People were talking about us, he told me. He was concerned for you. I knew my aunt and Pilar intended to come and see you. I must admit I hadn't quite intended that we should be discovered as we were... some things cannot be controlled,' he added with a wry mockery that brought vivid colour to her skin, 'and you were so sweetly responsive I forgot why I had come to your room and remembered only how much I wanted you... loved you,' he amended softly, 'because by then I did, although I was loath to admit it even to myself.'

'But when you married me you were so distant I thought you hated me!'

He cupped her face and looked at her sombrely. 'Why didn't you tell me you were a virgin? Was it to punish me, to make me suffer?'

Jessica didn't understand what he meant.

'I tried to,' she told him huskily, 'in the car on the way back to the *hacienda,* but you told me how relieved you were that I didn't need "initiating" and after that I just couldn't...'

'And so instead you make me suffer a thousand torments, hating myself for what I have done to you. It was bad enough when I simply thought I was forcing you into a marriage you didn't want. There was desire between us and I hoped that in time it might grow to something else. When I discovered that not only had I robbed you of your freedom, but that I had also taken from you the right to give your body and sweet innocence to the lover of your choice, I hated and despised myself...'

'You were so cold,' Jessica whispered, 'so distant, and so hateful.'

'Because it was the only way I could stop myself from taking you in my arms and making love to you again and again,' Sebastian told her whimsically. 'I wanted you so much, I had to erect a barrier between us for your sake. I wanted to get down on my knees and beg your forgiveness, kiss every inch of your beautiful, precious body and promise you that never again would it know pain, but to do so would be to inflict my desire and love on you again, and I told myself that was something I would never do.

'We both know how long my resolve lasted,' he added wryly, adding with a frankness that half shocked her, 'Your sweet cries of pleasure on that second occasion have haunted my nights like a siren song ever since.'

'You made me sleep on my own,' Jessica accused, still not daring to believe that it was true and that he loved her.

He smothered a groan. 'My sweet love, it was torture, but I had no alternative. I had promised myself that I would set you free, that it was wrong of me to hold you to our marriage. I couldn't forgive myself for taking your innocence when you didn't love me, and when I discovered you were to have my child...'

'You were so cold towards me I thought you didn't want it,' Jessica interrupted bleakly. 'Then Pilar came and told me that you wanted me to leave, and...'

'And you already believed that I had turned my back on my daughter,' he finished for her. 'Oh, Jessica, I can't tell you what it meant to me to think you carried my child! I longed fiercely to keep you here with me, but I couldn't do it. I couldn't hold you on so fragile a thread. I'm a proud man, as you have so often said, and my pride would not allow me to constrain my wife to stay with me only for the sake of our child.'

'But if she loved you...'

He cupped her chin, his eyes dark with emotion. 'If she loved me—if you loved me,' he corrected huskily, 'I would never let her go. When I saw that building and knew you were in it... If you had died then life would have had no meaning for me,' he told her simply.

'You risked your life for us,' Jessica said softly. 'I...'

'Do you think I would have let anyone else near you?' he demanded with a ferocity that surprised her. 'When everything a man holds of value in his life is in danger of course he trusts no one but himself to remove that danger. When you told me to take Lisa, even though I knew you were right, you'll never know what it cost me to go, leaving you there, possibly facing death.'

'And you'll never know how I felt, seeing you disappear,' Jessica told him softly, 'wanting you so badly...and then you were so cold, putting me in that bedroom when all I wanted was the warmth of your arms, your...'

'My...?' he questioned teasingly. 'Go on, *querida,* you are just about to get to the interesting bit, I think?'

'Your...body against mine,' Jessica admitted hesitantly, laughing at her own shyness. 'Oh, Sebastian,' she sighed ecstatically, 'I fell in love with you almost straight away, despite all those dreadful things you said to me!'

She frowned as Sebastian suddenly released her, picking up the piles of clothes from the bed and depositing them on a chair.

'What are you doing?' she asked anxiously. 'Sebastian...'

'I thought you wanted to be in my arms,' he reminded her with a slow smile, 'to feel my body against yours? Is that not right, *querida?*'

'Oh, but...' She tried to look scandalised and failed, laughing when he took her in his arms and said wryly,

'What is the matter? Is it not permissible for a man to make love to his wife in the afternoon?'

'I...'

He nibbled the delicate cord of her throat, sending tremors of pleasure coursing over her. 'Why else do you think we have the *siesta, amada?*' he questioned softly. 'It is for children to rest, and for their *mamás* and *papás* to make love.'

His fingers reached for her zip, pressing her against the taut length of his body, and the sudden urgency of the desire flooding through her made her expel her breath in brief shock.

'I love you,' Sebastian murmured smokily as her dress slid to the floor.

As he lifted her and carried her towards their bed Jessica wondered hazily if that first Rosalinda had known this heady, enveloping pleasure; this depth and intensity of love and need for her proud knight. Possibly she had, she thought lazily as Sebastian drew her against him, his fingers playing lightly against her spine, his mouth teasing her skin. Certainly if he was anything like his present-day descendant, she must have done!

He'd dialed the wrong number once...
Now he couldn't stop calling back!

HOTLINE

Gina Wilkins

1

THE ANTIQUE LAMP on the bedside table cast a soft amber glow across the Queen Anne bedroom furniture. Listening to the low rumble of thunder, Erin pulled her ballet-length nightgown over her head. She smoothed it over her slender hips, observing her image in the cheval mirror across the room. Erin knew she was considered beautiful—shapely, dark-haired, blue-eyed, delicately featured. Still, no one waited in the empty bed behind her; no one would step out of the adjoining bath to catch his breath in appreciation of the sight of her clad in thin, lace-trimmed silk.

Suppressing a sigh, Erin turned away from the mirror and brushed a strand of hair from her mouth, dreaming of a fantasy lover who would hold her, laugh with her, share the summer storm with her....

The telephone rang at almost the same moment thunder crashed loudly enough to rattle the doors and windows. She wasn't even certain she'd heard the phone until it rang again. With one eye on the open bedroom door across the hall, Erin snatched up the receiver, surprised the deafening boom hadn't woken Chelsea.

"Sis?" The voice was muffled by noisy static.

Erin smiled in pleasure at the call from her older brother. "This connection is terrible," she said, raising her voice. "Can you hear me?"

"Yeah. Am I coming through?"

"Yes. And it's about time you called! I was starting to worry. You sound kind of funny, though. Are you all right?"

"I've got a lousy cold," he answered glumly. "I could hardly talk at all, yesterday."

She reacted with characteristic worry. "Have you taken anything for it? Have you seen a doctor?"

"No, 'Mommy,' I haven't seen a doctor," he answered teasingly. "It's only a cold. Modern medicine hasn't discovered a cure, remember?"

"Sorry. I guess you're getting all the smothering care you need from the girlfriend." Erin tried not to sound too disdainful. Adam knew exactly how she felt about his latest inamorata. There was no need to start another quarrel about her.

After only a brief pause, he replied flatly. "That's over. She's history."

"Really?" Erin hoped she didn't sound too thrilled. Twirling a strand of her shoulder-length hair around one finger, she tried to sound nonchalant when she asked, "What happened?"

"Long story. Suffice it to say I finally saw beneath the pretty exterior and discovered that the interior wasn't nearly as attractive."

"Isn't that exactly what I told you?" she couldn't resist murmuring, not sure he'd hear her over the static.

He did. "No I-told-you-so's right now, okay? I'm sick and alone and tired. Save it until I'm in better shape to defend myself."

She rolled her eyes at the obvious play for sympathy. "All right, but the minute you're better . . ."

He laughed rather hoarsely. "I'll start practicing being defensive as soon as I hang up. You know, you sound a little strange, yourself. *You're* not coming down with something, are you?"

Erin shook her head, forgetting he couldn't actually see her. "Just tired, I guess. Long day at the grindstone."

"You're not overdoing it, are you? I've always said you try to do too much at once. You need to slow down, take some time to relax."

She frowned a bit, straining to hear him. Funny, he didn't sound at all like himself. That cold really must be a bad one. "I'm okay, really. I'm glad you called. I've missed talking to you. Especially now that Corey's moved off to the Ozarks to find herself, or some such nonsense. The two of you are the only ones who really understand my weird sense of humor."

A series of annoying pops made her wince and hold the receiver a few inches from her ear.

"*Who* moved away?" he asked when the noise faded.

"Corey," she repeated more clearly, wondering why he'd had to ask. "Come on, Adam, the cold hasn't affected your memory, has it? I mean, Corey's only my best friend, as you well know. I talk about her all the time."

"Honey, I'm sorry, but who—? Wait a minute. *Adam?*"

Confused, Erin began to worry that the cold really *was* affecting his mind. Could he be feverish? "What's wrong?"

"I thought you called me Adam," he explained during a respite on the phone line. The static on the line gradually lessened as the storm abated. His voice, hoarse from his cold, was clear—and not at all familiar! "Now, start over, Cheryl. Who's Corey? I honestly don't remember you mentioning her before."

Erin frowned. "*Cheryl?*" she repeated, tightening her grip on the receiver.

There was a moment of blank silence—and then: "This *is* Cheryl, isn't it?"

"No. You mean—you're not Adam?"

The voice on the other end of the line groaned. "Oh, boy. I'm really sorry. I must have gotten a wrong number. I thought you were my sister."

Even though he couldn't see her, Erin hid her flaming face with her free hand. "I thought you were my brother!"

His low laugh made her smile weakly despite herself. "Did I even get the right city? I was *trying* to call North Little Rock, Arkansas—555-2026."

"Well, you got the right city," Erin answered lightly. "But my number's 555-2029. You hit the wrong button."

He laughed again. "Talk about strange... I really thought you were Cheryl."

"And I really thought you were Adam," she repeated, her smile widening a bit. *How ridiculous!* The guys at the ad agency would love this one! Not that they'd ever believe it, she decided, chuckling.

"I don't suppose your brother lives in Boston, does he?" he asked, obviously amused. "Now that *would* be a wild coincidence."

"No, Adam's in California—most of the time. He travels a lot." But he wouldn't care about that, she told herself quickly. He was calling long-distance, and he wanted to talk to his sister. "Maybe you can get a refund on your call if you explain what happened to the operator," she suggested.

"Yeah." He didn't sound as though he cared one way or the other about the cost. "I guess you'd still like to hear from your brother, wouldn't you? Are you really anxious about him?"

Touched by his question, she responded reassuringly. "Oh, I'm sure he'll turn up soon. He does this sometimes."

"The Corey who's living in a cabin in the Ozarks—you said she's your friend?" It seemed as if he wanted to prolong the call. Strangely enough, so did she.

"Yes—my best friend," she answered. Even as she said the words, she realized what an understatement they were. Corey had been wonderful during Erin's divorce four years earlier, standing by her when others had drifted away. Most of the people she'd known during her marriage had been Martin's friends; and somehow, after the divorce, he'd retained custody of them. He'd wanted his friends—it had been his wife and daughter he considered inconveniences.

Since her divorce, Erin had been busy rebuilding her life—finding work as a free-lance illustrator, taking care of Chelsea, her three-year-old daughter, learning how to live within a budget. She'd made several new acquaintances, but no other truly close friends yet. As for her love life—well, that was practically nonexistent. The few dates she'd accepted had been disappointing, to say the least. Too many men thought she was in dire need of their services in bed, and didn't react very graciously when she firmly informed them that they were mistaken. And too many men had no intention of being responsible for another man's child.

Maybe that explained why she was finding this wrong-number telephone call so entertaining. She really *was* hard up for adult companionship. Maybe she should get up her nerve to accept another one of the dinner invitations she'd been receiving lately. They couldn't *all* be toads, could they?

"You know, you should try to call your brother. He'd probably like to hear from you, especially if you're feeling a bit down."

Rather than taking offense at the unwarranted advice, Erin smiled again. "I would if I knew where he was," she replied. "As I said, he travels a lot. He's somewhere in Central America right now, I think. He'll call me as soon as he gets back into this country."

"Oh. Well, I guess I'd better call Cheryl. Again, I'm sorry about disturbing you with the call."

"Thank you. But don't apologize. Actually, I rather enjoyed it," she admitted.

"Oddly enough, so did I." He paused as the phone line crackled one last, faint time, then said, "Well, goodbye."

"Take care of that cold," she couldn't resist advising him, slipping back into her pseudo-maternal voice. After all, he was *someone's* brother.

"Thanks. I will. Bye, again."

"Goodbye." Feeling strangely reluctant, she hung up. She wondered if she'd only imagined that he'd seemed disinclined, as well, to sever their accidental connection.

She had just gotten up from the side of the bed when the phone rang again. Who could it be this time?

"You know, I just thought of something," that now familiar, cold-roughened voice said.

She smiled. "What?"

"Your brother's still dating that terrible person you don't like."

Erin groaned. "Oh, dear, you're right. I hadn't even thought of that."

"Oh, well, keep working on him. Maybe you'll get to have your I-told-you-so speech yet. *My* sister's going to thoroughly enjoy hers."

Erin was laughing when he hung up as abruptly as he'd started speaking. She was still smiling when she tiptoed into Chelsea's room to make sure the storm hadn't disturbed her.

BRETT TRIED to concentrate on his work, but his thoughts kept wandering—wandering to the telephone on one corner of the desk that sat only a few feet from his drawing table. Frowning, he set pencil to paper one more time, then sighed and gave up. He wasn't in a creative mood that evening. He was fighting a strong, totally inappropriate urge to place a telephone call. A call to someone he'd never met, whose name he didn't know, but whose voice had haunted him for almost a week.

Impulsive by nature, Brett finally gave in to that urge and picked up the phone and dialed: 555-2029. He hadn't written the number down, but he hadn't forgotten it, either. If a man answered, he could always hang up, he reasoned with a wry grin at his rather juvenile thought processes.

"Hello?"

It wasn't a man. Definitely not a man. He tried to picture a face to go with that voice. He'd be willing to bet his brand-new T square that she was attractive. "I don't suppose you'd believe I dialed a wrong number again?"

She paused for only a moment. "If you did, we need to have a little lesson."

He relaxed. She didn't sound annoyed by his call. In fact, she sounded rather pleased. "What kind of lesson?"

"The difference between a six and a nine. A six has a little circle at the bottom, a nine has a little circle at the top. Your sister's number ends with the one with the circle at the bottom."

Grinning, Brett leaned back in the leather chair and crossed his argyle-covered feet on the desk in front of him. "I'll keep that in mind."

"Your voice sounds much better. Cold gone?"

"Yes, finally. I'm feeling a lot better now."

"That's nice. Um—" She paused delicately, then asked the question that had obviously been puzzling her ever since she'd realized who he was. "Why did you call?"

He thought about that a moment. Why *had* he called? "I don't know," he admitted at last. "I just wanted to talk to you again. I enjoyed our conversation last week. Besides," he added on a rush of inspiration, "you said you were a bit lonely. I was—um—worried about you."

The silence that followed expressed her surprise. "Why, that's very... thoughtful of you," she said at length. "But I'm fine, really. I have friends."

"I'm sure you have many friends," Brett replied quickly. So much for that excuse. He tried another. "Did you ever hear from your brother?"

"No, not yet." Her concern was evident in her voice. If he knew the guy, he'd go punch him out. Didn't the jerk know that his sister worried about him? Knowing his own sister, Cheryl, and her maternal instincts toward him, Brett could just imagine how this woman must feel at being so out of touch with her brother.

"You know," he said, rubbing the slight bump on the bridge of his once-broken nose in what was a habitual gesture, "the nice thing about talking to a stranger on the phone, long-distance, is that you don't have to worry about what you say, because you probably won't ever meet me. You don't even know my name. So, if you feel like talking, now's your chance. I have a feeling I'd even enjoy that weird sense of humor you say no one understands except Adam and Corey."

"Do you remember *every*thing I said last week?" she demanded with a startled laugh.

He did, actually. How could he have forgotten when he'd displayed an inexplicable tendency to replay the impromptu conversation over and over in his mind? "Most of it," he prevaricated, not wanting her to think he was some sort of nut case. "Tell me something you'd tell Adam if you were talking to him. Something you find funny," he added, curious about that sense of humor.

"Mmm," she murmured consideringly, and he realized in pleasure that she wasn't going to tell him to buzz off and hang up in his ear, which he'd half expected her to do. "Well," she began, "I had a call from my ex-husband's ex-wife today. I laughed myself silly when it was over, but some people may have questioned my sanity for doing so. Adam would've understood."

"Your ex-husband's ex-wife?" Brett repeated slowly, enjoying the conversation immensely.

"Yep. She was his first wife. She's forty now and still moping about being divorced by him six years ago. Now she wants me to join her in forming a 'support club' of former wives who were dumped for younger, prettier women. Can you believe that?"

"How old are you?" he asked, emboldened by anonymity.

"Twenty-six."

He blinked. "A forty-year-old woman wants someone who's only twenty-six to help her start a club for dumped wives? Does she think you're going to spend the rest of your life sulking because your marriage ended in disappointment?"

"That's exactly what she thinks. After all, it's what she's doing."

"Um, you weren't the 'younger, prettier' woman he left *her* for, were you?" he mocked, knowing she could always hang up if he insulted her.

"No, thank God. I met him a year after his divorce. He'd already been through a couple of younger women before me. I was twenty-one, he had just turned forty and was positively terrified of growing older—though I didn't realize it at the time. I noticed that he liked to show me off to his friends, but I thought it was because he really cared about me. I got the old story about how his first wife didn't understand him—and I fell for it, hook, line and sinker. I was one of the few of my friends who wasn't married at the time. I guess I was ready to be swept off my feet."

"Smooth talker, was he?"

"The smoothest. We were married six weeks after we met. On our honeymoon I suspected I'd made a mistake. Within a few months, I *knew* I had. And then, just after his forty-first birthday, he told me that I was cramping his style. He bought a Porsche sports car and a couple of gold chains, and let his hair grow enough to make a little ponytail at his nape. He's spent the four years since our divorce making an utter ass of himself. Poor schlemiel thinks he's living the true playboy life-style. I don't think anyone's had the heart to tell him that even Hef finally got tired of that and settled down."

"I know that guy!" Brett exclaimed, keeping his tone light. "Actually, I know several just like him. They think young women keep *them* young. I've always thought the young women just made them look old in comparison. Besides, what can you talk about with a woman who was born after the Beatles made their debut on Ed Sullivan's show?"

"*I* was born after the Beatles were on Ed Sullivan's show," she reminded him.

Brett winced and ran a hand through his curly brown hair. "Yeah, you were, weren't you? Oh, well, if it makes you feel any better, I don't remember that year very clearly myself."

"How old are you?"

"Thirty-four."

"Married?" The question was asked just a bit too casually.

"No," he told her. "I have to admit I haven't been in any hurry to tie myself down to a commitment like that. But I'm *not* another woman-user like your ex-husband, believe me."

"The woman who wasn't as pretty on the inside as on the outside—did you think about marrying her?"

He grimaced when he thought of Sheree. "No," he confessed. "But—"

"She was gorgeous," the woman said flatly. "She looked good at your side, knew a few interesting tricks in bed, kept your blood pumping for a while. I know the story. It's the one my husband gave me about the woman he dumped me for."

Brett whistled softly. "Wow! He *did* work you over, didn't he?"

"I'm not as bitter as that sounded. I know not all men are like Martin. I'm just still annoyed with myself for being so gullible." She sighed loudly.

"You were very young."

"And very naive. Thank goodness I've gotten beyond that stage now."

Brett smiled. "All grown up now?"

"You betcha."

Chuckling, he wished again that he knew what she looked like. Obviously she was attractive, or the idiot she'd married wouldn't have been interested in her in the first place. Somehow he'd known all along that she was someone a man would notice. After all, she'd captured *his* attention—and he hadn't even laid eyes on her. "You wouldn't fall for a smooth-talking Romeo now?"

"No way."

"Not even if he looked like Tom Cruise or Mel Gibson?" he teased.

"We-e-l-l . . ." She drawled the word deliberately, making him laugh.

"Typical," he goaded her. "Show a woman a handsome face and she forgets all her lofty pronouncements on wisdom and caution."

"Oh, and men are better?" she immediately countered. "You've just come out of a bad relationship, yourself, but I'd bet you'd walk through fire for a chance at meeting Kim Basinger."

"Actually, I prefer petite blond starlets," he teased.

"Ah. The protective type, are you?"

"Let's just say I've got normally active hormones. How are yours?"

After only the slightest pause, she replied a bit faintly, "How are my whats?"

"Your hormones. You've been divorced four years, you said. You surely haven't sworn off men altogether."

"There hasn't been anyone since the divorce," she admitted. "Mostly because I've been too busy getting back on my feet to even contemplate getting involved with anyone. I started seeing someone a year ago, but it didn't work out. Actually, it was a disaster. But that doesn't mean I've given up on men. They have their uses," she added tauntingly, obviously enjoying their sparring as much as he.

"You're talking about affairs," he suggested.

"That's right," she agreed equably. "A series of discreet, careful affairs, entered with open eyes, closed heart and a pocketful of protection against pregnancy and disease. And thank heavens I'm never going to see you," she added in the same breath, "because I *never* talk like this to people I know!"

Brett laughed, believing her. He attempted to ignore the discomfort her words roused in him. Why should he suspect that this woman would be terribly disappointed in the life-style she'd just described? He thought of a tender young heart torn by her husband's callousness. Wounds like that were healed with love and tenderness—not breezy, no-strings affairs. Would she listen if he tried to tell her that?

No. She wouldn't. Not from a stranger over the phone. He only hoped for her sake that some nice guy would come along and convince her that love didn't have to hurt; didn't always lead to heartache. "It's kind of fun to talk to a stranger, isn't it? Not to have to guard your words or worry about what the other person thinks of you," he mused.

"You know, it *is* fun," she said, laughing. "Maybe we've stumbled onto something here—the reason all those 900 numbers are making a fortune. Dial a stranger and pour out your secret thoughts. 'Telephone therapy.' What do you think?"

He chuckled. "I think you're right. Only *I* called you, remember?"

"Oops. I don't think you're going to make very much at this if you're the one footing the bill. Don't you have any deep-hidden anger you want to get out of your system while you've got me on the line? Just to make the call worth your money?"

Pleased at the smile he detected in her voice, he shook his head, forgetting for the moment that she couldn't see him. "I think it was worth my money, anyway. It's been very interesting."

"Better than TV, right?"

"Right."

"By the way, did your sister enjoy her I-told-you-so speech, or did you get out of it because you were sick?"

The memory made him cringe. "I wish. She went on for a good ten minutes about my lack of judgment and told me she wished I'd let her pick out a good woman for me."

"So, why don't you?" she teased.

"The last woman my sister introduced me to had dollar signs in her eyes and fangs behind her sweetly smiling lips," Brett replied bluntly. "The one before that had the IQ and conversational ability of a doorknob. The one before *that*—"

"Okay, I get the picture." She was laughing. "My brother has similar complaints about the women I've tried to fix him up with."

"What about him? Did he like Martin?" Brett couldn't resist asking.

"Hated him," she said with a sigh. "Too bad *I* didn't listen when he was the one giving advice."

"Did he say 'I told you so'?"

Her voice noticeably softened. "No, he didn't, though he certainly could have. He was wonderful. Still is."

When you hear from him, Brett thought, but kept it to himself. "Must be that brothers are more noble than sisters. We don't feel the need to rub your noses in it when we're right."

"Yeah, sure. If you only knew how many times he *has* gloated about being right when I was wrong . . ."

Remembering a few of those times between himself and his own sister, Brett refrained from comment. "It's getting late." It was already past eleven in Boston, though he knew it was an hour earlier in Arkansas. At last he knew now that there was no man impatiently waiting in bed for her. "Guess I'd better let you go."

"I suppose you'd better," she agreed quietly.

"I hope you hear from Adam soon."

"I will. He always keeps in touch when he can. It's just— difficult for him, with the way he travels."

"You know, I could give you my number. If you ever need to talk again—"

"I don't think so," she interrupted gently. "But thanks for the offer."

"Yeah. Well, goodbye. Be happy, okay?"

"You, too."

"Thanks. Bye."

"Bye."

Had her voice really sounded rather wistful when they'd said goodbye? Or was he only projecting his own feelings onto her? Why on earth should he find himself sorry that the conversation had ended, knowing he'd probably never talk to her again? They lived half a continent away from each other, for pete's sake, and she had indicated that she had no interest in pursuing any further acquaintance with him. Nor, if he was honest, was he all that interested in actually meeting her, beyond curiosity.

Fresh out of a disastrous relationship, he was in no hurry to enter another one—particularly with someone who'd been burned as badly as whatever-her-name-was. It was going to require someone very special to take away her scars; someone patient, selfless, infinitely loving. Someone extraordinary. *He* was about as ordinary as they came, Brett admitted matter-of-factly, catching a glimpse of his not-very-tall, not-terribly-handsome, brown-haired, brown-eyed reflection in the mirror on the opposite wall of his office. His sister accused him of staying young looking just to make her feel older. More than once he'd regretted the dimples and curls that, combined with his lack of impressive height, kept him from being a "major hunk," in the words of his best friend's teenage daughter. And the woman on the phone must be beautiful, judging by the tastes of the unpleasant Martin.

He really had to stop wondering about her. He didn't know her, had never seen her, would never meet her. Sure, she sounded nice, but he was notorious for being a sucker for a husky voice and feminine laughter. How many times had he been roped in by them only to find himself with a man-eating barracuda on his hands?

Get back to work, Nash. You're on a deadline, remember?

Trying to put her out of his mind, he sat in front of the drawing board again, reaching for his charcoal pencil. His creative mind was weaving stories again, and he needed to confine himself to the comic books he wrote and illustrated. The kind that made money. Mistaking fantasy for reality could lead to nothing more than disappointment.

ERIN SAT BY HER PHONE for several long minutes after the call ended, feeling like an idiot for telling her entire life's story to a stranger on the telephone. *What must he be thinking of someone with so little discretion?* she wondered with a low moan.

Then, after thinking about it for a few uncomfortable minutes, she decided that he really had seemed to enjoy talking to her, and to sympathize with her story of her failed marriage—something she rarely discussed these days. When *was* the last time she'd expressed her feelings so honestly?

Sure, she talked to Adam when she had the chance, but even with him she wasn't completely open, so that he wouldn't worry too much about her when he was away and had to concentrate on his own problems. Adam's job was a dangerous one—more dangerous, she suspected, than he wanted her to know—and he needed to focus all his attention on staying in one piece.

Corey was secluded in the mountains, and Chelsea was only three, so no wonder she'd done everything but open a vein when her mystery caller had offered an ear. All those words had been building up for a long time.

He was the one who'd made the call. He'd gotten what he'd asked for. And she felt much better for it. *So why feel badly?*

He'd never call again, of course. Why should he? They were total strangers. This second call had probably been an impulse just to satisfy his curiosity about the woman he'd accidentally talked to a week earlier.

He'd sounded so nice, she thought as she moved quietly through the house turning off lights, careful not to disturb her sleeping daughter. But then, lots of men sounded nice—and weren't, once you got to know them. Perhaps talking so frankly to a stranger on the telephone wasn't the brightest thing she'd ever done. Adam would probably have a fit if he ever found out. He was so overprotective of his only sister. It was because of him that her number wasn't listed in the telephone directory.

She'd be more careful from now on. No more chatty calls with strangers, no matter how safe the anonymous conversation might seem. She wasn't a silly girl any longer, but a mature, responsible mother who'd carved herself a secure, if sometimes just a tiny bit dull, niche. She was Chelsea's mom, and perfectly content with that role.

Climbing into her empty bed, she told herself that she really didn't mind sleeping alone. It was safer that way.

Lonely, perhaps. But safe.

Why didn't she find more comfort in that reassurance?

ERIN TURNED OFF the television with a sigh. *What garbage!*
She was annoyed with herself for watching the badly written disease-of-the-week movie. But Chelsea was asleep, she
had nothing new to read, and housework certainly wasn't
something she did for entertainment. What else was there
to do? She'd finished all her free-lance art assignments for
Redding & Howard, the advertising agency that was her
steadiest client. There was nothing else pending at the moment.

She was bored.

She stretched, then glanced at her watch. Nine-thirty.
Maybe she'd just go to bed.

The phone rang.

It couldn't be, she told herself even as her heart jumped.
It had been two weeks since she'd heard from Mr. Wrong
Number. She was certain he'd forgotten all about her. More
likely it was Adam. He'd called her as soon as he'd gotten
back into the country the week before. He'd missed her, and
was frustrated that he couldn't get away from work for time
with Erin and Chelsea.

It had been wonderful talking to him, but oddly enough
she'd thought of her mystery caller all during her long conversation with Adam. *Must be guilt*, she rationalized, determined not to let her brother know that she'd participated
in anything so imprudent. "Hello."

"Hi."

Funny that she recognized the voice. Even after two weeks. Even with only that one syllable. Helpless to restrain it, she felt a smile tilt the corners of her mouth. "Hi, yourself. Did you get the little circles on your numbers mixed up again?"

"I've got this terrible problem with curiosity. My sister's always said it was a good thing I wasn't born a cat."

"What are you curious about this time?" she asked, amused at his sheepish tone.

"Did you ever hear from your brother?"

"Yes, I did. He's back in California—for a while, anyway."

"What does he do?"

"He works for the government."

"Out of California?"

"That's right. He doesn't like D.C.," she explained as if that made perfect sense.

"Oh." He paused, then asked with studied nonchalance, "How are you? Everything going okay?"

"Yes, fine." She paused, unsure how to continue. Wondering why he'd called again. Wishing she weren't quite so glad that he had. "Um—how's Cheryl?"

He chuckled at the question. "She's fine. And Adam?"

"He said he was okay. Not that he'd tell me if he wasn't," she added candidly. "He's a bit overprotective when it comes to me."

He didn't respond. Instead he asked, "Heard any more from your ex-husband's ex-wife?"

"Yes, as a matter of fact, I did. I told her I had better things to do than sit around with a group of women whining about the men who'd done them wrong."

"Good for you!" he approved with a quick laugh.

Reveling in the compliment, she tossed her head, which made her dark hair fly out before settling in a sleek curtain around her shoulders. "She was highly indignant. Told me I didn't even have enough sense to know that I needed the support of other poor unfortunates."

"That's got to be one depressing woman."

"She'd be okay if she'd forget about Martin and get on with her life," Erin replied. "Which is exactly what I told her. I suggested that she go out and have a teeth-rattling affair. It would do her a world of good."

"This from a woman who hasn't—um—*been* with anyone since her divorce?"

She shrugged, hoping the gesture carried in her voice when she answered. "Haven't you ever heard the old saying, 'Do as I say, not as I do'?"

She heard a shuffling sound and a muffled squeak. She pictured him leaning back in a deep leather chair, then wondered what he looked like. She knew his age, but nothing else. Was he blond? Dark? Red-haired? Tall? Short? Lean? Fat? He didn't sound fat, she thought, smiling at her own foolishness.

"I suppose after four years of celibacy, you must be getting a bit . . . itchy," he said boldly.

Her cheeks heated and she was grateful he couldn't see her. He really did seem to remember every word she'd said to him. "Well . . . sometimes," she admitted.

He paused, seemingly intrigued by her tone. She could almost see him cocking his head in curiosity, though she still didn't know what color hair topped that head—if any at all. "Martin wasn't such a great lover?" he hazarded. "Not surprising," he went on before she had to respond. "The man you described would be much more interested in his own pleasure than his partner's."

"Unlike you, I suppose?" she taunted, amazed at her daring. What was it that got into her when she talked to this man?

"Are you asking if I'm any good in bed?" he challenged, sounding amused.

"I suppose I am," she acknowledged rather dazedly.

"Hmm..."

He drew the monosyllable out, as if giving the matter a great deal of thought. "It's hard to rate one's own performance, of course. But I haven't had many complaints."

"Many?" she repeated, fighting the urge to giggle.

"Well, there was one girl, back when I was a novice. She—um—she'd been around a bit, I guess you could say. I think I was a bit clumsy. Perhaps a little too...precipitate."

"And have you had a great deal of practice since that unsuccessful effort?"

"I'm not into one-night stands, if that's what you're asking. Even if I were, that sort of behavior is too dangerous, these days. Let's just say that I'm no longer a novice."

Erin sighed. "It's so different for men."

"In what way?"

"You can admit to having experience and it's considered admirable. A woman still has to worry about her reputation, about being thought easy—all that double-standard garbage."

"Oh, I don't think it's quite that bad anymore. Surely not."

"Oh, really?" she asked skeptically. "What would you say if I said I'd been with dozens of men?"

"Well, for starters, I'd wonder where you'd found the time in only twenty-six years. Then I'd point out that *anyone*, man or woman, who'd been with dozens of lovers is somewhat less than discriminating. I don't think you've had a great deal of experience."

"How do you know that?" she questioned.

"Call it a hunch. Am I right?"

She sighed heavily. "You're right. Martin was the first."

"Oh. I'm really sorry to hear that.'

This time she couldn't hold back a giggle. This man had the most incredible ability to make her feel better—about lots of things. "Believe me, I am, too. I haven't had a lot of luck with romance, actually. Something always goes wrong, someone always ends up being hurt. It's very difficult, isn't it?"

"If you want to fly to Boston, I'd be happy to volunteer my services in one area, at least," he offered humorously.

Hearing the teasing behind his words, Erin laughed. "I think not. I like our relationship exactly the way it is."

"But we don't even know each other's name."

"Right. There's a kind of freedom in that, don't you think? It's like—like having a pen pal without going to all the trouble of composing a letter."

"Telephone pen pals? Interesting concept."

"It is, isn't it? Of course, it's a bit more expensive than a postage stamp. You're going to have a hefty phone bill this month."

"That's okay. I make a hefty salary," he admitted airily.

That didn't surprise her. Somehow she'd sensed that he was successful at whatever it was he did. She didn't ask for specifics. As she'd said, she rather liked keeping him a fantasy man. It was fun, intellectually stimulating—and safe. Even if he knew her name, it would be unlikely that he could find her—if he were someone to worry about; and her instincts told her that he could be trusted.

"Does that mean it's okay if I call you again sometime—just to talk?" he asked a bit too casually, making her suspect that he really wanted her to agree.

"You don't think this is a little...strange?"

He didn't even hesitate. "No. You're the one who compared it to pen pals. There's not a lot of difference, is there?"

She was terribly tempted. It really was nice to have this new friend to talk to; someone with whom she didn't have to pretend, didn't have to guard what she said—almost like a child's imaginary friend. What harm could there be in it? "Sure, you can call again sometime."

"And will you do me a favor?"

"What?" she asked warily.

"Write down my number. You don't have to know my name, if you really want to keep it that way, but I'd like to know you have my number if you ever need to talk. Will you do that?"

She couldn't imagine ever having the nerve to pick up the phone and call him, but she sensed the genuine concern in his deep voice. "All right."

She could hear his smile when he recited the number, which she dutifully wrote down in the back of her telephone directory. No name beside it. She'd know whose number it was. "I have it."

"Good. So I'll talk to you again sometime."

"All right."

"Good night."

"Good night." Bemused, she hung up the phone. And then she started to laugh.

"WHAT'S YOUR FAVORITE food?" he asked, when he called again.

This was their fifth conversation in the six weeks since he first called her by accident. "Any kind of seafood—especially crab."

"What's your favorite movie?"

Erin thought about it a moment. There were lots of movies she liked, but her favorite? "Either *Somewhere in Time* or *Same Time, Next Year,*" she decided.

"Ah. A romantic," he teased. "And a bit of a maverick—not particularly interested in the critics' opinions."

"There was nothing wrong with either of those movies," she replied defensively. "They were both well written, well acted, and they touched my emotions. I always cry when Richard goes back to his own time in *Somewhere in Time*—the scene where he breaks down and cries. And when Alan Alda cries over the death of his—or rather, George's—son in *Same Time, Next Year*, it always gets to me, no matter how many times I've seen it."

"Oh, so you like seeing men cry."

She chuckled. "Poetic justice. Think of how many tears women have shed over men."

"You think men don't cry over women?"

"Have you ever?" she asked, curious and knowing he'd answer honestly. They'd both taken advantage of their odd circumstances to talk quite candidly. Better than therapy, they'd agreed.

"Yeah. As a matter of fact, I have."

She stretched comfortably on her stomach on the couch, propped on her elbows as she pressed the phone to her ear. "Tell me about it."

"My first serious relationship was when I was a senior in college. She dumped me because I was too short. And—I confess—I cried that night. I was really hung up on her and that seemed like such a stupid reason to break up."

"You're right, it does. Why would she dump you because you're too short? Didn't she notice how tall you were when you started dating?"

"Yeah, but she thought I was cute," he answered glumly. "Then I guess her girlfriends started teasing her—she was four inches taller than me. When she was elected homecoming queen, she started thinking about how it would look when I escorted her onto the platform. So she dumped me for a six-five basketball player."

"What a bimbo," Erin pronounced scornfully.

He laughed. "Yeah, I think she was. But she was gorgeous."

Her sigh adequately expressed her disgust. "This society is entirely too hung up on personal appearance. I mean, you've been hurt because you're not a six-footer. I was married because Martin thought I looked good beside him, which led to disaster. Appearance makes a difference in political races, hiring practices, social success. It's ridiculous. What we need is less emphasis on appearance, and more on character."

"A meeting of minds," he suggested.

"Exactly."

"Like we have."

That took her aback for a moment. "Well . . . yes, I suppose so."

"No, really. We've become friends without even seeing each other, just because we enjoy talking and have some things in common. I really like you . . . and I have no idea what you look like."

"None?" she teased.

"Well . . ."

Her feet kicked faster in enjoyment. "Tell me what you think I look like."

"You're pretty."

She all but snarled. "We've already established that—it's one of my problems, remember? Besides, 'pretty' is in the eye of the beholder. *I* don't think I'm all that special, but some men seem to think so. And didn't we just agree that had nothing to do with it?"

"Oh, it doesn't," he assured her. "I'd enjoy talking to you even if you bore a strong resemblance to George C. Scott.

But you asked what I picture when I think of you. And I think you're pretty."

"I want details."

He chuckled. "Okay. Your hair is either auburn or brunette."

She twirled a near-black strand around her finger. "Right."

"Which?"

"One of the two. What else?"

He sighed but continued. "Eyes either green or blue."

"Very good."

"One of the guesses is right?" he asked dryly.

"Yep. Anything else?"

"I have this sneaky suspicion you're tall," he said heavily.

She swallowed a giggle. "I guess that depends on whether I'm being compared to Dudley Moore or Magic Johnson."

"So how *do* you feel about Dudley Moore?" he asked hopefully.

"I think he's cute."

"Yeah. Somehow I thought you'd say that." He sounded thoroughly disgusted.

"See? You've got me down pat."

"Oh, sure. You're either auburn or dark-haired, blue- or green-eyed, and you're somewhere between Dudley and Magic in height. Perfect description. Any detective should be able to walk right up to you."

"Mmm." She tried to picture him. "I think your hair is brown."

"What shade?"

"Light—or medium. Your eyes, too."

"What about them?"

"Brown."

"Could be."

"Hey, I told you when your guesses were right."

"Yeah, but I gave you more choices. What else?"

"You're not very tall."

He snorted. "Gee, how did you ever figure *that* out?"

Ignoring him, she continued, "You have a nice smile. Probably dimples."

"You think so?" He sounded startled. She grinned, guessing that she was right on target with the dimples. "Why?"

"You just sound so cute," she crooned.

For the first time in five conversations, she heard him use an obscenity.

"*Cute* is not a favorite word?" she hazarded through a giggle.

"*Not* a favorite word," he confirmed. "Can't we talk about something else?"

"What's your favorite food?" she asked, mimicking his earlier cross-examination.

"Boston scrod. What else?"

"You know, there are times when you don't sound like a Bostonian. You sound like someone from around here, almost. Are you?"

"Close. I grew up in Memphis. I've been here long enough that my sister accuses me of sounding like a Yankee, but every time I visit her, I find myself talking Southern again. Guess I'm one of those who picks up the accents of people around me."

"Mmm. So that's how your sister ended up in North Little Rock?"

"Yeah. Married a guy from there. I came east to college and ended up staying."

"Harvard?"

"Yup. What else do you want to know about me?"

Wow. Harvard! "Are your parents still living?"

"Yes. They moved to Florida a few years ago. I see them a couple of times a year."

"Uh—do you like children?" Erin frowned as soon as the question left her mouth. She hadn't even realized she was going to ask that one. Why *had* she? she wondered, her gaze turning toward Chelsea's bedroom door.

"Sure, I like kids," he answered breezily. "From a distance." And then he laughed.

Damn. Another one. Some men just didn't like children, didn't want the responsibility. Martin certainly hadn't. Her own father had resented being tied down to a wife and two children; finally he'd walked out—when Erin was just a baby. Adam seemed to enjoy Chelsea, but admitted he was in no hurry to have any children himself, if ever. And then there'd been Scott, a man she'd dated briefly last year. She'd found out exactly how he felt about children in a most unpleasant way.

And now she'd discovered that her friend was another one. If she'd had any hope that anything could ever develop between them, it died then. She wouldn't risk another disaster like the one that had almost occurred with Scott.

"Hey—you still awake? No more questions?"

Erin forced herself to speak lightly. After all, this was still her telephone friend. No more than an enjoyable fantasy. Nothing had changed, right? "Okay, favorite movie."

"Almost any animated Disney film."

Erin blinked and pulled the receiver away to stare at it for a moment. Then she brought it back to her ear. *"Disney?"* she repeated carefully, wondering if she'd understood.

"Yeah. Their animation is incredible, isn't it? I mean, there have been a few clunkers, but on the whole, the stuff's great. Have you seen *The Little Mermaid?* Wonderfully done."

She'd rented the movie only a few weeks before, actually, and watched it with Chelsea. She didn't mention that fact because she hadn't mentioned Chelsea at all, telling herself it was for safety reasons. "I agree that the animation is wonderful, but surely you don't think it's better than *Fantasia.*"

"Oh, well, of course *Fantasia* is amazing—the ultimate in animation. But I prefer *The Little Mermaid*, because, not only is it beautifully done, but it has a strong story that holds the interest of children *and* adults. That's the real test."

"How about some of the other animated features—non-Disney work?"

"Puh-leeze."

She laughed, and named two of the more impressive animated features of the past few years—*The Secret of NIMH* and *An American Tail.*

"Hey, you really know about this stuff, don't you?"

She glanced at the open door of the spare bedroom that served as her office, the one next to the room in which Chelsea was sleeping. Her drawing board was just visible in the shadows. "Let's just say I'm very interested in art."

"Really? Me, too. In fact, I sort of work in the field."

"So do I."

"Yeah? What do you do?"

But that was getting too specific. She couldn't keep him in her fantasies if he started to get too real. "Art stuff," she answered vaguely.

"Oh." He sounded a bit disgruntled at her reticence, but he didn't protest. "Well, still, it's pretty interesting that we have this in common. If we ever actually meet, we'll compare work. What do you say?"

Her throat tightened. "Uh—meet? You mean—in person?"

"Well, yeah. Maybe sometime when I'm in Arkansas visiting my sister, we could get together for a drink or something. I don't have any plans to visit there now, but sometime, maybe—"

"*Mommy!*"

The sleepy, bad-dream cry brought Erin upright on the couch. "I've got to go."

"Was it something I said?" he asked, startled.

"No, of course not. It's just that—there's something I have to do," she explained hastily, as Chelsea cried out again. "Goodbye."

"Bye."

She'd hung up before he had the syllable out. Reality had intruded into fantasy.

BRETT WAS FROWNING when he hung up the phone. What had happened to make her hang up so abruptly? They'd been having a perfectly pleasant conversation. Had it bothered her that he'd even hinted they might meet at some point? If so, she was carrying this secrecy thing a bit too far. They'd become friends, in a way, and he was in North Little Rock every few years to see his sister. Why shouldn't he and . . . and— Hell, he wished he at least knew her name. Anyway, why shouldn't they get together sometime? Just a drink, maybe. Dinner, perhaps.

If anything else developed—well, what would be wrong with that?

Shaking his head, he shoved the phone across the desk and stood, telling himself that maybe he wouldn't call her again for a while. He needed a real flesh-and-blood woman in his life, not just a sexy voice on a phone line.

It *was* time for a visit with his sister. Deciding to do just that, he sauntered out of his office in search of a late-night snack.

BRETT'S RESOLVE lasted less than a week. He'd been working on a comic book for too long when he became aware of a peculiar sensation that the telephone on his desk was growing larger and larger the more he ignored it. Had he drawn that particular scene in a comic, he'd have had the phone sneaking a bit closer to the man's elbow when he looked away, only to stop dead in its tracks each time the man turned to check. He might even have sketched in a broken-line balloon above the instrument containing tiny letters spelling out, "Call her."

Sighing with disgust, he swiveled on his stool, glared at his phone and growled, "Shut up!"

Brett checked his watch. Ten in the evening. Just about the time he usually called her. Well, hell . . .

He picked up the receiver and punched out the digits he'd memorized.

"Hello?"

Funny how familiar her voice had become. Like that of a close friend. Or a woman with whom he was rapidly becoming obsessed.

"Hi. It's me."

"Oh, hi. How are you?"

He settled more comfortably in the chair for another long conversation with the woman whose name he didn't even know. "I'm losing my sanity."

"Oh? How can you tell?" she teased.

He grinned. Now he remembered why he kept calling her. She made him laugh. "Are you implying that I'm a bit shaky at the best of times?"

"Well, you have to understand that I haven't seen you under exactly normal circumstances."

"You haven't seen me at all," he pointed out.

"True. Why are you suddenly questioning your sanity?"

"I've been talking to my phone."

"That's what phones are for."

"Yeah, but there wasn't anyone at the other end of the line."

She paused for only a moment. "We may have a problem here."

He chuckled. "Didn't I say so? I think celibacy is dulling the old gray matter."

"So, who's been making you remain celibate?"

"I have, I guess," he answered after a moment's thought. "I've never been interested in sleeping with strangers and I don't particularly want to go to bed with anyone I know at the moment."

"Hmm. That *is* a problem. What are you going to do about it?"

"I'm considering flying to North Little Rock and seducing *you*," he murmured outrageously, just to test her reaction. "What do you think?"

"I think you were right earlier. You *are* losing your sanity," she informed him sternly, though she sounded more amused than insulted. That was another thing he liked about her. She knew how to take a joke.

Or had it been a joke?

Deciding not to dwell on that particular question, he carried the subject further. "Well, just in case I ever *do* try to seduce you, how should I go about it? I used to be a Boy Scout," he added, "and I like to be prepared."

"I'm not quite sure I understand the question. What do you mean, how would you seduce me? I assume you've conducted a few seductions in the past. A seduction's a seduction, isn't it?"

Brett pulled the receiver away from his ear and stared at it as if he were studying her face. Was she really that naive? "Boy," he said when he brought the phone back into place, "Martin really *was* a lousy lover, wasn't he?"

She murmured something he didn't quite catch and didn't ask her to repeat.

"A seduction," he went on meaningfully, "is *not* just a seduction. It's different for everyone. What turns one woman on may turn you completely off."

"I suppose that's true. I don't think I'd care much for leather and chains and whips."

Laughing, he raised one hand to massage the back of his neck, trying to ignore that his body was beginning to react to the suggestive conversation. It was all too easy to imagine himself seducing this particular woman—and he'd never even seen her, he reminded himself, rather dazed. "No? So what would turn you on?" he asked, trying to believe he was only teasing and not making notes for future reference.

"I can't believe we're having this conversation."

"Call it a fantasy. What would be your idea of the ultimate seduction?"

She hesitated for so long that he was beginning to think she wouldn't answer. He didn't for the life of him know why he wanted so much for her to do so.

"I guess I'm pretty traditional," she said at last, rather shyly. "Flowers, soft music, a crackling fire."

He'd half expected that from this woman. He already knew she was quite traditional in some ways. Delightful ways. "A bearskin rug?"

"Oh, no. I wouldn't want to make love on some poor animal's hide."

He choked on a laugh. "Um—yeah, right. So you've described the setting. Now, what about the man? Tall, dark and handsome? Hulking blond lifeguard?" He grimaced as he asked the question.

"We've talked about this before, remember? I'm not particularly interested in appearances. He just has to be... special. Amusing, interesting, caring. Unselfish."

Brett wondered if she was aware that she'd just revealed a great deal about her relationship with her ex. "Would you like for me—er—*him* to whisper pretty words in your ear? Snippets of poetry, perhaps?"

"I'd feel really stupid if some guy started quoting poetry to me," she returned with a laugh. "'Shall I compare thee to a summer's day . . . ?' Too Hollywood."

"What about the pretty words?"

"That might be nice," she replied slowly, a bit wistfully. "But only if he meant them," she added almost in the same breath. "And I'd know if he didn't . . . if they were just part of an act."

"Okay. So we have flowers, music, a fire, and soft, heartfelt words. What else? What about the actual love-making? You like it slow and easy? Hot and rough? Do you lie back and enjoy or take the initiative yourself? Do you like to make love once and go to sleep or keep at it all night?" Grinning enormously, he waited for her to stop him.

Her moan of embarrassment was just what he'd expected. "Stop," she begged. "I can't deal with this."

"Turning you on, huh?" He squirmed restlessly in his chair, realizing uncomfortably that the words held true in reverse.

"No, that's enough," she ordered firmly. "Really."

"Okay," he conceded. "I didn't mean to embarrass you."

"Yes, you did."

He laughed. "You're right, I did. You're cute when you blush."

"I— How did you know I was blushing?"

"Your voice was blushing. It's getting late. Guess I'd better let you go."

"All right. I think I'll go splash cool water on my voice."

"Do that. Bye."

"Goodbye. Um—?"

"Yes?" he prompted.

"*All* night?" she asked delicately.

Remembering what he'd asked her about keeping at it all night, he laughed again. "It's been done."

"Have you ever—er—?"

"Now *I'm* blushing. Good night."

"Good night."

Brett hung up, groaned, and decided he'd take a shower before turning in. Maybe he'd make it a cold one. He knew he wouldn't get much sleep that night.

Erin didn't sleep particularly well, either. She found herself squirming restlessly against the pillows well into the night, for some reason. She had only to close her eyes to picture herself lying on a thick, handmade quilt before a crackling fire, with flowers and candles scenting the air, her nude, aching body being caressed by a man with skillful hands—a man who murmured soft, seductive words in Brett's deep, now familiar voice.

She groaned and swallowed convulsively. Fantasies were exciting, but certainly proved uncomfortable at times. Trying to block them from her mind, she buried her face in the pillow and ignored the urgings of long-suppressed needs. She couldn't imagine why they had suddenly resurfaced after so many months of self-denial.

3

"IS IT DONE YET, Mommy? Can I have a bite?" Chelsea bounced eagerly at Erin's feet, her dark ponytail bobbing.

"No, darling. I haven't cooked them yet." Erin demonstrated that the square pan was filled with brownie mixture and ready to go into the oven. "It's not good to eat until it's been cooked."

Chelsea plopped into a chair at the kitchen table, her arms crossed resignedly over her chest. "Brownies take for*ever*," she proclaimed.

Erin closed the oven door. "I know. And they'll have to cool after I take them out," she warned. "They'll be too hot to eat at first."

Chelsea groaned loudly and hid her face behind chubby hands.

Chuckling at her three-year-old daughter's antics, Erin opened the refrigerator. "How about a glass of juice for now?"

"Okay. But don't forget the brownies," Chelsea warned.

Erin solemnly promised not to forget the brownies.

She'd just set the glass of juice on the table when the doorbell rang.

"I'll get it!" Chelsea cried, scrambling out of the chair and dashing for the door.

"No! Chelsea, don't open that door," Erin warned, hurrying after her. Though she was an exceptionally well-behaved and mature little girl, Chelsea's insatiable curiosity was the one trait that most often got her into trouble.

Lately she'd taken to answering the door and the phone, though Erin was trying to teach her not to.

She was glad her Boston telephone friend always called at night, after Chelsea was in bed and wasn't likely to grab the phone. They'd been carrying on their lengthy, laughter-filled, sometimes astonishingly frank conversations for eight weeks and Erin still hadn't mentioned Chelsea, though there was little else her mystery friend didn't know about Erin by now. She'd told him things about herself that no one else on earth knew—embarrassing incidents, private fantasies, lost dreams, past disappointments.

In return, he'd done the same. She'd learned so much about him, and had been startled to discover that men's private thoughts weren't so very different from women's, once the restraints of face-to-face conversation were dispensed with, thanks to the anonymity provided by the phone. Martin had certainly never been so candid. Nor had Adam who, though he never failed to provide a sympathetic ear for Erin, had never been one to talk much about himself.

All that honesty was another reason Erin looked forward to talking to her new friend—and another reason she told herself she'd never want to actually meet him, no matter what fantasies were beginning to weave themselves into in her dreams. Dreams in which his now-so-familiar voice murmured pretty words into her eager ears while his hands stroked her love-starved body and he looked down at her with a melting smile bracketed by deep, endearing dimples.

Trying not to think of those fantasies now, she looked out the small window of her front door before opening it, only to feel her eyes widen and her pulse quicken with pleasure. "Adam!"

Her brother's arms closed around her as soon as the door shut behind him. "Hi, sis."

"Adam, it's so good to see you." She lifted her face for his kiss without loosening her stranglehold around his neck, her toes dangling above the floor. Half an inch short of six feet, her brother stood well above her own five feet seven inches.

His dark, lean face softened only marginally with the half-smile he gave her—almost a grin for her usually serious sibling. His dark eyes, narrowed by hours of squinting into sun and shadow, reflected her own smile back at her. "You don't look half bad, yourself."

Her smile vanished abruptly. "Oh, Adam, what have you done to yourself *now?*" she wailed, her hand going up to his temple. He'd worn his fine, straight brown hair longer than usual, brushed to one side to fall over the temple on which she concentrated. Others might not have noticed the thin red scar beneath that thick lock. He'd probably known Erin wouldn't miss it even as he'd made a halfhearted effort to hide it.

"Nothing serious. Don't worry about it." He pulled away from her to turn to Chelsea, who was dancing impatiently at their feet. "Hello, pumpkin."

"Hi, Uncle Adam!" Chelsea launched herself into a vertical leap that took her straight into his waiting arms. She planted a noisy, juicy kiss on his cheek, then giggled as she poked a finger into the cleft in his chin. "Did you bring me something?"

"Chelsea—"

"Of course I brought you something," Adam said, overriding Erin's disapproval. "I brought you both something." He slanted a look at Erin. "I know you weren't expecting me, but I can stay a couple of days if you—"

"You know very well I'd throw a tantrum if you *didn't* stay," she broke in. "You don't need to make a reservation with me."

"Mommy's making brownies but they've got to cook and then they'll have to cool and where's my present?" Chelsea asked without pausing for breath.

With a husky chuckle, Adam tweaked the upturned tip of his niece's nose. "In my suitcase. You can have it if you promise that I can share your brownies."

"Well, of *course* you can share my brownies," Chelsea informed him. "Don't be ridic'lous."

Erin laughed at the quizzical look Adam gave her. "She's been watching television," she explained.

Adam nodded as if that made sense. Gravely, he tucked Chelsea under his arm and reached for his bag, listening to her chatter as he dug out the gifts he'd brought with him.

"MARTIN STILL MAKING a jerk of himself?" Adam asked laconically, as he sprawled on the couch with a beer clasped in one hand. They were sitting in her living room after a large dinner, enjoying the quiet now that Chelsea was finally asleep. Chelsea hadn't wanted to go to bed that night, claiming that she wanted to play with Uncle Adam, but he'd tucked her in, promising he'd be there when she woke the next morning.

Erin grimaced. "I keep hoping he'll get tired of being the laughingstock of the entire city, but he just gets worse and worse. He'll be forty-five next week, you know, and he's acting like a wild teenager." She shook her head in self-disgust. "I wish I knew what I'd ever seen in him in the first place."

"I think it had something to do with broad shoulders, blue eyes and a movie-star profile," he grumbled. "At least those were a few things you mentioned at the time."

Recalling her recent telephone monologue about judging people by appearance, Erin groaned. "I know. God, I was such an idiot."

Adam shrugged. "We all make mistakes."

"*You* don't."

He looked faintly startled. "The hell I don't."

Erin cocked her head. "Well, if you do, you always recover from them easily enough. And I can't imagine you ever letting yourself be taken in by a pair of blue eyes or falling for someone who's only using you to impress her friends."

He shrugged again. "So some of us make different mistakes than others."

Intrigued, she started to ask for specifics, but he forestalled her questions by asking another of his own. "Is Martin keeping up with his child-support payments?"

"Oh, yes, the checks come on exactly the same day every month. His secretary is very efficient. I'm surprised he doesn't send her over for a biweekly visit with Chelsea."

"He still doesn't visit her?"

"He told me he wouldn't when we split up. He reminds me occasionally that he never wanted a child in the first place and he'd told me so from the beginning. He heavily implies that the pregnancy was all my fault, then acts so self-righteous for fulfilling his financial obligations to her, anyway. How I'd love to tell him just where he can put his monthly checks."

"I know you haven't wanted to take any money from him from the beginning, but don't let him stop paying," he said flatly. "It's the least he can do for you and Chelsea. Dammit, Erin, it's the man's duty to see that the child he fathered is well cared for."

"*I* could support her," Erin argued stubbornly.

"Not working free-lance, you can't," he returned without hesitation. "And since you won't take any money from me, either, giving up the child support would mean you'd have to go back to work full-time. Is that what you want to do? I agreed with your decision to put her in that half-day preschool program to let her meet and play with other children, but do you really want to be away from her every day, all day?"

Erin leaned her head back against her chair and sighed. "No. I don't want to put her in day care. It's just pride talking, I guess."

"Exactly. And since you haven't spent one red cent of Martin's money on yourself, and you're putting most of it in savings for Chelsea's future, your pride shouldn't be in the least bruised. Hell, if you were any more self-sufficient you'd be living on a desert island somewhere," he added in a growl.

"Oh, you're one to talk," she retorted, her head lifting at his tone. "The original lone wolf—or are you still involved with that she-wolf who answered your phone that time I called and proceeded to inform me that she didn't want *any* other women calling you? Remember? The one who refused to believe I was your sister?"

The one whose parting she'd celebrated when she'd thought she was talking to Adam during that wrong-number call two months earlier, only to discover that some other sister had cause to celebrate. Erin didn't mention that, of course, knowing better than to tell Adam about her mystery caller.

"She was gone the next day," Adam muttered, looking down into his beer can.

"I can't say I'm sorry."

He shrugged. "Neither can I. I thought she knew the score from the beginning. Turned out I was wrong. Like I said, we all make mistakes."

"So, are you seeing anyone new?"

He shook his head. "Haven't had time to do much socializing lately. How about you?"

She cleared her throat, suddenly sorry she'd asked her question. She and Adam had had this conversation more than once during the past year and she already knew he disapproved of her reclusiveness. "No, not really."

Adam scowled. "When are you going to start living again, Erin? How long are you going to let one mistake ruin your life?"

"Not just one mistake," she reminded him. "The last one almost got Chelsea hurt. I'm not going to risk that again."

"Not all men are like Martin and Scott, you know. There are plenty of decent guys who like kids."

"Yeah. Well, I don't seem to do a very good job of finding them, do I?"

"Dammit, Erin, you're a young, beautiful woman. You shouldn't be so alone."

"I'm not alone, Adam. I have Chelsea. And I have you."

"And what about *you*? You don't even know who you are anymore. It's as if your own needs don't even exist."

"I know exactly who I am," she replied evenly. "I'm Chelsea's mom."

"Dammit, Erin—"

Whatever else he might have said was cut off by the telephone. She gulped and shut her eyes. *Oh, no! Not tonight. Adam will never understand.*

"Aren't you going to get that?"

Her eyes flew open to find him staring at the ringing phone on the end table right by his elbow. If only she'd turned on her answering machine. But, of course, Adam knew that she almost never kept it on when she was home, preferring to answer calls herself. He'd still suspect something. "Of course. I—uh—"

"Slow tonight, aren't you?" He reached for the receiver.

"No!"

But Erin's lunge was too late. His eyes narrowing suspiciously at her behavior, Adam spoke determinedly into the phone. "Yeah?"

Erin hovered beside him. She should have known. For some reason, she'd never been able to keep a secret from Adam.

"Yeah," Adam said again. "This is 555-2029. Who'd you want to speak to?"

He wouldn't know who to ask for, Erin suddenly realized. He didn't know her name. She could imagine him stumbling for an answer to Adam's less-than-gracious question. "Adam, give me the phone," she ordered, holding out her hand.

He scowled, but placed the receiver in her palm.

"Thank you," she told him, closing her fingers around the plastic instrument. She lifted it to her ear. "Hello?"

"Look, I can call another time," her caller said apologetically. "I didn't know you had company. I felt like a real idiot when he asked who I wanted to talk to."

Even with the awkwardness of the circumstances, she was warmed by his deep, rich voice, as always. "It's all right," she assured him quietly. "It's my brother, Adam."

She wondered if she only imagined that his voice lightened several degrees in what almost seemed like relief when he spoke again. "Oh, I thought maybe you'd found a likely prospect for that affair you're looking for."

"I told you I'm *not* looking," she replied gruffly, turning her back to her brother, who made no pretense of giving her privacy for the call. "And, don't you ever think about any-thing else?"

His husky chuckle reverberated through the receiver, causing a faint ripple of response to course down her spine. "Honey, it's been two and a half months since I've even been on a date. I'm afraid I've become a bit preoccupied with that subject lately."

Erin couldn't think of anything to say. Had Adam not been listening, she would have made some teasing remark about her friend's continuing complaints about his lack of a love life. After all, they'd gotten into the habit of saying whatever popped into their minds. But Adam *was* listen-ing—intently—and she couldn't do that. So she said in-stead, rather inanely, "How's your sister?"

He laughed at last. "I take it your brother's listening."

"Yes."

"Does he know about me?"

"No."

"Going to tell him?"

"No."

"Why not?"

"I— Because."

He didn't sound particularly pleased. "Oh, come on. It's not as if you have anything to hide. We're friends. And don't you think it's about time we started showing it? Tell me your name."

Her eyes widened. "No!"

He paused. "Because Adam's listening?" he asked after a moment.

"No."

"You mean you have no intention of *ever* telling me?" he asked incredulously.

"Look, we agreed." Her voice sounded thin, her hands were inexplicably damp. She fought to appear calm, though she knew how little chance she had of fooling Adam—no more than he'd had of hiding that new scar at his temple.

Her caller cursed beneath his breath. "We agreed not to meet. I thought the name thing was just an amusing game that we'd get tired of after a while and stop playing. But you weren't playing, were you? You never intended for me to know who you are."

"N-no," she admitted.

"So you really have just been using me for some sort of therapy," he said slowly, as if he hadn't really believed it until now. "Maybe a cheap thrill or two. Sorry I never gave you more of a rush. If you'd told me you wanted telephone thrills, I'd have made a few really obscene calls. You know— a bit of heavy breathing, followed by asking you what you're wearing."

Her fingers tightened on the receiver until they went numb. She chewed her lip, wondering how to beg him not to do this without having Adam snatch the phone from her hand and demand to know what was going on. If she didn't know better, she'd swear she heard pain in that deep, likable voice—almost as if she had hurt him.

"Look, I've got to go. I must have lost my mind to think that I could really become friends with someone over the telephone."

"No! Wait, please!" The words were torn from her throat. "Don't hang up—" But she didn't know what to call him. And it didn't matter, anyway, because he'd already slammed his receiver home.

"Damn," she muttered, hanging up her own phone. She kept her back turned to her brother, postponing the inevitable.

She'd known he wouldn't give her long and he didn't. "Who the hell was that?"

"Has it even crossed your mind that it's none of your business?" she asked quietly.

"Look, Erin, something strange was going on just now and I want to know what," he responded curtly. Overprotective brother on the job. "Who was that?"

Maybe her caller had been right. Maybe they'd both lost their minds. All of a sudden, the relationship they'd built over the past two months began to seem very odd. Crossing her arms defensively at her waist, Erin turned slowly to Adam. Adam, who'd always taken care of her. Adam, who always had the answers. Adam, who would never enter a relationship without knowing all the details.

"I don't know who it is," she told him, steeling herself for his reaction.

Adam rose deliberately to his feet. "You *what?*"

"I don't know who it is," she repeated more firmly. "Sit back down and I'll tell you about it."

"Have you lost your mind?" Adam almost yelled some five minutes later—familiar-sounding words. He was standing again, his hands on his lean hips as he loomed over the chair in which Erin huddled. "You've been having phone conversations with a total stranger whose name you don't even know? Just what the hell have you told this guy?"

"Nothing, really." *Only things I've never told anyone else—not even you, my dear, angry brother.*

"Does he know who you are?" The words came at her like bullets.

She exhaled impatiently. "No. I told you—neither of us knows who the other is. Only phone numbers and cities."

"Does he know about Chelsea?"

"No." *He doesn't even like children*, she thought sadly, though she knew better than to mention that right now. "Dammit, Adam, you know I wouldn't endanger Chelsea! If I thought there was any reason not to trust this man—"

"If you trusted him, then why didn't you tell him who you were?" Adam shot back.

Because I needed a fantasy and he fit the part beautifully. Because I was getting lonely and hadn't even realized it until he entered my life. And maybe I'm just a bit tired of always being responsible and careful and mature.

She said nothing.

"We'll have your phone number changed tomorrow," Adam announced grimly. "And you'll give me his number and I'll have it traced. I'll run a make on him, find out who the hell he is, what kind of game he's been playing."

"Now, wait a minute." Erin shoved herself defiantly out of the chair, standing up to her brother for one of the few times in her life. "You're not doing *any* of that, do you hear me? I'm not changing my number and I'm not giving you his. You're not running any makes on anyone. You're to stay out of it."

He probably wouldn't have looked more surprised if she'd punched him in the stomach. "Look, Erin, this is ridiculous. We're talking about your safety, here."

"Right. *My* safety." She lifted her chin even farther, matching her voice to his in volume. "I know I've come running to you plenty of times in the past, Adam, but this time I'm not asking for help. I've been on my own for four years now, wholly responsible for myself and my child, and I've learned to take care of myself during that time. I've also learned to make some decisions—maybe even some mistakes—and to take full responsibility for them."

She took a deep, steadying breath, then continued. "I won't pretend that I don't need someone to talk to at times. Obviously I do. But I don't need anyone telling me who I'll talk to on my own telephone, or screening the friends I make on my own. Do you understand? Now, I may never talk to that man again. I don't know. But if I do, then the decision is mine and mine alone. Got that?"

"Dammit, Erin, this is crazy!" Adam exploded. "You need a real flesh-and-blood man in your life, not some imaginary lover. You can't keep hiding from life, afraid to take chances, substituting a nameless, faceless voice for a shoulder to lay your head on."

"I don't need a shoulder," she answered flatly. "I don't need anyone. Except you. I need you to accept me, Adam, and to accept my ability to take care of myself."

They stared at each other for what seemed like a very long time. Always, in the past, Erin's resolve had crumpled beneath Adam's more forceful one. Not this time. He seemed to realize that she wasn't going to give in. "On one condition," he said finally, apparently determined to be difficult to the end.

"What?" she asked warily.

"If you *ever* suspect that something's not quite right about the guy, you'll let me check him out."

"All right," she conceded, knowing his dictatorial behavior was prompted by genuine love and concern for her.

"Promise."

"I promise."

He nodded. "All right. Then I'll stay out of it."

"Thank you."

They didn't speak of it again until Erin announced an hour later that she was turning in, laying out sheets and blankets for Adam, who would sleep on the couch, which made into a bed.

"Hey, sis," he said as she headed for her room.

She paused in the doorway. "Yes?"

He stood beside the sofa bed with his hands in the pockets of his worn jeans, his hard, unreadable face as soft as she'd ever seen it, his dark-eyed gaze unusually warm as it rested on her face. "I may not like this telephone game of yours, but I have to admit it took spunk for you to stand up to me like that. I know I have a reputation for being a bit — intimidating."

"A bit," she murmured dryly.

He inclined his head in response, but went on: "You've come a long way since you were twenty-two. If Martin were to meet you for the first time now, I don't think he'd find you such an easy mark."

She smiled brightly, touched by the atypical praise. "Neither do I, Adam. Good night. And thanks."

"Good night, kid. Sleep well."

"HOW'D YOU LIKE THE MOVIE?"

"Um — oh, it was, er, what did you think?"

Brett tugged viciously at the buttons of his shirt, muttering beneath his breath as the scene from his disastrous date played through his mind. He'd known she wasn't exactly a potential Nobel prizewinner when he'd asked her out, but he hadn't realized that there was nothing between her ears but cotton candy. If she even had any opinions of her own, she'd kept them well hidden, choosing, instead, to defer to his.

Unlike the woman in Arkansas, who not only had opinions, but didn't mind expressing them. And what fascinating, stimulating opinions they were.

Dammit. Was he going to compare every date he had to a woman he'd never even met? How long was he going to remain celibate because no other woman appealed to his mind in quite the way she did, despite the needs of his body?

One didn't fall in love with a voice on the phone, he told himself sternly, tossing his rumpled shirt to the floor. It had turned out one couldn't even make friends over the telephone. So why couldn't he stop thinking about her ten days after that last, irritating conversation?

He missed her, dammit. And he'd never even known her name.

He looked at his watch. Ten-thirty. He hadn't been home from a date at ten-thirty since junior high, when all the girls had curfews. But he and Ms. Airhead had finally had to concede defeat and he'd taken her home. She'd seemed more relieved than insulted. All in all, his ego and his mood had taken quite a beating tonight.

When the phone rang he almost cringed. Surely not the woman he'd just taken home, he told himself, though he was afraid it would be. Maybe she wanted to apologize or demand an apology from him, or something equally uncomfortable. He wouldn't answer it. His machine would get it on the fourth ring.

The answering machine intercepted the call with its usual brisk efficiency, informing the caller that he/she had reached the home of Brett Nash, who was tied up at the moment and to please leave a message after the beep. Brett cocked his head, standing by the phone to listen to the message.

"Brett? So that's your name. Um—mine is Erin Spencer. And I'm very sorry I hurt you. Please call me."

He had the receiver to his ear before she finished speaking. He was surprised to note that his hand wasn't quite steady. "Don't hang up. I'm here, Erin."

4

ERIN HAD DECIDED Brett wasn't home when she heard the answering machine. She hadn't expected him to pick up the phone. When he did, her mind suddenly went blank. Just what was it she'd wanted to say? she asked herself frantically.

"Erin? Are you still there?"

"I'm here, Brett," she answered finally, his name sounding strange on her lips. Brett. Brett Nash. The man who'd somehow become her friend.

"So your name is Erin."

"Erin Spencer," she confirmed, wondering why they were talking so awkwardly now. It had never been like that before.

"Why did you suddenly decide to tell me?"

The faint suspicion in his voice told her that he hadn't forgotten their last conversation. "I've thought a lot about what you said," she confessed. "And I realized you were right. I was using you. You'd become an emotional outlet for me, a no-risk fantasy friend who expected nothing from me. I'm sorry, Brett. I never meant to hurt your feelings."

"I've missed you, Erin."

His simple statement brought a lump to her throat. "I've missed you, too. Can you forgive me?"

"Of course. I understand. Our friendship hasn't exactly been a conventional one."

"Not exactly," she agreed wryly.

"I consider you a friend. I enjoy talking to you. You make me laugh and think, and you're a great listener when I need to talk. You never seem to be bored by what I say. Just as I'm never bored when you talk. Unlike my date earlier this evening," he added with a rueful sigh.

Warmed by his sincere-sounding praise, Erin chuckled at his last words. "You've been on a date tonight? Not a successful one, I take it, since you're home so early."

"Not successful at all." He launched into an exaggerated account of his miserable evening, making her laugh again and again. It was the first time she'd felt like laughing since their quarrel ten days earlier.

"I'm really sorry about your evening," she commiserated when he finished. "It sounds dreadful."

"It was," he assured her. "I'm getting desperate here, Erin. I may yet have to come to Arkansas and seduce you with flowers and flattery."

As she had in the past, Erin brushed off his suggestion, immediately changing the subject by asking about his sister. Which led to him asking about Adam. "Is he still visiting you?"

"Oh, no. He was only here for a couple of days. He couldn't take much time away from his job."

"What is it he does, exactly? You said he works for the government?"

"He's a DEA agent," Erin informed him, waiting for the usual reaction.

Brett gave a low whistle. "Whew. Tough job. Dangerous, too."

"Yes, it is. That's why I worry about him so much."

"Does he like his work?"

"I guess he does, since he's still doing it."

"Did you ever tell him about me?"

Erin winced. "He knows."

As if sensing something in her voice, he spoke quickly. "He doesn't approve?"

"He tends to be overprotective," Erin explained carefully. "He—uh—he didn't really understand."

Brett was silent for a moment. "I guess I can see his point. I'd feel kind of funny if it were my sister talking repeatedly to a stranger."

"Cheryl's married, isn't she?" Erin asked, wanting to distract Brett from her brother's reservations.

"Yeah." .

"Any children?"

"Two. Little monsters, the both of them." He sounded indulgently amused. "Every time I'm around them I thank the stars they're hers instead of mine."

At this new reminder of Brett's attitude toward children, Erin abruptly changed the subject. "So what movie did you see tonight?"

He named a recent release that had received quite a bit of publicity because of a steamy love scene between the two stars. "The movie was okay," he commented. "Not great, but okay."

"I saw it last week with a friend from work."

This time she knew she didn't imagine the meaningful pause before he asked in an unsuccessful attempt at casualness, "A girlfriend?"

"Yes. So what did you think of the notorious love scene in the middle?"

"I thought it was the best part of the movie, actually. Beautifully filmed and acted. Very sensual. I kept thinking what a shame it was I was seeing it with a woman who didn't interest me in the slightest."

She didn't like thinking of him on a date with another woman any more than he apparently cared for the thought of her with another man. She was going to have to think about that more carefully later, she decided. "It *was* a nice scene, wasn't it?" she remarked almost absently. "Using the amber filter was very effective. It made the scene dreamy— a nice contrast to the gritty reality of the main story line. As you said, it's too bad the rest of the film didn't stand up."

Brett responded with the husky chuckle that always made her smile. "You really are a sucker for romance, aren't you? Quite the traditionalist."

"I suppose so," she answered slowly. "Maybe because I've never really known the type of romance poets and novelists write about. It probably doesn't even exist, but it does make wonderful fantasy material."

"It exists, Erin. You just haven't found the guy to share it with yet."

"Spoken like another true romantic," she teased, keeping her tone light.

"You know, I didn't think I was a romantic until fairly recently. Now I'm beginning to believe I am."

"Oh?" Disturbed by the new intensity in his voice, she asked without thinking, "When did you come to this amazing conclusion?"

"When I found myself falling for a voice on the telephone," he replied.

The words made her tremble. How serious had he been? Was he only teasing, or . . . ?

"Um—" She swallowed, her fingers tightening on the receiver. "Gosh, it's getting late, isn't it?" she commented lamely.

"Yeah, I guess it is," he agreed, and he sounded patiently understanding. "We'll talk again, Erin."

It wasn't a question, but she answered it, anyway. "Yes. We will. Good night, Brett."

"Good night, Erin Spencer. Did I remember to tell you what a beautiful name that is?"

She couldn't help smiling. "Thank you."

"No." His voice deepened. "Thank *you*, Erin. Good night."

She hung up slowly, her hand lingering on the receiver as if reluctant to break the contact with Brett. She closed her eyes, wondering exactly what she'd just done. There was no more pretending that Brett was simply a fantasy friend, an outlet for anonymous conversations and a bit of harmless fun. He had a name now. He'd become real.

She should have known this would happen if the calls continued. She was too old for imaginary friends. Reality had been destined to intrude. She never should have encouraged him to keep calling. But he had. And now they knew each other's names. And he would call again. And again, until he grew tired of talking to her and found a more satisfactory relationship in Boston, or until he demanded something more from her. Like a face-to-face meeting.

The thought of actually meeting Brett still paralyzed her. As Adam had pointed out, there was something rather strange going on between Erin and Brett—a bond that shouldn't have developed, a connection with the potential to hurt if severed. Look how much she'd missed just talking to him in the past ten days. How much more would she miss after meeting him and then being disappointed in him, having this special friendship change or—more likely—end?

She didn't doubt that she would be disappointed. No one could be as perfect as the fantasy friend she'd created in Brett during the past few months. No man could be as patient, as understanding, as caring as he'd seemed. As much as she loved her brother, she couldn't even imagine living with him for an extended period. Brett was charming enough during telephone calls, but she knew too well how familiarity bred contempt.

And besides, she reminded herself, Brett had just as idealized an image of her. He'd admitted that he imagined her as a beautiful woman—a sleeping beauty, of sorts, only waiting for the right man to come along and seduce her back to life. A woman as footloose and unencumbered as he was, able to drop everything on a whim and go looking for fun. He didn't know that she was, primarily, Chelsea's mom. That the Erin he'd come to know was a pretense created to add a bit of excitement to her life. Someone he'd never been meant to meet.

She was satisfied with the way things were now, she tried to convince herself as she prepared for bed. Why risk messing things up by changing them?

ERIN SPENCER. Such a beautiful name. Lying in his bed, hands behind his head, Brett grinned into the darkness. She'd trusted him enough to tell him her name.

And then his smile faded. That was all she'd trusted him with, he reminded himself. There were still many things he didn't know about Erin. Chief among them why she was so terrified of the idea of meeting him.

She was becoming more intriguing, more important to him by the day. Whatever this was between them shouldn't have developed, logically. And yet it had, and it couldn't be ignored or denied. Their meeting was inevitable. He would probably have to take matters into his own hands to make sure that meeting occurred. Because he was terribly afraid his life would continue to revolve around a voice on the telephone until he made some effort to get over his obsession with her—even if it took a face-to-face meeting to do so.

And there was always a chance—a very slim, very fragile, very precious chance—that what they'd found during an accidental telephone call had been something that would last them a lifetime.

"AND HE *LOVES* KIDS. After all, he has four of his own. So what do you think, Erin?"

Erin looked up from the paperwork she'd been scanning, straightening her reading glasses on her nose. "What did you say, Eileen?"

The petite copywriter sighed and threw her hands in the air. "You weren't even listening! I was telling you about a wo-o-n-derful, definitely available man and you weren't even paying attention. My cousin, Bill. He's attractive, nice, loaded and single. So why don't I fix the two of you up for a date?"

"A date?"

Eileen grimaced again. "Honestly, Erin. Sometimes I worry about you. A date. You know—a man and a woman going out for dinner? Maybe a movie? Maybe a lifetime commitment? Surely you remember the custom."

Erin couldn't help but laugh at Eileen's disgusted expression. "Yes, I vaguely remember dates," she admitted.

"Great. Then you'll do it?"

"No." Erin spoke gently, but quite firmly.

Eileen exhaled, her never-idle hands swinging into motion again. "Why not?"

"Because I also happen to remember the custom of blind dates. They are almost always awkward, painful, embarrassing, degrading and generally disastrous. Thank you very much, but I'd just as soon pass on that particular pleasure."

"Believe me, I know about blind dates. I've had a few nightmares after them myself."

"Good. Then you understand why I have to decline."

Eileen shook her red head vigorously. "No, I don't. There's always hope. And Bill's different. He's a really nice guy."

"That's what they all say." Erin smiled to soften her refusal. "Sorry. Not interested." She reached out to gather the specs for her latest free-lance assignment from Redding & Howard, the advertising agency where Eileen worked full-time. "Is this everything?"

"Yeah." But Eileen wasn't quite ready to drop the subject or Erin's social life—or lack thereof. "I just don't understand it. You're drop-dead gorgeous. You have a figure I'd kill for. You've got a great personality. It's so depressing that I sometimes wonder why I even like you. And yet you live the life of an elderly widow. Why?"

"Let's just say I quit while I was relatively ahead," Erin answered with a faint smile. "I have Chelsea. She's enough to make me happy."

"And what are you going to have when Chelsea grows up and leaves home?" Eileen demanded sternly, hands on her rounded hips. "An empty house, that's what," she answered before Erin could speak. "Are you still going to be happy then?"

"Eileen, I haven't ruled out all future relationships," Erin pointed out. "I'm just not interested in going on a blind date."

She was half-tempted to tell Eileen about Brett—her regular "blind telephone date." She didn't, of course. She didn't expect anyone to understand about Brett. Except Corey, perhaps. She was seriously considering talking to Corey about her confusion where Brett was concerned next time Corey called. Corey had always had a different perspective on things than most people, and Erin had always valued her friend's opinions more than anyone else's—with the exception, perhaps, of Adam's.

"Okay," Eileen conceded reluctantly. "No blind dates. But how about if I give a party sometime—a party with lots of people there—and invite both you and Bill. Would you come, just to meet him? It wouldn't be a date or anything, just a social occasion. Would you accept then?"

"Maybe. I'll think about it," Erin promised. Placing her glasses in her purse, she gathered the paperwork for the assignment, impatient to get home and get to work. "Thanks for caring, Eileen," she added, knowing that the other woman's compulsive matchmaking was motivated by genuine concern. "I'll see you Friday."

She thought a great deal about Eileen's offer during the drive from the downtown Little Rock ad agency across the Arkansas River to her home in the adjacent city of North Little Rock. She hadn't even been tempted to agree to the blind date. True, she'd never cared for dates arranged in that manner, but for some reason she wasn't entirely sure she'd turned Eileen down just because of that. It was wholly illogical, of course, but for just a moment when Eileen had made the suggestion, Erin had felt almost . . . guilty, she decided uncomfortably. Disloyal. As if she were a woman committed to a monogamous relationship, not free to be listening to offers of dates with other men.

Ridiculous, she told herself, tightening her fingers on the steering wheel of her car. It was so foolish that thoughts of Brett had crossed her mind at that moment. She was hardly committed in that way to Brett. She'd never even met the man! So why in the world had she suddenly allowed her life to revolve around those continuing telephone calls?

No, she corrected herself immediately. Her life didn't revolve around those calls. Parking in front of her neat white-frame house, she reached to the passenger seat for her battered leather portfolio. Chelsea was the center of her life, followed closely by her brother, her friends and her work. Brett fell somewhere into the category of friend. Like Corey and Eileen and . . .

She winced, slamming her car door in a futile effort to deny the awareness that Brett was like no one else in her life. He was becoming entirely too important to her. And she didn't for the life of her know what she was going to do about it.

"Mommy, Mommy! Look what Mrs. Price made for me!"

Erin turned with a smile in response to her daughter's voice. Chelsea ran toward her from the yard next door, where she'd been staying with their neighbor while Erin ran her errands. She clutched a new rag doll of white muslin with brown yarn braids, a red flowered cotton dress and an endearing embroidered face. "What an adorable doll!"

"She's mine! Mrs. Price made her for me on the sewing machine. And she gave her brown hair and brown eyes, just like me. Isn't she beautiful, Mommy?"

"Very," Erin agreed solemnly. She looked at the smiling woman who'd followed Chelsea across the yard. "That was very sweet of you, Isabelle. Thank you."

The older woman beamed from behind her silver-framed glasses, one fragile hand resting on Chelsea's shoulder. "You know how I enjoy making things," she replied. "I found this pattern the other day and I couldn't resist making one for Chelsea. I hoped she'd like it."

"I love her," Chelsea breathed, hugging the doll tightly. "I'm going to name her Belle—after you, Mrs. Price. Is that all right?"

"I'd like that very much. You can keep her a long time and think about me every time you play with her."

"I will," Chelsea promised. "Always."

Erin regarded her daughter. How Chelsea would have loved Erin's mother, who'd died when Erin was only a teenager. Martin's mother, too, had died years earlier. Mrs. Price had become a substitute for the grandmother Chelsea had never had but always wanted. Erin was grateful to have found such a dependable, loving and willing baby-sitter for the few times she left the house without Chelsea.

She wanted so much for Chelsea to have everything she desired. She realized she was actually beginning to feel guilty because she couldn't provide her daughter with a grandmother. Wearily, Erin wondered if guilt had always been such an intrinsic part of motherhood, or whether she had a corner on that particular market. "Thanks for watching her, Isabelle. And for the doll. I know she'll treasure her."

"I'm going to go show Belle my room," Chelsea announced, running for the front door. "And she needs to meet my other dolls."

"Just a minute, sweetheart, I haven't unlocked the door yet," Erin called after her, sharing an amused look with her neighbor.

"I won't keep you. Chelsea's excited and you look like you have work to do." Isabelle eyed the bulging portfolio under Erin's arm.

"Yes, thank goodness. The bills will be paid for another month."

Isabelle chuckled and started toward her own house. "See you later, Erin."

"Hurry, Mommy! Belle wants to go in."

Erin smiled. How could she ever have thought there was something missing from her life? She gazed lovingly at her flushed daughter. Chelsea was all she needed, all she wanted. She couldn't wish for anything more. And she wouldn't allow herself to dwell on the most disquieting question Eileen had asked—a question that had hovered ominously at the back of Erin's mind ever since.

What are you going to have when Chelsea grows up and leaves home?

CHELSEA WAS SETTLED for the night, sleeping peacefully with
Belle tucked tightly in the curve of one arm, when Erin finally had a chance to relax. She'd worked all afternoon
while Chelsea had played with her new doll, stopping only
to have dinner with her daughter and then watch television
with her for an hour before bedtime. And then she'd worked
for another hour.

Putting one hand to the small of her back, Erin stretched,
wincing at the protest of muscles that had been frozen in one
position for too long. Hand cramping, she set down her
drawing pencil. She was tired. Her eyes burned behind the
glasses she wore for reading and close work. They felt
strained. She'd been meaning to make an appointment with
her optometrist for months. She'd better do it soon, she
thought wearily. For now, she needed rest.

She'd just slipped into her nightgown and crawled into
bed when the telephone rang. Her energy returned as if by
magic. Eagerly, she lifted the receiver of the bedside exten-
sion. "Hello?"

"Hi."

Erin curled beneath the covers, making herself comfortable for a long, cozy conversation. "Hello, Brett." His name
still felt rather strange on her lips. This was only the third
time she'd talked to him since they'd exchanged names.

"Are you busy? Can you talk now?"

"Of course," she agreed promptly. "I just put my work
away for the night. I was getting ready for bed."

A noticeable pause followed her words. When Brett
spoke, his voice sounded rather strained. "So—uh—what
have you been working on? You know, you've never told me
exactly what you do."

"I'm a commercial artist," she replied, no longer bothering with evasions. After all, he knew her name. The only
part of her life she still felt compelled to keep from him was

her daughter. For some reason, she couldn't bring herself to tell him about Chelsea. She didn't try to analyze her reasons. "I free-lance for some local advertising agencies."

"Really?" He sounded genuinely interested. "Another amazing coincidence. Our relationship has been filled with them, hasn't it?"

Her attention was caught briefly by the word *relationship*. She decided not to think about that, either. "You're a commercial artist, too?"

"In a way. I write a comic book. I don't suppose you've ever heard of *The Midnight Warrior?*"

She frowned. "No," she admitted. "I haven't. But I'm not very familiar with comic books. Only *Superman*."

"Ah, well, don't apologize. It's fairly new. I've only been writing it for two years. It's doing very well, though. There's talk about picking it up for a Saturday-morning cartoon."

"Wow!" She was impressed and didn't hide it. "I've never known anyone who wrote a comic book before. You do the artwork, too?"

"Yep. It's a hobby turned career obsession. Believe it or not, I used to be a stockbroker."

"Somehow I can't imagine you as a stockbroker," she said with a laugh. Comic-book author seemed much more suitable for the offbeat, funny, impulsive man she'd come to know, and despite the similarities of their professions, emblematic of the differences between them. Her artwork was practical, functional, meant to sell products; Brett lived in a fantasy world of his own creation. "Tell me about *The Midnight Warrior.*"

He launched into a sheepishly enthusiastic description of his hero, a vigilante who dispensed justice and retribution in an unnamed big city. Yes, he admitted, it was violent in typical comic-book fashion, but it also upheld old-fashioned values. "I'm not trying to moralize to my young readers," he added, "but I hope my hero's clear-cut sense of right and wrong serves as a positive influence against the evils of crime and drugs."

"I'm going to buy one of your comic books tomorrow," Erin promised him, smiling. "I can't wait to read one."

"It's not exactly written for adult women," Brett warned. "The stories appeal mostly to adolescent boys."

"I'm still going to read them. I'd like to know more about how your mind works."

He laughed. "You should talk to my sister. She has some very interesting theories on that subject. Most of them to my disadvantage, I'm afraid."

"She's a sister. It's her job to keep you cut down to size," Erin teased.

"Is that what you do with your brother?"

Erin thought ruefully of Adam. "As much as anyone could, I suppose."

They talked about their respective jobs for another half hour. And then Brett yawned in the middle of a sentence. "Sorry," he apologized. "It's been a long day at the drawing board."

Erin grimaced in empathy. "I know the feeling."

"I'm beat."

"Yeah. Me, too."

"You know what I'd really like to do now?" Brett asked after a pause.

She snuggled more deeply into her pillow, cradling the telephone to her ear. "Get some sleep?" she hazarded.

"Eventually. But first I'd like to build a fire, put on some music—Rachmaninoff, I think—pour some wine—no, better yet, hot chocolate, with marshmallows—and curl up on a soft sofa. With you."

She caught her breath, then swallowed. "That sounds lovely," she said casually. "But I guess you'd better settle for a hot bath and a good night's rest."

"I want to see you, Erin. The calls aren't enough anymore."

His words had caught her off guard. She could have cried. Why had he done this to them tonight, after such a pleasantly undemanding conversation. Why was he putting this pressure on her? Why couldn't he understand that what they had was too important to her to take a chance on losing it? "Brett—"

"Dammit, Erin. I'm human, you know? I need more in my life than a disembodied voice."

"Then find someone," she told him, though the words were difficult to push past the lump in her throat. "There must be hundreds of eligible women in Boston."

"I've tried that, remember? I can't stop thinking about you."

"Brett, you don't even know me." She looked at the picture of Chelsea on the nightstand beside the phone, and her vision blurred with tears.

"We can remedy that. I want to meet you, Erin. Face-to-face."

She closed her eyes, willing the tears away. "We'll...we'll talk about it some other time, all right? It's late tonight. We're both tired."

His sigh carried clearly through the lines. "Time isn't going to change anything."

"Brett, I—"

"I'm lonely, Erin. Can't you understand that?" The question was asked quietly, deeply, almost reluctantly. As if he'd had to swallow a healthy amount of masculine pride to make the admission.

Her bed seemed suddenly large and empty, her house all too quiet. She thought of sitting on a couch in front of a fire, sipping hot chocolate with someone who cared about her. Really cared. And she yearned. "Yes, Brett," she whispered. "I understand."

"Then—"

"Please. Not tonight. I'm just not ready to discuss this tonight. I'm so tired." Tired. Upset. Frightened. A little annoyed with him for pushing her this way. And so very confused.

"All right," he conceded quietly. "But we'll talk about it again. You know that, don't you?"

"I— Good night, Brett."

"Good night, Erin. Sweet dreams."

She already knew what her dreams would be, and set the receiver in its cradle. She knew that she'd wake flushed and frustrated, with Brett's husky voice echoing in her mind.

She suspected it would be a long while before she slept that night.

BRETT SLAMMED his own receiver down so hard the telephone jingled in protest. "Dammit!"

He shouldn't have pushed her. He hadn't meant to— hadn't even planned to mention a meeting tonight when he'd called her. The words had slipped out before he could stop them.

He needed to see her. To touch her. To find out if the woman he'd come to know and care about was real. He was a man with normal male appetites, and desire was beginning to eat a hole in his gut. If only he could find someone else to dull that hunger. The problem was that his hunger was a very specific one. No other woman interested him; no other woman intrigued him the way Erin did.

And he'd never even seen her.

Dammit, he thought again. Something had to give. He couldn't go on this way.

Meeting her would accomplish one of two things. Either he'd discover once and for all that he and Erin could never be more than friends and he'd be able to get back to a normal social life, or...

Considering the ramifications of that "or" had him breaking out in a cold sweat. It could be that he and Erin would be dynamite together.

Fantasies came easily to a man in his business. He could almost see himself with her, though he wished he had more than a hazy image of the woman in his daydreams. He imagined meeting her, of a spark of physical attraction as strong and immediate as the mental bond that had developed during that first telephone call. He pictured the two of them on outings, sharing the films and concerts they both enjoyed, dining on the Italian and Chinese cuisines they'd both claimed as favorites.

Carrying the fantasy even further, he thought of having her with him in Boston. Showing her around his city, strolling hand in hand through the Common, visiting the aquarium, spending an evening at his favorite Irish pub. Just the two of them. And, afterward... Well, anything was possible.

He was a normal man with a normal man's needs, a normal man's dreams. He needed someone to share his life with. Someone special. Someone real. Someone who could very well be Erin Spencer.

He had to meet her. One way or another, he would.

5

"SO MEET HER."

"Yeah, sure." Brett cradled the receiver against his shoulder and scowled at his feet, which were crossed on the desk in front of him. Cheryl tended to oversimplify things, he reflected, even as he told her, "It's not that easy."

"Sure, it is. You just walk up to her and say, 'Hi, I'm here. Let's get married.'"

Brett chuckled at his sister's teasing. Cheryl had been fascinated when he'd told her about Erin, amused by the series of telephone calls that had all started when he'd misdialed her number one stormy evening. He'd asked her, only half-hopefully, if she knew anyone named Erin Spencer. She didn't, but thought Erin sounded delightful. She asserted that it was time Brett met the woman who'd captured his attention so thoroughly.

"Cheryl, she doesn't want to meet me. I think she's concerned that it wouldn't work out, that the circumstances of our knowing each other are too strange."

"What's so strange about it?" Cheryl demanded. "It's no different than meeting through the mail, like those lonely-hearts-club things. Lots of people meet over the phone."

Brett privately agreed. He was beginning to wonder exactly what lay behind Erin's panic at the thought of seeing him. She wasn't going to tell him. There was only one way for him to find out. He had to meet her. "So, you think I should ignore her objections and meet her, anyway?" he asked his sister, wondering why he felt the need of reassurance on a decision that was, in effect, already made.

"You bet I do. I'm ready for a sister-in-law and some nieces and nephews. And Dad's starting to get anxious for grandsons bearing the family name."

"Yes, I know," Brett agreed dryly, thinking of his last conversation with his father—the old speech about Brett being the last of the line unless he got busy and had some sons. His father was the old-fashioned type, big on traditions. Brett hadn't acknowledged then that for the past several years he'd been subconsciously searching for someone to share his life. He knew now that he had been, though he hadn't given serious thought to the quest until he'd started talking to Erin.

"But, Cheryl, Erin may be right," he felt compelled to point out. "We may *not* hit it off in person. Maybe we're only meant to remain telephone friends."

"Why shouldn't you hit it off in person when you've been talking for months?" she returned logically. "Usually couples run into trouble when an initial physical attraction pales and they find themselves unable to talk. You and Erin shouldn't have that problem—you already know so much about each other. You have so much more in common than physical attraction. Of course, there is the chance that you won't find her attractive," she added reflectively.

He rejected that immediately. "It doesn't matter what she looks like. She still fascinates me more than any woman I've ever known."

"Well, hallelujah. Maybe there's hope for you, after all. How many times have I told you that if you'd quit chasing after empty-headed beauty queens, you just might find someone special?"

Not another I-told-you-so speech, Brett thought with a scowl. "That was a bigoted remark, Cheryl. Who said a

woman can't be beautiful *and* intelligent? Might I point out
that there are those misguided persons who find *you* appealing? You're no airhead, either. Most of the time."

"Why, Brett. That was almost a compliment. Thank
you."

"It might turn out the other way around, you know. Erin
may not be attracted to me. I'm hardly the male-model
type."

"That's ridiculous," Cheryl responded instantly, loyally.
"You're a very cute guy. Any woman with any taste would
appreciate you."

Grimacing at the hated word *cute*, Brett quickly changed
the subject. "All this is really academic, anyway. Erin
doesn't want to meet me. She's not going to agree if I try to
set something up."

"Hmm. That could be a problem." Cheryl was quiet for
a few moments, then he could almost hear the snap of her
fingers. "I've got it!"

"What?" he asked warily.

"Meet her without telling her!"

He frowned. "I beg your pardon?"

"You know—don't tell her who you are. You can meet her
incognito. That way she'll have a chance to get to know and
like you without freezing up."

"Cheryl, that's ridiculous. I couldn't do that."

"Why not? Tell her your name is—oh, B.J. After all, that
was your nickname in school. Since she won't have any ar-
tificial expectations from a total stranger, you'll have time
to charm her into giving you a real chance."

Brett was drawn into the fantasy despite his better judgment. "She'd recognize my voice."

"From telephone conversations? Hardly. Half your best
friends don't recognize your voice over the phone. You're
one of those people who sound different in person. Be-

sides," she added enthusiastically, warming to the plan, "Erin wouldn't be expecting to see you, which would make her even less likely to notice familiarities in your speech. What do you think?"

"I think you're nuts," he told her flatly.

She only laughed. "It could be fun."

"Uh-huh. And Erin could go for my throat when she finds out the truth. How would you like it if some guy did that to you?"

"I think it sounds very romantic," Cheryl answered loftily. "And it's similar to what Dwayne did with me, remember? Someone told him I wouldn't date cops, so he just didn't tell me he was one until after I'd been out with him a few times. By that time I was already hooked."

And then she gasped in exaggerated excitement. "Dwayne can help us find her! He can find out where she lives, whether she's ever been arrested for anything—"

"Cheryl," Brett interrupted, "you're insane. But, thanks. You've cheered me up considerably."

"Think about it, Brett. Okay? You really should meet her. Even if you don't like my plan of going undercover. Also, it gives you an excuse to visit me for a few days, which I've been nagging you to do for ages, anyway. Right?"

"Maybe," he temporized. "I've got to go to New York for a couple of days for my monthly meeting with my publisher. I'll think about it then and let you know what I decide."

Brett was still chuckling over Cheryl's wild plan later that evening as he dialed Erin's number. Meet Erin incognito Only his nutty sister could have come up with that one. It was earlier than he usually called, but he'd waited as long as he could. He wanted to talk to Erin.

He warmed, as always, when her voice came through the line. "Hi. It's me," he murmured, settling back for another pleasantly frustrating conversation.

"Oh. Hi, Brett. Would you mind if I call you back a little later? I'm—um—kind of busy now."

He scowled, but answered graciously enough. "Of course. I plan to be here for the rest of the evening."

"All right. I'll call after eight, okay? My time," she added.

"Yeah, sure. Talk to you then." He hung up in frustration, wondering what was making her too busy to talk to him. He'd had the impression that she wasn't alone. *A date?* he wondered, hating the idea of another man being with Erin when he was so far away from her.

And then he took some hope in remembering that she'd promised to call after eight. If she was with a man, at least he wouldn't be staying the night.

He really was going to have to do something about this. They simply couldn't go on this way.

"WHO WAS THAT, Mommy? Uncle Adam?" Chelsea asked curiously as Erin hung up the phone.

"No, it wasn't Uncle Adam. It was just a friend. Now, finish your peas so you can have your bath before bedtime." Erin tried to keep her voice light, hoping to distract Chelsea from the telephone call before there were any more awkward questions.

Brett had never called that early before. She hoped he wasn't going to make a habit of calling before Chelsea's bedtime. What if Chelsea had picked up the phone or called out to her during the brief call? How would Erin have explained why she'd never told Brett about her daughter when she wasn't even quite sure, herself, why she'd been keeping that particular secret?

He hadn't much liked her putting him off. She bit her lip, wondering why she suddenly felt she owed him explanations. She didn't owe him anything. Right? After all, it wasn't as if they were involved in a relationship or anything. Well, not exactly. Sort of. Oh, she was getting a headache just thinking about it.

"What's wrong, Mommy?" Chelsea questioned, looking up from the peas she'd been pushing around her Garfield plate.

Erin hadn't realized she'd moaned aloud. "Nothing, sweetie. I was just thinking."

"About what?"

"Stop stalling and finish those peas," Erin ordered, changing the subject yet again.

She'd just gotten Chelsea into bed later that evening when the telephone rang again. She sighed. He really was getting very impatient. Lifting the receiver, she said without preamble, "I was just about to call you. I promise."

A moment of silence greeted her words. And then a familiar, obviously amused voice replied, "Well, that's really nice. Tell me, Erin, when did you take up ESP? A new hobby?"

Erin laughed. "Corey?"

"What? You mean you didn't already know, after all?"

"No. I thought you were someone else."

"Ah. So just who *is* this someone else? Someone I should know about?"

"Possibly."

"So talk, pal. Tell me all about him."

"How do you know it's a him?" Erin countered, wondering where to begin.

"It had to be. And I can't wait to hear the details. I thought you were never going to start dating again."

"Look who's talking. I'm not the one holed up in the Ozarks. When's the last time you had a date?"

"The night I came home black-and-blue from wrestling with Juan-the-Latin-lover-insurance-salesman six months ago," Corey answered candidly. "I decided to rest up awhile before the next match. Enough about me. Tell me about *him*."

Erin did. From the beginning. Including a few of the things she'd purposefully neglected to mention to Adam. Like the way she was beginning to plan her days around Brett's calls. The way her pulse went into double time at the sound of his voice. The emptiness she felt whenever he hung up and she heard nothing but a dial tone from the receiver. His growing insistence on a face-to-face meeting.

"So what's holding you back?"

Erin had hoped Corey would understand. "Corey, weren't you listening? He doesn't even like children."

"Of course he likes children. Erin, he writes comic books. Who do you think makes up his audience?"

"So, he likes them from a distance. That was what he said when I asked him."

"All guys say that. It's macho, or something. I'm sure he'd love Chelsea. Anyone but a low-life creep like your ex-husband would love her. Even your spooky brother is nutty about her, right? Or so you've said."

Erin laughed again, always amused by Corey's frankness. "Adam isn't spooky."

"Couldn't prove it by me. I've never met the guy, remember? He sneaks into your house in the middle of the night, then wraps his trench coat around him and slips back out again before anyone can see him. If I didn't know better, I'd swear he was a figment of your imagination. But we're not talking about your brother. We're talking about Brett. When are you going to meet him?"

"I don't know." There'd been a time when she'd have said never. Now the meeting was beginning to seem inevitable. She wasn't sure how much longer she could stall him. "I'm scared, Corey."

"Of what?" Corey asked, no longer teasing.

"Of being hurt again. Of having Chelsea hurt again. If I thought Brett and I could just get together for drinks or dinner, have a good time together and then go our own ways . . . But I'm afraid it would be more complicated than that. Much more complicated."

"You may be right. You could fall in love with the man. And he with you. And would that be so terrible?"

"It might be for Chelsea. I have to think of her first, Corey. Surely you understand that. She shouldn't have to suffer because her mother has such rotten luck with romance."

"Erin, you know I think you're a wonderful mother—the best. But you have to take care of your own needs, as well. You can't put your own life on hold until Chelsea's grown."

"Yes, I can, if I think it's best for her," Erin countered. "I'm all she has."

"And you punish yourself every day because Martin doesn't want her. It's not your fault, Erin. You've more than compensated for her selfish slimeball of a father."

Erin sighed and ran a hand through her disheveled hair. "We've spent your whole long-distance call talking about my problems. I haven't even asked about you. How are you, Corey?"

"I'm fine. I really like it here. It's very peaceful. Exactly what I needed for a while."

"And the shop?"

"In the black last month," Corey announced proudly. "By almost a dollar eighty-nine."

"I want to come see it sometime."

"I'd love for you to. Anytime."

They talked a few minutes more. Before the call ended, Corey urged her once more to give Brett a chance. Erin promised to think about it. She knew she really had no choice since it had been hard to think about anything else lately.

And then she took a deep breath and dialed Brett's number. Their conversation was rather strained that evening. Though they avoided the issue, they both knew that soon they'd have to talk about Brett's insistence on meeting. Claiming a headache, Erin brought the call to an early end. She spent a long time thinking that night, though she was no closer to a decision when she drifted to sleep than she'd been before. And her manufactured headache had become real.

THE NEW YORK BAR was trendy and crowded. Brett sat at a table with an associate from his publishing company, his favorite drink in front of him. And he was miserable.

"Hey, Brett. Check the babe in the corner. She's been giving you the eye, man."

In response to Jarrod's urgent murmur, Brett looked over his shoulder. The woman was tall, improbably auburn-haired, her stunningly curved figure displayed in minute detail by a skintight black lace minidress. And she was looking straight at him. She smiled, lifted an elegant eyebrow in obvious invitation, and leaned back against the bar as if waiting for him to join her.

There'd been a time when he'd have broken his neck to get to her. After all, he wasn't the type who usually had gorgeous women throwing passes at him. He was the one who'd generally done the passing before, beginning with an announcement of what he did for a living—something some women found interesting. He'd been reasonably successful with that strategy. It would probably work quite well with the woman who was looking at him now. He smiled at her, made a rueful gesture with his shoulders and turned back to his drink.

He wondered if Erin's hair was auburn. Or black, maybe? He wondered if she ever wore lace dresses and smiled at men in bars. She'd damn well better not be doing it tonight.

"I don't believe this," Jarrod muttered in blatant disgust. "She just moved on to someone else. You turned her down, man. Are you crazy?"

Brett shrugged. "Just not interested tonight."

"She's not a hooker or anything, you know. I know her— well, sort of. She's an advertising account exec. There are men who would maim and kill for an evening in her company."

"Guess I'm not one of them."

Jarrod scowled. "All right, who is she?"

"Which she?" Brett stalled.

"The woman who's got you wearing a Private Property sign. You're off the market, dude. Someone's put her brand on you."

Rolling his eyes at the cheerfully mixed metaphors, Brett shook his head. "You're the crazy one."

"Going to deny it, huh?"

"Deny what?" Brett asked blandly.

Jarrod, the best inker Brett had ever worked with, only scowled more fiercely. "Yeah, you're hooked. Got a ring through your nose and your heart on your sleeve. So, when's the wedding?"

Brett only laughed and changed the subject. *Wedding?* he thought wryly. There hadn't even been a meeting yet. He didn't expect his friend to understand that.

He wasn't even sure he understood it himself. He only knew that sometime during the past few days he'd come to a decision. No more sitting in an empty apartment, gazing

longingly at the telephone. No more nights in bars, trying
to work up interest in a woman who wasn't Erin. No more
wondering what she looked like, who she was with when
she wasn't talking to him, what it was that scared her so
badly about meeting him.

He was going to find out for himself. He was leaving for
Arkansas as soon as he had the chance to get back home and
pack. He'd turned in a month's work that morning, so he
had a few days available. He would use them getting to
know Erin. Personally.

He glanced around the bar with a faint sense of smug satisfaction with his decision. Maybe he'd bring Erin here
sometime. He'd like to do New York with her, after he'd
shown her around Boston. There were a lot of things he
wanted to do with her. Just the two of them. It would be
great.

Now, all he had to do was convince her.

RUNNING A FINGER around the suddenly-too-tight collar of
his pale blue shirt, Brett stared at the neat, unassuming
home in front of him and wondered if he'd have the courage to ring the doorbell. What would Erin say when he introduced himself? he wondered for the thousandth time.
Would she be furious with him for tracing her address
through his reluctantly cooperative policeman brother-in-
law? For showing up on her doorstep when she'd told him
more than once that she wasn't ready to meet him?

Would she understand that he'd really had no other
choice?

He took a deep breath. Courage had never been something he'd lacked. Some might even call it foolhardiness. He
reached out to press the doorbell, listening in anticipation
as it buzzed inside.

Forgive me, Erin. I waited as long as I could.

She wasn't at home. Of all the scenarios he'd imagined—that hadn't been one of them. Deflated, he sighed, ran a hand through his humidity-curled hair and looked around. What should he do now?

"She's probably at the park," a friendly voice called from the yard next door.

Looking around hopefully, Brett spotted the middle-aged woman working in an autumn-thinned flower bed. "I beg your pardon?"

"Erin always goes to the park on Saturday mornings. It's just three blocks that way." The woman pointed a green-gloved hand holding a dirty spade as she spoke.

Were Erin's neighbors always so talkative with strangers? Brett wondered in mild disapproval. The woman didn't know him, had no idea what his purpose was for ringing the bell, and yet she was cheerfully telling him where Erin could be found. And then he smiled. Why was he complaining? That was exactly what he'd wanted to know, wasn't it? "Thank you. I appreciate it."

The woman gave him a long, measuring look, then returned his smile with what almost looked like approval. "You're welcome."

He had no trouble finding a parking space for his rented car beside the park the woman had indicated. He discovered it to be a couple of acres of trees and picnic tables and playground equipment neatly situated in the centre of the middle-class neighborhood. It looked like a family sort of place. Brett wondered about that. He hadn't really expected Erin to live in a house, having thought she'd probably have an apartment or a condo. And why did she come to this park every Saturday morning?

Calling himself a fool for searching for a woman he wouldn't recognize anyway, he shoved his hands in the pockets of his navy slacks and wandered through the park.

The place was crowded on this warm Saturday morning in mid-September. Children tumbled around him, squealing and squabbling, running toward the swings and slides and teeter-totters. Mothers of all shapes and sizes sat on benches, gossiping and keeping an eye on their younger kids. A few looked curiously at Brett, obviously unaccustomed to having strange men wander into their park.

He was just about to give up and leave when he saw the woman sitting alone on a redwood bench, reading a paperback book while she sipped at a canned cola. Her hair was dark, pinned loosely at the top of her head. Her face— a slightly squared oval, with delicate features—was enchanting, even behind the stylishly thin frames of the glasses she wore. Her pullover top clung attractively to full breasts, and a slender waist and khaki walking shorts made her golden legs seem to go on forever. She daintily licked a drop of soda from her full lower lip and his entire body tightened in response.

If this was Erin, he thought, he was a goner.

As if sensing him standing there staring at her, the woman looked up, her gaze meeting his. Her eyes were blue. Bright, vivid blue in delightful contrast to her dark hair. He had a sudden urge to see himself reflected in them. "Hi," he managed, gesturing awkwardly to the empty half of the bench on which she sat. "Mind if I sit down?"

She scooted closer to her end. "No, of course not. It's a public bench, after all."

Erin. He'd know her voice anywhere. Exhaling soundlessly, he sat down, still staring at her. So now he had a face to go with the voice. A beautiful, compelling face to match a bright, clever mind.

He felt the smile spread across his face as he slipped painlessly, hopelessly into love.

ERIN FELT HER CHEEKS warm beneath the man's intense inspection. She'd had other men stare at her, of course, attracted by whatever it was men found so appealing about her. But, for some reason, this one was different. There was something in his smiling, golden-brown eyes that she couldn't quite analyze.

She took a moment to study him in response before turning back to her book. He looked young, probably only a year or two older than her own twenty-six. His hair was brown, thick and curly, glinting with reddish highlights in the morning sun. His nose was appealingly crooked. His cheeks were square, slashed by disarming dimples. He was slim and fit, though not particularly tall. He looked nice. She couldn't help returning his smile.

As if encouraged by her reaction, he shifted to half face her. "Beautiful day, isn't it?"

"Yes, very nice," she agreed, amused by the bland, predictable opening line. At least he hadn't come out with something that sounded as if it belonged in a tacky singles-bar setting. She'd heard all of those already. They'd never worked for her.

"What's your name?"

He watched her face as he asked the question, as if hoping he hadn't become too personal, too quickly. She rather liked his diffidence. His uncertainty made her feel less wary than she might have been, had he come on too strong. "Erin," she supplied, not bothering with the surname.

"Erin. What a beautiful name," he murmured.

It sounded like something Brett would have said. In fact, this man could fit the mental picture she'd drawn of Brett during the past few months. But Brett was in Boston. This man's voice wasn't as deep and carried no trace of the Eastern accent that occasionally crept into Brett's. And she couldn't imagine Brett's smile edged with just the hint of shyness she found so appealing in this man. After all, why would Brett be shy with her? "Thank you," she said, then turned back to her book for lack of anything else to say.

She looked up when he cleared his throat.

"Uh—you come here often?" he asked, then winced. "Sorry. That was pretty lame, wasn't it? I might as well have asked your sign."

Disarmed by his self-deprecating smile, she laughed at his lapse into the singles-bar chatter she'd thought about only minutes before. "Actually, I do come here often. And I'm a Libra. What about you?"

He chuckled. "Sagittarius. Maybe I'd better go back to talking about the weather. Think it's going to get hot this afternoon?"

Intrigued, Erin closed her book, holding her place with one finger. "Yes, very. It's supposed to rain tomorrow, I hear."

Grinning broadly, the man nodded. "So they say. How's your book?"

"Interesting." She showed him the cover of the recent paperback bestseller, a romantic suspense by Nora Roberts, one of her favorite writers.

He glanced at it, then nodded. "I've read that. It's very good. Want to know who the murderer is?"

"No, not yet, thanks," she answered in amusement. "I'm surprised you read it. Her readers are usually women."

"A friend recommended it," he replied. "I think good writing appeals to everyone, don't you?"

She smiled. "It certainly should. Have you read any of her other books?"

"One. *Sacred Sins*."

"Oh, I loved that one! Did you know who the killer was? She had me completely stumped. I was so surprised by the ending."

They spent the next ten minutes discussing that book and several others they'd both read and enjoyed. Erin was surprised at how easily she and this attractive stranger conversed. She didn't generally talk so readily to strangers, particularly men. But it was nice to sit in a park, chatting with a man who regarded her with appreciation, a man with delightful manners and a touch of old-fashioned courtesy that appealed to her.

She couldn't help thinking of Brett. It was easy to talk to him, of course. But she wasn't sure it would be this easy if she agreed to meet him in person. After all, she'd told him things she'd never told anyone else. Their conversations had been almost embarrassingly frank at times. She wasn't sure she'd be able to look at him without blushing in recollection.

This man, on the other hand, knew nothing about her except her name and her taste in books, which made everything much less awkward. Nothing personal at all. Including, it seemed, the fact that she had a daughter. He looked stunned when Chelsea ran up to the bench to ask Erin to tie her shoe.

Studying him out of the corner of her eye, Erin bent to the tiny Reebok sneaker, wondering why he looked so surprised. Hadn't he known she was here with her child? She'd half assumed he had one running around somewhere. That was usually why adults found themselves in this park. If not that, why was he here?

Why hadn't she told him? Brett stared at the dark-haired little girl in dismay. She'd called Erin "Mommy." Not that the words had been necessary. The child was a miniature duplicate of her mother, with the same dark hair and almost-oval face. Only the eyes were different; the child's were dark, almost black—the dark, mysterious, slightly uptilted eyes of a future heartbreaker. "This is your—uh—?"

"My daughter," Erin supplied, straightening from her task. "Chelsea. Chels, this is Mr.—?"

"Hi, Chelsea," Brett said, smiling at the child as he deliberately ignored Erin's implied question. "It's very nice to meet you."

The little girl looked him over gravely, glancing at her mother to make sure it was all right to talk to the man. When Erin nodded permission, Chelsea turned to Brett with a smile that captivated him. "I'm going to be four after Thanksgiving. I'm getting a training bike for my birthday."

"Are you? Can you ride?"

"Not yet, but Mommy's going to teach me. Aren't you, Mommy?"

"Of course I am," Erin assured her. "But that's still a couple of months away, sweetie."

"I know." Chelsea sighed. "I have a dance recital next month," she announced. "I have a red-and-white costume and I get to wear a feather in my hair."

"I'm sure you'll look beautiful," Brett replied. "Do you like to dance?"

"Mm-hmm. I like tap better than ballet, though. Ballet's boring. Can I go slide, Mommy?"

"May I," Erin corrected automatically. "Yes, but be careful."

"Okay. Bye," she added to Brett, just before turning and dashing away, her ponytail swinging over her hot-pink-and-white playsuit.

Why hadn't she told him she had a daughter? Brett looked at Erin, hurt and even irritated by the omission. She'd told him so much about herself. Hadn't she considered a child a rather important part of her life?

A recently recurring fantasy replayed in his mind. Walking hand in hand in the Common on a beautiful, fragrant autumn day, the sounds of sidewalk performers and laughing conversations tangling in the air. Just Brett and Erin . . . and her three-year-old daughter. Somehow it just wasn't the same now.

"So you have a daughter," he said and his voice sounded a bit hollow even to him. "Any other kids?"

She shook her head, to his relief. "Just Chelsea. What about you? Are you here with children?"

"No, I don't have any kids. I was just—uh—" He hated lying to her, still wasn't even sure why he hadn't yet told her who he was. He decided to blame that on Cheryl. "Just strolling through the park enjoying the nice weather," he finished lamely.

Great, he thought with a mental groan. Back to the weather again. Chelsea's arrival had really knocked him for a loop.

It wasn't that he had anything against children, he reflected. It was just that he'd never lusted over anyone's mother before.

What should he do now? he asked himself, frantically trying to think of something to say. Should he tell her the truth? If he did, would she snatch up her daughter and storm away? Would she turn distant and awkward, suspicious of his sudden appearance? He ruefully suspected she wouldn't throw herself into his arms and welcome him to her town.

Dammit, Cheryl. What have you gotten me into now?

During his silence, Erin had turned back to her book, though he knew she was still aware of him. He cleared his throat. "Your daughter looks very much like you. Except for her eyes, of course. She—uh—has your husband's eyes?"

"My ex-husband's," Erin corrected.

"Oh." He looked at his hands, then at her. This wasn't going to work, he decided abruptly. He couldn't go on deceiving her about who he was, couldn't ask her out without telling the truth. "Erin, I—"

"Mo-o-mmy." Sobbing, Chelsea interrupted them, holding up two dirty hands as she approached them, both knees covered with dirt. "I fell down. My hands are bleeding."

Brett almost cringed at the sight of bright red drops of blood oozing from the tiny scraped palms. Erin didn't seem particularly disturbed as she took Chelsea's hands in hers. "Yes, I see they are," she said bracingly. "We'll go home and put some antiseptic on them."

Chelsea's lip quivered. "Will it hurt?"

"No, of course not. Remember the new brand we found that doesn't sting a bit?"

The child nodded. "Can I have orange pop?"

"Yes, with your lunch, after we clean your hands."

Tears already drying, Chelsea pressed her advantage a bit more. "And ice cream?"

Erin smiled ruefully at Brett. "Children become masters of manipulation at a very early age," she murmured before turning back to Chelsea. "We'll talk about it when we get home."

She tucked her book under her arm and stood. Suddenly realizing that she was leaving, Brett rose quickly to his feet. Erin turned to look at him and he realized that she had an inch advantage in height. He wondered glumly how she felt about guys who were shorter than she was. And then he wondered when he was ever going to have the chance to find out. "Erin, I—"

"Hurry, Mommy. My hands are still bleeding," Chelsea whined restlessly, fanning her stinging palms in the air. "They need 'septic."

"Yes, I'm coming, Chelsea." Erin looked apologetically at Brett. "It was nice to meet you."

He just managed not to wince. "Yeah. You, too," he muttered, conceding defeat this time. "Maybe we'll see each other again sometime."

"Maybe," she agreed, and he could tell by her expression that she didn't believe they would. "Goodbye."

He didn't repeat the goodbye. Unlike Erin, he knew they'd be seeing each other again. Soon. God help him.

CHERYL WAS PRACTICALLY waiting for him at her front door when he returned. "Well," she demanded, hardly giving him time to get inside. "Did you meet her? What's she like? Was she mad that you looked her up? Is she beautiful?"

Brett held up both hands. "Slow down, Cheryl. One question at a time, okay? And would you mind if I have a drink while you interrogate me?"

"There are cold colas in the refrigerator. Help yourself."

"Thanks." He walked past her into the kitchen. She followed right on his heels. "Where are the boys?" he asked, noticing the house was unusually peaceful. His nephews, ages five and four, were rarely still or quiet.

"Taking their naps," Cheryl explained with a sigh of relief. "It's always a hassle to get them down, but so wonderful while it lasts. We've got another hour of respite. So tell me about Erin. Did you meet her?"

"I met her," Brett answered, swinging a leg over one of the straight-backed chairs at the kitchen table and setting the canned cola in front of him. "Sort of."

"Have you had lunch? You want a sandwich or something? And what do you mean, 'Sort of'?"

Used to his sister's habit of carrying on at least two conversations at once, Brett only shrugged. "Yeah, a sandwich sounds good, if you don't mind."

She rummaged in the refrigerator. "What do you mean, sort of?" she repeated, obviously intent on learning every detail.

"I found her in a park close to her house. We talked a few minutes. I—uh—didn't tell her who I was."

Spreading mayonnaise on whole-wheat bread, Cheryl looked over her shoulder. "Why not?"

He shrugged. "Your fault. I guess I thought I was meeting her incognito."

She giggled. "Chicken."

"Yeah. When the time came to say my name, I couldn't do it. I thought I'd give her a chance to find out what a really nice, harmless—well, relatively harmless—guy I am, and then I'd confess the truth."

"It's a great plan," Cheryl assured him. "After all, it *was* my idea. So, did it work?"

"We got interrupted before I could make much headway."

"By what?" she asked, sliding a loaded plate in front of him.

"Her daughter." Brett picked up the thick sandwich she'd made. "She's got a three-year-old kid. She never told me."

"Oh." Cheryl waited until he'd taken a bite before asking, "Does that make a difference to you?"

Brett swallowed, trying to decide how to answer. "I'm not sure," he said finally.

"Well, why not? It shouldn't matter that she has a daughter."

"What matters," Brett muttered, "is that she didn't tell me. I can't help wondering what else she kept from me during the past few months."

"I see." Cheryl thought about it for the next few minutes while he ate, then asked carefully, "Could her daughter be the reason she was so wary about meeting you? You didn't give her any reason to believe you don't like kids, did you?"

Brett thought back to a conversation he and Erin had had not long after they'd started talking.

Do you like children? she'd asked.

Sure, he'd answered. *From a distance.*

He shifted uncomfortably in the chair. "Uh—well, maybe. I mean, she may have misinterpreted something I once said."

Cheryl rolled her eyes in disgust. "Men!" she muttered.

Was Cheryl right about Erin's reasons for putting him off? He sighed, finally understanding her hesitation. After all, she had a child to think of. She had more than herself to consider.

The question was, did he want to become involved with a woman with the responsibilities inherent in raising a child?

Did he really have any choice?

As if reading her brother's mind, Cheryl questioned, "*Does* it make a difference, Brett? Are you going to see her again?"

"Yeah," he said quietly. "I'm going to see her again."

"So, you're not mad at her anymore for not telling you about her daughter?"

"I guess I understand why she didn't," Brett conceded, though he still wanted to hear Erin's explanation.

"And you don't mind that she has a child?"

He shrugged. "I guess not. I mean, why should it? She seemed like a nice kid. And there are always baby-sitters."

Cheryl looked concerned. "There's a bit more to it than that," she murmured. "Children aren't a minor inconvenience you have to work around, Brett."

"I know," he replied defensively. "Just—let me take it one step at a time, okay?"

Cheryl leaned against the table across from him, resting her chin on her fists. "So, how did you find her in the park? How did you recognize her?"

Brett chuckled, shaking his head. "You probably won't believe this, but I walked straight to her. And as soon as I heard her talk, I knew I'd guessed correctly."

"Wow. It must be fate," Cheryl mused, her brown eyes going dreamy.

"Maybe it is," Brett agreed, remembering the almost-physical impact Erin's beautiful blue eyes had had upon him. "Maybe it is."

ERIN WAS THINKING about the man from the park as she cleaned the kitchen that evening. Chelsea was tucked into bed and the house was quiet except for the radio playing from the kitchen counter. *A very nice man,* she found herself thinking again. *Attractive, too, in a wholesome, guy-next-door way.* It was the first time a man had appealed to her in that way in quite some time. She'd sensed that the attraction was mutual. In fact, if Chelsea hadn't interrupted when she had, Erin thought he might have asked her out.

What would she have said if he had? After all, he was a total stranger. Yet she realized in some surprise that she would have been tempted to say yes. Very tempted. It had been so long since she'd been on a date, since she'd eaten in a restaurant where the food wasn't served on carry-yourself trays by people with clowns on their ID badges. Hadn't she been telling herself she needed to get out more? Hadn't Adam insinuated that the reason she was so fascinated by her telephone friend was because she was sublimating her natural need to spend more time with adults—in particular, male adults?

Would a more active social life help her sleep better? Make her stop tossing and turning and dreaming of a fantasy lover who was no more in reality than a voice on the telephone?

And why, dammit, was she suddenly feeling guilty for considering going out with a man she'd met in the park, a man she'd probably never see again? What was this misguided sense of loyalty to Brett? She'd told him she didn't want to meet him. If only she could make herself believe it.

As if her thoughts of Brett had prompted it, the telephone rang. Erin stared at it for a moment before picking it up, again plagued by a nagging sense of disloyalty. Then, telling herself she was being an idiot, she picked up the receiver. "Hello."

"Hi, Erin."

The deep voice went straight to her knees. She sank into a chair at the kitchen table. "Hi, Brett."

"How are you?"

"I'm okay," she returned vaguely. "How about you?"

He sighed through the line. "I'm getting damned frustrated."

She winced, knowing what was coming next. She was right.

"I want to see you, Erin."

"Brett, don't start this again."

"I'm not going to stop. It's getting ridiculous. You're important to me. You're a part of my life. I want to see you."

"Brett, I—"

He broke in with a new note in his voice that she hadn't heard before—a firm, no-nonsense, very male note that made a shiver of awareness course down her spine. "All right, Erin, let's have it. What, exactly, is holding you back? What aren't you telling me?"

She widened her eyes, thinking immediately of Chelsea. Should she tell him? If so, what words could she use to explain that she was afraid her relationship with Brett could only end up hurting her daughter? How could she make him understand that Chelsea came first, would always come first with her? "What makes you think there's something I'm not telling you?" she countered.

"I've gotten to know you pretty well during the past few months. I know the way you sound when you're not being entirely honest with me. What is it, Erin? Was your relationship with Martin so horrible that you can never trust another man?"

"That's part of it," she admitted candidly. "Martin changed me, Brett. I went into our relationship naive and optimistic and hopelessly romantic. I came out hurt and bitter and with very few illusions left. It's taken me a long time to get over the anger and the pain. I don't want to go through that again."

"What makes you think we'd end up like you and your jerk of an ex-husband?" he demanded. "There's no comparison. Martin wanted you for your youth, your beauty. I'm interested in your mind, your opinions, your wonderful sense of humor. We have so much in common, Erin. So much more going for us than most couples just starting out in a relationship. Why are you so sure we're doomed to failure? What do I have to do to convince you I'm not like him?"

"I've never said you were like Martin," Erin answered defensively.

"You've implied it. And yet I've just told you that I'm not particularly concerned with appearances. I'm not worried about growing older, the way he was. Actually, I'm looking forward to a few interesting lines and gray hairs," he added, striving for a lighter note. "Maybe they'll help me get away from the 'cute' look and take on a more distinguished air."

"Maybe they will," Erin agreed.

"I don't wear gold chains and I'd never pull my hair back into a little ponytail. I don't carve notches into my bedpost. How did Martin feel about kids and animals?" he asked deliberately, still in that teasing vein but oddly serious with the question.

"He—uh—" She cleared her throat. "He didn't like either of them. Never wanted either a pet or—or a child."

"Well, there you go. Something else different about the two of us. I happen to like pets. And children."

"From a distance," she reminded him faintly.

"I was only teasing when I said that. Really. I like kids."

She couldn't help but be suspicious about his sudden preoccupation with that particular topic. It was almost as if he knew about . . . But he couldn't, she reminded herself. How could he have found out about Chelsea? She remained silent, not quite knowing what to say.

"Erin, what would you do if I suddenly showed up on your doorstep? Would you close the door in my face, refuse to talk to me?"

"I don't know," she whispered, having asked herself that same question more than once. "But you don't know where I live, so I don't suppose I have to worry about that, do I?"

He hesitated. "I just want to know what you'd do," he insisted without answering her question.

Erin wearily pushed a strand of hair out of her face. "You're giving me a headache," she accused him, rubbing at her temple with her free hand. "Why don't you give me time to think about what you've said tonight?"

"How much time?"

"I don't know," she murmured again. "I just . . . need to think, Brett. About a lot of things."

"Well, think fast, Erin. I want to see you. Dammit, I need to see you. And I don't know how much longer I can wait."

"You're pushing me."

"Yes," he admitted without hesitation. "I know I am. But I can't help it. Don't you see that I really have no other choice?"

Maybe he was right, she thought despondently. Maybe neither of them would ever be able to go on with their normal lives until they'd gotten the meeting out of the way. But she couldn't quite work up the nerve to agree yet. She needed more time. "I'll think about it," she promised again.

"You do that," he suggested. "I'll talk to you soon, Erin."

"All right. Good night, Brett."

"Good night, Erin."

She hung up with the sense that control of this unusual relationship was about to be taken out of her hands. If it hadn't been already.

THAT NIGHT Erin dreamed, as she had before, that she and Brett were making love. His deep, so-familiar voice murmured words of love and appreciation into her ears as he caressed her. Only this time he had a face to go with the voice. Oddly enough, she'd given him the face of the man she'd met in the park.

She woke with a start, blinking at the morning light pouring through the bedroom window. What a strange dream! She got out of bed and headed for the kitchen. She needed coffee.

She was still thinking about the dream, still puzzling over its meaning, when a familiar tap on the back door made her cross the kitchen and pull the door open. "Good morning, Isabelle. I just made coffee. Would you like a cup?"

Her neighbor shook her gray head with a smile. "No, thanks, dear, I have to get ready for church. But I had these fresh blackberry muffins left over from breakfast and I thought you and Chelsea might like them this morning."

Erin took the basket gratefully. "They smell heavenly. Thank you."

"By the way, did that attractive young man find you yesterday?"

Surprised by the question, Erin looked curiously at Isabelle. "What attractive young man?"

"The one who came calling while you were at the park yesterday morning. I normally wouldn't have told just anyone where you were, but he looked so nice. He reminded me of my nephew, Andrew. Curly brown hair, lovely smile. And very courteous. A new suitor?" she asked hopefully.

Curly brown hair. Lovely smile.

What would you do if I suddenly showed up on your doorstep? Brett had asked. But Brett was in Boston. He'd called from there only the night before. Hadn't he?

Of course, he'd never actually said he was still in Boston. She'd only assumed . . .

"You said you told him I was at the park?" she asked Isabelle slowly.

Beginning to look concerned at whatever she read in Erin's face, the older woman nodded. "Yes. I hope I did the right thing. Maybe I shouldn't have . . . ?"

"No, it's all right, Isabelle," Erin assured her quickly, not wanting her friend to worry.

Isabelle didn't look convinced. "Maybe I shouldn't do that again?"

"Maybe not," Erin agreed gently. "But, really, don't worry about it. This time it was a friend." *Or, rather, an ex-friend.*

She was an idiot, she told herself as she closed the door behind her neighbor. A full-fledged, gullible idiot for falling for his clever smile and skillful evasions.

He'd deceived her.

She must have known all along, subconsciously. That's why she'd had the dream, she reflected, growing angrier with every passing minute. And that's why he'd looked so stunned when he'd found out about Chelsea. He had known where to find Erin, but he hadn't known she had a child.

Her cheeks flaming, she paced the kitchen, her steps short, crisp, forceful. Snatches of frank, intimate, sometimes risqué conversation ran through her mind. Why had she talked so candidly to him, secure in the misguided belief that they'd never meet? She should have known better than to play games that had no rules. She should have listened to Adam.

How had Brett found her? That was one of the questions she intended to ask him, just before she told him exactly what she thought of him for deceiving her. She didn't doubt that he'd be back. Soon. Probably today.

When he came, she'd be ready for him. *The rat.*

Turning toward her bedroom, she decided to get ready, not wanting to be caught off guard. She'd practice her speech to him in the shower. She wanted to make her displeasure perfectly clear when she talked to him.

He was the one who'd wanted honesty. Who'd insisted on a face-to-face meeting. Fine. That's exactly what she'd give him.

7

BRETT PULLED HIS RENTAL car into Erin's drive, determined to get the confrontation behind him. He'd waited until early afternoon, but he couldn't wait any longer. He'd been wrong to deceive her, wrong not to tell her who he was in the park yesterday. Now it was time to confess and then try to salvage something from the resulting explosion.

Now that he'd actually seen her, he was even more obsessed with her than he'd been before. He'd spent most of the night adjusting to his new knowledge about her: the fact that she had a child. He'd decided it didn't matter. He wanted Erin. If she came as a package deal, fine. He'd take her any way he could get her.

If only he could convince Erin to forgive him—for the deception, and for forcing a meeting she'd resisted.

He rang the doorbell with a not-quite-steady finger. The door was thrown open more quickly than he'd expected, catching him off guard. Almost as if she'd been waiting for him. Something in her eyes made him catch his breath.

She knows, he thought, startled. *How could she possibly know?*

"Hello, Erin," he said quietly, studying the fiery glitter in her vivid blue eyes with wary interest. She wasn't wearing the glasses this time, he noted automatically.

She tilted her head in obviously feigned surprise, her dark hair swaying at her shoulders. She wore jeans and a rather militarily styled black shirt that only enhanced the femininity of her delicate features. His body tightened in fierce response; the desire he'd felt the day before was only strengthened by seeing her again.

"Why, it's the man from the park," she murmured, her voice much too smooth.

"Well—um—"

"Please, come in." She stepped aside, waving an invitation with one slender hand.

Since she didn't even ask how he'd found her or what he was doing there, Brett was even more positive that she already knew who he was. He stepped carefully past her, looking around for her daughter. "Where's Chelsea?"

"She's making chocolate-chip cookies with our neighbor, Mrs. Price. You should remember her—she's the one who gave you directions to the park yesterday."

Brett winced. So that was how she'd figured it out.

"So, tell me, stranger," she continued, planting her hands on her slender hips and looking him straight in the eye, "what can I do for you? Are you, perhaps, selling insurance? Encyclopedias?"

"Erin—"

She cocked her head. "No? Then perhaps you're a reporter, looking for a story. Something having to do with a woman you assume to be a naive idiot."

"I don't think you're a naive idiot," Brett said wearily. This was going to be worse than he'd expected.

"How would you know? After all, we just met yesterday, didn't we, *stranger?*"

"That's enough, Erin. You obviously know who I am."

"All I know is what you told me yesterday, remember?"

His own temper was beginning to ignite, despite his awareness that he deserved her anger. Perhaps *because* of that awareness. "I said that's enough, Erin. We need to talk and we can't do that as long as you're taking potshots at me."

Her eyes widened, her cheeks darkened with emotion. "You have the *nerve* to criticize me for being furious with you? *You lied to me!*"

"I didn't—" He stopped with a sigh. "Yeah, I guess I did, in a way. I'm sorry."

She wasn't appeased. "That's supposed to be enough?"

"It's the best I can do," he answered evenly. "I *am* sorry, Erin. I wanted a few minutes to talk to you without scaring you off or making you self-conscious. And I enjoyed talking with you for those few minutes. I would have told you the truth if we hadn't been interrupted. I knew I couldn't deceive you for long."

"You shouldn't have deceived me at all," she snapped, arms crossing defensively at her waist. "You should have told me who you were from the beginning. Or at least you should have said something during that call last night. Dammit, you shouldn't have even been there in the first place! You agreed to give me time."

He narrowed his eyes, clenching his fists in his tight jeans pockets. "I think I've groveled just about enough," he informed her in clipped words. "Okay, so what I did was wrong. But I'm not the only one who hasn't been exactly honest, am I? At least I only deceived you for a few minutes. You've been lying to me for nearly four months!"

Stung, she lifted her chin defiantly. "I have *not* been lying to you!"

He crossed his own arms, tucking his hands into the crooks of his elbows to keep them from reaching out for her. Even furious, she was the most striking woman he'd ever seen. He couldn't remember ever wanting anyone like this. The wanting was a hunger gnawing voraciously inside him, making it hard for him to think clearly, hard to control his volatile emotions.

"I suppose you simply forgot to mention that you had a three-year-old daughter?" he said sarcastically.

Her cheeks flamed. "No, I didn't forget," she muttered. "I didn't think it was any of your business!"

He felt as if she'd slugged him. "None of my business?" he repeated incredulously, staring at her.

She shifted uncomfortably on her feet, not quite meeting his eyes. "It's just that we—that I—"

He didn't allow her to finish whatever she'd tried to say. Catching her forearms in his hands, he barely resisted the impulse to shake her. Eye to eye, toe to toe, he faced her, speaking in a low, clear, furious voice. "I've told you things I've never told anyone. Things no one else could possibly understand. But *you* did—or at least, I thought you did. I thought we had something special. If nothing else, I thought we were friends. And you didn't think it was my business that you have a child?"

"Brett," she whispered, "I—"

"Tell me, Erin, do your other friends know about Chelsea? Do you make it a regular habit to conceal her existence?"

"No, of course not. All my friends know about her. But—"

"All your *real* friends, you mean," he cut in bitterly. "Just how did I fit into your life, Erin? If not a friend, what was I to you?"

She tossed her head in agitation, her dark hair flying around her face. "You were a fantasy! An escape. Someone with whom I could pretend, just for a few precious hours, that I was more than Chelsea's mom. Someone to talk to and laugh with and share witty repartee and inside jokes. Someone—the only one, I thought—who didn't expect anything from me, didn't care about my responsibilities or obligations."

He deliberately eased his hold on her, his fingers caressing rather than binding. "That wasn't a fantasy," he murmured huskily. "I don't care about those things. And I know you're more than Chelsea's mom. You're Erin."

Her eyes sad, she shook her head slowly. "You still don't understand. I *am* Chelsea's mom. First and foremost. I'm not free to jump into impulsive relationships or become involved with any man who catches my interest. What I do affects her. The men I date become a part of her life, as well. Men look at me and they see—I don't know—someone different from who I really am. Someone suitable for fun and games and free-spirited affairs. Well, I can't be that person. I have Chelsea."

Genuinely confused, he tried to understand. "You didn't want to meet me because you thought I wouldn't understand about your daughter? Because you thought I'd try to separate you from her?"

"You wouldn't be the first," she replied in little more than a whisper. "And you can't convince me that you were overjoyed to find out about her. I saw your face when she ran up to the park bench yesterday. I didn't understand why you looked so stunned then. Now I do."

"Yeah, I was stunned," he agreed dryly. "How could I not have been? I had no idea you had a child. And, I have to admit, it took me a little while to adapt to this new image of you. But it hasn't changed anything, Erin. I still think we're special together. That we have a better foundation for a relationship than most couples who have dated for months. That we'd be crazy to give up on it without even trying to see where it leads."

"And if it leads nowhere?" she asked tightly, her hands lifting to rest on his chest as she searched his face.

"Isn't that a risk everyone has to take sometime?"

"I don't want Chelsea hurt," she insisted stubbornly.

"I'm not going to hurt your daughter, Erin. Or you. Give me a chance to prove it, will you?"

She looked at him suspiciously. "How?"

The urge to shake her returned—not as strongly this time, but he was still exasperated. "How does anyone find out more about someone? Go out with me. Have dinner, talk—you know, date? Don't you think it's past time we had a first date?"

She frowned suddenly. "How did you find me, anyway?"

"My brother-in-law's with the NLRPD," he answered. "And, yeah, he shouldn't have looked you up for me, so I hope you won't turn him in. He owed me a couple of favors. Will you have dinner with me tonight, Erin?"

She gnawed on her lower lip while she thought about her answer. The unconsciously seductive act was almost his undoing. He wanted to kiss her so badly he ached with it; wanted to taste her, to imprint himself on her so she'd stop fighting the inevitable. He'd been wanting her for months—even before he'd ever set eyes on her. Now that he had, the wanting was almost more than he could take.

"Erin?" he demanded hoarsely.

She released her lip, moistening it with the tip of her tongue. He almost groaned. "All right, Brett," she murmured. "I'll have dinner with you tonight. I'll see if I can find a baby-sitter for Chelsea."

"You don't have to do that," he said, remembering that she worried about him not wanting to have anything to do with her daughter. Though he'd rather have Erin to himself, at least this first time, he wanted even more for her to know that he could deal with her responsibilities to her kid. "Bring her along. We'll have burgers or pizza or something, and get to know each other."

She shook her head, with an expression that was hard to read. "No. I think it will be better if she stays with a baby-sitter this time."

"You do whatever you think best."

"When it comes to Chelsea, I always do," she answered immediately.

It was impossible to continue standing so close to her without wanting to be closer. His fingers tightening on her arms, he drew her an inch nearer. "I know you don't want to hear this, Erin, but you really are beautiful. More beautiful than I'd ever imagined."

"I never said I didn't want to hear compliments," she responded with a half smile. "I'm as vain as any other woman."

Compared to some of the women he knew, there wasn't a vain bone in Erin's body. He didn't bother to tell her so. Instead, he smiled and pulled her even closer, so that her full breasts just brushed his chest. Her lips were only inches from his. She moistened them again, nervously, but didn't draw away. Her gaze locked with his and he saw curiosity there, as well as sensuality.

She wanted him to kiss her, he thought exultantly.

She wanted him to kiss her, she realized in dismay.

Reading the intent in his eyes, Erin swallowed and tried desperately to think clearly. She was still angry with him—wasn't she? Still furious, even hurt, that he'd deceived her, that he'd ignored her requests to give her time to decide whether she wanted to meet him. She tried to focus on those negative feelings. Instead, she could only think of how very much she wanted him to kiss her.

"You shouldn't have come here," she whispered—a weak reminder to him—and to herself—that there were still many problems standing between them.

He lifted a hand, sliding his fingers into her hair as his palm cradled her cheek. "Are you really sorry I did?" he asked, looking at her with a mixture of challenge and entreaty.

"I—" Was she? At the moment, she honestly couldn't have said. "I don't know," she answered candidly.

The silence lingered. His hand was so warm against her face, tempting her to snuggle more deeply into the light embrace. How long had it been since anyone had touched her so tenderly? Why hadn't she realized how much she'd craved that tenderness?

His thumb slid slowly over her lower lip. "Erin," he murmured, somehow making her name a caress.

She trembled. "Brett, I—I'm not a spontaneous, impulsive person," she managed, her voice strained with emotion. "I need time. I have responsibilities . . ."

His hand slid to the back of her head as his mouth covered hers.

Erin closed her eyes and melted into him, forgetting responsibilities, forgetting everything except the longings that had been building inside her with each intimate telephone conversation they'd had. Longings to be held, to be kissed, to be wanted by the man who'd laughed with her and talked with her and listened to her so many times; who'd brought excitement and fantasy and desire back into her life after the long years of duty and self-denial. He wasn't a stranger, wasn't a man she'd met only the day before. He was Brett, and she'd been dreaming of his kisses for months.

The kiss was thorough, yet gentle, making her feel pampered and cherished and so very special—feelings she hadn't had in years, if ever. Her willpower dissolved. Her arms slid around his neck and she strained closer to him, losing herself in the pleasure he gave her.

Brett pulled his mouth away slowly, tightening his arms around her. His eyes mirrored the same dazed awe she felt. "Erin," he murmured hoarsely, "I've wanted you for so long. You couldn't possibly know how much I've wanted you."

Couldn't she? She brought her mouth back to his to show him differently. He groaned his approval, his tongue sweeping past her parted lips to tangle eagerly with hers.

Participating wholeheartedly in the kiss, Erin wondered at how beautifully they fit together. Martin stood well over six feet, as had most of the other men she'd dated, making her feel small and, at times, vulnerable. With Brett she was an equal. Their mouths met effortlessly. Her breasts pressed tightly against his solid chest. Their thighs brushed and hers cradled his straining manhood. It took very little effort to imagine them together in bed, tangled in perfect alignment. The erotic images made her moan into his mouth.

Responding to that sensual sound, Brett pulled her even closer, sliding one hand to the small of her back to mold her against his bold need. "Erin, I—"

"Mommy?"

The child's voice broke into the sensual haze surrounding them. Erin pulled out of Brett's arms with a gasp, turning to find her daughter standing in the kitchen doorway, a basket clutched in her tiny hands. "Chelsea." She cleared her throat, automatically straightening her hair. "Did you finish making cookies with Mrs. Price?"

"They're all done. She gave me some to bring home." Chelsea stared at Brett. "Why were you hugging my mommy?"

"Because I like her," Brett replied easily, dropping to one knee to bring himself on a level with the child. "Don't you hug people you like?"

Chelsea nodded, dark braid bobbing. "I hugged Mrs. Price when I left. I like her a lot."

"There, you see? Boy, those cookies smell good."

Chelsea smiled in shy pleasure that made Erin wary. There were so few men in Chelsea's life. Erin was particularly concerned that Chelsea would become attached to Brett before any of them knew where this relationship would lead. She would simply have to take steps to make sure that didn't happen, she told herself firmly.

"You were at the park yesterday," Chelsea informed Brett, cocking her head in recognition.

"Yes," he confirmed. "My name is Brett."

"I think we'd better make it Mr. Nash," Erin corrected quickly.

Brett only looked over his shoulder at her. "Mr. Nash is my father. I'm Brett."

Chelsea looked from the man kneeling in front of her to her mother, visibly confused. Reading the determination in Brett's steady gaze, Erin relented rather than cause an awkward scene. "All right. Brett."

Chelsea smiled. "I like that name," she told him.

Brett returned the grin, reaching out to tug lightly on the child's braid. "I like your name, too."

"You want a cookie? I put the chocolate chips in by myself. I only had one so I could eat more with Mommy, but it was really good," she assured him earnestly.

"I'd love to have a cookie. Thank you."

Chelsea was already digging into the basket. Sighing, Erin stepped forward. "Let's take them into the kitchen and I'll pour everyone a glass of milk to go with them. And then Brett has to go," she added with a meaningful look at him. "I have some things to do before tonight."

Brett only smiled. She knew he'd contented himself with his victory in talking her into having dinner with him that evening. She still wasn't exactly sure how he'd done it, but she needed time alone before they left for that date. Time to think about what had just happened. To decide whether she wanted it to happen again. As if she had any choice in the matter. She knew that Brett would only have to touch her to have her falling into his arms again.

She definitely had a lot to think about before dinner that evening.

ERIN GAZED ACROSS the linen-covered table at Brett. Why had they been able to talk so easily over the telephone as strangers when they were having such trouble making conversation tonight?

Pleating her napkin in her lap, she tried to think of something to say to break the tense silence. Nothing came immediately to mind. She moistened her lips and looked to Brett for help.

Reading the entreaty in her expression, he grimaced and set his fork on his half-empty plate. "It's awkward, isn't it?"

"What is?"

"Getting to know each other again. For some reason, I thought it would be easier."

She looked down at her lap. Hadn't this been why she'd resisted a meeting? Hadn't she known their special friendship would change with the end of anonymity?

"Erin." Brett leaned across the table and covered her hand with his own. "It wasn't a mistake. We had to do this."

She sighed. "So you keep saying."

"Trust me."

She looked at him gravely. "You're asking for something that's very hard for me to give."

Scowling, he sat back. "I've figured out that for myself."

She didn't know what to say to that, so she said nothing.

"So, tell me about your family," Brett prompted, obviously determined to keep the conversation moving. "I'd like to know more about your childhood. All I know is that your parents were divorced and your mother died several years ago. Have you always been very close to your brother?"

"Very," she replied, comfortable with that particular subject. "Adam is nine years older than I am. My mother had three miscarriages between us. My parents split up when I was only three. Adam was twelve and he became the 'man of the house' after our dad walked out. He was the one I turned to with my problems, the one who fixed my broken toys, the one who made sure I did my homework and brushed my teeth before bedtime."

"Your mother?"

"My mother had very little education and no job skills, having dropped out of school in her junior year to marry my father. She was always rather fragile physically, which, I think, was what attracted my father to her in the first place. But then she had those miscarriages and her health suffered. She had a very difficult pregnancy with me. The bills piled up and she became very depressed and she and my father started having problems. I don't remember those years very well, of course.

"Anyway, he left us with nothing but a few dollars in the bank, so Mother had to go to work. She found a job as a waitress in a cocktail lounge. It was very demanding work—too taxing for her, really—but she was afraid to give it up for fear of not finding anything else. She was very insecure about her lack of education and skills. She'd go to work late in the afternoon and come home very early in the morning. She slept during most of the days. Adam was the one who took care of me, on the whole, though I think Mother did the best she could. She was so tired all the time."

"What happened to her?" Brett asked gently, when Erin fell silent for a moment of painful remembrance.

"She insisted that Adam attend college when he graduated from high school, though he wanted to find a full-time job to support all of us so Mother could quit working. She convinced him that he could make more after obtaining a degree, so he attended a local college on a full academic scholarship. He worked after school and on weekends, but Mother refused to quit her job until he graduated."

"So your brother attended school, worked and took care of you. Quite a guy."

"Yes," Erin agreed proudly. "He is. It nearly broke his heart when our mother died two weeks after he graduated from college. I was thirteen."

"What happened to her?" Brett asked again, his eyes dark and sympathetic in the flickering light from the candle at the center of their table.

"Pneumonia," Erin answered simply. "She contracted it at work one night, but just kept going. By that time, she'd gotten into the habit of putting everyone but herself first and she waited too long to seek medical treatment. Adam was too immersed in finals and work to realize how sick she was—he's never gotten over that—and I was too young and too involved with my own adolescent problems. She collapsed at work one night. She never came home from the hospital."

"God, I'm sorry." His hand covered hers again, squeezing supportively. "That must have been a horrible time for you."

"I don't know what I would have done if it hadn't been for Adam."

"He raised you?"

"Yes. He got a job in a bank—a job he truly hated," she added with a grimace. "For the next five years, he dedicated his life to me, to making sure I didn't lack for anything, that I didn't get into trouble in school or elsewhere. He was a tough guardian, but I knew he loved me and I didn't rebel very often. When I graduated from high school, he gave me a bank book—the money he'd saved for my college education—and told me that he needed to go away for a while. He'd lived his life for my mother and me since he was twelve years old. He needed to do something for himself. He told me he'd always be there for me if I needed him, that all I ever had to do was call and he'd be here—and he has been."

"He gave you your independence."

Erin nodded, pleased that he understood. "Yes. Just as he claimed his own. I handled my freedom very well during my college years. I didn't get into trouble, kept my grades up, didn't get into the wrong crowds. After all, I had teachers and guidance counselors and dorm monitors to keep an eye on me, and that didn't bother me, because I was accustomed to answering to someone. And then, when I graduated with a fine-arts degree, I realized I was on my own. I panicked," she said frankly. "I'd gotten so used to having someone take care of me that I wasn't sure I could handle life on my own."

"Enter Martin," Brett murmured.

"Exactly. He was older and sophisticated and so very attentive that I was swept off my feet and into his arms almost before I knew it. He told me he wanted to take care of me. I wanted him to do that. It seemed the perfect match."

"You once told me you knew almost from the beginning that you'd made a mistake."

"I knew on my wedding night," Erin confirmed, looking away. "I found out then that Martin was basically selfish, that his own pleasure would always come first."

"You didn't sleep with him before you married him?"

Her cheeks burned and she looked quickly around to make sure no one had overheard. It had been much easier to talk frankly to Brett when they couldn't see each other.

"No. I think he rather liked the idea of a young, virgin bride."

"The bastard," Brett muttered.

She smiled weakly. "Oh, yeah."

"But you tried to make it work?" It wasn't really a question; Brett knew Erin well enough by now to know that she would honor her commitments.

"Yes. I tried. And it wasn't too bad at first. As long as I provided Martin with the coveted trophy of a pretty young bride at his side for his many social functions, he treated me like a queen. But then I got pregnant. I was delighted. I thought the baby would finally give us a common goal, a common interest. He wanted me to get an abortion. When I refused, he told me that he was very sorry, but a baby simply didn't fit the plans he had for the remainder of his life. He left me when my figure started to go because of the pregnancy. He's never seen his daughter, though he's been very generous with his child-support payments. Never missed a one."

"He *is* a bastard," Brett said savagely. "How can you compare me—or any decent guy—to a shallow, selfish, lowlife creep like him?"

"I wasn't comparing you to him," Erin replied defensively. "Not really. I just know that most men aren't interested in women who have children."

"More bad experiences, Erin?"

"Yes. I've had men ask me out and then make excuses when I mention finding a baby-sitter. One man asked if I've ever considered boarding schools for my daughter. Boarding school! She's not even four yet."

"But, surely—"

"Oh, I know there are lots of nice, decent men out there," she said wearily, having heard that speech from Adam, Corey and Eileen so many times. "I just haven't been able to find them. I thought I'd met someone nice just over a year ago, but even he turned out to be more interested in his toys and things than in a little girl's feelings."

"What happened?" Brett asked, sounding resigned to hearing another story that cast his sex at a disadvantage.

"He asked me to dinner at his place one night after we'd been dating for several weeks. I think he'd planned to take me to bed that night. I—" She hesitated, blushing. "I was thinking along the same lines. After all, Scott was attractive and charming and he'd always been nice enough to Chelsea the few times he'd seen her. And it had been so long since . . . Well, you know."

"I know," Brett muttered grimly.

"Anyway, at the last minute, my baby-sitter canceled. I had to take Chelsea with me. Scott wasn't particularly gracious about it. During the evening, she got bored—as two-year-olds do—and she broke an expensive stereo component while investigating it. Scott lost his temper. I snatched her away from him just as he was drawing back to hit her. I replaced the equipment, of course—it took nearly a month's earnings to pay for it—and then I never saw him again."

"He would have hit a two-year-old child?" Brett repeated in disbelief.

"Yes. I'm sure he would have if I hadn't intervened. As I said, he was already sulking because the evening hadn't gone exactly as he'd planned. He accused me of bringing Chelsea along as a test—a way for me to find out what kind of father he would make before committing myself to making love with him."

"And had you?" Brett asked quietly.

Erin opened her mouth to furiously deny the question— and then stopped herself. "I don't know," she answered finally—something she'd never even admitted to herself.

"Maybe I could have found another baby-sitter. Maybe I had reservations about going to bed with Scott without knowing where our relationship was leading. Maybe I sensed that there were things about him I wouldn't like, once I knew him better. I don't know. The point is, it has been better for Chelsea and for me since I stopped dating and concentrated on raising her."

"You haven't been on a date since that evening?"

She shook her head. "It just didn't seem worth the trouble."

Brett was silent for a long time. When he did speak, it was only to ask if she was ready to leave.

Glancing at her nearly empty plate, Erin wondered absently if she'd enjoyed the meal she hardly remembered eating. "Yes. I'm ready."

"Then, let's go." He threw some money on the table and held out his hand to her.

Studying his unsmiling expression, she placed her hand in his, wondering what he was thinking. Did he understand now why she was so reluctant to get involved with him? Was he going to tell her that he, like the others, wasn't interested in a woman who would always place her child first?

And had she really hoped, if only for a short time, that this one would be different from the others?

WHILE ERIN CHECKED on her sleeping daughter, Brett paid the teenage baby-sitter—generously, making the girl's eyes widen appreciatively. Erin waited until the teenager had left before turning to Brett in indignation. "You didn't have to pay for my daughter's baby-sitter. I would have taken care of it."

He only shrugged. "I asked you out. The evening was on me. Why does it bother you so much?"

Since she couldn't put her qualms into words—even to herself—she crossed her arms at her waist and turned away from him, her eyes on Chelsea's open bedroom door, concentrating on the dark silence inside the room. "It's getting late."

"We've talked on the phone much later than this."

She felt him moving closer, then knew that he'd stopped only inches behind her. "Do I make you nervous, Erin?" he asked with what sounded like only mild curiosity.

Her fingers tightened on her forearms. "No, of course not," she lied briskly, hoping he wouldn't notice that she was trembling like a leaf. *Nervous?* No. Somehow that mild, innocuous word didn't convey the half of it.

His hands landed gently on her shoulders and she nearly jumped. "Erin."

She closed her eyes, too vividly aware of how close he stood to her, of the warmth of his palms through her blue silk dress, the whisper of his breath at her nape. "What?"

"Would you look at me?"

She moistened her lips. "I—uh—"

His lips touched her neck. "Look at me, Erin."

Very slowly, she turned. He was smiling, his golden-brown eyes crinkled at the corners, his dimples carved deeply into his tanned cheeks. "Don't be nervous, Erin. It's only Brett."

Only Brett, who'd entered her life so unexpectedly and become important to her before she'd realized it. Only Brett, who'd made her want things she'd thought were long ago put behind her. Only Brett, who made her tremble with his smile.

He cupped her face in his hands, still gazing into her eyes. "I have a confession to make."

"You do?" She cleared her throat to make her voice less husky. "What?"

"I'm really glad you didn't wear high heels tonight. I'm not normally intimidated by women who are taller than I am, but—just for tonight—I'm glad you aren't towering above me."

She couldn't help smiling. "Why tonight?"

"Well, you see, I'm a bit nervous, myself. It makes it easier that we're on the same level."

"Why would *you* be nervous?" Erin asked, startled, half-skeptical about his words.

His smile deepened, and his eyes looked warm enough to melt her willpower. "You don't feel it?"

Standing very still, hardly breathing, she felt the fine tremors in the fingers cupping her cheeks. Brett was trembling, too! "Why?" she whispered.

He touched his lips to hers—a butterfly caress too brief to require a response. "I've never wanted anyone like this. I've never needed anyone this much. And I'm so afraid of doing something wrong, something stupid, something that would make you push me away."

His admission of uncertainty twisted her heart, further weakening her shaky resistance to him. She lifted her hands tentatively to his chest. She felt his heart beating beneath her palms, rapidly, forcefully. In response to her touch, he drew a deep, slightly ragged breath. His smile remained, but she saw the strain at the corners of his mouth. "Are you going to push me away, Erin?"

She should. She knew she should. But, oh, how she wanted to kiss him! To be swept again into that whirl of pure sensation she'd experienced earlier when he'd kissed her. Had memory exaggerated her incredible response to that earlier kiss? Would she react the same way if they were to kiss again? Would it be utterly foolish of her to try to find out?

She could only look at him, willing him to take the decision out of her hands.

His gaze still locked with hers, his mouth brushed hers again. A bit longer this time. A bit harder. Still, not nearly enough.

She almost moaned her frustration when he drew back. He wasn't going to make it easy for her, she realized abruptly. He wasn't going to make her decisions for her, leaving himself open to reproof later. She would have to make the first move.

Her fingers gripped the finely woven fabric of his shirt. Very slowly, she leaned toward him. He met her halfway, his lips curved upward in a satisfied smile when they touched hers. And then the smile was gone and he was kissing her with the same rapacious hunger she'd sensed in him earlier. And, as before, she lost herself in his need and her own. Her arms went around his neck even as his locked behind her. They strained together, mouths and tongues expressing everything they hadn't been able to say with mere words.

Madness claimed them both during the kiss. Unrestrained, uncontrollable madness. It swept away doubts, reservations, inhibitions, leaving in its wake only aching need. "So long," Brett muttered, clasping her fiercely against him. "I've wanted you for so long."

"Brett," she whispered. "I want you, too."

She couldn't remember ever wanting like this, ever needing like this, ever feeling like this. She wasn't certain she'd survive if she acted upon those needs, wasn't sure she'd want to if she didn't. She didn't even know if she had a choice.

Brett seemed to think she did. He pulled back only enough to allow him to see her face. His eyes were dark, turbulent. "Let me love you tonight, Erin. Please."

She caught her lower lip between her teeth, feeling torn. Feeling desire. Fear. Hunger. Uncertainty. Her gaze went to her daughter's bedroom door.

Following the look, Brett seemed to understand. "I won't be here when she wakes up. But please, don't send me away yet."

Through half-lowered lashes, she studied the face that had already become so familiar to her. She no longer felt as though they'd just met. He'd seduced her long before, in intimate, candid conversations, shared laughter, hazy dreams. Seduction of the mind, she realized, could be just as powerful as a conventional courtship. He'd made her want him before she'd ever seen him. Now she could touch him, taste him, feast on the physical attraction of curly hair and golden-brown eyes, masculine dimples and a flashing smile. And she wanted him even more.

She released a sigh of surrender. Or was it anticipation? "I don't want you to go. Not yet."

The words had been a mere whisper, but he heard them. His smile was blinding. He held his hands out to her, and she placed hers in them in an instinctive gesture of trust.

She led him into her bedroom, locking the door behind them, turning to him. The look in his eyes as he undressed her excited her. Her body seemed to delight him more with each inch he uncovered. His murmured praises rippled through her, taking away any shyness she might have felt. She stood proudly before him, letting him take his time exploring her with his eyes and his hands.

He paid slow, loving homage to her full, firm breasts, teasing them with his tongue, then drawing each nipple deeply into his mouth until she was forced to cling to his shoulders for support. Her head fell back and her eyes closed when his hair brushed her bare shoulders as he moved downward, his open mouth trailing a moist path from her breasts to her navel. He paused there only a moment, then dropped to his knees to nuzzle warmly at her thighs and the dark triangle between as he slowly lowered her hose and panties. She bit her lip to hold back a cry of pleasure and anguish, her hands clenching his shoulders convulsively. Unable to bear any more, she tugged at him, urging him back to his feet.

She was on fire when she reached for the buttons of his shirt, craving the feel of him against her. Eagerly she spread the fabric, exposing the warm, glistening skin beneath. His chest was sleek and tanned, and rippled with subtle musculature that testified to his healthy fitness. She drew her palms slowly down from his shoulders to his waist. He held his breath, his eyes heavy lidded, watching her as she'd watched him only moments before. She hoped her pleasure with his body was as obvious to him as had been his delight in hers.

The shirt fell unnoticed to the floor. Brett drew her closer until her breasts lightly brushed his chest. They both caught their breaths in ragged unison at the sensation. His fingers traced her spine from shoulder to hip. Then, molding his hands against her flesh, he pulled her even closer until their bodies were pressed together from breast to knee, with only the fabric of his trousers separating them. Even that was too much—she wanted all of him.

Reaching between them, she tugged impatiently at his belt buckle, making him laugh huskily and move back to give her better access. His laughter had died by the time his slacks and briefs dropped to the floor.

Just as he had explored her, Erin wanted to know every inch of the man whose mind she knew so well. She tasted the corded strength of his neck, feeling the pulse pounding there, reveling in his excitement. She lowered her head to sweep her tongue across his small brown nipples, feeling him flinch in response. He was sensitive there, she observed with delight, tugging delicately at one nub, then the other, with the edges of her teeth. His choked moan made her laugh breathlessly.

"Witch," he accused, bringing her hard against him as he sought and found her mouth with his. She thought fleetingly of the parts of him she had yet to investigate, but then the room tilted around her and she found herself on the bed, with Brett leaning over her. He murmured her name and she held out her arms to him, no longer doubting that this was what she wanted. He paused only long enough to ensure her protection from pregnancy, and then he covered her, his tongue surging into her eager mouth in a bold imitation of the more intimate joining to come.

It was as if it were the first time. New sensations, new emotions flooded her, carrying her higher than she'd ever been. And yet she was grateful for previous experience that had taught her ways of pleasing him in return. She was an active participant in their lovemaking, not a timid recipient. And she did please him. He left her in no doubt about that.

She'd never believed a man could be so generous, so unselfish in his lovemaking. So unconcerned over who was the leader, who the follower. He led her, yet seemed just as eager to grant her every unspoken wish. She'd never imagined her own greed could drive her so relentlessly, nor that her own hunger could make her so anxious to satisfy his.

Their limbs became fluid, their bodies sinuous, as they rolled, shifted, undulated—hands skimming, caressing; mouths seeking, sampling. There were husky moans and urgent whispers, pounding pulses and harsh, ragged breaths. It was pleasure that bordered the boundaries of pain.

Brett's fingers stroked the silky, moist flesh buried in the nest of curls between her legs and Erin arched with a pleading cry. She grasped the heavy, throbbing evidence of his arousal and he shuddered, growling her name.

"Now, Brett," she whispered, clutching frantically at his perspiration-dewed shoulders. "Please. Now."

"I know it's been a long time," he muttered, his muscles rigid with restraint. "I don't want to hurt you."

She wrapped her long legs around his hips and moved enticingly against him. "You won't," she promised. "I need you, Brett. Now."

He groaned and flexed forward. His mouth covered hers when she would have cried out in delirious pleasure, so lost in passion that she'd forgotten the need for discretion. Buried deeply inside her, he paused to allow her to adjust to him. Her heart beating against his, her body entwined with his, Erin opened her eyes to find him looking back at her, his glowing eyes penetrating the shadows surrounding them. And abruptly she realized that what she felt was more—much more—than desire.

Too afraid to put a name to the emotion swelling within her, she squeezed her eyes shut and concentrated on the physical, the definable. She tightened around him, lifting her hips in the initiation of a slow rhythm that he picked up immediately. His hands moved on her and rational thought fled, taking with it the fears that had temporarily assailed her. His head bent to her breast and she bowed beneath him, blindly striving toward something she couldn't understand, having never experienced it before.

"That's it, sweetheart," he murmured, his deep voice barely audible. "Let go. Just let go, Erin. Trust me."

Willingly surrendering the trust he requested, she clung to him in breathless anticipation. And then his fingers slid between them and her entire body strained in reaction. Her toes clenched, her breath locked in her throat, her face flushed with heat. She tried to cry out, but her voice was gone; she could do nothing more than gasp.

The powerful climax rocked her, rippling through her again and again. Hot tears blinded her to everything but the feel of Brett against her, inside her. She wanted to share those incredible feelings with him, wanted him with her on that higher plane of existence. She tightened her legs around his hips, pulling him deeper within her. His muffled groan signaled the beginning of his own release and then he was shuddering in her arms. Tears streaming down the sides of her face, Erin held him more tightly, her heart aching with the love she'd tried so desperately to deny, so vainly to resist.

Afterwards, they didn't sleep, but lay silently wrapped together, slowly recovering. With Brett's heart beating beneath her cheek, Erin closed her eyes and savored. How could she have known it would be like this? How could she have anticipated something she'd never even experienced in dreams? How could she regret knowing such ecstasy, even if only for this one time? She couldn't. Her only regret was that the end had come so quickly.

For just a little while, she hadn't been Erin Spencer. Hadn't been mother or sister or breadwinner or home-maker. For just a little while, she had been someone alto-gether different: a creature of passion, a woman conceived in fantasy, nurtured by love. She wouldn't—couldn't—ex-ist in daylight, but, oh, these moments in the darkness had been glorious!

She smiled and nestled more deeply into his arms, knowing he would soon have to go.

Brett tightened his arms around her, wondering about her silence. Was she sorry that they'd made love? Did she have any regrets? Could she possibly understand the significance of what had happened between them?

Just remembering made his blood start pumping faster again, his body tense. Though he'd thought himself a man of experience—discriminating, but well practiced—he'd never known anything like what he'd just shared with Erin. He'd had sex before, even great sex on occasion. But he'd never made love until Erin.

Already he wanted her again, wanted to know if any-thing could possibly be that spectacular twice. But he had to go. And he still didn't know how she felt about what they'd done.

"Erin?"

She stirred lazily, stretching with feline grace. "Mmm?"

He reached out to snap on the small lamp on the night-stand, causing both of them to blink in its golden glow. "Are you—um—okay?"

She lifted her head to smile radiantly down at him. "Are you kidding?"

He began to relax. "Does that mean yes?"

Chuckling, she dropped a kiss on his lips. "That means I feel wonderful. Glorious. Fantastic!"

Brett blew out a deep breath and made a show of wiping his brow in relief.

Erin laughed softly. "You're so silly. How could you doubt how good it was for me? Couldn't you tell?"

"Honey, I'm still so dazed, I wouldn't be surprised if I'd dreamed the whole thing," he admitted.

She looked surprised, then pleased. "So it was good for you, too?"

Shaking his head in exasperated disbelief, he thought in disgust of her ex-husband. "Sweetheart, it was unbelievable," he assured her. "It's never been that good with anyone before."

What might have been skepticism crossed her face, but then she smiled. "You're very sweet," she told him before kissing him again.

He sighed. How was he supposed to convince her that he wasn't just telling her what he thought she wanted to hear? If he told her what he was really feeling, she'd probably bolt from the room in panic. He didn't think she was ready for the truth. "I guess I'd better go," he said reluctantly, glancing at the clock. "It's getting late."

"Yes." She sounded no more enthusiastic than he had. "How long will you be in town?"

"I haven't decided. I can probably take a couple of weeks off. It's really up to you."

Her eyes widened. "To me?"

He nodded without taking his gaze from her face. "Yes. Do you want me to stay that long? Will you arrange to spend time with me if I do?"

Chewing her lower lip in the gesture he'd already recognized as characteristic, she thought about the question. And then she seemed to reach some conclusion that satisfied her. "Yes," she told him with a nod. "I'd love to spend time with you during the next two weeks. Chelsea attends preschool in the mornings three days a week and I'm usually able to find a baby-sitter for occasional evenings."

He'd almost forgotten her daughter. Hoping she hadn't noticed, he caught her hand in his. "You don't have to find a baby-sitter every time. I don't mind if Chelsea joins us. I'd like to get to know her better."

Erin didn't answer.

Brett began to scowl. "Look, Erin, how many times do I have to tell you that I'm not like your ex-husband? I'm not worried about maintaining some sort of macho image that would be spoiled by the presence of a child. And I'm not like the last jerk you dated. I won't have a tantrum if Chelsea breaks one of my toys."

"I just don't think you understand what it's like to have a three-year-old around for long," Erin countered almost apologetically. "It's a very demanding age. Chelsea's exceptionally well behaved, if I do say so myself, but she's a normal child. She wants attention, and she's sometimes too curious for her own good and—"

"And I'd like to have a chance to find out about her for myself," Brett interrupted. "I'm sure she's as delightful as her mother."

Erin only smiled and kissed him yet again. This time he held her when she would have pulled away, making the kiss a deep, thorough one. He groaned when it ended. "If I don't leave now, I never will. Will you see me tomorrow?"

"Yes. I'll be here in the morning. Chelsea's in preschool from eight-thirty until noon."

He stepped into his slacks and reached for his shirt. "I'll drop by around nine, then."

"All right." She watched as he finished dressing, then walked him to the door. "Drive carefully."

He smiled at the advice that sounded as if it could have come from his sister. And then he kissed her until his ears buzzed, just to make sure she knew there was nothing fraternal about his feelings for her. "Good night, Erin."

"Good night." She watched him step outside, started to close the door, then opened it again. "Brett."

Running a hand through his disheveled hair, he turned on the walk, admiring the way she looked, silhouetted in the doorway in her thin, silky robe. "Yes?"

"I'm glad you're here," she said in a rush. "We're going to have such fun for the next two weeks."

And then she closed the door, leaving him staring wryly at its dark, unrevealing surface.

Fun. The word repeated itself in his mind as he drove toward his sister's house on the mostly deserted streets. It seemed that Erin had forgiven him for descending on her, was even welcoming his presence now. Why did he have the feeling that she was planning on taking a vacation, of sorts, and that he was the resort she'd chosen?

He wasn't particularly pleased by the analogy that had popped into his head. He'd go along with her for now, but he intended to make sure this was one vacation she'd never want to end.

AS PROMISED, BRETT arrived at Erin's house at nine the next morning. Precisely. Her heart beating faster, her stomach clenched in an unexplainable attack of nerves, she cleared her throat and smoothed her embroidered ivory sweater over her jeans before opening the door in response to his knock.

He looked wonderful—his thick hair wind-tossed into an unruly cap of curls, his trim, so-talented body clad in an oversize blue pullover and jeans so tight they were just short of shocking. "Good morning," she said, feeling strangely shy as her gaze met his smiling one.

"You're blushing," he observed in amusement, stepping inside to slip his arms around her waist.

His comment, of course, only made her blush deepen. "Have you had breakfast?" she asked, quickly changing the subject.

He laughed. "Hours ago." And then he kissed her. Thoroughly. "Good morning," he murmured when he finally released her mouth.

That quickly, embarrassment had become searing desire. She clung to his shoulders, trying to stiffen knees suddenly gone weak. "Has anyone ever mentioned," she asked huskily, "that you are one fantastic kisser?"

His eyes darkened. "Never so delightfully," he murmured, drawing her back to him for another long, devastating kiss. By the time it ended, they were both trembling.

Expecting to be hustled straight into the bedroom, Erin blinked in surprise when Brett cleared his throat, stepped out of her reach and waved vaguely toward the front door. "Are you ready?"

She was most definitely ready, but she wasn't certain they were thinking about the same thing. Following his gesture toward the door, she frowned and asked, "For what?"

"Are you ready to go? Need to turn off lights, or get your purse or anything?"

She hadn't known they were going anywhere. Looking longingly toward the bedroom, she stuttered, "Well, I—"

"I'll wait for you outside, okay? I could—uh—use some fresh air." And he all but bolted outside, leaving her looking after him in a mixture of frustration and bewilderment. Would she ever learn to predict this man? she wondered, even as she snapped on her answering machine and went in search of her purse.

Standing on the small porch outside her front door, Brett took several long, deep breaths of warm, late-September air, wishing he'd worn jeans that weren't quite so tight. His aroused state was rather painful, but he took comfort from the knowledge that it would ease. Eventually.

It had been a close call, he thought ruefully, running his fingers through his hair. He'd decided sometime during the night that Erin needed reassurance that he wanted more from her than sex; that they had more than that as a foundation for a relationship. And then he'd nearly blown his own plan by taking her right there on the floor of her living room. *Great willpower, Nash!* he thought in self-disgust.

He turned as Erin stepped out to join him, her beautiful face still a bit dazed and kiss-flushed. And the jeans that had just begun to loosen grew painfully tight again.

It was going to be a *long* day!

THEY SPENT THE MORNING at MacArthur Park browsing through the Arkansas Arts Center and the Museum of Science and History. Brett confessed, to Erin's obvious amusement, that he'd always been fascinated by General Douglas MacArthur, who'd actually been born in the building that now housed the museum.

"Why is it," he mused at one point, studying a studio portrait of the famed military hero, "that I always visualize him looking like Gregory Peck?"

"Possibly because of Hollywood casting?"

Grinning, he glanced at her. "Could be." And then he looked at his watch. "What time are you supposed to pick up Chelsea?"

Catching his wrist so that she could see the time, she sighed. "Soon. We'd better go."

"Yeah." Looping an arm around her waist, he walked with her through the exit. "We'll get the kid and then find a burger joint for lunch. One with a playground. I'll bet she likes those, doesn't she?"

He felt Erin stiffen against his arm, though he didn't release her. "I really wasn't planning on going out to lunch," she murmured.

"You have other plans for the afternoon?"

He studied her face as she prevaricated. "Well, not really, but—"

"Now you do." Without giving her time to answer, he urged her into the passenger side of his car and circled the hood toward his own door. He wasn't exactly sure why Erin seemed so compelled to keep him away from Chelsea, but he was becoming more determined to include her in their activities. How could he show Erin that he could accept her daughter when she never gave him a chance to even talk to the kid?

Reluctantly, as if sensing that his mind was made up and wouldn't be changed without a major scene, Erin gave him directions to Chelsea's preschool. Chelsea seemed surprised, but not displeased to find Brett accompanying her mother. "Hi, Brett! Look at the picture I drawed today."

"Drew," Erin corrected even as Brett examined the colorful drawing of stick figures.

"Chelsea, these are really good," he assured her. "And, trust me, I'm an authority."

Hanging over the seat back beside his shoulder, Chelsea beamed at his praise, but frowned at the wording. "What's a ath-auth—"

"Authority," he repeated clearly. "Someone who knows what he's talking about. I draw people like this all the time. I draw a comic book."

"Yeah?" Tilting her dark head in appraisal, she studied him with huge, dark eyes. "Like the ones Mommy buyed last week?"

"Exactly like the ones your mother bought last week," he assured her gravely, knowing Erin had probably purchased copies of *The Midnight Warrior.* She'd already admitted she didn't read any other comics.

Clearing her throat self-consciously, Erin slid into the front passenger seat and turned to her daughter. "Sit down and buckle your seat belt, Chelsea."

Grinning to himself, Brett waited until the child had complied before turning to look at her, his arm slung casually over the back of the seat. "Want to go out to lunch with us?"

Chelsea bounced twice in approval. "Yes, *sir!*" she answered eagerly.

"You choose. Where's your favorite place to eat?"

Erin groaned dramatically even as Chelsea unhesitatingly named a pizza parlor.

Brett looked questioningly at Erin. "Is there a problem?"

"It's not the best pizza in town," she answered with a grimace. "It's a place custom-designed for kids, and the kids couldn't care less about the food."

"It's really neat, Brett," Chelsea assured him anxiously. "They have games and rides and big puppets that sing and everything. You can play Skee-Ball and win prizes, too."

"Skee-Ball?" Brett repeated, rubbing his jaw. "Gosh, I really love that game."

Erin rolled her eyes. Chelsea clapped her hands. "What are we waiting for?" she demanded.

"We're waiting for your mom to say it's okay," Brett explained, his eyes focused on Erin's face.

She looked impassively back at him for a long moment. Then she sighed and nodded. "All right. Just don't say I didn't warn you."

He only smiled and started the engine.

9

IT WAS LATE AFTERNOON before Erin unlocked her front door, as Brett and Chelsea waited behind her. Chelsea's chubby hands were filled with plastic and stuffed toys from the pizza parlor's selection of prizes, and her face was streaked with the ice cream and candy Brett had insisted on providing despite Erin's protests.

"You might have mentioned," Erin said to Brett when Chelsea dashed to her room with her treasures, "that you'd been to that place a few times before."

Brett grinned. "How'd you guess?"

Erin shook her head, remembering his boyish enthusiasm in the game room, not to mention the money he'd spent on game tokens. Chelsea, of course, had been enthralled. "You tipped me off when you just happened to know the names of all the animated characters on the stage," she answered dryly. "As well as the lyrics to all their songs."

His grin deepening, Brett pulled playfully at a strand of her hair. "I told you Cheryl has two small boys, didn't I? I took my nephews there a few times last year when I visited them."

"I should have known," she said with a sigh. "I should have realized you'd love a place like that."

"I even like their pizza," he confessed cheerfully.

"I noticed." She had been amazed at how much he'd eaten.

"Speaking of food, you wouldn't have any cookies or anything, would you?" he asked, his expression reminding her very much of Chelsea's at times. "Skee-Ball makes me hungry."

She couldn't help smiling. "I'm beginning to think everything makes you hungry."

"You noticed that, too, huh?"

"Did you say cookies?" Chelsea asked from close behind them.

Brett grinned and caught Chelsea up in his arms. "My kind of kid," he informed her, making her giggle as he tossed her into the air.

Instinctively, Erin started to step toward them, but stopped herself just in time. It bothered her that Chelsea was so taken with Brett. She was hungry for masculine attention, having never known her father and seeing her only uncle so rarely. Erin was concerned that Chelsea would be hurt when Brett left. She couldn't even bear to think about how *she* would feel when he was gone.

Trying not to dwell on it, to just enjoy the moment for now, she turned to the kitchen to prepare snacks for Chelsea and Brett.

She hadn't intended for him to stay all day. But then somehow she found herself serving him a steak and salad for dinner while Chelsea chattered happily beside him. Brett was still there when Chelsea's bedtime arrived. Erin led Chelsea to her room, her thoughts already dashing ahead. Was Brett staying to make love to her? He'd been quite restrained during the day, but there'd been times when she'd caught him looking at her with an expression that had stopped her breath in her throat. She'd seen the sensual preoccupation in his eyes, and she had shared it.

And she was deluding herself if she believed she could resist him tonight, particularly now that she knew how fantastic they could be together.

Brett was waiting for her in the living room. He'd made coffee, she noticed. He smiled and nodded toward the cup waiting for her, patting the couch with his right hand to invite her to sit beside him. "You take cream and sugar, don't you?"

"Yes." She settled on the couch and picked up her cup, watching him from beneath her lashes. Lounging against the cushions, Brett looked completely relaxed. If he was only biding his time until pouncing on her, she reflected with a ripple of wry humor, it certainly didn't show in his expression.

"It's been a great day, hasn't it?" he asked, meeting her gaze with a smile.

"A very nice day," she agreed.

Holding his cup in his left hand, he reached out with his right to toy with a strand of her hair—a habit he seemed to have developed during the day. He twirled the dark curl around his finger, then released it, then twirled it again. "You have the softest hair. It's as fine and silky as Chelsea's," he murmured.

She didn't quite know what to say. She took a sip of her coffee.

"Tell me about your work," Brett said unexpectedly, abruptly releasing her hair to wrap both hands around his coffee cup. "How long have you been a commercial artist? Do you ever dabble in other forms of art? Do you have aspirations of being a world-renowned painter?"

Startled into a smile, Erin shook her head. "No. I'll never be a great artist and I'm content with that. I like what I do. It's quite a challenge to take my assignments and make them appealing to the average buyer. I like designing logos, too— coming up with something so eye-catching and unique that it will serve for years to identify the business or product. My friend Corey—I've mentioned her to you before, I think—"

Brett nodded.

"Well, she's a commercial artist, too, but she's the one with the real art talent. Her paintings are spectacular, but I'm afraid she still has a problem with self-confidence. Her family never encouraged her much and she had a professor in college who was a real . . . But you're not really interested in that, are you?" she asked, stopping herself when she noticed that Brett's gaze was focused on her mouth, his attention obviously elsewhere.

He frowned and quickly looked her in the eye. "Of course I am," he argued. "I'm interested in everything about you, including knowing about your friends."

"Well, we always end up talking about me," she argued, trying to ignore the ripples of awareness still cruising through her, all because he'd looked at her mouth. Simply looked at it, she reminded herself in mild disbelief. *Amazing*. "Tell me more about *The Midnight Warrior*. Do you still enjoy drawing it, even after two years?"

"I love it," Brett answered simply. "Those years I spent as a stockbroker nearly did me in. I never quite fit the image. Always drove the wrong car, wore the wrong watch, forgot what labels I was supposed to be wearing inside my clothes. Even worse—" he lowered his voice conspiratorially and leaned closer "—I don't like white wine. Or mineral water."

Erin raised a hand to her throat and looked seriously shocked. "How gauche," she pronounced in tones of dismay.

His eyes smiling at her teasing, he nodded gravely. "Yes, I know. Imagine the looks I got when I ordered domestic beer—or worse, Coke Classic—at the yuppie bars we frequented on Friday nights. And imagine the scorn I encountered when I admitted that my hobby was drawing cartoon characters."

Erin shook her head. "You must have been a real wash-out."

"Hopeless," he agreed solemnly. "I sold a lot of stocks, but of course that's only half the game in that sport."

"I read a couple of your comic books."

"Did you?" He smiled as if he hadn't already guessed. "Did you like them?"

She tried to think of a way to answer without offending him. "Well . . . they were very interesting. And the artwork was amazing. Do you do all the drawings yourself?"

"Yes. What didn't you like about the story lines?" He'd cut right through the "interesting" to the reservations beneath.

She shifted uncomfortably and avoided his eyes. "They're a bit . . . violent, aren't they?"

"In typical comic-book-adventure style, I suppose."

"And would a mild-mannered businessman suddenly turn into a midnight vigilante after the murder of his family? Don't you think this man is really in need of serious counseling?"

Brett only laughed at her hesitant questions. "It's fantasy, Erin," he reminded her. "Typical male-oriented fantasy of good taking on evil and winning one-on-one. Justice, retribution, triumph. I realize that good and evil are rarely as clearly defined as they are within the pages of the comics, but I think there's still a need for that type of escapist adventure. I'll bet you read romance novels," he added with startling accuracy.

Erin had to admit she did.

"And you accuse me of writing improbable fantasies?" he retorted, grinning cockily.

She lifted her chin. "At least women's fantasies don't usually involve mass bloodletting."

"You don't have to defend women's fantasies to me. I'm a great believer in fantasy in any morally and socially acceptable form. Sometimes I think our fantasies are all that keep us sane in an insane world. They're what keep us going, keep us striving, keep us optimistic even after reading a depressingly realistic newspaper from front to back. And, speaking of fantasies . . ." He scooted closer, his expression going from briefly serious to devilishly mischievous.

Holding her half-empty cup of coffee between them, Erin backed away. "Now, Brett—"

"Yes, Erin." Still smiling, he took her cup, set it on the low table in front of the couch and reached for her. "Now."

Obligatory protest out of the way, she settled into his arms with a sense of inevitability. Hadn't she known this was coming? Why not admit that she'd hoped it was? She lifted her face to his.

Fingers spearing into her hair, Brett exhaled deeply, his lips hovering only inches above hers. "I've been wanting to do this all day."

"I've been wanting you to," Erin confessed, sliding her hand to the back of his neck. "Kiss me, Brett."

His mouth covered hers almost before she'd finished saying his name.

Had it only been hours since he'd last kissed her? She threw herself into the embrace as if it had been days, weeks, even longer. He'd kissed her for the first time only the day before and yet she was already seriously addicted. How would she ever live without his kisses when he went back to Boston?

Shoving that depressing thought out of her mind, she snuggled closer into his arms, determined to enjoy every minute she had with him. She sighed into his mouth with pleasure when his hand covered one swelling breast. She fit him quite nicely, she observed, shifting to press herself more snugly into his palm. Thinking back to the night before, she realized contentedly that the words applied in many ways.

"Erin. God, how I want you." Brett's voice was ragged—the deep, husky voice of her telephone fantasy lover. Only then did it occur to her that he sounded quite different in person. She wondered why she hadn't noticed before. And then she forgot to wonder about anything as his weight shifted and they tumbled back into the cushions.

He was heavy and yet gloriously so. Delightfully crushed beneath him, Erin reveled in the sensation as he continued to move his lips over hers, his tongue probing the depths of her mouth. Her body, sexually reawakened after such a long deprivation, flared into overdrive, demanding the fulfillment she'd discovered only the night before. His arousal ground deliciously into her abdomen, telling her that he, too, sought satisfaction. She knew that in granting his, she would find her own.

She thought longingly of her bedroom, the privacy accorded by a locked door, the comfort and convenience of her big bed. "Brett," she whispered, turning her head to free her mouth. "Let's—"

"Mommy?"

The cry made Erin stiffen and her hands move immediately to push against Brett's shoulders. He groaned and rolled to the side, allowing her to slide out from under him.

"Mommy!"

Hesitating only a moment, she glanced at Brett, who lay on his back, one arm over his eyes. "You'd better see about her," he suggested, his voice still gritty from the arousal evident in his rigid body.

Her knees not quite steady, Erin turned and hurried to her daughter's bedroom, wishing she could have seen Brett's eyes. How was he reacting to this interruption? Had it made him more aware of the difficulties of dating a woman with a child? He'd been wonderful with Chelsea earlier, but Chelsea had been on her best behavior, so far. This was reality.

Chelsea was sitting up in her bed, whimpering, one hand pressed to her stomach, the other clutching Belle, the beloved doll Mrs. Price had made for her. "My tummy hurts," she whined the minute Erin stepped into the room. "Make it stop hurting, Mommy."

Erin sighed. She should have been more firm about the ice cream and candy, she thought regretfully, pulling the child into her arms. "Do you feel sick?" she asked, resting her hand against Chelsea's forehead, which felt damp, but cool.

"Maybe," Chelsea moaned, cuddling into her mother's shoulders to make the most of the attention. "It hurts," she repeated.

"What is it?" Brett stood in the doorway, silhouetted by the hall lights behind him.

Erin looked apologetically at him. It hadn't been anything she could have avoided. She'd been as eager as Brett to continue what they'd been doing. "She's not feeling well," she told him.

"What's wrong with her?"

"Her stomach's upset. Too many sweets and too much excitement, I think."

He grimaced. "Oh. Sorry."

"It's not your fault."

Chelsea moaned and buried her face in Erin's shoulder, her doll crushed between them. "I don't feel good," she whimpered, sounding queasy.

Erin looked again at Brett. "This may take a while."

He sighed and walked into the room. "Is there anything I can do to help?"

"Thanks, but no, there's really nothing you can do."

"Then I'll go and let you take care of her." He leaned over to brush a kiss lightly across her lips. "See you tomorrow?"

"I have some things to do tomorrow. Why don't you call in the morning and we'll see what we can work out."

"All right. Good night, Erin." He touched a gentle hand to Chelsea's back. "Good night, Chelsea. I'm sorry you don't feel well."

"G'night, Brett," Chelsea murmured without lifting her face out of Erin's shoulder.

Brett hesitated only a moment longer, then turned and left the room. Slowly rocking her daughter on the edge of the bed, Erin heard the front door close behind him, then the fainter sound of his car starting.

She should have expected this, she thought despondently, rubbing Chelsea's back with a tender hand. She'd known it would happen, of course, but had hoped she'd have at least tonight with him.

She'd fallen in love with him. Real love, this time—not the naive infatuation she'd felt for Martin. She'd probably loved Brett before she'd ever even seen him. She hardly expected anything permanent to come of this whirlwind affair. Nothing about their relationship had been predictable so far, from their initial contact to that unexpected meeting in the park. She didn't know what to expect from the future, except the certainty that their "affair" couldn't last.

She simply didn't know how to deal with a spontaneous, impulsive, footloose type like Brett, endearing as she found those qualities. She knew he wasn't shallow, materialistic and selfish as Martin had been; but would Brett be any more willing to sacrifice his long-accustomed freedom for a life of schedules, regular bedtimes, fun impulses dashed because of the lack of a baby-sitter?

Probably not.

Chelsea moaned and grabbed for her stomach. "Mommy?"

Putting Brett out of her mind to concentrate on more immediate concerns, Erin rose and, carrying her daughter, hurried toward the bathroom.

CHELSEA'S TUMMYACHE turned out to be stomach flu. It lasted forty-eight hours. Erin talked to Brett on the telephone a few times during those two days, but firmly refused to see him. She didn't want him exposed to Chelsea's illness, she said when he offered to come over, and she wouldn't leave her daughter when the child was ill.

"I'd understand, of course, if you have to get back to Boston now," she added, obviously trying to sound casual.

Brett informed her crisply that he would still be in town when Chelsea recovered. "This will give me a chance to visit with Cheryl and the boys," he added. "Why don't you and I plan to have dinner Friday night? Chelsea should be fully recovered by then."

"All right," Erin agreed. "I'll arrange for a baby-sitter."

"I'll call you tomorrow, okay?"

"Sure. Bye."

"Yeah." He hung up with a sigh.

"No one ever said parenthood is a glamorous job," Cheryl reminded him, having entered her kitchen in time to hear the end of the conversation. "I couldn't even tell you the last time Dwayne and I had a weekend to ourselves."

"I'm pond scum," Brett admitted, hanging his head.

Cheryl laughed. "Why is that?"

"I'm actually sitting here being jealous of a three-year-old kid with stomach flu."

Still smiling, Cheryl ruffled his hair, much the same way as she had when they were kids. "Don't feel too badly.

Dwayne feels like that at times. There are just days when we moms have to put the kids first and the grown-up boys second."

Brett scowled at her. "You're patronizing me."

"Yes, I am. So, what are you going to do about it?" she challenged.

Nothing. Absolutely nothing. He was having a good time visiting his family and he'd be seeing Erin Friday.

He intended to make sure it was one evening she'd never forget.

ERIN CHECKED her appearance in the mirror. Brett had told her to wear something sexy. "Not that appearances matter, of course," he'd added, a smile in his voice. "I'd think you were sexy if you were wearing a garbage bag."

She wasn't wearing a garbage bag.

The dress was silver—a glistening, clinging fabric that hugged her from the deeply draped neckline to the knee-length hem. Diamonds glittered at her ears, throat and wrist, rhinestones sparkled in her upswept dark hair, silver sandals with impossibly high heels barely supported her silk-sheathed feet. Her gaze lingered on those sandals. They were definitely sexy. Much better suited to this particular dress than flats. But they would make her at least three inches taller than Brett. Would that bother him? Should she change?

The doorbell rang, letting her know she was out of time. She could still slip the sandals off and . . .

No. Shaking her head in irritation at her own waffling, she turned and headed for the door. She and Brett had agreed that their relationship was based on more than appearances, right? So the disparity in their heights shouldn't matter.

The bell rang again just as she reached for the doorknob. Brett was getting impatient, she thought with a secret smile.

She knew the feeling. It seemed like weeks, rather than days, since she'd seen him.

His eyes rounded when she opened the door. "Remember what I said about appearances not mattering?"

She smiled. "Yes."

"I lied. You're the most beautiful woman I've ever seen. And I love it."

She felt warmth flood her cheeks. She'd heard such compliments in the past, of course. But they'd never meant the same to her before she'd heard them in Brett's voice, before seeing the almost-stunned appreciation in his eyes. "Thank you. You look very handsome, yourself." He looked wonderful, she thought, studying the way his dark suit molded his athletically trim body as he walked past her into the room.

"Where's Chelsea?"

"She went over earlier for hot dogs and a Disney movie before bedtime." Erin had told Brett when they'd made arrangements for the evening that Chelsea would be spending the night with Mrs. Price, though Erin had promised to pick her up early Saturday morning.

"Good. Then I can do this." He slipped one arm around her waist and snagged the back of her neck with his other hand to bring her mouth to his. If it bothered him that he had to reach up a bit to do so, it certainly didn't show in his kiss. He stormed her mouth like a man who'd been starving for her, like a man who delighted in everything about her. She closed her eyes and responded to the embrace with very similar emotions.

Brett's breathing was discernibly accelerated when he drew back. Erin thought hers had stopped altogether.

Brett checked his watch. "Are you ready to go?" he asked huskily, and again she had the impression of impatience.

She nodded and reached for her purse.

They said little during the drive. Erin wasn't particularly surprised when Brett turned into the parking lot of a luxurious downtown Little Rock hotel. After all, the restaurant there was very good, and quite popular. She did lift a questioning eyebrow, however, when he led her to the glass elevators on the opposite side of the lobby from the restaurant entrance and pushed the call button. The only place she knew of upstairs was a piano bar on the top floor. Perhaps they were having drinks before dinner.

Instead, the elevator doors opened onto a floor of rooms. Grinning at her expression, Brett took her elbow and escorted her out of the elevator and down the hallway to a heavy wood door with a discreet brass number plate. He slipped a card into the lock.

Erin couldn't help smiling. Brett was obviously more impatient than she'd guessed earlier. He must have stopped on the way to her house to secure a room. She certainly wasn't complaining, but she'd thought they'd at least have dinner before they—

The sight that greeted her took her breath away again.

The suite's sitting room was gorgeous. Crystal and brass. A pale rose carpet so deep and soft she could have comfortably slept on it. An open doorway gave her a glimpse of a bedroom done in the same elegant theme. In the center of the sitting room was a small round table covered in white linen and beautifully set for two. Champagne cooled in a silver ice bucket. Flowers and candles were everywhere. From somewhere in the background, instrumental music played softly. Rachmaninoff.

She hadn't realized that her eyes had filled with tears until the room blurred in front of her and she was forced to blink to clear her vision. "Oh, Brett."

A trace of uncertainty, a touch of vulnerability that wrenched her heart, colored his voice when he asked, "Do you like it?"

She turned to give him a smile that trembled at the edges. "I love it. No one's ever done anything like this for me before." Though she didn't want to think of her ex-husband just then, she couldn't help thinking that Martin would never have arranged an evening like this. His pleasure in Erin had been showing her off to others, not sharing the intimacy of a candlelight dinner for two.

Brett caught her hand and lifted it to his lips. "I wanted to give you your fantasy," he murmured.

"You have," she whispered, as tears threatened again. "More than once." Didn't he know he *was* her fantasy?

Brett kissed her at the same time the discreet knock sounded at the door. He drew back, smiling. "Dinner is served, I believe."

They lingered a long time over the exquisite meal he'd ordered, talking quietly, savoring tastes and scents and the pleasure of being together.

The champagne bottle was empty, the dessert plates cleared away, the waiters gone before Brett rose from the table. The room seemed to flicker with the illumination of the dozens of candles arranged on every glossy surface, which were also reflected in the depths of his golden-brown eyes when he smiled down at her. And then he shrugged off his dark jacket, draped it over a chair and held out his hand. "Dance with me."

Smiling, she placed her hand in his. A seductively slow instrumental version of "Unchained Melody" had just begun to drift from the hidden speakers. Kicking off her shoes, she stepped into Brett's arms, closed her eyes and enjoyed, not particularly surprised to hear the tune, which was one of her all-time favorites. Such things happened in fantasies.

The carpet was too plush to allow for fancy steps. Erin didn't mind, and was content to sway in Brett's arms, her cheek against his, their bodies pressed so tightly together a breath of air couldn't have passed between them. His hand rested warmly at her waist, then slowly moved inward to the base of her spine, exerting just enough pressure to mold her hips more intimately to his. He was aroused, strongly aroused, but seemed in no hurry to end their leisurely dance.

His slightly ragged breath ruffled the fine hairs at her nape that had escaped her upsweep. She turned her head to taste the firm line of his jaw, her lips nibbling delicately at his smoothly-shaven skin. His responding groan rumbled deep in his chest, vibrating against her. His hand tightened on her back, then slowly slid downward to press against one firm, soft hip through the clinging silver dress.

Erin tickled his right earlobe with the tip of her tongue before catching it briefly between her teeth. Brett swallowed audibly, then released her hand, which he'd been holding in dance position, to place it against his chest before reaching up to her neatly styled hair. The rhinestone clips fell like glistening raindrops around their feet, unnoticed. Freed, her dark hair tumbled to her shoulders. He buried his fingers in it.

She worked her hand between them and tugged at the knot of his silk tie. She left it hanging loose and began to unbutton his shirt, still moving to the strains of the music, brushing her lips across his cheek. She felt Brett tugging at the long back zipper of her dress. She spread the sides of his

shirt at the same time he lowered the dress to her waist and
pulled her close again.

The low front of the silver dress hadn't allowed for a bra.
She was glad, now, that it hadn't. Her unbound breasts, already swelling for his touch, brushed his bared chest, causing them both to shiver in sensual response. Erin slipped her
arms around his neck, beneath the collar of his open shirt,
bringing herself more snugly against him.

"God, I love being alone with you like this," he muttered, his arms drawing her even closer.

He was warm. So very warm. And strong. Pulsingly
strong. She felt the ripple of muscles against her and luxu-
riated in the differences between male and female. How
beautifully they meshed.

The song ended. Another began. In time to the new
song—"Misty," Erin noted distantly—Brett rocked her
against him. He pushed one leg between hers, making her
aware for the first time that he'd lifted her straight skirt to
allow him better access. Her silk-covered legs were exposed to midthigh. His hand slid beneath the hem of her
skirt. He inhaled sharply when he discovered that she was
wearing high-cut bikini panties, a frivolous scrap of a gar-
ter belt, and stockings—which left several inches of thigh
bare to his touch.

"You meant to drive me to the edge tonight, didn't you?"
he asked hoarsely.

"Yes," she answered, then caught his lower lip between
her teeth.

Brett groaned and caught the back of her head to grind
his mouth against hers in a kiss that sent the room spinning
around her. The leg he'd inserted between hers thrust forward at the same time his fingers clenched into her but-
tock, rubbing her aching feminine mound against his rock-

hard thigh. The blatantly sexual move made her shudder, and her fingers dug into his shoulders. "Brett!"

His eyes glinted wickedly when he lifted his head to give her a pirate's smile. "I hope you weren't planning on getting any sleep tonight."

"As a matter of fact, I wasn't," she assured him, her hips moving now without his guidance, her voice thick with a hunger for something totally different from the food they'd just eaten.

"Good," he replied, then covered her mouth with his again.

10

"I HAVE TO GET DRESSED," Erin murmured, expressing regret at bringing an end to the perfect night.

Brett's arm tightened around her bare shoulders. "Don't do that."

She smiled and lifted her head from his chest to look at him. "But I must," she informed him. "I have to pick Chelsea up at nine. I'd like to go home and change first. I don't think I want to go to Isabelle's door dressed in the clothes I left home in last night."

Shifting lazily against the pillows, Brett stroked his hand from her shoulder to her hip, dislodging the sheet that had covered her. "I'd like to keep you here—just like this—forever."

Still smiling, she brushed her mouth against his. "That sounds lovely. But not possible, I'm afraid. I've got a life to get back to. And so do you."

He sighed. "I guess you're right. Dammit."

Her smile faded. "Last night was the most beautiful night of my life, Brett. I want you to know that."

He slid a hand into her tousled hair and pulled her mouth down to his. "Thank you for telling me," he whispered against her slightly swollen lips. "It was for me, too."

The kiss was deep and tender. They'd kissed many times during the long, glorious night—too many times to count—and yet this one was different. This one said things Erin wasn't sure she was ready to hear. She drew back, shaken, her smile wavering. "I have to get dressed," she repeated, avoiding his eyes as she scooted toward the side of the bed.

The reflection she saw in the bevel-edged bathroom mirror made Erin moan in dismay. She looked...she looked... She looked as if she'd just spent a long night making strenuous, passionate love. Which, of course, she had.

She showered quickly, scrubbing away her faded makeup. Then she pulled a comb through her tangled hair and stepped back into the silver dress that was so appropriate for the evening, so unsuitable for the dawn. She carried a few cosmetics in her purse; she used them now to conceal, as best she could, the evidence of the long hours with little sleep. Studying her image again, she decided she looked better than she had earlier. Not her best, certainly, but at least presentable.

The blessedly welcome scent of coffee greeted her when she stepped back into the bedroom. Wearing a thick terry robe provided by the hotel, Brett smiled and held out a filled cup. "I thought you might like to have coffee while I shower," he said. "They just brought it up."

"Thank you," she breathed, eagerly accepting the delicate cup from him. "I really need this."

"I ordered croissants, too. Help yourself. I won't be long." Giving her a smile over his shoulder, he disappeared into the bathroom. Her gaze lingering on the closed door, Erin remembered a long, lazy bath sometime during the night in a marble tub that had simply begged to be shared. A shiver of arousal coursed down her spine. It would be a long time, if ever, before she could remember last night without reacting quite physically, she realized.

She heard the shower start as she stirred sugar and cream into her coffee. Sipping her coffee, she reminded herself that the night was over. It was time to get back to reality. And reality was Chelsea, probably waiting impatiently for her mother to come home.

Brett came back into the room with his hair damp, wearing only the slacks from his suit and his dark socks. In reaction, Erin's fingers clenched around her coffee cup, and suddenly she was all too aware of the wildly rumpled bed temptingly beside her. She tried to ignore it. "There's still hot coffee in the carafe," she said, hoping her voice sounded normal enough.

He slipped his arms into the sleeves of his shirt. "Thanks, but I had a quick cup while you dressed. I don't need any more right now."

She set her own empty cup on the table. "Then I guess we should go."

Shoving his feet into his shoes with somewhat more force than necessary, he nodded and reached for his coat and tie. "Yeah, I guess we should. It's almost seven."

She didn't like the sudden awkwardness between them, the uncharacteristic lack of expression in his eyes. It was as if he were deliberately distancing himself from her for some reason. Had he reached the same conclusion she had? That it was time to put the night behind them and get back to reality? That the fantasy had ended?

Casting one last look at the bed, Erin stepped into the sitting room and walked toward the door to the hallway. She'd just reached it when Brett's hand fell on her shoulder, turning her around to face him. Leaning into her, pressing her back against the door, he framed her face in his hands and kissed her until they were both gasping for air.

"Now we can go," he told her when he finally drew away.

She moistened slightly swollen lips with the tip of her tongue. "Yes," she repeated dazedly. "Now we can go."

As they walked out into the corridor and closed the door of the suite behind them, Erin wondered if anyone ever had the chance to visit paradise twice in one lifetime. Once a fantasy had ended, could it ever be replayed? Or was it destined to remain only in heartrending memories that would haunt her for the rest of her life?

BRETT WATCHED AS Erin unlocked her door. He'd already assured her that he wouldn't be staying, but he had no intention of leaving without one last kiss shared out of range of curious eyes. He noted with almost-idle interest that his body, thoroughly sated by a night of lovemaking like nothing he'd ever experienced before, still responded when she brushed against him as he held the door open for her. *Amazing.*

She turned to him as soon as they'd entered her living room. He couldn't stop looking at her. She was so lovely, even with her eyes a bit shadowy from a near-sleepless night, her hair falling in sexy disarray around her face and shoulders, her silver dress somewhat wrinkled. Those reminders of their night together only made her more beautiful to him.

He loved her. Last night had only confirmed what he'd already suspected. He loved her as he'd never even dreamed of loving a woman before.

He couldn't help wondering how that love was going to change his life.

Seeming to grow uncomfortable because of the intensity of his gaze, Erin glanced away. "I'd better change and get Chelsea."

"I know." He caught her hands in his, still unable to stop himself from staring at her lightly flushed face. "Dinner tonight?"

"I can't leave Chelsea with a baby-sitter again tonight."

He frowned impatiently. "Of course not. I'm not asking you to. We'll take her with us."

"I don't think so. After spending the night with Isabelle, Chelsea will need a quiet evening to settle into her normal routine. We'll probably turn in early. To be honest, I could use the rest."

He waited for her to invite him to join them for the quiet evening. His frown deepened when she didn't. "I'll call you later, then. Okay?"

She nodded and he thought he detected a hint of relief in her eyes. Had she expected him to push? "All right. Thanks again for the beautiful evening."

"No," he murmured, tugging at her hands to pull her close. "Thank you, Erin." He kissed her slowly, reluctant to step away from her.

She was the one who finally pulled back. "See you later, Brett."

"Yeah." He shoved his hands into his pockets. "See you, Erin." *The next time you'll allow it,* he added silently and with a degree of resentment that rather surprised him.

Maybe it was best that they spend a few hours apart, he decided as he backed his rented car out of her driveway. After their night of loving, his emotions were a little too close to the surface, a bit too raw. He could use the next few hours to regain some emotional distance, to think logically about what he wanted to do now that he'd acknowledged his love for Erin.

Cheryl was serving breakfast to her husband and sons when Brett let himself into her house. The family had obviously slept in on this nice Saturday morning. Brett was vividly conscious of his rumpled clothes from the night before as four pairs of curious eyes turned his way.

"So there you are," Cheryl murmured, grinning at Brett's expression. "Should I ask if you had a good time?"

Dwayne, the husky six-two redhead who'd married Brett's sister seven years earlier, shot a look of warning at his irrepressible wife. "Now, Cheryl, don't start on him."

Cheryl widened her brown eyes in exaggerated innocence. "But, Dwayne, I was only trying to make conversation."

"Yeah, sure you were."

"Did you go to a sleep-over party, Uncle Brett?" five-year-old Danny asked. "How come you didn't take extra clothes?"

"Didn't you even take your pj's?" four-year-old Kevin asked, studying his uncle's empty hands.

Brett cleared his throat, glaring at his giggling sister. "If everyone will excuse me, I believe I'll go change now."

"Why don't you do that," Cheryl agreed. "Then come back down and I'll make you something to eat."

Knowing he was in for an interrogation, Brett took his time changing into jeans and a cotton-knit sweater. He wasn't sure how much he wanted to tell Cheryl about his relationship with Erin. It would be nice to talk about it, share his confusion and uncertainty with someone who cared. But how could he put into words what he didn't understand completely himself?

He'd hoped her husband and children's presence would serve as a buffer—at least temporarily—from her questions. He was surprised to find her alone in the kitchen when he went back downstairs. "Where are Dwayne and the boys?"

"Dwayne had to run to the store for a part for the car. The boys went with him." She motioned him to a chair at the kitchen table and slid a coffee mug in front of him. "How do you want your eggs?"

"However you want to make them." He sipped his coffee, remembering that first cup he'd downed while Erin had showered and dressed. It had been all he could do then to prevent himself from joining her in the shower. He knew that if he had, they'd still be in the hotel suite.

He sighed.

"Want to talk about it?" Cheryl asked quietly, setting a well-filled plate in front of him.

He'd expected teasing, not obvious concern. He cocked an eyebrow in question. "Do I have a choice?"

"Of course, you do. Have I ever interfered in your life?" she asked indignantly.

He only looked at her.

She had the grace to blush. "Well, if you want me to stay out of it, just say so."

He reached across the table to pat her hand apologetically. "No, it's okay. I'm just a little shell-shocked this morning."

"Shell-shocked? Was the night that good?"

"Better," he muttered, spreading margarine on a slice of toast.

"This is getting serious, isn't it? I mean, really serious."

"It *is* serious. Really serious," he added in a weak imitation of her. "And I don't for the life of me know quite what to do about it."

"You're falling in love with her?"

"You may as well use the past tense. I fell. I tumbled. I went down for the count."

"You love her," Cheryl translated.

"I love her." He took a bite of toast.

"And?"

He swallowed the toast along with a slug of coffee. "And?"

"What *are* you going to do about it?"

"I—uh—I think I'm going to ask her to marry me," Brett answered slowly, as if even he didn't believe he was actually saying those words. He was rather dazed at hearing them coming from his own mouth.

Cheryl's lips twitched with the smile she considerately suppressed. "You think?"

"Well, yeah. I mean, it's only been a week since I first laid eyes on the woman," he temporized, dragging his fork through his eggs to keep from looking at his sister.

"So why did you really come to Arkansas, Brett?" she asked perceptively.

He sighed. "I think I came to ask her to marry me."

"Before you'd ever even set eyes on her?"

"Well, at least I came to see if the possibility existed that we— Oh, hell, Cheryl, I think I fell in love with her the first time I talked to her on the phone. It was like something just clicked—something I'd been waiting for for so long that I didn't have any trouble at all recognizing it when it hit me. I don't want to live without her anymore. I don't want our relationship to consist of telephone calls and stolen weekends. You know?"

She smiled tremulously, lovingly. "I know. And I'm so happy for you."

He grimaced. "Don't start throwing rice yet. I haven't asked her. I haven't even mentioned the possibility. I don't think Erin's even thinking beyond this weekend. She'd probably bolt in panic if I mentioned marriage."

"Because she doesn't know you well enough?"

"There's that. And she doesn't trust me," he added reluctantly.

Cheryl sat up straighter, immediately defensive. "Doesn't trust you about what?"

"Her daughter. She doesn't think I understand what's involved in raising a child."

Cheryl suddenly looked thoughtful. "Oh. I guess I'd sort of forgotten about Chelsea."

He grimaced. "I've done that once or twice myself."

"Oh, Brett. I can't say I don't understand Erin's fears. I'm a mother. I know what's involved. I know that you don't, because you've never had to deal with it. It isn't easy to raise a child. It's a full-time, lifelong commitment, taking precedence over everything else for years to come. You've been so footloose and responsibility free for the past few years. Are you sure you want to give that up for an instant family? Are you sure you can offer Chelsea the kind of love and commitment she deserves from a stepfather?"

Stepfather. The word made a bite of egg stick in his throat. Brett hastily washed it down, asking himself the same questions. He knew how he felt about Erin. He loved her. He wanted her. Always. And, to be painfully honest, he wanted her all to himself. He was selfish enough and newly enough in love that he wanted to smuggle her away from everyone else, wanted to hoard her like a treasure he'd discovered after years of searching. Sharing her with a three-year-old—a child who'd always take first priority with her—wouldn't have been his first choice.

But Chelsea existed, and Erin was a good mother. A wonderful mother. He admired her dedication to her daughter, the sacrifices she'd made to compensate for her poor choice of a father for her child. She wouldn't be the woman he loved if she were any different. Could Brett possibly be as selfless—for a child he hadn't fathered, hadn't spent nearly four years growing to love? She *was* a beautiful child—bright, inquisitive, well behaved, enjoyable. But he'd only been with her for a few hours. And already she'd come between him and Erin on more than one occasion. What would it be like to share Erin with her full-time? Would Chelsea be any happier about sharing than Brett was?

"I feel like a heel," he muttered, furious with himself for having such doubts. "No better than her selfish creep of an ex-husband."

"You're wrong there," Cheryl defended him firmly. "It's only human to ask yourself questions before taking a step this momentous, but you're nothing like the man you told me about. He's a shallow, insensitive, self-glorifying playboy. You're a kind, loving, generous man with a heart big enough to hold a dozen children if you choose."

"And you're just a bit biased," Brett reminded. He shoved his half-empty plate away and leaned both elbows on the table, looking to his older sister for advice for the first time in years. "What should I do, Cheryl?"

"The obvious answer is to spend more time getting to know both Erin *and* Chelsea," Cheryl answered briskly. "You'll never know how you feel about parenting until you give it a shot, will you?"

"Erin's not being particularly cooperative in that area," Brett admitted wryly. "She's worried that Chelsea will be hurt if things don't work out between us. She's had some unhappy experiences with guys treating Chelsea badly."

"Then the time you spend with them will also have to convince Erin that you know what you're getting into and that you can handle it. How long can you stay?"

"I can probably swing another week. But I hate to impose on you and Dwayne. I can get a room—"

"You'll do no such thing! We love having you here. You're my brother, for heaven's sake."

He smiled for the first time since sitting down. "Thanks, sis."

"You're welcome. And when are you going to introduce me to this woman?"

"Soon. I hope."

"Good. I'm dying of curiosity."

His smile deepened. "You'll like her, Cheryl. She's really very special."

Cheryl returned the smile affectionately. "She must be." And then she turned her head as the sound of car doors slamming came from outside. "Dwayne and the boys are home. So much for a chance to talk in peace."

Brett chuckled and stood to put his breakfast dishes in the dishwasher. Behind his show of amusement, however, lay a deep-seated concern about his future. Would he leave Arkansas a happy man, content with the family fate had brought him? Or would he leave a shard of broken heart behind if he and Erin couldn't work things out between them?

For one of the first times in his life, happy-go-lucky Brett Nash found himself afraid.

CHELSEA WAS ALREADY asleep and Erin had just gotten ready for bed when the telephone rang. Smiling at the familiar routine, she picked up the receiver of her bedside phone. "Hello?"

"I miss you."

Brett's deep voice coursed through her like the expensive champagne they'd shared the night before. She closed her eyes and gave herself up to the intoxication. "I miss you, too."

"How's Chelsea?"

It pleased her that he asked about her daughter so quickly, though she couldn't help wondering if that had been his intention. "She's fine. She and Isabelle had a wonderful time together last night. She's been talking about it all day."

"Is she asleep now?"

"Yes."

"And where are you?"

"I was just getting into bed," Erin admitted, curling her feet beneath her.

"So—uh—what are you wearing?" Brett inquired, hoarsely nonchalant.

She glanced down at her French silk nightgown with a slight smile. "Nothing much."

Brett moaned.

Erin's smile widened. "Is this an obscene telephone call?"

"It might become one if we don't change the subject. How about going to the fair with me tomorrow?"

"The fair?" Erin repeated, surprised.

"Yeah. The Arkansas State Fair. It's in full swing at the fairgrounds in Little Rock, you know. The boys have been talking about it all day. They wanted to go tonight, but Cheryl and Dwayne had to attend some kind of awards ceremony for the police department. I kept the little monsters for a couple of hours. Anyway, Dwayne has to work tomorrow, but as a bribe for one entire evening of exemplary behavior, I promised the boys I'd take them to the fair tomorrow afternoon. I'd like for you and Chelsea to come, too."

"I—uh—"

"It'll be fun. I love fairs. And Chelsea will like the boys. They're pretty decent kids. In fact, she can bring a friend and they can have a munchkin double date. What do you say?"

"I can't believe you're trying to fix up my three-year-old daughter," Erin accused him, swallowing a laugh.

"Hey, she and Kevin will be perfect for each other. Trust me. Of course, he's a little young to get a job—he's only four—so they'll probably have to move in with you after they're married, but I'm sure you're about ready for grandkids to spoil, right?"

The laugh escaped in a ripple of giggles. "You're insane, do you know that?"

"It's been suggested a few times. I like to think of it as artistically eccentric. So, is the answer yes?"

"Yes," she replied, quickly, because she really wanted to go. Chelsea would love the fair. And Erin would be with Brett again. How could she turn him down?

"Guess we'd better get some rest," Brett suggested, obviously reluctant to end the call. "Three kids under six at the fair may be just a bit strenuous."

"Oh, just a bit."

"Good night, then. Dream of me."

"I have been. For months," Erin murmured. Something about Brett made it hard for her to remember to be circumspect.

"Damn, I wish I were with you." The words were little more than a groan.

There was a long moment of silence, and then Brett muttered a hasty "Good night" and hung up.

Erin was breathing raggedly when she recradled her own receiver. She turned with a sharp exhalation to bury her face in a pillow, trying to pretend she was snuggling into Brett's arms.

ALMOST BESIDE HERSELF with excitement, Chelsea could hardly stand still long enough for Erin to help her dress for the fair. These last September days were warm, though the nights were turning cooler. To accommodate the weather, Erin dressed her daughter in layers of brightly colored knits, folding a jacket into the tote bag she would carry at the fairgrounds. She looped Chelsea's silky dark hair into a neat French braid to keep it out of the way, clipping a hot-pink bow at the nape. "You look adorable," she said, indulging herself with one long hug.

Chelsea wriggled impatiently. "Is it time to go yet? When's Brett going to be here?"

"Soon," Erin promised, standing to smooth her light-weight purple-splashed black sweater over her black acid-washed jeans. She put a hand to her own French braid to make sure it was still neat. It was.

"Can I take Belle? She'll love the fair."

"I'm afraid she would get dirty, Chelsea. Why don't you just tell her all about it when you get back?"

Chelsea sighed but agreed. "Maybe Brett will win me a teddy bear," she said. The ragged three-foot-tall stuffed dog Adam had won for her on a brief visit last year sat proudly in a corner of her bedroom.

"Now, Chelsea—"

The doorbell rang before Erin could deliver the lecture she'd intended. "Just don't pester Brett to play the games, you hear?"

"Yes, ma'am. Aren't you going to get the door?" Chelsea hopped from one sneakered foot to the other as she pushed her mother.

Erin headed for the door. She could only hope Brett's nephews proved enough distraction that Chelsea wouldn't drive Brett crazy with demands for his attention.

Danny and Kevin, two cute denim-clad redheads who hadn't yet entered the girls-are-yucky stage, took one look at dark-haired, dark-eyed Chelsea and fell in love. Both of them. A spirited competition for her attention began almost immediately. Erin smiled, aware that Chelsea would be quite happily diverted for the afternoon.

Brett grinned cockily, watching his nephews' macho posturings. "What'd I tell you? You should have brought another hot babe. Chelsea's going to have her hands full."

Erin watched as Chelsea smiled through long, dark lashes at Kevin before turning with interest to Danny. "I think she can handle it," she remarked dryly.

"I can tell we're going to have to keep a close eye on her in the future," Brett murmured, then immediately opened the door. "Ready to go? We're burnin' daylight," he added in his best John Wayne imitation.

Dazed by his subtle insinuation that he'd be around in Chelsea's future, Erin smiled weakly and reached for her tote bag before herding the children outside to the car. She decided not to think about his words at the moment. She'd save them for later, when she was alone.

ERIN HAD ALWAYS LOVED the fair. The smells and sounds took her back twenty years to her own childhood, when Adam had escorted her and her mother around the midway, making sure Erin had every snack she craved, rode every ride, owned every prize he could win for her. Staring at the crowded merry-go-round, she could almost see herself sitting on a pink horse beside her rather embarrassed teenage brother on his purple one. She blinked back tears.

"Erin? What's wrong?" Brett demanded.

She smiled and shook her head. "I was just thinking of times I used to come to the fair with Adam. He was so sweet to me. I thought he was the best big brother in the world. I think he must have been."

Brett took her hand, keeping his eyes on the three hand-linked children hurrying through the sawdust just ahead of them. "You're really close to him, aren't you?"

"He was the closest I had to a father when I was growing up," she answered candidly. "I adored him. I suppose it's safe to say I still do. He made so many sacrifices for me. Took care of me so well."

"He let you marry Martin," Brett grumbled.

"He couldn't have stopped me," she assured him.

Brett grimaced in mute apology. "Sometimes I'm a bit jealous of him," he admitted.

"Jealous of my brother?" Erin repeated in astonishment. "Why?"

"I guess you'd have to hear the way you talk about him to understand. So, where do you think the kids would like to begin? Rides or animal exhibits?"

"Rides!" all three children simultaneously cried out.

Brett grinned and allowed himself to be guided through the crowds toward the section of small-children's rides. While he was busy convincing Danny that some of the larger rides were too dangerous for five-year-olds, Erin considered what he'd said about Adam.

Seconds later, she decided she'd think about that later, too. She had the entire afternoon to spend with Brett. She wasn't going to spoil it by analyzing everything he said.

11

THEY STAYED AT THE FAIR until after dark. Even then, they had to practically drag the grubby, exhausted children away. Brett carried Chelsea to the car, both boys stubbornly proclaiming they were too old to be carried. All three were asleep before Brett had navigated the crowded, narrow Roosevelt Road to the freeway that would take them into North Little Rock.

"They're out," Erin stage-whispered, looking over her seat at the snoozing trio in the back, held upright only by their seat belts as they nodded bonelessly, surrounded by stuffed animals, balloons and toys. Brett had spent a small fortune on the kids, refusing to allow Erin to contribute a dime. She knew none of the children would ever forget this outing.

"Whew!" Brett breathed. "I didn't think they'd ever run out of energy. Lord knows, I did a long time ago."

She smiled. "I thought you kept up admirably well."

"I was trying to impress you with my stamina," he replied with a suggestive grin.

"You did that Friday night," she shot back, making him laugh softly and reach for her left hand with his right.

"You're good for my ego, Erin Spencer," he told her, bringing her knuckles to his mouth to brush them with his lips.

Her fingers curled around his.

None of the children awoke when Brett pulled into Erin's driveway and killed the engine. He walked around the car

to open the back door. Handing Erin Chelsea's goodies in
the big plastic bag they'd obtained at the Hall of Industry,
he unbuckled Chelsea's seat belt and slid his arms beneath
her. He lifted her without waking her, nestling her head into
his shoulder. Erin had to swallow a sudden lump in her
throat at the sight of him holding her daughter so comfortably.

"The boys will be okay while you carry her in?" she asked,
looking at his sleeping nephews. "I really can manage her
alone if you—"

"They'll be fine," he assured her. "I'm only going to carry
her inside and then I'll come right back out. Besides, your
hands are full."

She had to admit he was right. Between the tote she'd
carried and the stuff Chelsea had hauled home, she never
could have made it alone, despite her claim.

Following Erin's instructions, Brett deposited Chelsea on
her bed on top of the bedspread. "I'll have to clean her up
and change her into pajamas," Erin explained, setting the
enormous bear he'd won next to the big dog in the corner
of the room. There was something symbolic about Brett's
prize sitting next to Adam's in her daughter's room, she was
sure, but she was simply too tired to think about it now.

"Guess I'd better go, then. Cheryl will be worrying about
the boys."

Erin walked him to the front door. They lingered there in
a moment of silence, the usual disinclination to part hanging between them. It was getting harder each time to say
good-night, and Erin read the same sentiment in Brett's sober eyes. "Thank you for taking us today," she told him,
clinging to his hand. "Chelsea had a wonderful time, and I
did, too."

"Me, too," he agreed. "Even when I nearly got sick on the
Tilt-A-Whirl ride with Danny."

She smiled faintly, remembering how green Brett had looked when he'd staggered off the ride. Only then had he admitted that he had problems with rides that spun in circles. She'd thought it sweet that he'd ridden a "grown-up" ride to please his oldest nephew even though he'd known it would be difficult for him. "You were wonderful," she assured him.

"I wasn't half-bad, was I?" he replied cockily. "Did you hear that woman tell me what a good father I was?"

"Yes, I heard her." Erin clearly remembered the incident. Kevin had tripped over a power cord and scraped his hands. Obviously embarrassed to cry in front of Chelsea, whom he was trying so hard to impress, he'd turned to Brett for help. Brett had scooped the boy onto his shoulder and headed for the rest room, "To help him wash up," he'd called back, giving Kevin a few moments of privacy to recover.

Having seen the whole thing from her booth, one of the fair employees had complimented Brett when he'd returned with a smiling child. "I've seen fathers yell at their sons for crying and making the kids even more humiliated," she'd added, scowling. "Nice to see a young dad like you who understands that sometimes a kid needs to cry without being embarrassed about it."

Brett had blushed faintly with pleasure, twisting Erin's heart with pride for him. It hadn't been the only time during the evening they'd been taken for a family. There'd even been a few raised brows that Erin had interpreted as consternation at how closely the three children were spaced. She might well have had another child soon after Chelsea, as Brett's sister had done having her two, if Martin had been the type of man who loved children the way Erin did. Many times she'd regretted that Chelsea might never have a brother or sister. Erin had thought her longing for another child had been put firmly behind her. Admittedly her maternal instincts were as active as ever.

These were very dangerous thoughts, she decided, shoving them away. "You'd better go. The boys will be frightened if they wake up alone in the car," she urged him.

"I know. I'm leaving." He kissed her, then opened the door. He'd just stepped outside when he turned and looked back at her. "Erin?"

"Yes?"

"What do *you* think about what that woman said? Do you think I'd be a good father?"

"I—uh—" Her throat tightened. Just how was she supposed to answer? Was his question only hypothetical or did he have something more personal in mind? "I think you'd make a wonderful father," she answered honestly. "If you'd decided that was what you wanted."

He smiled, obviously pleased. "Thanks. I'll call you tomorrow."

"All right. Good night, Brett." She closed the door before he could make any other unsettling remarks.

She thought about his words as she undressed her sleepy daughter and used a soapy washcloth before placing limp, weary limbs into the sleeves of a pair of soft pajamas. "Good night, sweetheart," she murmured, putting her partially clean child into bed and kissing her chubby cheek.

"Night, Mommy," Chelsea mumbled, half asleep. "I liked the fair."

"I'm glad. See you in the morning."

"Mommy?" Chelsea asked just as Erin was about to step out of the room.

"What is it, Chelsea?"

"Could Brett stay with us forever? I like him."

It must be the night for questions that knocked the breath right out of her, Erin thought, her hand tightening on the doorknob. "We'll—um—we'll talk about it later. Okay, sweetie? Go to sleep now."

"Okay. I love you, Mommy."

"I love you, too, baby."

Just what was Brett planning for them? Erin asked herself as she lay in bed later, staring at the darkened ceiling, so tired and yet too disturbed to sleep. She knew Brett would have to go back to Boston soon, though he'd avoided the issue so far. What then? A long-distance affair? Would either of them be content with their frequent telephone calls, perhaps an occasional visit? Would he ask her to go with him when he left? He hadn't mentioned marriage, hadn't even told her he loved her. So, what had he meant by that question about whether he'd make a good father?

Did Brett love her? There were times when she was convinced he must. The way he looked at her, the way he touched her, the way he'd made love to her Friday night—all night. Yet he'd never said the words.

She loved him. More deeply each hour she spent with him. She couldn't bear the thought of parting from him, going back to knowing him only as a voice over the telephone line. And yet—marriage? Uprooting herself and her child from the only state either of them had ever lived in and moving to a new town to start a new life with a man she had known such a relatively short time? How could she even think about doing that? Chelsea would be devastated if things didn't work out after such a drastic step. And Erin would very likely be destroyed by the shattering of another dream.

She tried to calm herself with the reminder that Brett hadn't asked her to marry him, that she was anticipating problems. Somehow she didn't find much comfort in that. If not marriage, what did he want for them? Or did he intend to tell her goodbye for good when he left Arkansas?

Had this only been a vacation affair, a pleasant interlude before getting back to his real life? No, she couldn't find any comfort at all in that possibility.

The telephone rang at ten-thirty, just as her eyes were drifting shut. She turned to reach for the phone. She hadn't expected Brett to call tonight. She wasn't sure if she was pleased that he had. "Missing me already?" she asked lightly, trying to hide her anxiety behind flippancy.

"I miss you frequently," the male voice answered dryly. "But for some reason I don't think that question was directed at me."

She relaxed into the pillows. "Adam! I wasn't expecting it to be you."

"Obviously. So who did you think it was—as if I didn't know?"

"Brett," she admitted. She'd told Adam Brett's name several weeks earlier, after learning it herself, though she'd warned her brother then that she still didn't want him interfering in the unusual relationship.

"Yeah. That's what I thought. So your telephone romance is still going strong, I take it?" He made little effort to hide his disapproval.

"It's a little more than that now," Erin conceded. "Brett's here. Well, not *here*, but in Arkansas. He's staying with his sister."

There was a moment of silence, and then, "How long has he been there?"

"A week yesterday."

"How long's he staying?"

"I'm . . . not sure. Another week, maybe."

"And?"

"And what?"

"What's going on between the two of you?"

Erin bristled. "That's really none of your business," she told him crisply.

"Look, it's only natural that I would have concerns about this. It's not like this is the most normal courtship on record, you know. I mean, he seems okay—makes a good living, stays out of trouble, pays his bills and taxes—but you really don't—"

"Dammit, Adam, you checked him out, didn't you?" Erin interrupted furiously. "You promised you wouldn't do that."

"No," he reminded her. "I didn't. You ordered me not to, but I never promised I wouldn't."

"Why?"

"Look, Erin, I've been watching out for you since you were a baby. Just because we don't see each other very often now doesn't mean I can break that habit. I let you down with Martin. I don't want to see you get hurt again."

"You didn't let me down, Adam," Erin argued, remembering that Brett, too, had implied that Adam should have interfered with her disastrous marriage. Why couldn't either of them see that she had to make her own mistakes, had to be responsible for her own life? That she was an adult, capable of taking care of both herself and her child?

"Erin, I love you. I'm concerned about you. Is that so terrible?"

Weakened, as always, by his sincerity, Erin sighed. "No, Adam. It's not terrible. I love you, too, even when you're being arrogant and overprotective. But you have to let me make my own decisions, Adam. Give me credit for knowing what's best for me, will you?" She could almost laugh at her own words—she only wished she *did* know what was best for her.

"All right. So tell me about Brett. What's he like?"

She smiled. "He's wonderful. Funny and charming and thoughtful."

"Does Chelsea like him?"

"Very much. Particularly after today. He took us to the state fair. His nephews came along. They're five and four and they both want to marry Chelsea."

Adam groaned. "You mean, now I have to start worrying about her love life, too?"

She laughed. "It's okay, Uncle Adam. I think you've got a few years before you have to worry seriously about her."

"So the fair was back in town, huh? I'm sorry I couldn't have been there to go with you this year."

"So am I. I thought of you often today."

"I'm glad." There was a comfortable pause filled with happy memories before Adam spoke again. "You'll call me if you need me for anything?"

"Of course I will. Are you going to be in the country for a while?"

"A few more weeks, probably."

"Good. I hate it when you leave. I always worry so about you."

"I know. It comes with the territory of family."

"Yes," she agreed, catching his hint. "I know it does. I love you, Adam."

"Love you, too, sis. Just be careful, okay?"

"You, too. Bye."

"Yeah." He hung up without further comment—Adam never said goodbye.

Surprisingly enough, Erin fell asleep quickly after Adam's call. The questions, the worries were there at the back of her mind. But she pushed them aside, choosing, instead, to snuggle into the warm feelings remaining from a day with Brett and a call from her brother.

THOSE QUESTIONS and worries haunted her during the next few days, when Brett seemed determined to insinuate himself into her life as deeply as possible. Painfully aware of how much she'd miss him when he was gone, Erin tried at first not to get too accustomed to having him around. She quickly gave up that effort as futile. She loved having him around. She wanted him around all the time.

Twice during the week he took her out alone, leaving Chelsea with a baby-sitter. The other nights he spent at her house with the two of them, sharing meals and television programs, staying after Chelsea's bedtime to make love with Erin until—in deference to Erin's wishes—he forced himself to leave before Chelsea awoke.

FRIDAY MORNING, while Chelsea was in preschool, Erin drove into west Little Rock for her appointment with her optometrist, guiltily aware as she did so that she'd been letting her work slide while Brett was in town. She had to get busy again to make her deadlines and earn the salary she needed to support her daughter. She suspected that Brett would be leaving Sunday or Monday. She'd get right back to work after he left. She would need the work to keep her from sitting around missing him.

"Well, you were right, Erin. Your prescription does need to be changed," the optometrist, an attractive blonde in her early thirties, confirmed an hour later. "No wonder you were having headaches after a day at the drawing board. Your eyes were going into accommodation spasms."

Erin smiled at the woman who'd been taking care of her eyes for several years. "I won't even ask what that means."

"I'd be happy to explain," Dr. Spring McEntire assured her, sitting back on her stool with a smile, and indicating a technical-looking chart on her clipboard.

Erin shook her head. "I probably wouldn't understand if you did. Just write me a prescription and I'll wear the glasses."

The other woman laughed. "It's nice to know you have such faith in my judgment."

"Why shouldn't I?" Erin countered. "You've never given me any reason to doubt you." She looked around the examining room, smiling at the photograph displayed proudly on a shelf above the desk. "Your son is really growing," she remarked, studying the golden-haired, four-year-old sitting in a handsome blond man's lap, both of them dressed in bright, eye-catching colors. "He looks exactly like his father, doesn't he?"

"Identical," Spring agreed with a wry smile. "And they're just alike in other ways, too. I've really got my hands full with the two of them."

Erin had met Spring's husband socially a time or two and knew that the well-respected psychologist was a bit eccentric, to say the least. She also knew that the couple had been happily married for several years.

She remembered sharing a table with them at a country-club New Year's Eve party the year she and Martin had been married. Erin had envied their closeness and love for each other—something that had been missing almost from the beginning in her own marriage. Spring had been pregnant then. Erin had particularly craved the kind of joy the other couple had shared during that pregnancy. It was something that would be denied her throughout her own, which had begun by accident only two months later. Several times during those lonely, unhappy months, she'd thought of Spring and Clay McEntire, longing for the sort of love and support they'd shown each other.

"How's Chelsea?" Spring asked as she scribbled something on a prescription pad. She'd given Erin's daughter her first eye examination only a few months earlier.

"She's fine, thank you."

"She's a beautiful little girl," Spring complimented. "I'm hoping for a girl this time, though of course it doesn't really matter what we have, as long as it's healthy."

Startled, Erin looked at the other woman's flat waistline. "You're pregnant?"

Spring smiled brightly. "Yes. Three months."

Vague feelings of envy became outright jealousy. "That's wonderful news. I'm very happy for you." Erin forced a smile.

"Thanks. Clay's been wanting a second child ever since Easter when my family had a reunion and my sisters both brought their new babies, both girls. He played with my nieces all afternoon and has been dropping hints ever since. Even Sean's been nagging me for a baby brother or sister, though I think he's leaning toward a brother. Between the two of them, it wasn't too hard to talk me into it."

Erin took the prescription Spring held out to her and reached for her purse, still wearing her determined smile. "I really am happy for you," she repeated. "Give Clay my best, will you?"

"I will. Let me know if you have any trouble with those glasses, okay?"

"Yes, I will. Thanks, Spring."

Erin handed a check to the dark-haired woman at the front desk and left the office, still smiling. The smile faded the moment she slid behind the steering wheel of her car and closed the door. She couldn't help thinking again of how very much she would like for Chelsea to have a baby brother or sister. She couldn't help worrying again that it would never happen. Brett was the only man she could even imagine having children with—and yet, conversely, she was terrified to make that commitment to him.

She groaned and started the car.

"CAN WE REALLY GO in an airplane, Brett?" Chelsea asked excitedly from the back seat of the car.

He smiled at her in the rearview mirror. "We won't be going up in the air in one," he reminded her. "But I understand there will be air-force planes on display that we can go through. It'll be fun."

"And then we can see the Thunderbirds?"

"Yes. Then we can see the Thunderbirds," he promised.

Smiling, she hugged her doll and looked out the car window, counting the minutes until they reached the Little Rock Air Force Base, which was holding its annual open house and air show. Having read about the event in the local newspapers, Brett had assured Erin and Chelsea that they'd love it, particularly if he was the one escorting them. Chelsea had been only slightly disappointed that his nephews weren't accompanying them this time. Brett had explained that the boys were planning to go the next day with their parents, and had added that he hoped Chelsea wouldn't mind too much.

Chelsea had smiled, given Brett a hug and assured him that she would have a wonderful time with him and her mom. He had only to remember that hug to experience again the warm feelings it had sent through him. He could easily get used to this little girl's hugs. Just as he had her mother's.

He glanced over at Erin. She'd been awfully quiet today. What was bothering her? Was she aware, as he was, that their time together would have to end soon—that he had to get back to Boston within the next few days? He wanted to think she dreaded that separation as much as he did. He wanted to believe there was a chance she would go with him when he left, though he hadn't yet had the nerve to make that suggestion. He intended to find that courage today. He was going to charm the socks off her today, show her again what a terrific father he'd make for her daughter. And to-night he planned to ask Erin to marry him.

Just thinking about her answer made his hands tremble on the steering wheel. Would it be yes? Or was she going to break his heart with a no?

"Looks like it's going to be crowded," Brett commented, subtly urging Erin to talk to him as he drove past the front gates of the base.

"Yes. Very crowded."

Clearly something was bothering her and he couldn't ask now, with Chelsea listening so avidly to everything they said.

Chelsea didn't seem to mind standing in long lines wait-ing to walk through the transport planes on display for the public. Clinging to Brett's hand, oblivious to the heat of the afternoon sun, she chattered nonstop about everything she saw. She could hardly wait for the air show. Brett had ex-plained about the air-force flying team, the Thunder-birds—six F-16 jets flown by the best pilots in exhibitions all over the world. He kept Erin's hand in his left one as he held Chelsea's in his right, aware that they looked like a family and pleased they gave that appearance. He was ab-surdly proud of both Erin and Chelsea.

One enormous hangar had been cleared for a crafts show sponsored by the Officers' Wives Club. Brett, Erin and Chelsea strolled from booth to booth, examining the hand-made wares. One woman displayed handmade doll clothes just the right size for Chelsea's Belle. To Chelsea's delight, Brett bought her an entire wardrobe.

"You're spoiling her," Erin murmured, frowning as Brett handed over the money.

"I know," he acknowledged ruefully. "But look at her. How do you resist that?"

Erin's expression softened at the pleasure shining in her daughter's dark eyes. "It isn't easy," she admitted. "But you really should stop. It's not good for her to be so indulged."

Brett wasn't convinced. What could be so bad about making a kid happy? Still, he promised Erin he wouldn't buy anything more. Fortunately, Chelsea didn't see anything else she particularly wanted, which meant that Brett's willpower wasn't put to a test.

It was almost time for the air show to begin when they left the hangar. Brett noticed that a lot of people had brought lawn chairs. Since he hadn't thought of that, he found a small cleared patch of pavement where he and Erin could sit Indian-style, with Chelsea perched on Brett's knee.

Brett hadn't thought to warn the child that the Thunderbirds would be very loud. When the first plane roared over their heads from behind in a crowd-delighting surprise appearance, Chelsea squealed in fright and turned to hide her face in Brett's shoulder, sobbing pitifully.

"Hey, it's okay, baby. It's just an airplane," he reassured her, holding her close and patting her back. He noticed that Erin had instinctively reached out to her daughter, but he didn't release the little girl who'd thrown her arms around his neck and buried her face in his throat. He was stunned by the sense of protectiveness he felt in response to her trembling, the tenderness her vulnerability brought out in him.

He continued to murmur words of comfort until Chelsea had grown accustomed to the noise and turned to watch, though she continued to cling to him for the duration of the earsplitting demonstration. Catching a glimpse of Erin's expression, Brett realized belatedly that she wasn't used to sharing Chelsea in this way. She obviously wasn't quite sure how she felt about having her usual position as comforter usurped by someone else. He wanted her to be comfortable with his relationship with Chelsea. He intended to be a part of the rest of their lives.

They had dinner at a family seafood restaurant in North Little Rock. Then they returned to Erin's house, where Brett waited in the living room, watching a television program while Erin bathed Chelsea and got her ready for bed. At a noise from the doorway, he looked up to find them standing hand in hand, Erin still in her jeans and sweater, Chelsea freshly scrubbed and clad in a lace-trimmed white nightgown. Looking at the dark-haired, blue-eyed woman and the dark-haired, dark-eyed little girl, Brett fell in love all over again. With both of them.

How could any man want more than this? he asked himself. What a fool Martin had been to walk away. Brett had no intention of being so stupid.

"I came to tell you good-night," Chelsea announced.

Brett grinned and held out his arms. "Well, c'mere, then."

She laughed and threw herself across the room, landing in his lap with a thud. Her chubby arms closed around his neck, her rosy lips smacked against his cheek. "Good night, Brett. Thank you for taking me today and for buying me the airplane and the doll clothes." The speech had obviously been rehearsed with her mother, but sounded convincingly sincere.

Holding her soft, sweet-smelling little body close, Brett found his eyes suddenly misting with unexpected tears. "Good night, Chelsea. Sweet dreams."

His gaze locked with Erin's for a moment. Erin's eyes looked suspiciously bright. Were hers filmed with tears, too?

Chelsea wriggled out of his arms and off his lap. Erin led her from the room. Brett could hear the child chattering down the hallway.

It was time, he told himself, rising from the couch to wander restlessly around the room, trying to build his courage. Time to put his entire future in Erin's hands. *God, please let her say yes!* he prayed, his hands clenching at his sides.

How would he bear it if she said no?

He turned when she came back into the room. She smiled. "She'll probably be asleep in minutes. She couldn't wait to put Belle's new nightgown on and snuggle under the covers with her."

"I'm glad she liked the doll clothes." *Make conversation,* Brett ordered himself. *Be cool. Bring up the subject of marriage gradually so you don't scare her off.*

"Would you like some coffee?" Erin offered, turning toward the kitchen. "It'll just take me a few minutes to make some."

"I love you, Erin. I want you to marry me."

Brett winced in self-disgust the moment the words left his mouth. That certainly hadn't been the way he'd intended to ask, he thought irritably, remembering his plan to introduce the subject gradually. The words had simply left his mouth before he realized he was going to say them.

Judging from the look on Erin's face as she slowly turned to stare at him, his words had been even more startling to her. She looked . . . stunned, he decided, shoving his hands into his pockets to conceal the way they'd suddenly started to shake.

12

STUNNED was too mild a word to describe her reaction to his proposal. It had, quite literally, been the last thing she'd expected to hear just then. She wasn't even certain she'd heard him correctly.

"Married?" she repeated faintly. "You want to get married?"

Brett's face softened. His smile was spine-melting. "Yes. More than anything I've ever wanted before. I love you."

He loved her. A wave of hot, pure joy rushed through her. Then she forced herself to think rationally. How could she marry a man she'd actually known only two weeks? Risk her future—and, more important, Chelsea's—on a whirlwind courtship? "Brett, I—"

"I know you're going to say it's too soon," he said, forestalling those very words. "But we've known each other for months, Erin. As long as lots of people who decide to marry. Our courtship wasn't a conventional one, perhaps, but it was valid. It was enough to make me fall in love with you before I even saw you."

She locked her hands behind her back. "Brett, a string of telephone calls can't really be considered a courtship. You didn't even know my name for the first couple of months."

"I didn't *need* to know your name," he argued stubbornly. "I knew everything that was important about you."

"You didn't know I had a daughter."

His eyes narrowed. "Only because you deliberately kept that from me. I've dealt with that during the past two weeks. My feelings for you haven't changed."

She took a step toward him, lifting her hand in an almost-imploring gesture. "Brett, you have to understand that I can't give you an answer now, not like this. I have responsibilities. I can't—"

"Not another responsible, mature-adult speech, Erin, please." Shoving his hand through his thick hair, he took a deep breath. "Look, I know I'm impulsive and that worries you. But you needn't worry that I'll ever regret proposing to you. I've thought this out. I know what I want."

"You think you know," she corrected him gently, unwilling to hurt him but determined to make him see reason. How could he expect her to just marry him so spontaneously? A decision like that would have to be given months of thought, of preparation. So much was involved, so much at stake. And he still hadn't had time to come to terms with the demands of parenthood. Chelsea hadn't always been an angel around him during the past two weeks, but he'd seen mostly the good side of parenting. He still had no experience with all that was involved.

"I know," he repeated flatly, his gaze holding hers prisoner. "I may be impulsive, Erin, but I'm not naive, and I'm not stupid. I know it won't always be easy. But I believe we can make it. And I know I want to try. I can learn to be a husband and I can learn to be a father, with your help. It's what I want."

She thought she detected a touch of desperation in his golden-brown eyes and her heart twisted. Couldn't he understand it was for his sake as well as her own that she was hesitating?

Brett took the extra step between them and closed his hands around her forearms, holding her tightly. "Erin, I love you," he said again, tersely. "Just tell me if you feel the same way. I need to know what you really want."

She moistened her lips. Why did he suddenly look so anxious? Didn't he know, hadn't he guessed that she'd loved him from the first time they'd made love, if not before? And, as far as what she wanted . . . She thought of her visit with the optometrist, the rush of jealousy she'd felt at the other woman's happiness in her marriage and pregnancy. Erin wanted those things so badly she could taste them. And yet she was so afraid to reach out for them, so afraid of failing again.

"I—I think I love you," she began cautiously, her eyes focused somewhere in the vicinity of Brett's chin. "But—"

He pulled her closer, with hope flaring in his eyes. "Then, what's holding you back?"

She lifted her gaze to his mouth—his sexy, talented, usually smiling mouth. He wasn't smiling now. "Is there really any reason to rush?" she whispered. "Can't we take our time to make sure—really sure—that this is the right step for us."

He frowned. "The thought of returning home alone is what makes me want to rush. I don't want to be alone anymore."

Erin closed her eyes in a spasm of pain. She'd been on such intimate terms with loneliness. It ripped her heart apart to think of being without Brett now, to picture him alone in Boston, missing her the same way. How she wanted to say yes, to abandon all caution and go away with him. But . . .

"I can't," she whispered achingly. "Brett, I can't."

His fingers clenched convulsively, almost bruisingly. "You're a coward," he accused her, his anger almost, but not quite, concealing the underlying vulnerability. "You're afraid to take risks, afraid to trust, afraid to love. You're not doing yourself *or* Chelsea any favors by hiding you both away, the way you've been doing for the past three years."

Stung, Erin finally looked at him, straight in the eye. "It's easy for you to make those accusations. Easy for you to take risks. You have nothing to lose. I have a little girl who has no one to depend on except her mother. I can't—I won't—risk her security until I'm very sure about what I'm doing."

Brett dropped her arms as if his palms had been scalded, his eyes widening in blatant disbelief. "That is the most arrogant thing I've ever heard you say," he exclaimed. "Nothing to lose? You honestly think I have nothing to lose? You think men can't hurt, can't bleed? You think I like the idea of having you reject me after what we've shared the past two weeks? I am in *love* with you, Erin Spencer, and you could break my heart with very little effort. You don't think I'm taking a risk opening myself up for that kind of pain? Think again, lady."

She reached out to him in agitation, her fingers just brushing his arm. "Brett, I'm sorry. I didn't mean— But you have to understand. I don't know what to do. You have to give me time. If it were just me—if it were only my happiness placed at risk—it would be so much easier for me to give you the answer you want. But I have to think about Chelsea. I have to."

"And you don't trust me to think about her happiness, as well," he added, his voice curiously flat. "You still think I'd do something to hurt that little girl. You're still comparing me to the shallow, aging playboy you married."

"No," she denied. "I know you're not like Martin. I just need time, Brett. Please."

His jaw working, he nodded and half turned away. "All right. I'll give you time. But I have to get back to Boston. I can't wait here, put my life on hold indefinitely, until you decide you can trust me. I'm leaving tomorrow."

"I understand," she whispered, crossing her arms over her aching heart.

"There won't be anyone else," he told her, turning suddenly to stare intently into her tear-filled eyes. "There won't ever be anyone else for me. I'll do whatever I have to do to prove to you that I know what I'm doing, what I'm feeling."

Though she knew she was doing the right thing by waiting until she was very sure before giving him an answer to his proposal, the thought of saying goodbye to him tore her apart. She couldn't bear the thought of not seeing him, not touching him, having him in her life only as a voice on the telephone. Desperately, she pictured her daughter, drawing strength from the image of Chelsea's trusting dark eyes. But still she hurt.

With a thin cry, she stepped into Brett's waiting arms. "Hold me, Brett. Please hold me."

"I'll do more than that," he promised roughly. "I'm going to leave you with a night to remember. Something to think about when we're both alone, both lonely. A taste of what we could have every night if only you trusted me, trusted your own feelings."

His mouth covered hers, hard, his arms going around her as if to chain her to him for eternity. Her own closed around his neck and she held him tightly, trying to pretend she'd never have to let him go.

And they made love over and over, their pleasure edged with the awareness that their hours were numbered. It was dawn when he left, weary, grim-lipped. He'd already told her he hated airport goodbyes, that he would call her the next night from Boston. He stepped into Chelsea's room on his way out, standing by the sleeping child's bed for several long, silent moments while Erin watched from the doorway, wrapped in her robe and her pain. Brett leaned down to brush a kiss across Chelsea's chubby cheek and then turned away as though the contact had hurt him, his hands shoving fiercely into the pockets of his jeans.

Erin's throat tightened, her eyes flooding with tears again. Was it really possible that Brett had learned to care for her daughter as much as he said? That he could adapt to an instant family, to the demands parenthood would place on his previously unrestricted life? She hoped so. Oh, how she hoped so! All she needed, she told herself bracingly, was time to be sure. Time for both of them to be sure.

He held her for a long time at the door, his face buried in her throat. And then he kissed her quickly and turned away, hiding his expression. "I love you, Erin," he muttered, his voice choked, his hand on the door.

He was gone before she could answer. She'd wanted to tell him that she loved him, too. Leaning against the closed door, one hand on its smooth, cold surface, she gave in to confusion and exhaustion—and wept.

BRETT WANDERED around his empty apartment, telling himself he really should get to work, wondering how he was ever going to find the enthusiasm to draw his mythical hero when his own life was in such a shambles. It was hard to lose himself in fantasy when reality kept intruding into his once-fertile imagination.

He stood in his room and stared at his big bed picturing himself and Erin rolling on it. That thought made him groan and pace, restless, painfully frustrated. He paused at the door of the guest room, studying its sterile, professionally done decor, thinking how much prettier it would be with Chelsea's toys scattered on the expensive carpeting. He imagined the silence filled with Erin's soft voice, Chelsea's musical laughter. Just as he'd been imagining those things for the past month, ever since he'd made himself return to his real life, giving Erin the time she'd requested to consider his proposal.

He was alone and he wanted a family. His family. The one he'd found in Arkansas.

He glanced at his watch. It was still early afternoon, but maybe he'd call Erin. He could talk to Chelsea, too. Ask her how she was doing, how preschool was going, what she'd learned in her last dance class. Erin had sent him a picture from the dance recital; Chelsea had looked adorable in her sequins and feathers and tights. He should have been there, he thought for at least the hundredth time. Should have been in the audience with a video camera and a proud smile. And afterward, he could have taken his family out to dinner and then gone home to make love to his wife before drifting into a contented, satisfied sleep.

Dammit, why was Erin denying him those experiences? She was refusing them both the pleasures inherent in marriage and parenthood, just because she didn't trust him to handle the inevitable rocky times. He knew it wasn't all good times and laughter. Knew there'd be days of frustration, of conflict, of tension. Hell, that was all part of it. And he wanted it all.

With sudden decision, he grabbed his coat and headed for the door. He needed to get out, away from the haunted silence, the taunting images. He needed to see people, hear them, watch other families enjoying what he'd been denied—just being together, sharing their lives.

He didn't look at the telephone as he passed it on his way out. This time the cold, plastic instrument couldn't give him what he needed.

LEAVING CHELSEA watching her favorite PBS children's program, Erin drifted into the kitchen, telling herself she needed to put something out to thaw for dinner. She paused, instead, by the telephone, looking longingly at it. It was hours earlier than Brett usually called, and yet she wanted so badly just to hear his voice.

For the past month, her life had revolved around the telephone. She seemed to exist from call to call, going through the motions of working woman and devoted mother during the daytime, fully content only when she was talking to Brett each night. And then she had to amend even that thought. She would never be fully content as long as she and Brett were so far apart. She wanted to see him, wanted to touch him. She wanted him.

She knew he was as miserable as she was. She heard it in his voice every time they spoke. Time and again she'd found herself on the verge of surrender, ready to promise anything he wanted just to end the torment of being without him. Time and again a vision of Chelsea's trusting little face had floated into her mind, stopping the words in her throat. How could she be sure? she asked herself over and over. How could she know she was doing the right thing?

Corey thought she was crazy for putting herself through this. During their last telephone call she'd urged Erin to take a chance at happiness, to fight for what she wanted. After all, Corey had walked away from a successful job and a hectic social life to hide herself away with her art and her books and her own company. She'd assured Erin she'd never regretted that decision, that it was something she'd needed to do to find herself. One couldn't live one's whole life worrying about the consequences of every decision, she lectured. Sometimes a person just had to take a chance.

Adam had said little when Erin had told him about Brett's proposal. This was a decision she had to make on her own, he'd told her reluctantly. He'd been telling her for some time that she needed to find someone, to start living her life again. He couldn't tell her whether Brett would make her happy, couldn't predict the future for her. He only wished he could, to spare her any pain. All he could do was be there if she needed to talk. "Whatever you do," he'd added, "I love you. I'll always be on your side."

Though his words had warmed her, they hadn't been enough. She'd wanted him to tell her what to do. Adam had always seemed so competent, so infallible. Why couldn't he tell her what to do now? For the first time in years, she just wanted to let someone else make the decisions, someone else worry about the consequences.

She wanted to be with Brett. She wanted to do what was right for her daughter. She wanted to crawl into bed and pull the covers over her head.

Sighing, she reached for the phone. She really needed to talk to Brett.

He wasn't home. She let the phone ring for a long time before she finally gave up and replaced her receiver. He'd obviously forgotten to turn on his answering machine. She wasn't sure what she would have said if he had.

HE CALLED AT HIS USUAL time, around ten. Erin had been waiting for the call ever since she'd tucked Chelsea into bed two hours earlier. Drawing her knees up to hug them with her free arm, she sat on the bed, the telephone cradled to her ear. "I tried to call you earlier," she told Brett almost immediately.

"Did you? I was out."

"Yes, I know." She didn't ask where he'd been, though she would have liked to. She trusted him, of course. But she really would have liked to ask.

"So, what have you been doing?" Brett asked, stiltedly making conversation.

"Just the usual," she answered with a shrug she knew he couldn't see. "I finished my assignments for Redding &

Howard today. I should be getting some more next week. How about you? Will you make your first-of-the-month deadline?"

"Maybe," he answered rather grimly. "By some miracle."

She was instantly concerned. "You're having trouble working?"

"Don't worry about it. It happens sometimes. Is Chelsea asleep?"

"Yes."

"Thanks for sending me the pictures of her dance recital. She looked really cute. I wish I'd seen her."

"I wish you had, too," Erin murmured, remembering how empty the chair next to her had seemed that evening.

"I miss you, Erin."

He always told her, always sounded so sincere. Yet tonight there was a new intensity in the quietly spoken words, a trace of despair. Erin's heart twisted. "I miss you, too, Brett."

"All I have to do is close my eyes and I can see you. Sometimes I can see you so clearly that I can almost reach out and touch you. Almost. It's not enough."

"No." She closed her eyes.

"I want you," he said starkly. "So much I hurt. I go to sleep hurting and I wake up the same way. I want you in bed beneath me. I want to kiss you, to touch you. I want to feel your breasts against my chest, your legs wrapped around mine. I want to be inside you, loving you, hearing the little sounds you make when you come."

Erin moaned. "Brett, please. Don't."

"Do you want me, Erin? Does your body tremble for my touch? Are your breasts aching, hungry for my hands, my mouth?"

"Yes," she breathed, her aroused nipples brushing almost painfully against the fabric of her nightgown. She hugged her knees more tightly, trying to ease the discomfort. The pressure only made it worse.

"I want to kiss them. I want to take you into my mouth and feel you arch against me. I want to run my hand up your soft thigh and slide my fingers between your legs. You're already hot and wet for me, aren't you, Erin?"

Her eyes tightly closed, she squeezed her thighs together, almost whimpering at the moist, pulsing emptiness between them. She tried to beg him to stop but she couldn't speak. Her breath came fast and ragged, escaping her lips in a gasp of need.

Brett's voice was raw, gritty. "All I have to do is think of you and I get hard. Cold showers don't help. Exercise doesn't help. I can't concentrate on anything else to make the ache go away. I need you."

"Brett—" His name was little more than a sob.

"The calls aren't enough now. Not since we've been together, not now that I know how incredible we are together. I need to be with you. How much longer are you going to torture both of us by keeping us apart?"

"I don't—"

"Come to Boston, Erin. Please."

Tears welled in her eyes and began to cascade down her cheeks. "I can't."

His sigh was weary, heartrendingly dispirited. "Maybe I'd better go," he said heavily. "I'm not feeling quite in control tonight. I'm only going to make us both miserable, say something I'll probably regret. I'll talk to you tomorrow, all right?"

She was still struggling to control her breathing. She clutched the receiver so tightly her hand cramped. Finally she swallowed and murmured, "Yes."

"I love you, Erin."

The hoarse murmur brought fresh tears to her closed eyes. "Good night, Brett," she whispered, then quickly dropped the receiver into its cradle. She wrapped both arms around her raised legs and rested her face on her knees, her tears soaking through the thin nightgown. Her body throbbed with need and her heart ached until she thought it would shatter. Her breasts were swollen so tight they hurt, aroused by nothing more than Brett's words.

How much longer could they go on like this? How long until one or both of them broke?

Why couldn't someone tell her what to do?

BRETT SLAMMED his phone down and rolled onto his side on his big, empty bed, cursing himself for starting something he couldn't finish. His blood pounded heavily in his veins, his breath sharp-edged as it slashed in and out of his lungs. His hand brushed that part of him that was so painfully, throbbingly swollen and he dully considered easing the ache in the only way available to him at the moment. He refrained because he couldn't bear the thought of the heart-deep emptiness afterward.

He couldn't go on this way much longer. He needed Erin, loved her until he was half sick with it. If this was his penalty for living on his own terms for so long, then he had surely paid in full for every selfish, irresponsible action.

A hundred times he'd told himself to go after her, stay on her heels until she couldn't run any farther. A hundred times he'd told himself that the only chance he had of winning her was to wait for her to come to him.

He buried his face in the pillow, his fist clenched at his side, willing his body to cool. Something had to give, he thought again. Soon.

He could only hope it wouldn't be his sanity.

IT WAS THREE in the morning when Erin reached again for the phone. She hadn't slept, hadn't been able to do anything except lie on her back in the darkness and stare at the ceiling as if hoping to find the answers there to all her questions. She didn't stop to think that it was an hour later in Boston, that the middle of the night wasn't the time to make calls. The phone rang twice on the other end and then Brett answered, his voice sleep-thick and disoriented. "Yeah? What?"

"I'll marry you, Brett. If you're sure it's what you want, I'll marry you." Even as she said the words, Erin prayed that the decision was the right one—for her, for Chelsea, for Brett. She only knew she'd never be truly happy again unless she took this chance.

A long, stunned pause followed her announcement. And then Brett spoke again, tentatively. "Erin?"

She couldn't help smiling through her tears. "You've proposed to someone else?"

"Wait a minute." She could hear bedsprings creaking quietly, the rustle of fabric. She closed her eyes and pictured him, sleep tousled and heavy eyed, wearing nothing but his oh-so-sexy smile. "Okay, I'm awake," he told her clearly. "Now, say it again."

"I'll marry you," she repeated obediently.

His laugh was quick, breathless. "That's what I thought you said. God, I hope this isn't a dream."

"You're not dreaming."

"How soon can you get here?"

"You want me to come there?" she asked, her fingers nervously pleating the sheet that covered her. She thought wistfully of the state she'd grown up in, that she loved so dearly. Could she really be happy in Boston?

She only knew she couldn't be happy without Brett, wherever they chose to live.

"Yeah. I want to show you around, see how you like it. We've got a thousand plans to make and I want to do it together. In person. You'll stay here, of course. There's an extra bedroom for Chelsea."

"You want me to bring Chelsea?"

"Of course, I want you to bring Chelsea," he answered impatiently. "Did you think I'd ask you to leave her behind? We're going to be a family, Erin. The three of us. The sooner we start, the better. So, when can you be here?"

"How soon do you want us?" she asked, clinging tightly to her courage.

"Now," he answered promptly.

She smiled. "How about later in the week?"

He sighed. "I guess I can wait that long. Barely. I'll be working my buns off in the meantime to clear some free time for us."

"I'll get things together here, then. I'll let you know when we'll be there."

"I'll send you the tickets."

"That's not necessary."

"I'll send you the tickets," he repeated firmly.

She knew when to give in. "All right."

"Erin?"

"Yes, Brett?"

"I love you."

"I love you, too," she whispered. *God, please let me be doing the right thing.*

THINGS STARTED GOING wrong almost as soon as the airplane took off from the Little Rock Regional Airport, headed for Memphis. Originally excited about her first plane ride, Chelsea was frightened by the sounds and movements of takeoff. Her ears hurt from the changing altitude and she was too young to know how to relieve the pressure herself. Tearfully, she accepted the bubble gum Erin had brought for that purpose, huddling into her seat with Belle and chewing fiercely.

Chelsea had just gotten used to her surroundings when it was time to change planes. She sobbed through the second takeoff, despite Erin's crooning comfort. She was finally distracted when the stewardesses served lunch. Intrigued by the novelty of being served in her seat on the fold-down tray, Chelsea grew much more cheerful, even eating nearly every bite on her plastic plate.

Erin, on the other hand, could hardly touch her meal. She was tormented by doubts and questions. Had she done the right thing? Would Brett adjust to having his bachelor home invaded by her and her child? Would she ever be comfortable in Boston after living all her life in Arkansas? Would she fit in? Would Brett be ashamed of her provincial ways?

What about the crime rate she'd read about? The violence? The pollution? Wouldn't it be better to raise Chelsea in the less stressful, less urbanized atmosphere of North Little Rock?

Was she doing the right thing?

Brett was waiting at the airport. He hardly allowed them to step through the gate before catching Erin in his arms for a welcoming kiss that nearly singed her eyelashes. She was bruised and breathless when he released her to sweep Chelsea into his arms for a less powerful, but equally enthusiastic hug. He'd bought flowers for Erin, an adorable stuffed monkey for Chelsea.

Tired and overly excited by the trip, Chelsea was very quiet during the ride across Boston to Brett's town-house apartment. Erin was having trouble, herself, finding things to say. Even Brett's broad smile had begun to dim by the time they arrived. He and Erin exchanged long, grave looks when he opened the front door, saying, "Welcome home."

Chelsea immediately ran inside to investigate. Erin was as impressed as her daughter by the lovely decor. Brett's apartment had been furnished in a contemporary style that was quite comfortable looking despite its modernness. He gave them a tour, showing them the state-of-the-art kitchen, the spacious dining room and living room, and his office.

Chelsea seemed fascinated by the oversize comic-book drawings littering his desk and drawing board. "You're welcome to look at them when I'm with you," Brett told the child. "But don't touch, okay? This is almost a month's work."

"I don't want you in this room without me or Brett, Chelsea. Understand?" Erin added to reinforce Brett's mild warning. He probably wasn't aware that understatement had little effect on an almost-four-year-old, she thought with nervous amusement.

The next stop on the tour was the master bedroom. His eyes on Erin, Brett set her bags at the foot of the bed. "Do you like it?" he asked quietly.

She looked from him to the enormous bed, refusing to even consider how many other women might have shared it with him. "It's a lovely room," she replied firmly. "It looks quite comfortable."

His grin conveyed a masculine confidence. "I think you'll enjoy it."

She flushed and turned away.

"And this, Chelsea, is your room," Brett announced, opening the door to the guest room. "What do you think?"

Chelsea looked around the strange room with its trendy adult furnishings, then turned uncertainly to Erin. "It doesn't look like my room," she declared.

"It will when we bring all your things here," Erin assured her. She'd been trying to prepare the child for the upcoming move, though she'd wondered if she should have waited until a definite date had been set. And then she'd told herself that Chelsea should be included from the beginning in the plans Erin and Brett were making. After all, this marriage would affect the rest of Chelsea's life, too.

"So—um—would you like to freshen up or anything? I have reservations at a new restaurant for dinner, but I thought we could look around Boston a little first, if you like."

"That sounds fine," Erin responded. "Doesn't it, Chelsea?"

Clinging to her doll and her mother's hand, Chelsea nodded gravely. "Yes."

Brett cleared his throat loudly and made an awkward motion toward the door. "Let's go, then. I'm sure you'll really love my town."

13

Boston was big. And busy. And crowded. Erin couldn't
help feeling dwarfed by the buildings towering over her
head as they drove down a bustling street. Downtown Little Rock wasn't this crowded and hectic even at rush hour,
and the sky-touching towers at home were spaced several
blocks apart rather than side by side. She and Chelsea huddled into their coats, unaccustomed to the cold—it was still
comfortably warm at home.

Chelsea stared around her silently, not at all impressed
by the historic sights. Erin was surprised at the age of some
of the sites Brett pointed out. Arkansas, of course, had still
been inhabited by Native Americans when some of these
places were built. She spent a lot of time trying to understand the rapid, flat-voweled speech patterns of the people
around her, and was painfully aware of her own slower,
obviously Southern accent.

"What do you think, so far?" Brett questioned, holding
her hand and searching her face with his anxious gaze.

Even Brett sounded different here, she noticed with a hard
swallow, hearing the way he unconsciously dropped the *r*
in *far.* "It's a lot different from home," she admitted with a
weak smile.

"I suppose it seems that way at first. I hope you'll learn
to love it here, as I have," he said, glancing around with an
almost-proprietary air. Erin could tell that he really loved
his adopted city. She hoped he was right about her growing
to love it, too.

"Erin." As if reading the doubts in her eyes, Brett tightened his fingers around hers. "If you don't like it here, if you decide it's not right for us, we'll move. We'll find someplace where you can be comfortable raising our children. Just give it a chance, okay?"

Bemused by his mention of their children, Erin smiled shakily and nodded. "I will. I promise."

He pulled her close for a quick kiss. "I'm not sure I can wait until Chelsea goes to bed tonight," he murmured. "It's been so long since I've held you properly."

Her knees already weakening in anticipation of the night, she clung to him for a moment, until Chelsea demanded her attention. She gave Brett a quick smile of promise before turning to answer her daughter's question.

FROM THE TIME they arrived at the popular new Cambridge restaurant, it was glaringly apparent that Brett wasn't accustomed to including a young child in his evening plans. It wasn't a family restaurant. The snooty hostess rolled her eyes in poorly veiled annoyance at having to find accommodations for a small child. She finally produced a booster seat with the air of someone who'd had to look long and hard for the distasteful item. Erin's cheeks were warm when she settled Chelsea in the seat, aware of the surreptitious looks from other diners, all of whom looked like trendy, upwardly-mobile types who hadn't yet scheduled children into their lives.

An equally snooty waitress offered to take their drink orders. Intimidated by the woman's hauteur, Erin asked for water. The woman sighed and asked, "What brand?"

Since she didn't think she should answer "Tap," Erin named the first brand she could remember, hoping it was still in vogue. "With a twist of lime," she added, trying to appear more sophisticated than she felt at the moment.

Giving Erin a faint smile, Brett ordered a drink, then asked Chelsea what she'd like. "Chocolate milk," the child answered promptly.

The waitress sighed noisily. "We don't *do* chocolate milk," she grumbled, obviously irritated. "We probably have regular."

"That will be fine," Erin replied hastily.

Brett waited until the woman was out of hearing before chuckling. "She's a real sweetheart, huh? Sorry, Erin, I had no idea the service here was so lousy."

She managed a smile and told him not to worry about it.

The meal went downhill from there. The Waitress from Hell obviously didn't approve of Erin's order, could hardly hide her disbelief at Chelsea's request, and was marginally pleasant to Brett only because she seemed to sense he belonged there. Erin was feeling more and more out of place. Maybe she should have stayed in Arkansas, she thought miserably. She and Chelsea could be eating at a McDonald's or Bonanza or Po'Folks restaurant.

The seemingly interminable meal finally drew to an end—but only after Chelsea had become so uncomfortable in the tense atmosphere that she began to whine. Erin drew a deep breath of relief when they were finally in Brett's car.

"I'm sorry," he said again, shaking his head in disgust. "What a terrible place. I'd never been there before, and I had no idea it was one of those joints so impressed by its own image that patrons are treated like interlopers. I'll never go back."

"You couldn't have known how they felt about children," Erin responded, trying to reassure him. "I suppose having a child around cramps your style a little."

He pulled his brows downward in obvious annoyance. "Don't be ridiculous. It wasn't Chelsea's fault the staff was so obnoxious. Next time, I'll ask some of my married friends to recommend a child-friendly place to eat."

Though she was so tired her head drooped pitifully, Chelsea didn't want to go to bed in the strange bedroom alone. Erin lay down beside her until the child finally dropped off, her doll clutched tightly in her arms. And then Erin slipped from the bed and tiptoed out of the room.

Brett waited for her in the den, his eyes shadowy. "I guess you've had more enjoyable days."

She didn't want him to blame himself. "Maybe we just tried to do too much at once," she suggested. "Chelsea and I were both tired from the trip."

"Tomorrow will be better," he reassured, and she wondered which of them he was trying to convince.

"I'm sure you're right," she replied, wanting to believe it herself.

He stepped closer to her and cupped her face between his hands. She covered them with her own. "I've missed you so much," he murmured, his thumb tracing her trembling lower lip. "I've wanted you here for so long. It's going to work out, Erin. I promise you that."

"I know," she whispered, searching his golden-brown eyes for any sign of doubt. She found none. Brett truly believed that they were doing the right thing. She smiled and touched the tip of her tongue to his thumb.

He groaned and tugged her closer, covering her mouth with his. "God, I want you," he muttered against her lips. "I'm going crazy with it."

She kissed him lingeringly, then stepped back to hold out her hand to him. "What are you waiting for?" she urged quietly.

Smiling, he took her hand, his fingers squeezing hers tightly as he led her to the master bedroom.

Quickly abandoning their clothes, they tumbled onto the big bed. Their hands sought out intimately remembered territory, their mouths clinging, tongues dueling. They couldn't linger to savor slowly the first time in so many weeks. Their coupling was hot and frantic. Erin peaked almost immediately when he thrust into her. Brett wasn't far behind. Their muffled cries mingled, their harsh breathing echoing in the shadowy corners of the room.

And then they began again. This time they lingered. And savored. This time they climaxed together in deep, blissful, seemingly endless swells.

"I love you," Brett repeated again and again, his hand stroking her damp, trembling flesh as he calmed her afterward. He still found it hard to believe she was actually here with him, as he'd imagined it so many times. "I love you so much."

She turned her face into his sweat-beaded shoulder, tasting his warm, salty skin. "I love you."

"I want to get married soon. I want to adopt Chelsea and make another baby for her to play with. Okay with you?"

She lifted her head with an effort, obviously surprised. "You want to adopt her?"

He answered her very seriously. "Yes. I've thought about it a lot. I want us all to have the same name, be a real family. I want to be her father, not her stepfather. I want her to call me Daddy. If she wants to, of course," he added a bit less certainly.

"I think she'd like that," Erin murmured, her voice sounding suspiciously thick. "She's always wanted a daddy."

"I'll be a good one, Erin. I promise."

"I know you will," she whispered, fighting tears. "Oh, Brett."

He wasn't quite finished. "I want you to tell Martin to take his child-support checks and spend them on his latest jail-bait girlfriend. Chelsea doesn't need anything from him."

Erin smiled. He knew she'd been anticipating that call for a very long time. "All right."

Answering her smile with a deeply sensual one of his own, Brett reached for her again. "Erin—"

"Mommy!"

Erin sighed and reached for his robe, which he'd left across the foot of the bed that morning. "I may be a while," she warned him.

"I could go to her," he offered, surprising both of them.

She shook her head quickly. "No. I'll take care of her. You rest."

He watched her hurry from the room in response to another cry. And he realized that she was still uncertain about his role in her daughter's life. That she still wasn't totally convinced he was ready for the responsibilities of parenthood. It hurt, but he was determined to prove her wrong—no matter what he had to do to convince her.

FOR THE NEXT THREE DAYS Brett dedicated himself to entertaining Erin and Chelsea. He and Erin discussed their wedding plans, deciding to fly back to Arkansas to be married so that his sister and her friends and brother could attend. Brett would make arrangements for his parents to be flown there for the ceremony. They would leave the following week, after Brett had mailed his next comic-book installments. They'd spend another week making arrangements to sell Erin's house and ship her things to Boston. And then they'd be married in the little church she'd attended most of her life.

Erin called her minister from Boston, and was pleased that he'd be able to work them into his schedule on the date they requested. Even Adam promised to attend, telling Erin he was sure she had made the right decision this time. She sounded happier, he told her, than she had in a very long time.

Things seemed to be working out very well, indeed.

Brett went out of his way to find things to do that Chelsea would enjoy. She loved the harbor area, particularly the aquarium. They spent hours there. He took her to a toy store and bought her an armload of playthings. He bought her clothes from the trendiest children's store he could find, decking her out like a little model. Chelsea was blissful, her every whim satisfied. Brett asked her how she felt about calling him "Daddy." Chelsea agreed that she'd like that very much—especially when she discovered that Brett couldn't bring himself to deny her anything whenever she used that particular word.

Erin began to worry. "You're spoiling her, Brett. Believe me, you're going to regret it."

He only smiled. "C'mon, Erin, I've never had a kid to spoil before. What could be the harm?"

"The harm," she answered seriously, "is in having her expect you to give her whatever she wants. That isn't always possible, you know, or even preferable. A child needs limits. You're letting her get away with murder. You don't even want me to discipline her."

He shrugged. "She really hasn't done anything that needed disciplining. She's a very good little girl, Erin."

"I know," Erin admitted, softening reluctantly at his praise of her daughter's behavior. "But, please, Brett, trust me to know what's best for her."

Brett frowned. She knew he was trying very hard to demonstrate that he'd be a good father, and that touched her. But she worried about what would happen when he tired of pampering Chelsea; when he realized that he'd created a tiny monster. It was becoming harder for Erin to balance Brett's indulgence. Blessed with every child's innate talent for manipulation, Chelsea knew she had only to turn to Brett for whatever she wanted.

They were spending a quiet afternoon at home when the crisis occurred.

Brett and Erin sat in the den, making lists of things that had to be done before their wedding, immersed in details. The last time they'd checked, Chelsea had been happily playing in her room with some of her many new toys. It was Erin who realized that the child had been too quiet for a bit too long. "I'd better make sure she's still playing," she announced, uncoiling her legs from beneath her to stretch lazily.

Catching a glimpse of smooth, silky skin when her sweater lifted an inch from the waistband of her slacks, Brett couldn't resist reaching out to touch. "Maybe she's taking a nap," he suggested hopefully, thinking of the delightful ways they could spend an hour or so of privacy.

Erin gave him a look that mocked his optimism. "Yeah, sure," she murmured, catching his hand in its sneaky foray and returning it firmly to his knee. "I'll be back in a minute."

She'd been gone less than that when he heard her calling Chelsea. "What's wrong?" he called out.

"I can't find her," she answered, appearing in the doorway with a frown of concern. "She's not in her room. I'll check our room."

Brett pushed himself off the couch to join the search, smiling faintly at Erin's words. "'Our room,'" she'd said. He really liked the sound of that. It sounded so—so settled. Permanent. Married.

Yeah, he liked that a lot.

And then he turned his thoughts to Chelsea's possible whereabouts. Where was she? What was she getting into that was keeping her so suspiciously quiet? Some nagging instinct made him check his office first.

The bellow escaped him before he could hold it back.

"*Chelsea!*"

Starting guiltily, Chelsea looked up from his desk, her hand still clutching a red felt-tip marker. Before her lay nearly a month's work. Or, rather, the remains of nearly a month's work, now liberally smeared with bright red ink. "I wanted to color the pictures," Chelsea told him warily, her dark eyes widening in response to his expression.

Torn between anguish and fury, Brett studied the results of her mischief. *Ruined*, he thought grimly. It would take him at least a week of sixteen-hour days to make his deadline now. "Chelsea, didn't I tell you to stay out of here?" he demanded, his hands clenched at his hips as he glared at the little girl huddled in his chair. He really couldn't remember the last time he'd been this angry. With anyone.

"Yes, sir," she replied. "But, Daddy, I wanted to color," she added, tilting her chin up and looking at him the way she had every time she'd wanted anything during the past few days, he realized sickly. And he'd given her whatever she'd wanted, then. She had no reason to expect him to set limits now.

Hearing a choked groan from the doorway, he turned to find Erin standing there, her face stricken as she took in what had happened. "Oh, Brett, I'm sorry."

He drew a deep breath and made a gesture he intended to mean that he was turning the situation over to her. But, though he could tell she was holding herself back with the greatest effort, she didn't move. She only looked at him with an expression that said quite clearly, *You wanted to be a father. Now's the time to start.*

I can't! he thought in panic, trying to convey the message with his eyes as Chelsea watched intently. *I don't know how to do this!*

Erin only waited, watching him steadily.

She trusted him, he realized abruptly, staggeringly. She trusted him to deal with her daughter, despite his obvious anger with the child. And he'd never felt more helpless in his life. What did he know about disciplining children? What if he screwed up? What if he ruined the kid's life?

Turning slowly to Chelsea, he tried to remember what his own father would have done. That wasn't hard. His dad would have tanned his hide but good. Though he'd never doubted his father's love and concern, Brett wasn't about to resort to that. Instead, he relied on carefully selected words spoken in a low, serious tone.

"I'm very angry with you, Chelsea. I asked you not to touch these. I told you how important these papers were. And now you've scribbled on them and I'll have to work very hard to redo them."

Chelsea's lower lip trembled. "But I wanted to color," she repeated, as if that explained everything.

"I bought you two new coloring books," he replied evenly. "You should have colored in those."

Her enormous brown eyes filled touchingly with tears. "Are you going to spank me?"

"No," he answered. "But I think you'd better go to your room while I clean this up. Sit on the bed and don't play with your toys, understand? I want you to think about how you'd feel if someone tore up something very important to you. We'll talk about that when I finish in here."

She sniffed and nodded, tears rolling copiously down her pink cheeks. Dragging her feet, she headed for the door, risking one peek at her mother, who stood with arms folded, brows drawn into a reproving frown. And then she paused to look up at Brett. "Do you still like me?" she asked, her little voice just barely audible.

He melted, though he did his best to conceal it. Trying to keep his voice even, he said, "Chelsea, I love you. Very much. Just because I'm angry with you doesn't mean I love you any less. You're probably going to be mad at me at times. That's what happens in a family. And it's important that we learn to respect each other's property. Do you understand?"

Her brow crinkling, Chelsea nodded. "I have to leave your stuff alone."

He fought the beginnings of a smile. "Yeah. Unless you ask permission first and unless I tell you it's okay, you have to leave my stuff alone."

"Come on, Chelsea. We're going to your room. Now," Erin added, taking her daughter's shoulder in a gentle, though firm grip. She glanced briefly at Brett as she led the child from the room.

Brett tried to decide what that look had meant. Did she disapprove of the way he'd handled the situation? Had he been firm enough? Maybe he'd been too firm. Maybe he shouldn't have told Chelsea that he was angry with her. Maybe he shouldn't have ordered her to her room. Maybe he should have just shrugged the whole thing off and complimented her on her artistic talent. What if he'd traumatized her so severely that he'd stifled all her budding creativity.

Sighing in self-disgust, he began to gather his ruined pages. Surely he'd done the right thing. After all, Chelsea had to learn that his work was off-limits. He was certain that Erin would never allow her daughter to get away with destroying assignments she did for the Little Rock advertising agency. Chelsea had simply gotten spoiled, and it was past time he persuaded her that couldn't go on.

He hoped he'd done the right thing.

"What's the damage?" Erin asked quietly from the other side of the desk.

He hadn't heard her come back in. He looked up slowly, trying to read her expression. All he could detect was concern as she anxiously examined his desk. "It's not as bad as it looked at first," he replied. "But it may put our trip to Arkansas back a few days. The wedding's still on as planned, but we won't have quite as long beforehand to get your things in order, I'm afraid. And I guess our sight-seeing trips are over for the time being. I'm going to have to concentrate on redoing these pages so I can get them to my publisher in time."

"I understand," Erin assured him. "Chelsea and I will do everything we can to help you. We'll stay out of your way while you're working. In fact, maybe we should go on home and I can be taking care of things there while you—"

"No," Brett cut in quickly. "I don't want you to go back without me."

"Now, Brett, be reasonable. We'd only be in your way here and I have a thousand things I could be doing at home. There's no reason for us to stay."

"Erin, I'm not going to stop working after we're married. I can work with you and Chelsea here."

"I know you can. I'll make sure of that after we're married," she answered with a smile. "But this time I think it would be best if I take care of things in Arkansas while you're doing this. It will give us much more free time for each other after the wedding," she said, supplying the one argument to which he couldn't object.

He capitulated, as she knew he would. "All right. But I'll miss you. I'll resent every minute that we're apart."

"I know. So will I. But it won't be long," she promised. "Soon we'll be together for always. No more separations."

"I like the sound of that."

She smiled. "So do I."

His own weak smile faded. "Erin, did I—I mean, was I okay? Was I too hard on her? Should I have—?"

She advanced steadily around the desk, her loving gaze locked with his. "Brett . . . Darling. You are an excellent father. You're exactly the kind of father I always wanted for Chelsea. You're loving and kind and funny and sweet. And you were wonderful today. You'll make mistakes sometimes—God knows, I've made my share and will make more—but that's all part of it. We can only follow our instincts and hope for the best."

He almost sagged in relief. "Thank you for trusting me, Erin. I know how hard it was for you."

She cupped his face in her hand and leaned toward him to brush her lips across his. "When it came right down to it, it wasn't hard at all," she murmured. "It was probably the easiest thing I've ever done. I love you, Brett."

He pulled her into his arms, burying his face in her throat. "I love you. Oh, Erin, I love you so much. How did I ever survive without you?"

She laughed quietly and sought his mouth for another kiss. He kissed her eagerly, telling himself that he had to be the luckiest man on earth. He'd found a beautiful, witty, loving wife and an adorable, if normally mischievous daughter—all because he'd once pressed the wrong button on his telephone.

Only it hadn't been the wrong number, after all, he reflected with a surge of satisfaction.

It had been the right number all along.

Epilogue

HER STILL-SLIGHTLY-DAMP body wrapped in a thick terry robe, Erin stepped out of the bathroom, toweling her wet hair. The telephone on the bedside table rang, startling her. One brow lifted as she answered it, looking around the room with a frown. "Hello?"

"Oh, excuse me," a deep voice said. "I was trying to call my sister."

Smiling, Erin shook her head in amused exasperation. Now she knew why the elegant hotel room had been deserted when she'd finished her shower. "I'm sorry, you must have the wrong number," she replied, playing along with his whimsical game. "But you sound very nice. I'd like to meet you sometime."

"Gee, I don't know. What if it didn't work out?"

"Oh, I have a feeling it will work out," she responded in a sultry voice.

"In that case, why don't we get married?"

"I think we already did," she answered with a grin, smugly examining her shiny new gold band. "Five hours ago, to be exact."

"Then what am I doing in the hotel lobby?"

"That's what I'd like to know."

"I'm on my way," he promised her.

"Hurry," she urged, letting the terry robe fall to the floor. "I've learned not to waste precious time." And she gently

hung up the phone. She stood where she was, waiting for
him, happily anticipating the night ahead of them. Chelsea
was staying with Brett's sister and her doting new cousins.
Brett and Erin had three whole days ahead of them. Alone.
Just the two of them.

She was sure they'd make excellent use of those three
days—and nights.

He was there in a matter of minutes, sweeping her into his
arms with a broad grin. "Relationships are so much nicer
in the flesh," he observed, his hands stroking her bare skin
as he pulled her closer to his already aroused body.

"Yes, they are," she agreed, lifting her hands to unfasten
the buttons of his shirt.

They tumbled together onto the bed, laughing breathlessly as they rushed to rid Brett of his decidedly unnecessary clothing. And then they began an all-night celebration
of the odd whims of fate.

FORBIDDEN SURRENDER

Carole Mortimer

He was engaged to one woman...
and in love with her double!

CHAPTER ONE

'MARIE! How are you?'

Sara blinked up at the tall attractive man in front of her, smiling her regret. 'I'm sorry.' Her American accent was very noticeable against his English one. 'I'm afraid you have the wrong person.' She turned away with an apologetic smile, wishing that she could have been the absent Marie. This man was very good-looking, possibly in his mid-twenties, and by the expression in his twinkling blue eyes he looked as if he could be fun to be around.

He took hold of her arm, stopping her from crossing the road. 'Hey, I'm not going to tell Nick that you were wandering around Soho on your own.'

Sara frowned, her deep brown eyes puzzled, a startling contrast to her long golden blond hair, hair bleached by years under the Florida sun. Having lived in America most of her life she had been curious to see the country she had been born in, the country she had lived in until she was a year old, taken to start a new life in America by her mother after the untimely death of her husband.

'I'm sorry,' she repeated to the young man, 'but you really are mistaken.'

He remained unconvinced. 'I love the accent.' He grinned. 'But I know you too well to be fooled by that.' He put his arm about her waist, his fingers spread dangerously close to her breast.

Sara stiffened, revising her opinion of him. He was obviously a flirt, and he sounded as if he and Marie were more than just casual acquaintances.

She gave him a cold stare. 'Would you kindly take your hands off me?' she requested haughtily, flicking her long hair back over her shoulder.

He frowned down at her but made no effort to let her go. 'There's no need to be like this, Marie. I admit I'm a bit sore about the way you ended things between us last year, but Nick—'

Sara squirmed away from him. 'I don't know any Nick, and I don't know you either. And if you don't let go of me I'll call a policeman!' She looked around for one, never having thought a man would try to pick her up so openly. It was the middle of the afternoon, she had got lost during a sightseeing session, and she certainly hadn't expected to be accosted like this.

'Okay, okay.' The man grimaced. 'There's no need to get nasty. If you want to keep up this pretence of being an American tourist then that's all right with me.' He shrugged.

She wasn't pretending to be anything, an American tourist was exactly what she was, although this wasn't a very high class area to have got lost in. She only hoped Aunt Susan didn't go home without her. Only having been in the country a couple of days herself she had no idea of the way back to Aunt Susan's house.

'Maybe I could be your guide?' The man gave her a sideways glance. 'Hey, that could be fun, Marie. We could—'

'I already have a guide,' she interrupted him, annoyed by the fact that he still believed her to be this other woman. It would seem he knew Marie very well, which made his obstinacy about her identity all the more surprising. Unless this was the way he usually picked his women up!

'Oh, I see.' He smiled bitterly. 'I bet Nick doesn't know about this—and I wish to God I didn't!' He bent and kissed her briefly on the mouth. 'See you at the weekend' was his parting shot.

Sara stared after him dazedly. She wasn't a prude, she had been kissed before, but never by a complete stranger. And he had been so respectable to look at too, his black pinstriped suit and snowy white shirt immaculate.

'Sara!' Her plump Aunt Susan arrived breathlessly in front of her. 'Thank goodness I've found you!'

Sara turned, the flirtatious stranger already swallowed up in the crowd. 'I must have lost you in that last shop.' She smiled her apology.

Susan Ford was a pleasantly plump lady of forty-eight, her blond hair kept the same gold as Sara's by a light tint every couple of months, her face still youthfully smooth and attractive. She was Sara's mother's sister, and although the sisters had been parted for the last twenty years their letters to each other had been numerous, so much so that Sara felt as if she already knew her aunt when they had met two days ago, had found herself instantly liking her aunt.

This trip to England wasn't exactly a holiday to Sara, more of a convalescence. Six months ago her mother and stepfather had been killed in a car accident, and besides leaving her orphaned it had also left her with two broken legs, utterly ruining the modelling career that had just been starting to get off the ground.

It had taken six months for the scars to heal, both the emotional and physical ones, and on her final dismissal from the doctor she had arranged this trip to visit her English relatives, finding herself to be a very rich young woman on the death of her stepfather, Richard Hamille. They had been a close family, Sara being adopted by Richard when he had married her mother, and to suddenly find herself alone was very bewildering.

Her Aunt Susan had instantly taken her to her heart, she and Uncle Arthur having no children of their own. Sara felt at home with them, felt at home with England, and in a way she would be sad to leave when the time came. Still, that wouldn't be for another couple of weeks yet.

'Who was that man?' Her aunt frowned. 'The one I saw you talking to?'

Sara shrugged as they fell into step together, making their way back to the busy city centre. 'I have no idea,' she answered her aunt.

Her eyes widened. 'You didn't know him?'

Sara shook her head. 'No.'

'But I saw him kiss you!' Her aunt sounded scandalised.

Sara grinned. 'I think he was trying to pick me up. It wasn't a very good approach, though—he pretended that he thought I was someone else.' She shook her head. 'Not very original!'

'Who did he think you were?'

She shrugged. 'Someone called Marie. I wouldn't have minded, but he seemed so insistent. Oh well.' She dismissed. 'He'll have to chalk this one down to a no-go.'

'Yes, I suppose so,' her aunt agreed vaguely. 'Now, where were we? Oh, yes, if we turn here we should be near the underground. Shall we go home and have a cup of tea? I'm dying for a cup.'

Sara grinned at her, her face alight with mischief, her features strikingly beautiful, the eyes wide and a deep dark brown, heavily fringed by long black lashes, the nose short, the mouth wide and smiling, her teeth very white against her golden skin. Her body was tall and supple, long-legged, and very slender. Her looks were invaluable in her profession, and she hoped to return to modelling when she went back to the States.

'You and your tea!' she chided. After only two days she was well aware of her aunt's weakness for the brew, the other woman seeming to drink gallons of the stuff. Sara preferred coffee herself, but she readily agreed with the idea of going home for refreshment; the visit to Buckingham Palace and the Houses of Parliament had tired her out.

Uncle Arthur came in soon after they did, a short stocky man, going a little thin on top, his sparse brown hair going slightly gray now.

'I have a surprise for you, love.' He beamed at Sara as they ate their dinner. 'I've invited Eddie round tonight, my nephew by my sister Jean. I thought you would like a bit of young company for a change.'

Sara masked her irritation. Her aunt and uncle had been so kind to her, and it was ungrateful of her not to appreciate this extra act of kindness. They had no way of knowing of her recent disillusionment, of the way Barry had let her down when she needed him the most, had walked out on her when the accident had temporarily robbed her of the ability to walk into a room with him and make one of his grand entrances. Barry was an up-and-coming actor, had appeared in several television serials, and he ranked his worth much higher than any television producer had yet had the foresight to do. Sara had been dating him a couple of months before the accident, not realizing that her main attraction had been her undeniable beauty and her original way of dressing. Barry had replaced her within a day of the accident, having no time for her bereavement or her own injuries.

So at the moment she wasn't particularly keen on men. 'That will be nice,' she said, giving a bright smile.

'I hope so.' Her uncle nodded, settling back in his armchair. 'He's a good lad, works in a garage.'

'He doesn't work in a garage, Arthur,' his wife chided. 'He owns one, dear,' she told Sara. 'And he lets other people do the work.'

Sara felt sure Eddie wouldn't agree with that, the poor man was probably worked off his feet. It wasn't easy running a business, she knew that. Her stepfather had run an advertising firm, and he had often come home absolutely exhausted. Eddie probably felt the same way on occasion.

'It's nice of him to spare me the time,' she said in all honesty.

'Well, he took a bit of persuading,' her uncle told her, 'but I managed to talk him round.'

After Barry's desertion of her this wasn't exactly a booster to her morale. It was because of Eddie's apparent reluctance to meet her that she took special care over her appearance that evening.

Her silky suit was in a pale lilac color, the narrow belt that fitted over the shirt top in a deep purple color. Her shoes matched the color of the belt, her legs were long and silky beneath the straight skirt. She was aiming to knock his eyes out, so her make-up was dramatic, just to show him that his time hadn't been wasted.

When she heard him arrive she checked her appearance. Her hair, newly washed, fell in gentle waves halfway down her back, shaped in casual curls either side of her face. Yes, she looked the top model she had rapidly been becoming until the accident, and if Eddie wasn't impressed now he never would be.

He was. It was obvious by the widening of his deep blue eyes, by the way he slowly rose to his feet, his gaze appraising.

'Hi,' she greeted huskily, giving him her most dazzling smile. 'I'm Sara, and you must be Eddie.' She held out her hand politely.

He took her hand, seemingly reluctant to let it go again. His own hand was strong and work-worn, the nails kept short and clean. He was a man possibly in his late twenties, his hair sandy blond, his face attractive, his dress casual in the extreme, his denims faded, his shirt unbuttoned partway down his chest.

'Nice to meet you.' He gave a wide appreciative smile. 'Uncle Arthur didn't tell me how—Well, he didn't say— You're gorgeous!' He grinned.

Sara gave a happy laugh, at last managing to release her hand. 'Thank you, kind sir.' She curtseyed. 'Uncle Arthur wasn't too descriptive about you either,' she admitted, instantly liking this man.

Eddie nodded understandingly. 'You expected me to be wearing an overall, with oil under my fingernails,' he derided.

'Something like that.' She gave a rueful smile. 'Although Aunt Susan assured me you didn't actually work in your garage.' Her eyes twinkled mischievously.

'Charming!'

She burst out laughing at his disgusted expression. 'I'm sure she didn't mean it the way I made it sound.' Her aunt and uncle had taken advantage of Eddie's visit and gone to visit some friends for the evening.

'Hey, you're all right.' Eddie smiled at her. 'Fancy coming out for a pint? A beer,' he explained at her puzzled expression.

'I'd love to.' She accepted eagerly.

She had never been into a 'local' before, had never even been into a bar. Her mother and stepfather were quite protective of her, vetting most of her friends, and keeping her close within their own circle.

She loved the pub they went to, loved the beer Eddie made her try, loved the friendly, warm atmosphere, and most of all she loved the people. She was instantly accepted into Eddie's crowd and persuaded to join in a game of darts, a game she was totally hopeless at. But she had a lot of fun trying, and no one seemed to mind her inability to hit the board twice in a row.

'That was fun!' She gave Eddie a glowing smile on the drive back to her aunt and uncle's house.

'Glad you enjoyed it. Care to come out with me again?' He quirked one eyebrow enquiringly.

'I'd love to!' Sara's face glowed.

'Tomorrow?'

She looked uncertain. 'I'm not sure what plans Aunt Susan and Uncle Arthur have for me. You see—'

'It's okay, Sara,' he cut in dryly, 'I realize I'm not the sort of man you usually go out with.'

She blushed at his intended rebuke. 'I didn't mean that.'

'But it's true, isn't it? You were like a child tonight, enjoyed each new experience with eagerness. Uncle Arthur told me you were a rich kid, in the executive bracket.'

Sara bit her lip, knowing she had hurt him. 'I did enjoy tonight, and I—I'm sorry if I embarrassed you with my enthusiasm. I didn't mean to.'

Eddie sighed. 'You didn't. You were a success, you know you were. Maybe that's why I'm so annoyed—I was jealous of half the men there tonight.'

Sara relaxed somewhat, back on territory she could handle. 'You had no need to be. I always remember who took me on my date, and I always make a point of leaving with that person.'

'So it's still on for tomorrow, if Aunt Susan and Uncle Arthur don't have any other plans for you? And this time I'll take you somewhere I can have you all to myself.'

She wasn't so sure his single-minded interest was a good thing. She would be going back to the States soon, two or three weeks at the most, and it wouldn't do for Eddie to become involved with her, not deeply involved. When she got back home she intended concentrating exclusively on her career. There would be no time for romantic involvement.

'Sara?' Eddie prompted.

'I—er—What did you have in mind?'

He shrugged. 'A meal and then on to a club?'

'It sounds lovely.' She accepted, deciding she could deal with Eddie's interest in her if and when it started to become serious. She liked him, he was fun, and there could be no harm in them going out together. 'What time shall I be ready?'

'Oh, about eight.' He stopped the car outside the house.

'Like to come in for coffee?' she invited.

'Not tonight, thanks. If I know Aunt Susan and Uncle Arthur they'll have gone to bed long ago, and I wouldn't want to disturb them. You'd better ask them for a door key for tomorrow, we could be late.'

'Not too late, I hope.' Sara frowned. 'I need my beauty sleep,' she added lightly.

'I hadn't noticed,' he teased.

She smiled. 'I really don't want to be too late. I—I don't keep late hours any more.' Since leaving the hospital she had taken life at a slow pace, retiring early and rising late.

'Okay.' Eddie sighed. 'I'll have you home by midnight—Cinderella. But I should still ask for a key, they're usually in bed by ten.'

She knew that, and for the last two nights she had done the same thing. 'I'll ask,' she promised. 'And thanks once again for tonight, I had a great time.'

'Enough of a great time to kiss me goodnight?'

She leaned forward and kissed him lightly on the mouth. 'Goodnight,' she called before hurrying into the house.

They had both been wrong; their aunt and uncle weren't in bed at all, they were still in the lounge.

'But it's still worrying,' Aunt Susan could be heard insisting.

'You're worrying over nothing,' her husband chided her. 'Just forget about it, it didn't mean a thing.'

'But, Arthur—'

'Susan!' he said sternly. 'I think I just heard Sara come in, so let's just drop the subject.'

Sara shrugged to herself, coughing to let them know of her presence. Her mother and stepfather had often had minor arguments, but they usually passed within a day or so, and she felt sure things were no different between her aunt and uncle. The middle-aged couple seemed very happy together.

'Did you have a nice time, dear?' her aunt asked as she came into the room.

'Lovely.' She nodded agreement.

'Going out with him again?' Uncle Arthur eyed her over the top of his horn-rimmed glasses.

Sara blushed. 'Tomorrow.'

'Hear that, Susan?' He turned to his wife. 'Before you know it we'll have a wedding on our hands.'

'Arthur!' she warned.

'I'm not getting married for years yet, Uncle Arthur,' Sara told him hastily. 'I'm only twenty, almost twenty-one.'

'Susan and I had already been married two years by that time.'

'It was different when we were young, Arthur,' his wife chided. 'There's so much for young people to do nowadays, places to see, that they don't want to tie themselves down to marriage too young.'

He raised his eyebrows, his eyes twinkling with mischief. 'After all these years she finally tells me she married me out of boredom!' He winked at Sara.

'Go on with you!' his wife scolded. 'Where's Eddie taking you tomorrow?' She turned to ask Sara.

'Out to dinner and then on to a club, he said.' Her aunt and uncle's interest in her evening out was nothing unusual to Sara. Her mother had always been interested in such things too, and it was in fact quite like home sitting and chatting like this after an enjoyable evening out.

'Better than a trip to a pub,' Uncle Arthur teased.

'I liked the pub.' Sara had been quite disappointed that Eddie had decided not to take her back there.

Aunt Susan stood up, putting down her knitting. 'Well, I'm for bed. Arthur?'

'I am too.' He stood up, stretching. 'It's nice having you with us, love,' he told Sara huskily.

She moved to hug him, tears in her eyes. 'It's nice to be here. I wish now I'd come sooner, instead of waiting until—' She broke off, stricken.

Her uncle patted her shoulder awkwardly. 'It's all right, Sara. We're your family now, for as long as you want us.'

'Thank you.' She kissed them both on the cheek before hurrying to her room.

The tears flowed readily once she closed her bedroom door; the loss of her parents was still a raw wound. Without Aunt Susan and Uncle Arthur's support the last few days she didn't know what she would have done; some of the moods of depression she had suffered in the States had been very black indeed.

AFTER AN exhaustive perusal of most of the museums the next day Sara didn't feel up to going anywhere that evening. But she had told Eddie she would go out with him and she couldn't let him down. If they were dining out he had probably had to book a table.

'Oh, you look lovely!' her aunt exclaimed as Sara came into the lounge to wait for Eddie.

She felt quite confident of her appearance, knowing her black dress would be suitable for any occasion, would blend in both at the restaurant and the club, its style demure while still managing to show the perfection of her figure, her breasts firm and uptilting, the slenderness of her waist emphasized by a thick black belt, her hips narrow in the pencil-slim styling of the dress. Her legs were long and smooth, her slender ankles shown to advantage in the high-heeled sandals she wore, a slender gold chain about one of her ankles. She had needed to wear it for one of her photographic sessions, and now found it an attractive piece of jewellery.

She sat down opposite her aunt, her long hair secured on the top of her head, leaving her neck slenderly vulnerable. 'Where's Uncle Arthur?'

'Gone for a drink with a few of his friends.' Her aunt carried on with her knitting, halfway through making a cardigan for her husband. 'It's a regular thing. It does him good to get out for an evening.'

Sara frowned. 'You should have told me, then I wouldn't have arranged to go out tonight.'

'You go out and have a good time,' she encouraged. 'To tell you the truth,' she confided with a smile, 'I usually doze off about nine o'clock.'

'I see.' Sara laughed. 'A bit of peace and quiet, hmm?'

'That's the idea. That will be Eddie,' Aunt Susan said as the doorbell rang.

Sara went and answered the door herself. Eddie was looking very smart in a navy blue suit and contrasting light blue shirt. His eyes widened as her saw her. 'You're ready.' He stepped into the hallway.

'Of course.' She frowned. 'It's eight o'clock, isn't it?'

'Oh, yes.' He nodded. 'I just thought I'd be kept waiting until at least eight-fifteen.'

She smiled as she led the way back to the lounge. 'I always try to be punctual. My mother always told me that if someone has taken the trouble to arrive on time then it's only polite to be ready.'

Eddie smiled. 'I think I would have liked your mother.'

They said their goodbyes to Aunt Susan. The drive to the restaurant was a short one, their table secluded in one of the corners of the room.

'I quite like Chinese food myself,' Eddie told her once they had given their order. 'But not knowing your preferences I played it safe and chose an English restaurant.'

Sara eyed him teasingly. 'You were taking a risk thinking I like to eat at all. Most of the models I know live on milk and lettuce leaves.'

'Hey, that's right—you're a model, aren't you? Are you open to offers? And I meant for work,' he added dryly.

She shrugged. 'I will be, when I get back to the States. I don't have a permit to work over here. This trip is strictly pleasure.'

'Pity. I have a friend who's a photographer. No, really,' he insisted at her dubious expression. 'Pete and I were at school together. He's quite successful over here.'

'Maybe some other time,' Sara said regretfully.

'Okay. Maybe I'll be able to introduce the two of you before you go home, then you'll have a contact over here if you ever should decide to work here.'

Sara smiled, her skin a glowing peach color, her eyes deeply brown. 'That's really nice of you, thank you.'

'No trouble,' Eddie dismissed.

It was after ten when they left the restaurant for the club, by now the two of them firm friends. Sara's eyes were glowing from the amount of wine she had consumed during her meal, her smile more ready than usual.

The club was plush and exclusive, not really the sort of place she would have thought Eddie would have enjoyed frequenting.

'I know what you're thinking.' Eddie grimaced. 'But I've been here a couple of times with Pete.' He shrugged. 'I like watching the rich lose their money.' He referred to the gambling tables, jewel-bedecked women and quietly affluent men gazing avidly down at the tables. 'Pete's a member,' he explained the fact that they had actually been able to get in. 'And the people here know me.'

Sara felt slightly uncomfortable among such people. 'That sounds as if you've been here more than a couple of times,' she teased.

He looked sheepish. 'Maybe a few.'

She put her arm through his, determinedly putting any feelings of shyness behind her. 'Let's go and take a look.'

She had never been in a gambling club before, and for the first half hour she found it all fascinating. They were standing behind a middle-aged woman who to Sara's knowledge systematically lost every bet she placed. Sara stood back away from the light, finding it all very sickening, the only word she could think of to describe that mindless addiction.

'I'll get you a drink,' Eddie suggested.

She would rather have left, but she didn't want to be a killjoy. Eddie was enjoying himself, and they would probably be leaving quite soon. She accepted the offer of a drink, continuing to watch the play in front of her, not understanding it at all but becoming more and more fascinated by the spin of the roulette wheel as she waited for Eddie's return.

A woman on the other side of the table finally gave up, standing up to leave. A man moved to take her place, and Sara watched him as he began to win. This man had the look of an experienced gambler, a deadpan face, his blue eyes shrewd.

Sara watched him, her interest in the roulette reawakened. His movements were made without haste, his hands slender and lean, the fingers long and tapered. Her eyes were drawn from his hands to his face—a hard face, the deep blue eyes narrowed, the nose hawk-like, the mouth compressed, his jaw set at a strong angle. The evening suit he wore was impeccably styled, as was his dark over-long hair, his manner assured and speaking of wealth. The staff of the club treated him with deep respect, making Sara wonder who he could be. He was in his mid-thirties, maybe a little younger, and yet he seemed to be a man of affluence.

Suddenly he looked up and caught her watching him, and his face darkened into a frown, any attractiveness about him instantly disappearing. She recoiled from the angry dislike in his blazing blue eyes and turned away in search of Eddie. He was a long time getting their drinks.

Someone grasped her arm and she was roughly spun around to face the man she had been watching at the roulette table. He must have left the table immediately she turned away.

'What the hell are you doing here?' he rasped, his fingers painful on her arm.

Sara frowned at this attack on her, both physically and verbally. 'I—We—I was signed in.'

His mouth twisted—a perfect mouth, the lower lip fuller, pointing to a sensuality this man would take pains to hide. 'So you aren't alone?'

'No—'

The man pulled her away from the table and over to a quiet corner of the room—if it could be called quiet in a room like this. 'Who are you with?' he demanded to know.

'I—Let me go!' Sara tried to pry his fingers loose, looking up at him with wide apprehensive eyes. If she had done something wrong by being here why didn't he just say so and let her leave? There was no need for him to get rough with her. And where was Eddie? He could explain that he had signed her in, that his friend was a member. 'You're hurting me!' she cried as his strong fingers refused to be dislodged from her arm.

His teeth snapped together, white teeth, very even. 'I'd like to do more than that!' He thrust her away from him. 'Who's the man?' he asked tautly.

Sara rubbed her bruised skin. 'Eddie Mayer,' she muttered.

The man's expression was grim, frighteningly so. 'I don't know him, but then I never do, do I? Well, you got this Eddie Mayer to bring you, so he can damn well take you home again. We'll discuss this tomorrow.'

She blinked up at him. 'Tomorrow...?'

'Yes, tomorrow. And make sure you're there. I'm getting a little tired of these exploits of yours, Marie. I thought they were over.' He sighed. 'God, if your father knew . . .' He shook his head.

It was Marie again! For the second time in two days she had been mistaken for this other girl, Marie. This man must be another of her men, and the man Nick that the man of yesterday had warned her about was obviously this girl's father. Considering she didn't know the girl she was finding out a lot about her!

Well, this man was a definite improvement on yesterday's, although he was no less wrong about her identification. 'There's been a mistake—'

'Yes,' he hissed angrily, 'and I'm beginning to think I made it!' He gave her a disgusted look. 'We'll talk tomorrow.' He turned and walked out of the club with long controlled strides.

Sara was left feeling as if she had just survived an earthquake, or something equally disastrous. Whoever this Marie was she led an interesting and varied life, and it looked as if this last man had had enough. The other girl was obviously a flirt, but that didn't make it right that she was going to get the blame for something she hadn't done.

She was curious to know the man's identity, and walked over to the doorman. 'That man . . .' she paused hesitantly. 'The one that just left . . .'

'Mr. Thorne?' the man enquired politely.

'Oh, Mr. Thorne.' She feigned disappointment. 'It seems I made a mistake, I thought it was Gerrard Turner.' She hastily made a name up.

'No, miss.' The doorman shook his head, 'that was Mr. Dominic Thorne. He's in engineering.'

'Thank you.' She smiled. 'Wrong man.' She shrugged before walking away.

When the man said Dominic Thorne was 'in engineering' she felt sure he meant that he ran these firms. There had been an air of authority about the man, a determination that wouldn't let him be ruled by anyone. Despite his rough treatment of her, Sara had found him attractive. A shame he was interested in someone called Marie, a girl who appeared to be her double.

She had read that everyone had a double somewhere in the world, but it seemed hers was living in London, and that their likeness was so extreme that even this Marie's lovers seemed to have been fooled. And Sara was sure both those men had been her lovers; they had both had a strong sense of familiarity about them towards her—or rather, Marie.

'Sara!' Eddie appeared in front of her. 'I thought for a minute you'd left without me.' He sighed his relief. 'Sorry I was so long, but I ran into Pete. Come over and meet him.'

She went willingly enough, just relieved to have him back with her, before any more of Marie's men accosted her. Pete proved to be an extrovert, even the sober suit and tie did not diminish his exuberant nature.

'Wow!' he exclaimed when he saw her, pulling her on to the bar stool next to him. 'I bet you're a natural,' he enthused, studying her with the practised eye of a photographer. 'Boy, would I like to get you the other side of my camera,' he spoke softly to himself. 'No chance of that?' He quirked a hopeful eyebrow.

Sara grinned at him; this enthusiasm was doing wonders for her ego. 'Not this trip.' She refused him. 'I've already explained to Eddie that I don't have a permit—'

'I could get you one,' Pete cut in eagerly.

She shook her head. 'I'm still convalescing.'

'Mm, Eddie explained.' Pete was studying her closely. 'Have you ever worked in this country?'

'I've never even been here before, except as a baby, so I certainly haven't worked here before.'

'I have this feeling I've seen you before.' He frowned his puzzlement.

'Not you too!' Sara sighed. 'You're the third one since I've been here.'

'At the club?' Eddie enquired, sitting the other side of her.

'No, in England. People keep thinking I'm someone else.'

'A pick-up!' He dismissed.

'No.' She shook her head. 'The first time it happened I thought that, but it happened again tonight, here, and both men thought I was the same person.' She shrugged her puzzlement.

Eddie put his arm about her shoulders. 'I refuse to believe there are two like you.' He smiled at her warmly. 'Nature couldn't have been that generous!'

Sara ignored the pointed show of possession, realizing that Eddie was warning his friend off her. Not that she particularly minded, one man was complication enough for her stay here. 'It was all very odd, though. Still.' She dismissed it from her mind. 'It doesn't matter. Could we possibly leave now, Eddie? It's getting late, and Aunt Susan and Uncle Arthur seem to have taken to waiting up for me.'

They made their goodbyes to Pete, and Sara promised to get in touch with him if she ever decided to work in England.

'Lucky we ran into him,' Eddie remarked on the drive home. 'He can be an elusive man, impossible to find at times.'

Sara was preoccupied, unable to put the thought of the man at the casino out of her mind. He hadn't been the sort of individual you forgot in a hurry; his manner was forceful, his attractiveness mesmerizing, animally sensual. Whoever Marie was, she was a lucky girl to have had him for a lover.

'Eddie.' She bit her lip thoughtfully. 'Tonight, at the club, there was a man called Dominic Thorne. Do you know him?'

He spluttered with laughter. 'You have to be joking! He's out of my league, love,' he added less scornfully.

'But you have heard of him?'

'Who hasn't?' He shrugged, halting the car outside the house. 'He has his finger in every business pie going, every one that's legal, that is. He and his partner—well, his father's partner, actually, but the old man's dead now—they're in the millionaire class.'

'Is he married?' Sara made the query as casually as she could, not wanting to show her extreme interest in Eddie's answer.

'No.' He grinned. 'But he's going to be. He's done the sensible thing, he's got himself engaged to his partner's daughter, Marie Lindlay.'

Sara swallowed hard. 'Marie . . . ?'

'Mmm. One day Dominic Thorne will have it all, all the business interests plus the lovely Marie.'

Sara was no longer listening to him. This Marie everyone kept confusing her with was actually going to *marry* Dominic Thorne. Surely he couldn't mistake another woman for the girl he was going to marry?

CHAPTER TWO

IT WAS ALL a puzzle to Sara, one there seemed no answer to. She mentioned it to her aunt, but she dismissed it as a coincidence.

'But even her fiancé thought I was this other girl.' Sara frowned.

Her aunt shrugged. 'It was dark in there, it was probably just a case of mistaken identity.'

'It feels weird to be so like another person.'

'Maybe you aren't really.' Aunt Susan dismissed. 'As I said, the lighting probably wasn't very good in this club you went to. Mr. Thorne's girlfriend probably has blond hair too, and in a bad light maybe you do have a resemblance to this other girl. I should just forget about it, Sara.'

'I suppose so.' She sighed. 'Although it might be interesting to actually see this Marie Lindlay.'

'Is that her name?'

'Eddies says it is.' She nodded.

'I—Oh, damn!' Her aunt swore as she dropped a cup, watching in dismay as it smashed on the floor. 'One of my best set, too.' She tutted, bending down to pick up the pieces. 'I hope they're still making these, I'd like to buy a replacement for it.' She put the pieces in the garbage.

'I'm sure they do.' Sara swept up the shattered fragments still scattered on the floor.

Her uncle came into the room. 'Did I hear a crash just now?'

'It's as well I hadn't fallen over,' his wife snapped. 'It took you long enough to get in here.'

He looked taken aback by this unexpected attack. 'I knew Sara was in here helping you wash up.' He frowned. 'It was only a crash, Susan, not a thump.'

'It's all right, Uncle Arthur,' Sara soothed. 'Aunt Susan's just broken one of her best china cups, and I'm afraid she's rather upset about it. Take her into the lounge and I'll make you both a nice cup of tea.'

He nodded. 'Come on, Susan. It was only a cup,' he chided as they went through to the lounge.

'It wasn't that, Arthur. It was—' The kitchen door closed, cutting off the rest of the conversation.

Poor Aunt Susan, the tea set obviously meant a lot to her. It was rather lovely to look at, very delicately made, with an old-fashioned floral pattern. She would see if she could get a replacement this afternoon when she went shopping.

'Where's Eddie taking you tonight?' her uncle asked as she took their cups of tea in to them.

'I'm not seeing him tonight.' She had turned down his invitation for this evening, deciding that three nights in a row was just too much. 'But he's taking me out for a drive tomorrow,' she added ruefully. Eddie had been adamant about seeing her again, and she had finally agreed to let him drive her to see some of the English countryside.

London was interesting, there was certainly plenty to see, but she was well aware that there was a lot more to England than its capital. Her mother had never forgotten the greenness of the countryside here, it had been the one thing she really missed by living in America, and Sara was determined to see some of it before she left.

'As long as it isn't another casino.' Her aunt shook her head disapprovingly.

Sara laughed. 'It was quite an experience.'

'Not one I'd like to see repeated,' Aunt Susan said sternly. 'I gave him a piece of my mind last night after you'd gone to bed. Taking you to a gambling hall, indeed!' she added disgustedly.

'You make it sound like a den of iniquity,' her husband teased.

'I'm sure Rachel wouldn't have approved of Sara going to such a place, and I don't either. And Eddie introduced Sara to that mad friend Pete of his.'

Uncle Arthur smiled. 'He isn't mad, Susan. A bit of an extrovert maybe, but there's no harm in him.'

It wasn't like her aunt to be bad-tempered, and Sara could only assume that breaking the cup had upset her more than they had realized.

She managed to find a replacement that afternoon, although she seemed to have walked most of London to find it. Her aunt was suitably pleased with her purchase.

'Eddie telephoned while you were out.' Her aunt put the cup with the rest of the set.

Sara looked up. 'Did he happen to say what he wanted?'

Her aunt smiled. 'He didn't "happen" to say at all—I asked him. He said something about a party tonight.'

'I see.' She bit her lip. 'He'll be calling back, then?'

'Mmm. Soon, I should think.'

Ten minutes later a call came through, only this time it was Pete. 'Do you fancy going to a party?' he asked her.

'I think Eddie intends inviting me to one.' She refused.

'On my behalf. I'm the one who wants to take you to the party. Eddie has to work.'

Sara bristled angrily. 'I went out with Eddie because he's my uncle's nephew. I don't expect to be passed around to Eddie's friends!'

'Hey,' Pete chided, 'that isn't the idea at all.'

'Then what is?' she snapped.

'I suddenly realized why I thought you'd worked in this country before, and I wondered if you would like to meet your double.'

'Double . . . ?' she repeated dazedly.

'Mmm, you look exactly like Marie Lindlay.'

Sara frowned. Again someone had noticed the similarity. Her curiosity was aroused once again. To be able to see this girl, to see exactly what their similarity was would be fun, even if this apparent likeness turned out to be a myth in the end.

'What sort of party is it?' She delayed making a decision.

'Given to amuse the idle rich,' he said scornfully.

'Then how did you get an invitation?' she teased, her anger leaving her.

'Naughty!' Pete chided. 'Actually I'm a friend of a friend, and I have it on good authority that Marie Lindlay is going to be there, with her fiancé, no less.'

Dominic Thorne. It would be interesting to see his face when he saw her, and at least she would be able to prove to him that his fiancée was telling the truth when she denied being at the club the evening before. Besides, she just wanted to get another look at him, to see if he really was as good-looking as her imagination told her he was.

'Okay,' she agreed. 'What shall I wear?' She didn't want to turn up wearing completely the wrong outfit.

'As little as possible.' She could almost hear Pete grinning. 'To tell you the truth, I usually take one of my models to these parties, and she wears the most shocking clothes. I like to make an entrance,' he added with humor.

Another one! 'Right.' Sara knew exactly the dress she was going to wear. 'I'll be ready at eight.'

'Make it nine,' Pete advised. 'These parties rarely get going until at least ten-thirty.'

'And the later we are the more of an entrance we can make,' Sara guessed dryly, knowing this from her experiences with Barry. 'Okay, nine it is.'

She was searching through her clothes in her wardrobe when her aunt came into the room. She had just found the gold dress and matching cape, and she quickly buried them beneath her other clothing. Aunt Susan would certainly not approve.

'Dinner's ready,' her aunt told her.

'So am I.' Sara smiled. 'I'm starving.'

She mentioned the party as they were eating their meal, and her uncle talked down Aunt Susan's objections.

'Let the girl enjoy herself,' he said affectionately. 'Lord knows she'll be leaving us soon enough.'

'But, Arthur—'

'Stop fussing, woman!' Sara's usually mild uncle spoke very firmly. 'Sara's quite old enough to know what she's doing. Pete may seem a little on the wild side to us, but to Sara I'm sure he seems a lot of fun.'

'He does.' She grinned, agreeing with her uncle. There was no harm in Pete, he was just a joker.

'Then that's all that matters. Are there any more potatoes, Susan?' He quirked an eyebrow at his wife.

She gave an impatient sigh. 'I thought you might say that, which is why I did the normal amount of potatoes.' She went into the kitchen to get them.

Sara's uncle turned to wink at her. 'After thirty years she knows me better than I know myself.'

Sara hoped, if she ever got married, that she and her husband were as happy together after being married the same number of years.

She was glad of the cape top when she was at last dressed in the gold dress, it served to hide the scantiness of the gown's bodice. The material barely covered her naked breasts. The gown was still daring, but not as much as when the cape was removed.

When she heard Pete at the door she put her head around the lounge door and made her hurried goodbyes, dashing outside to join Pete before her aunt and uncle could see what she was wearing, not because she was ashamed of the dress but because she knew they wouldn't understand why she was wearing it. A dress like this would be perfectly acceptable in the company she would be mixing in this evening, in fact she had attended a party with her parents in it, but she was sure her aunt and uncle would be slightly shocked by its daring.

Pete wasn't so much shocked as delighted. 'Beautiful,' he murmured appreciatively.

Sara gave a happy laugh. 'Stop drooling and drive,' she ordered.

He did, driving to the more exclusive part of London. The cars in the driveway they finally arrived at were all in the expensive Rolls-Royce and Jaguar bracket. Pete's car was a Jaguar too, a vintage model, so it wasn't in the least out of place.

He grinned at her appreciation of it as he locked the doors. 'I bought it cheap. It was a wreck when I found it,' he explained. 'Eddie did it up for me.'

'Nice to have a friend who can see to your cars for you,' she teased.

'A friend who doesn't mind me taking his girl out for the evening.' He raised one eyebrow questioningly.

Her smile faded. 'I'm not his girl, Pete. We're just friends.'

'I know.' He grinned. 'Eddie told me he'd been politely but firmly warned off. Don't worry, Sara,' he said at her frown. 'He doesn't mind. Eddie isn't into serious relationships either.'

'I'm not into *any* sort of relationships!'

He quirked his eyebrow again. 'Bad love affair?' he asked softly.

Sara gave a scornful snort. 'No affair, and no love either. What it was was just bad.'

'And it's over now?'

'Very much so,' she continued vehemently.

'Right, then let's go in and dazzle the crowd.'

'In that case I'd better take this off first.' She whisked the cape off, and her blonde curls cascaded down one shoulder and over her breast, pinned by a comb at the nape.

'Wow!' Pete gasped his appreciation. 'Dazzle is the right word. Come on,' he took her arm, 'I'm going to enjoy this.'

Sara walked beside him into the entrance hall of the house. 'Do I really look like this Marie Lindlay? My aunt and—no, just my aunt, she thinks that it's probably just superficial.'

'Well, I hope you don't have Marie's nature. She can be a bit of a flirt on occasion, or so I've heard. But as far as the face and body are concerned you're identical.'

She shook her head. 'It's hard to believe.'

'But true. I looked at some photographs of her today.' He shook his head. 'It's unnatural. Let's go inside, then you can see for yourself.'

The long room they entered was crammed full of people, all of them talking in loud refined voices, and sparkling with diamonds. Several people turned to look at them as the butler showed them in, and a tall redhead broke away from the crowd of people she had been talking to and made her way towards them.

'Our hostess,' Pete had time to mutter before the woman descended on them in an expensive cloud of perfume.

'Pete darling!' she cried before hugging him, kissing him lightly on the cheek. 'And I see you've brought Marie with you.' Her tone cooled somewhat. 'What have you done with Dominic, darling?' she spoke to Sara, her blue eyes hard.

'I—'

'This is Sara Hamille, Cynthia,' Pete interrupted.

The blue eyes became even harder, the beautiful face assessing. 'What game are you playing, Marie?' she finally asked.

Sara looked confused. 'No, really, I—'

'A change of accent doesn't make you any less Marie Lindlay,' the woman scolded. 'And Dominic is going to be furious when he arrives. Oh, well,' she said dismissively, 'it's your funeral. Drinks are over there.' She waved her hand vaguely in the direction of the bar. 'Help yourselves to food.' She moved gracefully back to the people she had previously been conversing with.

'You see?' Pete dragged Sara over to the bar. 'If you can fool Cynthia, you can fool anyone. She and Marie have been friends since boarding school.'

Sara grimaced. 'Are you sure "friends" is the right description?'

'They're like that in this crowd,' he said dismissively. 'They stab each other in the back every opportunity they get. For instance, they're probably all looking forward to the scene between Dominic Thorne and the supposed Marie Lindlay.'

'How nice!' she said with unconcealed sarcasm.

'Come on, let's have a drink,' Pete encouraged. 'We might as well enjoy ourselves now we're here.'

An hour later, when Dominic Thorne and Marie Lindlay still hadn't put in an appearance, Sara was beginning to wonder if they were coming, and she said as much to Pete.

'Don't worry,' he assured her gaily, 'they'll be here. It's only just gone ten o'clock.'

'I wouldn't mind.' She grimaced. 'But everyone here seems to think I really am Marie Lindlay. A couple of people have turned nasty because I refuse to admit to being her.'

'Then they're going to get a shock when the real one walks in. Have another drink.'

She was beginning to think they should leave. It was all turning out to be very embarrassing, these people convinced she was the other girl trying to make a fool of them, so much so that she was even beginning to doubt herself. Cynthia Robotham-James, their hostess, had become very annoyed with her a few minutes ago when she had again insisted her name was Sara Hamille.

'Here we go,' Pete suddenly whispered in her ear. 'Look over at the door,' he said fiercely.

Sara looked. Dominic Thorne was instantly recognizable in black velvet jacket and matching trousers, his snowy white shirt emphasizing his tan. She held her breath as her gaze passed down to the girl at his side, gasping at what she saw. The hairstyle was different, the dress even more daring than the one she was wearing—if that were possible, and yet looking at the girl at Dominic Thorne's side was like seeing a mirror image. No wonder everyone kept insisting she was Marie. The two of them looked exactly alike!

'You see?' Pete said excitedly. 'Didn't I tell you? Let's go over there.'

'No!' She hung back, too confused at the moment to actually meet the other girl.

'Come on,' Pete insisted. 'I'm not going to miss out on the fun now.'

Sara allowed herself to be pulled towards the doorway, too numb at the moment to offer any resistance. How could two people possibly be so much alike unless they were related in some way, and yet she had no cousins and was an only child herself. She shook her head dazedly, then looked up to find steely blue eyes fixed on her.

Dominic Thorne registered her appearance with a narrowing of those eyes, his body tensing. He looked down at his fiancée and then back to Sara, frowning darkly. He bent down to whisper something in Marie's ear, and she lifted her head, her eyes the same deep brown as Sara's as the two girls stared at each other.

Pete was the only one in the group of four who remained immune to the sudden tension. 'Hi,' he greeted Marie brightly. 'Permit me to introduce Sara Hamille.' He made the announcement with a great deal of pleasure, obviously enjoying this situation immensely.

'Miss Hamille,' Dominic Thorne was the first to break the silence, his voice just as deep and attractive as Sara remembered it, all of him just as attractive as she remembered.

'Mr. Thorne,' she acknowledged, still staring at Marie Lindlay, and the other girl stared right back.

Suddenly that beautiful face broke into a smile, a mischievous smile. 'So you're the girl who's been going around London impersonating me?' she accused jokingly.

'Hardly impersonating,' Dominic Thorne replied, completely in control of himself again, *and* the situation. 'Miss Hamille has been acting as herself, it's others who have taken her to be you.' He looked at Sara with narrowed eyes. 'I believe I owe you an apology,' he said, as if the words didn't come easily to him, as if he rarely had to admit to being in the wrong.

'Let's move away from the doorway,' Marie suggested lightly. Her voice was completely different from Sara's, her education obviously having been in one of England's finest boarding schools. 'We're attracting a lot of attention standing here.'

'I'm afraid that's my fault,' Sara admitted as they moved to a less prominent part of the room. 'The people here refused to believe I wasn't Marie Lindlay, and now that you've arrived . . .' She shrugged.

'Ooh, how lovely!' Marie clapped her hands in delight. 'Isn't this fun, Dominic?' she exclaimed.

'I doubt Miss Hamille has thought it so, it can't have been easy being thought to be you,' he added dryly.

'Oh, Dominic!' Marie pouted prettily.

He turned to look at Sara, his eyes once again registering his shock at her likeness to his fiancée. 'I really must apologize for my behaviour yesterday evening.' His voice was stilted, his manner haughty. 'You must have thought me very strange.'

Sara flushed. 'And you must have thought me even stranger.'

'Not really.' He shook his head.

Marie gave a tinkling laugh, her long blond hair brushed freely about her shoulders. 'Dominic has this mad idea that I keep going off with other men.' She looked up at him through dark, silky lashes. 'Don't you, my jealous darling?'

Sara found Marie's clinging behaviour where Dominic
Thorne was concerned rather uncomfortable to watch. The
reason for this feeling was easily explained; it was like
watching herself—and she knew she could never act that
way with this arrogant man.

But maybe Dominic Thorne had reason to be suspicious of Marie. The man in Soho had certainly been more
than a friend to her.

'I'm sure Miss Hamille isn't interested in what I do or do
not think,' he said curtly. 'Now don't you think we should
make our presence known to Cynthia?'

It was a deliberate snub, but not one Marie seemed
about to endorse. 'I can't lose sight of my double now. Just
think of the fun we could have, Sara.' Her eyes lit up with
pleasure. 'We could play some terrific tricks on people!'
She turned Sara towards the mirror that adorned the wall
behind them. 'It's incredible,' she said breathlessly, staring at their reflections.

And it was incredible, the likeness was uncanny. Sara's
hair was possibly a little lighter in color, bleached by years
under the Florida sun, and her skin was a more golden
color against Marie's magnolia coloring, but other than
that they were identical—the same height, the same features, even the same slender fingers, but a huge diamond
ring sparkled on the third finger of Marie's left hand.

'I think unbelievable is a more apt word.' Dominic
Thorne came to stand between them. 'Have you always
looked like this, Miss Hamille?' The question was almost
an accusation.

She flushed at his tone. 'Are you implying I've had
plastic surgery to make me look like Marie? Because I can
assure you I haven't,' she said indignantly.

'No, she hasn't,' Pete cut in, indignant on her behalf. 'I can spot that sort of thing a mile away. Sara was born with that face.'

'Well, I can assure you *I* haven't had plastic surgery. Dominic,' Marie told her fiancé.

'Considering I've known you since you were ten years old I would say that was obvious,' he said scornfully. 'But there has to be some explanation for this.'

'I can't think of one,' Marie said dismissively. 'Come on, Sara, we'll go and show Cynthia you aren't a liar at all.' She took Sara by the arm and led her away.

Sara was fuming, aware of the fact that Dominic Thorne didn't like her, distrusted her. Plastic surgery indeed!

'You mustn't mind Dominic.' Marie seemed to read her thoughts. 'He's suspicious by nature.'

Sara couldn't dismiss him so easily, although she did her best as Marie led her from group to group, the other girl loving the sensation they were causing.

'I really must get back to Pete,' Sara insisted at last, having noticed that he was having extreme difficulty conversing with the taciturn Dominic Thorne, those steely blue eyes never leaving Marie and herself.

Marie looked regretful. 'And I suppose I should get back to Dominic.' The smile she gave him was radiant, her hand once again through the crook of his arm as she looked up at him affectionately.

'I think we should be going now,' Sara told Pete.

'Surely not?' To her surprise it was Dominic Thorne who made the objection. 'I was just going to ask you if you would care to dance.'

Sara loved to dance, although Pete assured her that he was absolutely tone deaf and so hopeless at dancing. But despite her love of dancing she didn't relish the idea of being relatively alone with Dominic Thorne.

'I really think we should be leaving now.' She put as much regret in her voice as she could in the circumstances.

Those hard blue eyes remained fixed on her face. 'One dance isn't going to delay you too long, surely?' he persisted.

'I—'

'Oh, go on, Sara,' Pete encouraged. 'Five minutes isn't going to make that much difference.'

'It never pays to argue with Dominic.' Even Marie added her argument in favor of the dance.

Sara gave a resigned shrug. 'Very well, I'd love to dance, Mr. Thorne.'

'Dominic, please,' he could be heard saying as he manoeuvred her onto the space that had been cleared for dancing, some of the couples around them doing more than dancing as the alcohol they had consumed hit their bloodstream. Sara was quite embarrassed by some of the things that were going on. 'Ignore them,' Dominic advised, seeing her shocked expression.

'I—That's a little difficult.' She gasped as she saw one man blatantly touching the bare breast of his dancing partner.

Dominic saw it too, not bothering to dance any more but taking her hand and leading her out of the double doors that led to the garden.

Sara snatched her hand away, eyeing him warily. 'Is it always like that?' she asked disgustedly.

'It gets worse,' he derided.

Then thank goodness she was leaving. And thank goodness she hadn't actually got to dance with this man. Even in the brief moment he had pulled her into his arms she had been aware of his masculinity, of the sensual air that surrounded him. Not that she felt any safer completely alone with him out here, where the noise of the party sounded strangely muted. And she soon realized why—he had closed the doors behind them.

He took a packet of cigars out of his breast pocket, lighting one with a gold lighter. 'You've obviously never been to one of Cynthia's parties before,' he mocked.

Sara moved restlessly, wishing he would stop staring at her with those curiously intent eyes, as if he were trying to see into her very soul. 'No,' she confirmed nervously.

'Have you been in England long?' The query sounded casual, and yet Sara had the feeling it wasn't any such thing.

She shrugged. 'A few days.'

He nodded. 'Are you here with your parents?'

'They were both killed in a car accident six months ago,' she said jerkily.

'I see. I'm sorry,' he added as an afterthought. 'So you're over here on holiday?'

'Yes.' No point in mentioning that she was slowly recovering from her own injuries in the car accident, it wasn't of interest to this man.

'So Mr. Glenn is a relatively new acquaintance?'

'Very new.' She frowned. 'I don't understand the reason for these questions, Mr. Thorne.'

He shrugged. 'You didn't seem surprised by Marie's likeness to you, and as you are obviously an American and have only just arrived in England I wondered how you'd learnt of Marie's existence.'

Sara stiffened. 'I'm not sure that I like your tone, Mr. Thorne.' He sounded almost accusing, as if he suspected her of something but hadn't yet stated these suspicions.

'I'm sorry if you take exception to what I've said.' But he didn't look in the least sorry; his expression was hard, his eyes narrowed to icy slits. 'But I'm sure you can understand my puzzlement as to your reason for seeking out my fiancée.'

'I didn't seek her out!' Sara snapped resentfully. 'I admit that I wanted to see her, but only because so many people had taken me to be her, yourself included,' she added pointedly. 'I had no ulterior motive for meeting Marie, as you seem to be implying I have.'

Dominic Thorne remained unmoved by her heated outburst. 'Did I do that?' he asked silkily.

'You know you did. Just why do *you* think I wanted to see Marie?' There were two spots of angry colour in her cheeks.

He shrugged. 'She's rich, and—'

He didn't get any further. Sara's hand swung up to strike him forcibly on the side of the face, and she watched with satisfaction as angry red welts appeared on his rigid cheek. This satisfaction soon faded as she saw the angry glitter in glacial blue eyes.

'You deserved that!' she spluttered, backing away. 'You—'

Now it was his turn to render her speechless—only his method was much more destructive! Barry had liked to kiss her, in his practised way he had believed he was arousing her, but this man, Dominic Thorne, ravished her mouth with his lips, bent her curves to mould against his hard muscled body, rendered her breathless—and aroused her against her will.

'How dare you!' she demanded when he at last released her mouth, pushing away from him.

Her indignation only served to amuse him. 'Couldn't you have come out with something a little more original than that?' he mocked. 'You disappoint me, Miss Hamille.'

Her eyes flashed. 'And you disappoint me too, Mr. Thorne!' She wiped her mouth with the back of her hand, watching his expression darken. 'I had expected more than brutality from the celebrated Dominic Thorne,' she added insultingly.

'You know,' he drawled slowly, 'your similarity to Marie is only skin-deep.' His look was contemptuous of her slender curves and flushed face.

'Maybe she appreciates your—your savagery.' She spat the words at him angrily. 'But I don't! Excuse me, Mr. Thorne, I hope I never have the misfortune to meet you again.' She spun on her heel, but was stopped from leaving by his hand on her arm. 'Let go of me!' she ordered coldly.

He looked down at her, his jaw rigid, a pulse beating rapidly in his throat. 'I hope we never meet again, Sara,' his voice was husky. 'But for a completely different reason from yours.'

'Goodbye, Mr. Thorne!' She swung away from him, and this time he made no effort to stop her.

'Goodbye, Sara...' he said softly as she closed the door behind her.

She marched straight over to Pete as he still stood talking to Marie, her anger making her look even more beautiful in that moment. 'I'm ready to leave,' she told Pete tautly.

Marie burst out laughing. 'Has Dominic been upsetting you?' she chuckled. 'I can see he has.' She put her arm through Sara's. 'You mustn't mind Dominic. If he's been insulting you, which I think he must have done, he was probably only trying to protect me. Dominic always thinks he has to protect me from something.'

'Then this time he's done a good job of it,' Sara said distantly. 'I'm sorry I bothered you, Miss Lindlay. I can assure you I had no intention of upsetting you in any way.'

Marie's smile was openly scornful. 'I'm not upset. I've had the most fun tonight that I've had in a long time. If you give me your telephone number perhaps I can call you some time and we can have lunch together.'

Sara hesitated, Dominic Thorne's determination for Marie and herself never to meet again fixed firmly in her mind. He had made his opinion more than clear, and she doubted if many people opposed that strong will of his.

'Oh, please do,' Marie encouraged. 'Dominic doesn't even have to know about it. Please,' she added with a beguiling smile.

Sara knew this sort of persuasion of old—she must look exactly the same when she tried to get her own way. How could she possibly refuse! 'All right.' She wrote out her aunt's telephone number on the piece of paper Marie provided. 'But I'm only here for another couple of weeks at the most.'

'Oh, I'll call you before then,' Marie assured her.

Sara saw Dominic Thorne fast approaching their little group and so she hurriedly made her goodbyes. She had had enough of him for one evening.

'Where did Thorne take you?' Pete asked on the drive home.

'Outside,' she revealed furiously. 'He seemed to think I was trying to pull a stunt on them.'

Pete laughed. 'Men like him don't understand coincidence. How did you like Marie?' He gave her a sideways glance.

'How did *you* like her?' She quirked an eyebrow at him. She hadn't missed their slightly flirtatious manner when she had rejoined them.

'I liked her a lot,' he acknowledged softly. 'It's strange, the two of you look exactly alike, and yet there's a difference. You have an air of sexual challenge about you that Marie doesn't have, and I'm into the innocent look at the moment. Not that I'm complaining,' he added hastily, 'but I think Thorne probably spends most of his time fighting men off her.'

'He certainly watches over her well,' Sara said moodily.

'So would I.' Pete grinned.

'Lecherous beast!' She started to relax a little, her indignation about Dominic Thorne's treatment of her put firmly to the back of her mind. 'I doubt if Marie would stay innocent for long around you.'

He shrugged. 'Marie has these vibrations... and I felt them.'

Sara gave him a worried look. 'I wouldn't advise stepping on those particular toes.' Dominic Thorne would deal far more ruthlessly with a man.

'If the lady's willing...'

'Ah, but is she?'

'I think she could be,' he nodded.

She shrugged. 'Then I wish you luck.'

If Dominic Thorne found out about it then Pete was going to need more than luck!

Her aunt and uncle were already in bed when she got in, although her aunt called to her as she changed into her nightclothes. Her uncle was fast asleep, but her aunt had her own bedside lamp on and had been reading. She put the book down when Sara came quietly into the room.

'Oh, don't mind your uncle,' her aunt said at her questioning look. 'He can sleep through anything, and often does. Did you have a nice time, dear?'

'Quite nice, thank you.' But she wouldn't be seeing Pete again. They had parted as friends, but he was just another man who found Marie more attractive; Dominic Thorne had already made it known that she in no way compared to his Marie. 'I'm not seeing Pete again, he's going to be very busy the next few weeks,' she said to excuse herself to her aunt.

'Were they nice people at this party?'

Sara smiled. 'Or slightly mad like Pete?' she teased.

'Yes,' her aunt admitted guiltily.

'They were all—very nice.'

'Well, I'm glad you had an enjoyable evening.' She plumped up her pillow. 'I think I'll go to sleep now that I know you're home.'

' 'Night,' and Sara quietly left the room.

For some reason she had been loath to mention her meeting with Dominic Thorne and Marie Lindlay to her aunt.

CHAPTER THREE

EDDIE WANTED to know all about her evening when he took her for her drive the next day.

'Was Marie Lindlay really like you?' he asked her.

She smiled. 'Pete didn't think so, he found her infinitely more attractive.'

'The man has no taste!' Eddie scoffed.

'Marie's fiancé seemed to agree with him.'

'Thorne? Well, I suppose he does—after all, he's going to marry her.'

'Yes.'

Eddie quirked an eyebrow. 'You don't sound too sure.'

'Oh, I'm sure they'll marry. It's just that—well, they're an odd couple. Dominic Thorne must be years older than her, for one thing.'

He shrugged. 'Thirty-five isn't old.'

'On him it is!'

Eddie laughed. 'He certainly hasn't made a conquest out of you.'

'Does he usually?' Sara scorned.

'Has them queueing up,' Eddie nodded. 'Before his engagement to Marie Lindlay this last year he was the most sought after man in town. Come to think of it,' he said with a grin, 'he still is.'

'Mmm, he doesn't look the faithful type.' He had been a man completely in command, who did what he wanted when he wanted, and woe betide anyone who got in his way. Besides, he hadn't hesitated about kissing her.

'Then they make a good pair,' Eddie said dryly.

Sara gave him a sharp look. 'Meaning?'

'Meaning Pete has a date with the lovely Marie this evening.'

She couldn't hide her surprise. Dominic Thorne would be furious about that if he ever found out. And why on earth was Marie doing it? Having seen for herself how angry Dominic Thorne had been when he had thought *she* was Marie out with Eddie, then Sara thought Marie ought to have more sense. After all, she must know him so much better than Sara did, must realize the full force of his anger—and the full force of his lovemaking too! No one seemed to wait for the wedding any more.

Except Sara! Barry had constantly tried to persuade her into a more intimate relationship, and she had always refused, something she was glad of when he let her down in that way. How much more awful it would have been if they had been lovers!

There was such a lot of pressure about sex nowadays, from television, advertising, and most of all from society itself. Sara had been thought something of a freak by her model friends because she had no tales of bedroom romps to tell them.

They had found great pleasure in recounting whose bed they had slept in—although from all accounts sleep was the last thing they did!—the evening before, and although Sara had politely listened she had found it all rather sordid, instead of the excitement the other girls insisted it was.

Not that she was a prude, and she certainly didn't say to herself before she went out with a man, 'I must not sleep with him'; she just hadn't ever met a man that she loved, a man who excited her so much she gave herself to him

willingly. If that day ever came she would go to him without thought of the future, would give herself body and soul
into his keeping.

What her friends in the States didn't seem to realize was
that they were invited out for the evening, perhaps two
evenings, and when these men had taken the thing they
were really interested in they didn't want to know any
more.

'Hey, you weren't interested in Pete yourself, were you?'
Eddie broke into her thoughts.

'No,' she could deny with ease. 'I was just wondering
why Marie took such risks.'

He shrugged. 'For the hell of it, I should think. Thorne
must be something to see in a jealous rage.'

Not really. He had treated *her* more like a naughty
schoolgirl when he had ordered her home from the casino. And he hadn't taken her home himself, but had told
her to get her escort to take her. Not exactly a jealous rage!

'Is it almost lunchtime?' she changed the subject. 'I'm
starting to get very hungry.'

Eddie grinned. 'I thought you'd never ask! I don't mind
being your chauffeur, but all this green countryside and
pure fresh air is making me thirsty.'

Sara felt very guilty, because she had hardly noticed the
countryside she had come out to see, being much too
wrapped up in thoughts of Dominic Thorne and Marie
Lindlay. Not that she ever expected to hear from the other
girl; she felt sure her arrogant fiancé would make sure that
she didn't.

'Where are we?' she asked with interest.

'Royal Berkshire,' he announced.

'Oh? Anywhere near Windsor Castle?'

Eddie grimaced. 'Very near. Don't tell me you want to
see that too?'

'Well...I wouldn't mind.' She gave him a coaxing smile.

'Okay.' He sighed. 'But a beer and lunch first,' he added as her face lit up with excitement.

'Lunch in a pub?' Her eyes glowed. 'Oh, good.' She grinned. 'I'm really getting to like your English pubs.'

Eddie drove into a pub car park. 'For goodness' sake don't tell Aunt Susan I've taken you to another one. She gave me an earful the last time!'

'I won't tell her,' Sara assured him.

It seemed there were a lot of things she was keeping to herself lately, and not normally being a secretive girl she was surprised at herself.

Lunch was delicious, a lovely prawn salad served to them out in the garden. Sara also enjoyed the lager and lime Eddie bought her. She enjoyed going around Windsor Castle, too, and although Eddie moaned about it she thought he secretly enjoyed it, too.

'I bet it's years since you went there,' she teased on the drive home. The time was now well on the way towards dinner.

Eddie looked shamefaced. 'Well, actually, I—I've never been before,' he admitted.

Her eyes widened. 'Never been to Windsor Castle?'

'There's no need to look so surprised.' He looked sheepish. 'It isn't unusual not to visit a place that's more or less on your doorstep. You've probably never been to Disney World!' he said scornfully.

'Wrong.' Sara smiled. 'I've been dozens of times—I love it. It's absolutely fantastic. I feel like a little girl again when I go there.'

'You probably look like one too. You're very easy to be with, Sara,' Eddie said suddenly. 'And I mean that in the nicest way possible.'

'I know,' she accepted huskily. 'I've enjoyed today.'

'So have I.' He seemed surprised by the fact.

'It's just like having a brother,' she said sleepily, leaning tiredly back against the headrest.

'It's okay.' Eddie laughed. 'I wasn't moving in for the kill.'

Sara smiled at her own conceit, then dozed off in the warmth of the car and the monotonous hum of the engine.

She woke with a jerk, a curious feeling of foreboding hanging over her.

THE FEELING PERSISTED over the next few days, so much so that she found she wasn't sleeping at night. The doctor had warned her of this delayed shock, the long air flight on top of her already weakened state sapping what little energy she had, and she spent the next three or four days resting, not going far from the house.

Consequently she was at home when Marie Lindlay telephoned her, and answered the call herself. The idea of meeting for lunch appealed to her, and the two girls arranged to meet at a restaurant in town.

There was no sign of Marie when she arrived at the arranged time, although the doorman insisted on calling *her* 'Miss Lindlay.' Sara found the situation too complicated to explain, leaving him under the misapprehension that she really was Marie. The poor man would think himself intoxicated when Marie did arrive.

She came into the restaurant twenty minutes later, and the first five minutes of their conversation were taken up with her apologies.

'It was Dominic.' She sighed, ordering a Bacardi and Coke from the hovering waiter. 'Whenever Daddy's away he seems to think he has to keep checking up on me. It's nonsense, of course, but he still does it. He kept me on the telephone ten minutes trying to find out where I was going.'

'When are you getting married?' Sara asked, wondering what she was doing here now that she was actually here.

'Oh, not for ages yet.' Marie dismissed the question, nodding at the waiter as he put her drink on the table. 'Dominic's in no hurry, and neither am I.'

'But surely you've been engaged for almost a year.' Sara frowned, not seeing Dominic Thorne as the patient type.

'Just under six months,' Marie corrected. 'And to tell you the truth, I'm not sure I'd be very good as a wife for Dominic. He's such a perfectionist.'

Sara smiled. 'I'm sure he would make allowances for a new wife.'

'Maybe.' Marie dropped the subject. 'I love your accent. Where in America do you come from?'

Sara told her, also explaining about the accident that had killed her parents and injured her. She found it so easy to talk to the other girl, and Marie seemed to feel the same.

'How sad!' Marie looked genuinely upset. 'I hate death.' She shuddered. 'My mother's dead too.'

'I'm sorry.'

Marie seemed to shake off her dark mood, and gave a dazzling smile. 'Let's order lunch.'

Sara was amazed at the other girl's capacity for passing from topic to topic, from mood to mood, and it seemed that during lunch they discussed every subject possible. By the end of the meal Sara felt that they were friends.

'I still can't get over our likeness,' said Marie as they went from the restaurant into the lounge for coffee. 'Dominic's convinced it's all a trick on your part,' she giggled.

Sara stiffened. 'I'm well aware of your fiancé's opinion of me.'

'And he's aware of yours.' Marie grinned. 'Did you really hit him?'

Sara kept her eyes down on her coffee cup. 'Did he say I had?'

'He didn't need to, it was pretty obvious. God, he was in a foul temper the rest of the evening! I've never seen him in such a black mood.' Marie didn't seem perturbed by the fact, grinning widely.

'He deserved it,' Sara said tightly.

'I'm sure he did.' Marie nodded. 'The trouble with Dominic is that he's perfect himself, and he expects others to be the same.' She shrugged. 'I'm afraid that even I don't meet up to his high standards.'

That Dominic Thorne made her feel totally inadequate was obvious, and that Marie admired him tremendously was also obvious.

'Dominic thinks you're trying to get money out of me in some way,' Marie added guilelessly. 'Or Daddy.'

Sara frowned. 'But I've never met your father, nor have I made any effort to contact him.'

'No.' Marie grinned. 'But Dominic thinks my father may have met your mother, about nine months before you were born.'

An angry tide of red color passed in front of Sara's eyes. Dominic Thorne had a disgusting mind. How dare he imply that about her mother!

Marie laughed at her expression. 'Don't worry, I soon disabused him of that—my father was devoted to my mother. That's the reason he's never remarried.'

'And my mother loved my father. Your fiancé really does have a twisted mind! Besides, I didn't make any effort to see you again, and if I'd been up to something underhand surely I would have done.'

'Dominic said that was just a clever move on your part.' Marie shrugged.

Sara drew in an angry breath. 'Your fiancé says altogether too much!'

'Actually, he doesn't,' Marie said seriously. 'He doesn't talk much at all, but when he does you can bet it's something important. Now I'm the opposite, I chatter on for hours and none of it makes much sense.'

Sara had already noticed that, and she liked it. She liked Marie too, found her bubbly, flamboyant nature the complete opposite of her own more reserved one.

She considered they had talked about Dominic Thorne quite enough for one day. 'What do you do?' she asked Marie.

'For a living, you mean?' Marie sounded scandalized.

Sara laughed at her expression. 'By your reaction I take it you don't do anything.'

'Is that terribly naughty of me?' Marie looked like a guilty little girl.

'No.' Sara smiled. 'I wish I could do the same.' Although she wasn't sure she really meant that. Her months of enforced inactivity had made her long to go back to work, although she accepted that the injuries to her legs had made it impossible for her to do anything too strenuous. But nevertheless she didn't think she would enjoy being idle. Her mother and father had been quite well off, and that money had now been left to her, but she had never been encouraged to sit at home and live off that wealth. Even her mother had been her stepfather's chief assistant at the advertising agency.

'I'm kept quite busy,' Marie told her. 'Daddy's always entertaining, and I have to be his hostess. And then there's the sports club, I go there a lot. And then—'

'Okay, okay.' Sara laughingly silenced her. 'I believe you!'

'You're a model, aren't you?' Marie said interestedly. 'Pete told me,' she explained.

'Oh, yes.' Sara bit her lip, undecided about saying anything to Marie about her date with Pete. After all, it was none of her business who the other girl went out with. And yet... 'Did you have a nice evening with him?' she queried.

Marie shrugged. 'He's okay. I—Hey, I didn't step on any toes, did I? He told me there was nothing between the two of you.' She frowned.

'There isn't. I wasn't thinking of me.' Sara quirked one eyebrow.

'Then who—? Oh, you mean Dominic,' the other girl said dismissively. 'Mmm, I don't suppose he would like it much.'

'He would have a right not to. You are engaged to him,' Sara gently reminded her.

'He's kept very busy, he works very hard. And then he's often away on business. I get very lonely. Anyway, I won't be seeing Pete again.'

That didn't particularly bother her. Marie could have a hundred other men besides Dominic Thorne if she wanted to, but she had the feeling that he wouldn't stand too much of that treatment, and unless Marie wanted to lose him she would have to curb her activities with other men.

Marie didn't seem to agree with her when she pointed that out to her. 'He'll forgive me.' She dismissed it lightly. 'He always has.'

Then Dominic Thorne must be a more understanding man than she would have given him credit for. Maybe he loved Marie more deeply than he appeared to on the surface. He was definitely a deep character.

'My marriage to Dominic will make things all neat and tidy,' Marie told her, at her frowning look. 'He and my father are partners, you see. When we marry Dominic is assured of eventually becoming sole owner. He's been so good to me, it's the least I can do for him. And he's so gorgeous, isn't he? So distinguished.'

'Yes.' Although marrying him because he had been good to her didn't seem a very good reason to Sara. Perhaps they loved each other in their own way, but it wasn't the way she wanted to love her life's partner.

'Mmm, I love to be seen with him.' Marie's expression was dreamy. 'And he's so masterful. Daddy says he's a brilliant businessman.'

Sara hastily revised her opinion of Marie not loving her fiancé. She obviously adored him, although she took pains to hide it. Their relationship was too complicated for her to understand, so she decided not to probe any further. The two of them obviously understood each other, and really that was all that mattered.

'I—Oh, look, there's Suzanne,' Marie exclaimed. 'Suz— Oh, damn, she's gone into the restaurant.' She turned to Sara. 'Would you mind if I left you for a few minutes? I just have to see Suzanne.'

'No,' Sara smiled. 'You go ahead.'

Marie stood up, hesitating. 'You won't leave?'

She shook her head. 'No, I won't leave. I'll finish drinking my coffee and wait for you here.'

Marie was gone considerably longer than a few minutes, so much so that Sara started to get fidgety. When she saw Dominic Thorne enter the restaurant her heart sank.

Verbal abuse from him was not something she welcomed right now, not after the things Marie had told her he had said about her, the insults he had made about both her and her mother.

He came straight over to her, his strides long and purposeful. 'I thought I'd find you here.' He stood looking down at her. 'Why couldn't you have told me earlier instead of all that evasion?' He sat down in the chair Marie had recently vacated, his dark suit impeccable, as was the rest of his appearance.

He thought she was Marie! Her anger at his accusations concerning her mother and herself came to the fore. She tried to recall Marie's husky tone of voice, hoping she could pull this off. This man was arrogant, condescending, and totally wrong about her, and it was time she got her own back on him.

'Maybe I didn't want you breathing down my neck.' Was that really her talking? She had managed to get quite a good impression of Marie's husky tones, good enough to fool Dominic Thorne, she could tell.

He sighed, his anger barely contained. 'I merely like to know—'

'—What I'm doing every minute of the day and night,' she finished in that highly educated English voice. Maybe she should take up acting? 'I'm only out to lunch, Dominic.'

He put his hand over hers, and Sara only just stopped herself from pulling away. 'I feel responsible for you while your father is away.'

Sara pouted as she had seen Marie do. 'But, Dominic, surely I can't come to any harm while I'm out to lunch?'

He gave an indulgent smile, looking the most pleasant she had ever seen him, his harshly attractive features softened. 'You could come to harm just sitting at home,' he teased. 'Who are you lunching with?'

'Well, actually—'

Dominic's face darkened, his eyes narrowed to icy blue slits. 'You haven't seen the Hamille girl again, have you?'

Sara bristled angrily on her own behalf. 'And why shouldn't I?' Amazingly she still managed to maintain Marie's accent.

'I've already told you why,' he said sternly. 'The girl is out to cause trouble.'

As far as Sara was concerned this charade had gone on long enough! 'And in what way am I doing that, Mr. Thorne?' She dropped the pose, talking to him in her own voice, her anger obvious.

He instantly dropped her hand, his face an angry mask. 'Very amusing, Miss Hamille,' he snapped. 'Perhaps you should take up acting as a profession.'

Her mouth twisted. 'I had just thought the same thing. Let me assure you, Mr. Thorne, I am not out to cause "trouble". I met Marie today at her suggestion, and because I like her. But now that I know your opinion of my mother and myself—and incidentally, my mother didn't meet Marie's father at any time, let alone nine months before my birth. I'm sorry, Mr. Thorne, did you say something?' she asked coldly.

His expression was fierce. 'I said damn Marie and her loose tongue,' he rasped.

'If the remarks hadn't been made she wouldn't have been able to repeat them. Twenty-one years ago my mother was married to my father, and that is the time I was born. The comments you made about her are slanderous.' Her eyes sparkled with fury. 'And I'm not going to sit back and let you make them!'

'It was merely conjecture,' he said smoothly. 'Your similarity to Marie is—amazing. I was merely trying to find a reason for it.'

'Well, that isn't it!' Sara snapped.

'No, I accept that. Your age would seem to veto that idea. Twenty-one, I think you said?'

'Almost,' she confirmed resentfully. 'Next month.'

'Mmm, and at the time Marie's father was also happily married to her mother.'

'I require an apology for your remarks, Mr. Thorne,' Sara told him stubbornly.

Anger flared in those narrowed eyes. 'Miss Hamille—'

'An apology!' she repeated tightly. 'My mother is dead and so unable to defend herself, but I demand an apology on her behalf.' She looked at him challengingly, refusing to withdraw from their silent optical battle. Marie might enjoy his domineering attitude, but Sara just found it infuriating, and she refused to be cowed by it.

Dominic Thorne looked as if he were going through a battle of his own, with himself. That he was unaccustomed to admitting to being wrong about anything she had no doubt, but she remained firm. He *would* apologize.

'All right.' The words came out in a hiss, blue eyes glittering resentfully. 'I apologize. It would appear I'm mistaken.'

Sara could thankfully see Marie coming back, the other girl bending to lightly kiss her fiancé on the lips before sitting down beside him.

'Sorry I was so long,' she spoke to Sara. 'I'm afraid Suzanne is as much of a chatterbox as I am!' She gave a glowing smile in Dominic Thorne's direction. 'What are you doing here, darling? Not that I'm not pleased to see you.' She entwined her fingers with his. 'But I thought you'd be hard at work this afternoon.'

'I had some spare time.' His voice showed none of his fury of seconds earlier, his manner at once indulgent. 'I thought I might find you here.'

So that he could spy on her, Sara silently fumed. And it seemed that Dominic Thorne loved Marie in return, a possessive over-protective love that would suffocate Sara.

'Sara and I are going shopping,' Marie surprised her by announcing. 'Do you want to come with us?' she asked her fiancé.

'No, thanks.' He gave a teasing smile. 'But you can show me later what you bought.'

Marie gave him a mischievous smile. 'I thought I might buy some lingerie.'

Dominic laughed, at once sensually attractive. 'In that case you can definitely show it to me later!' He stood up. 'I'll leave you two girls to enjoy your shopping.'

'Goodbye, Mr. Thorne,' Sara said pointedly, meeting his sharp look unflinchingly.

He nodded curtly. 'Goodbye, Miss Hamille. Until later, Marie,' and he bent to kiss her, a tall compelling man who drew much attention as he left the restaurant.

Marie gave a pleasurable shiver. 'I don't think I'll ever get over how attractive he is.' She smiled. 'Or the fact that I'm engaged to him. Oh, well, shall we go and do that shopping now?'

It was late when Sara got back to her aunt's house, her leave-taking from Marie having been difficult. Marie had wanted them to meet again, but Sara had claimed that she would be too busy during her time left in England.

Marie called her again a couple of days later, and Sara did her best to get out of seeing her.

'Please,' Marie coaxed. 'I like you, Sara, I feel I can talk to you. I know.' Her husky laugh sounded down the telephone. 'I never do anything else! But I feel I can *really* talk to you. Maybe it's because we're so much alike, I don't know, but I feel as if there's a bond between us.'

Sara felt it too, so much so that it felt weird. She wasn't even sure that she and Marie had anything in common, she just felt close to the other girl, wanted to help her if she was troubled about anything.

'Oh, go on, Sara,' Marie encouraged, sensing her weakening. 'I'll pick you up, shall I?'

'No!' Her voice was sharp. She still hadn't mentioned her first two meetings with Marie to her aunt and uncle, and she didn't want to have to tell them now. 'I—I'll meet you somewhere.'

They arranged a place to meet, and Sara duly turned up there at the appropriate time. Marie was late, but then time never seemed to mean much to her, possibly because she had so much of it on her hands.

After a quarter of an hour she was starting to worry, after half an hour she was convinced something had happened to Marie. Luckily the other girl's telephone number was in the book, and she rang through to the house. The maid told her that Miss Lindlay was resting in her room, and that she certainly didn't have an appointment to meet anyone this afternoon.

Sara didn't know what to make of that, standing dazedly in the callbox, until an irate person outside began to knock on the window. She slowly moved out of the callbox, stunned by what she had just been told. It sounded like a brush-off to her, and considering that Marie had been the one who wanted the meeting she didn't think it was her doing. There could be only one person behind this—Dominic Thorne!

She waited until the other person left the callbox before putting a call through to Dominic Thorne's office. Without even asking her name his secretary told her he wasn't available, and would she like to leave a message. What she had to say to Dominic Thorne couldn't be relayed through a third party!

'Could you tell him Sara Hamille called,' she said stiffly before putting the receiver down.

So that she didn't completely waste her time she went for a walk in one of the parks, amazed that you could find such peace and beauty in the middle of this teeming city.

The fresh air did her good, giving her an appetite for her dinner. She had taken to spending her evenings quietly at home with her aunt and uncle, remaining friends with Eddie but not accepting any more of his invitations. After all, she was here to rest, and she had enough exercise during the day.

She was watching a film on the television when her aunt told her there was a caller for her.

'Take him into the other room,' her aunt said in a whisper. 'It's tidier in there.'

Sara wasn't really surprised by the identity of her caller; he had to be someone quite important for her aunt to suggest using the lounge. Even her aunt had recognised the individualism of Dominic Thorne.

'Yes?' Sara's manner wasn't forthcoming as she fought off feelings of inadequacy. He looked so distinguished in the black evening clothes, showing her denims and T-shirt up for the casual attire they were.

Dominic Thorne was obviously aware of her clothing too, as his narrowed gaze passed slowly over the length of her body. 'I hope I haven't called at an inconvenient time,' he drawled.

'Not at all.' She put her thumbs through the loops of the waistband of her denims, adopting a challenging stance. 'I'll probably miss knowing who the murderer was after watching the other hour and a half of the film, but what does that matter?' Her sarcasm was unmistakable.

His expression hardened. 'My secretary said you telephoned.'

She raised her eyebrows. 'I didn't expect a personal visit for the call.'

'And you aren't getting one.' His patience seemed to be wearing thin. 'I was in the area and I thought I would come and explain the reason Marie let you down this afternoon.'

'I think I can guess that,' Sara mocked, her head tilted back defiantly.

'I doubt it.' He scowled. 'Marie suffers from migraine. She had one this afternoon.'

'I'm sure!'

Dominic stiffened. 'I am not in the habit of lying.'

Sara's shrug was deliberately provocative. 'Once or twice doesn't make you a habitual liar.'

His hands came out to painfully grasp her arms. 'I'm sure Marie will call you herself tomorrow and explain why she was unable to meet you.'

'I'm sure she will. You've probably instructed her very well.' She was being childish now and she knew it. 'It wasn't my idea that we meet, Mr. Thorne. Marie seemed upset about something—and I think I can guess what that something was,' she said scornfully.

His eyes glittered dangerously as he stood looking down at her, their bodies so close they were almost touching. He shook his head. 'Why did you have to appear in our lives?' he muttered, seeming to be talking to himself, certainly requiring no answer. 'You're a complication I don't need.'

'Don't worry, Mr. Thorne,' she snapped. 'Another week and I shall leave as suddenly as I arrived.'

He pushed her away from him. 'I don't think so.'

Sara stepped back, relieved to be away from his blatant masculinity, having found his warm sensuality disturbing in the extreme. He was engaged to be married, it didn't seem fair that he could still command attraction in the way that he did, seemingly without volition.

'Oh, but I shall, Mr. Thorne,' she assured him.

'No.' Again he shook his head. 'Would you like to see Marie tomorrow?' he asked suddenly.

'I—If she's feeling better.' Sara nodded dazedly.

'She will be,' he said with certainty. ''Well, enough to see you, anyway.' He took out a card, writing on the back of it. 'Come to this address at twelve-thirty tomorrow. It's Marie's home,' he explained as he handed her the card. 'I'm sure she would like to see you for lunch.'

'You're actually encouraging me to see her?'

He shrugged. 'Why not? I'm sure you'll meet anyway, if you want to.'

'Yes.'

'Then come to lunch.'

'Will you be there?'

Dominic smiled, a totally mocking smile. 'I'm afraid so. Has that put you off coming?'

Sara rose to his challenge. 'Certainly not!'

'Very well. Twelve-thirty tomorrow.'

She went with him to the door. 'I'll be there.'

He gave a mocking inclination of his arrogant head, and Sara had to restrain herself from slamming the door after him.

'A friend of yours, dear?' her aunt asked as she rejoined them.

Sara gave a casual shrug. 'Just a friend of a friend,' she dismissed. 'I met him at the club I went to with Eddie the other night,' which was basically true. 'He was in the area and just thought he would call in,' which was also true.

'Nice-looking man,' her aunt remarked.

'Very nice.' If you were partial to arrogant, bossy men! And she wasn't, especially ones who thought themselves omnipotent into the bargain.

She felt hesitant about keeping the luncheon appointment the next day, knowing that her pleasure in seeing Marie had already been dampened by the fact that Dominic Thorne would be there, too. She finally decided it would be an act of cowardice not to go. Besides, she didn't even have to speak to Dominic Thorne unless she wanted to.

It seemed he had other ideas about that. As soon as Sara arrived at the Lindlay house she was shown into what turned out to be a study, and the occupant of that room was none other than Dominic Thorne.

His gaze took in her appearance, the finely checked brown tailored suit and contrasting tan blouse a complete antithesis of her attire of the evening before.

'Marie will be down in a moment—she's still dressing,' he explained her absence.

'Is she feeling better?' Her voice was stilted, distinctly unfriendly.

'Much better. Actually I'm glad she's late, because I have something I wanted to discuss with you.'

'Oh, yes?' She was at once on the defensive.

'Yes.' He gave an abrupt nod of his head. 'Please, sit down.' He waited until she had done so before becoming seated himself. 'Now, I'll come straight to the point.' He leaned forward over the desk. 'You lied to me, Miss Hamille,' he told her quietly.

Sara's hackles rose indignantly. 'I beg your pardon? I have never at any time lied to you.' Her tone gave the impression that she didn't consider him important enough in her life to bother with such things.

'There is such a thing as lying by omission,' he said coldly. 'I had you checked out, Miss Hamille—'

'You had no right!' Her eyes flashed angrily.

'I had you checked out,' he repeated calmly, 'and I found that your father was not Richard Hamille.'

'I never said he was!'

'Would you kindly let me finish,' Dominic Thorne snapped. 'I also found out that you aren't American by birth, you're English, that—'

The door behind them swung open and another man walked in. Dominic gave Sara a sharp look before greeting the other man.

'You're back early, Michael,' he said almost enquiringly.

'I heard about Marie. I—You aren't Marie!' the man accused, his face paling, going a sickly gray as he continued to look at Sara. 'My God,' he said dazedly, 'if you aren't Marie then you have to be—'

'Sara,' she supplied huskily, feeling as if the world were revolving around her. 'And you're my father!'

The face was much older, the hair grayer, but this man was still the same man her mother had shared her first wedding day with, the man who stood beside her in their wedding photographs, the man her mother had said was dead!

CHAPTER FOUR

THIS WAS ALL like some horrendous nightmare. The man standing in front of her couldn't be her father—and yet he was, she knew he was. She had a photograph of him in her handbag somewhere, and although it had been taken twenty-two years ago, on the day of his marriage to her mother, there could be no doubting his identity.

And if this man, Michael Lindlay, was her father, then that made Marie her half-sister. No wonder they were so much alike!

'Sit down,' Dominic instructed as she seemed to pale even more.

She hadn't even been aware of standing up, but she sat down thankfully, staring speechlessly up at her father. He seemed to have been struck dumb, too, and the two of them stared at each other in silence.

He was a very distinguished man, tall, with gray wings of color over his temples, the rest of his hair the same blond as her own and Marie's. His face was handsome, although she guessed him to be in his mid, possibly late, forties. And he looked kind, a touch of sadness in the depth of his brown eyes. Sara found it strange that she should have the same coloring, and look so much like a man she didn't even know.

She turned to Dominic Thorne, to find him watching them warily. 'You knew, didn't you?' she accused huskily.

He shook his head. 'Not at first,' he denied softly.

Michael Lindlay seemed to gather his thoughts together with effort. 'Is this your doing, Dominic?' he demanded to know.

'Not guilty.' Dominic shrugged resignedly. 'I think you'll find it's not been the conscious act of anyone, just a co-incidence.'

Brown eyes narrowed. 'You mean that after all these years Sara just turned up here by accident?'

'Not by accident, but *because* of an accident,' Dominic corrected softly. 'Rachel is dead, Michael. She died six months ago in the same accident that killed her second husband and left Sara badly injured.'

Michael Lindlay swallowed hard. 'Rachel—dead?' he repeated raggedly.

Dominic nodded. 'I'm afraid so.'

He turned to look at Sara. 'Is it true?'

She frowned her puzzlement. 'Yes.'

'Oh, God!' her father groaned. 'And you were badly injured. Are you all right now?'

'Yes, thank you,' she answered in a stilted voice, still dazed by this whole affair.

'Did Rach—your mother.' He swallowed hard. 'Did she suffer at all?' There was raw pain in his eyes.

Sara shook her head. 'The doctors said not.'

'And Richard?' A certain coolness entered his voice.

'The same,' she answered abruptly. She turned to Dominic Thorne. 'Could you please tell me what's going on? How can my father—Mr. Lindlay,' She felt guilty as she saw him wince. 'How can he still be alive when my mother always told me he was dead?'

'For the same reason,' Dominic answered her, 'as Marie was always told her mother was dead.'

Sara gasped. 'Are you saying that my mother was also Marie's mother?'

'I'm saying more than that.' He frowned. 'You still haven't realised, have you?'

Now it was her turn to frown. 'Realized what?'

'That Marie isn't just your sister, but your *twin* sister.'

'No!' she cried, her eyes wide with horror, looking in desperation at her father's gray face. 'That isn't true! Tell me it isn't true,' she pleaded.

He seemed unable to speak, and it was left to Dominic to answer her once again. 'I'm afraid it is true, Sara.'

'But it *can't* be! Tell him.' She grabbed her father's arm. 'Tell him he has it all wrong!'

Michael Lindlay looked at her with tormented eyes. 'But he doesn't, Sara.' He choked, turning away to stare out of the window, his back rigid.

Dominic picked up a sheet of paper from the desk, obviously the report he had received about her. 'I was suspicious from the first,' he told her. 'But I was thrown by the fact that you seemed to be an American. And then there was the fact that you said *both* your parents had been killed in the accident.'

'I always called Richard Dad,' she said stiffly.

Dominic nodded. 'Well, on the basis of those two facts I concluded that your likeness to Marie was just a freak of nature. Then the other day you told me you were twenty-one next month—so is Marie. That was too much of a coincidence for me. Here,' he said, handing her the report, 'read the last paragraph.'

Sara took it from him. The last paragraph was short and to the point. 'And so we have proved beyond doubt that Sara Hamille is in fact Sara Lindlay, the daughter of Michael Lindlay, and the twin of Marie Lindlay.' Her eyes went to the name printed at the top of the sheet; the reputation of the firm was indisputable. She looked up at her father with an agonized expression, having read the information to herself. 'But why?' she groaned in a choked voice. 'Why did you do it?'

'Here,' Dominic picked up the sheet and held it out to his partner. 'You'd better read this too.'

Michael Lindlay made no effort to take it. 'I can guess what it says,' he said dully, a haunted expression to his face.

Dominic shrugged, dropping the report back on to the desk. 'Then I second Sara's query, why?'

'Why did Rachel take Sara and I take Marie?'

'Exactly!' Sara said bitterly.

Michael drew a ragged breath. 'I think Marie should be here to listen to this.' He sighed. 'I only want to have to say it the once. Will you go and get her, Dominic?'

'Sara?' Dominic frowned at her.

The man she had regarded as her enemy until a few minutes ago now seemed her only hold on reality. 'Don't leave me,' she pleaded, her hand on his arm as she gazed up at him beseechingly.

His breath caught in his throat before his hand came out and grasped hers, his fingers firm and reassuring. 'Maybe you should go and get Marie, Michael,' he suggested quietly, still looking at Sara.

'Of course,' the other man agreed jerkily. 'I—I won't be a moment,' and he closed the door with a decisive click.

Sara swallowed hard, shivering even though the day was warm, and removed her hand from Dominic's. 'I'm sorry,' she told him softly. 'I—I'm just so confused.'

'It's all right,' he reassured her. 'You really thought he was dead, didn't you?'

'Yes. You see, my mother always said—well, she said—'

'Michael's told Marie the same thing about her mother.' He shook his head. 'It's going to take some understanding.'

Sara didn't think she would ever understand the cruelty of separating two babies not yet a year old. Why, she might have gone through her whole life without knowing the bond of her twin. What on earth had possessed her mother and father to do such a thing? She found it cruel in the extreme, and totally incomprehensible.

'But, Daddy,' Marie could be heard complaining as she came into the room. 'I haven't finished my make-up yet. Whatever can be so important that I can't—Sara!' She had turned around and seen her, and her face lit up with pleasure. 'You came!' She came over to take Sara's hand in her own. 'I'm so sorry about yesterday. I have these headaches, you see, and—But you don't want to hear about that.' A beaming smile banished all thought of yesterday's painful migraine. She turned to look at her father. 'You only had to say Sara was here, Daddy. There was no need to be so mysterious. Don't you think the way we look so alike is just amazing?' She held Sara at her side for her father's opinion.

He was obviously too choked to speak, looking at the two of them in silent wonder.

'Daddy?' Marie prompted impatiently.

'You'll have to excuse your father,' Dominic cut in. 'I'm afraid he's had rather a shock.'

Marie's gaiety instantly left her, and she went to her father's side. 'What is it, Daddy?' She searched his face with a worried frown. 'What's happened?' she asked sharply.

'It's all right, Marie, just calm down,' her father instantly soothed. 'You've just got over one attack, don't bring on another one.' He smoothed her hair back from her face. 'Now, let's all go into the lounge and then we can talk in private—and comfort.'

Michael Lindlay—for Sara couldn't bring herself to call him her father—seemed to have regained his equilibrium, taking control of the situation now that he had himself under control.

'Would you like me to leave, Michael?' Dominic asked him. 'Let you talk to the two girls in private?'

'No!' Sara hadn't meant her protest to be made quite so vehemently, but she couldn't let Dominic go. She needed him.

'She's right,' Michael Lindlay told him. 'You have a right to be here. After all, you're almost a member of this family yourself.'

'What's all this about?' Even the lighthearted Marie had sensed the tense atmosphere.

Michael Lindlay bit his bottom lip, obviously having trouble knowing where to start.

'At the beginning, Michael,' Dominic advised him, sitting in one of the armchairs while Marie and Sara sat side by side on the sofa.

'Yes. Yes.' He began pacing the room. 'Rachel and I were very young when we married, only eighteen and nineteen, too young really to know what it was all about. But nevertheless things were going well until Rachel became pregnant.' He sighed. 'We couldn't afford to have a child. I hadn't met your father then, Dominic, and I was still training to be an engineer, living on a pittance. A child was the last thing I needed at that time. But Rachel went into ecstasies about the coming baby, and for a while I think she forgot she had a husband. I'm not proud of what happened next—'

'Another woman?' Sara put in bitterly.

He ran a hand through his gray-blond hair. 'It was a stupid thing to do, stupid and childish. Rachel found out soon after—after the twins were born—'

'Twins?' Marie echoed in an astounded voice. 'Sara and I...?' she asked dazedly.

'Yes.' Their father nodded.

Marie turned to Sara with glowing eyes. 'You really are my sister?' she said excitedly.

Sara gave a shy smile, not knowing what reaction she had expected from Marie, but it certainly hadn't been such unreserved pleasure. Resentment had been the more expected emotion.

'That's wonderful!' Marie cried happily. 'I've always wanted a sister, but a *twin*—! That's really fantastic!'

Sara wished she could share her sister's questionless enthusiasm, but there was too much she still wanted to know, to try and understand. Unable to answer Marie, she simply took her hand in hers, holding on tightly. 'Go on,' she told her father.

He drew a ragged breath, a catch in his throat as he looked at the two of them sitting so close together. 'When Rachel found out,' he continued huskily, 'she ended our marriage right then and there, wouldn't have anything to do with me. Oh, we continued to live together, a case of her staying with me for the sake of the children. Then Rachel met Richard.' He swallowed hard. 'He was over here on business, and they fell in love. Rachel wanted to go back to America with him, taking the twins with her. I wouldn't allow that, and she—she wouldn't leave without them. In the end—'

'In the end you compromised!' Sara finished shrilly. 'You parted Marie and myself, took a child each.'

Her father looked at her pleadingly. 'Try to understand—'

'There's nothing *to* understand,' she told him angrily. 'You and my mother selfishly parted my twin and myself, because neither of you wanted to miss out! My God, you disgust me!' Her voice rose to a shout.

'Sara!' Dominic warned. 'Sara, don't!'

She looked at him with tears in her eyes. 'I know you mean well,' she stammered. 'But I can't *ever* forget what they did.' She ran to the door. 'I'm sorry, Marie. I'll call you.'

'Sara!' Dominic caught hold of her arm. 'Your father—'

'No!' Her eyes flashed deeply brown. 'Don't ever call him that! Richard was my father. He certainly never hurt me as Mr. Lindlay has. Now, please, let me go.'

He looked down at her with compassionate eyes. 'I'll take you home if you want to go. All right?' he said softly.

She frowned, unable to think straight. 'I—No—'

'Yes,' he insisted firmly.

'Shall I come with you?' Marie wanted to know.

'No, stay with your father,' Dominic advised.

'Could we please leave now?' Sara muttered. 'Before I make an absolute fool of myself and faint.'

'Sara—'

'Not now, Michael,' Dominic cut him off harshly. 'Can't you see what you've already done to her?' he said savagely. 'For God's sake don't say any more. Let's get out of here,' he muttered to Sara.

Sara sat miserably hunched up on her side of the Rolls-Royce, too numb to care where he was driving or where he was taking her. To think that her mother, a woman she had always loved and admired, had committed that atrocity! How could two people do that to innocent children, change their lives so completely before they had even begun?

'I really had no idea,' Dominic broke the silence. 'No idea at all,' he repeated with a shake of his head. 'It seems incredible to think I've known Michael all these years, and all the time he was hiding this secret.'

'I knew my mother all my life,' she said bitterly. 'And I would never have thought her capable of something like this.'

Dominic shrugged. 'She was very young, only your age—'

'You think I could do a thing like that?' she asked him angrily.

He gave her a sideways glance. 'No, I don't think you could. But put yourself in her place. Go on, Sara,' he said firmly as she went to protest. 'Right. Now you're married to a man you no longer love, you have two children by him. Suddenly you meet a man you do love, and you want to be with him, but your husband refuses to give up his children. What do you do?'

'I—Why I—He should have let my mother take both of us,' she declared. 'It was pure selfishness—'

'Wasn't it selfish of your mother to want both the children, to take them thousands of miles away? She already had the man she loved, your father was left with nothing?'

'He—I—' She frowned. 'Separating us was not the answer!'

'I agree. But what was? Can you tell me?'

Sara bit her lip. 'No...' she finally admitted.

'Your father has suffered for that one lapse in their relationship,' Dominic told her quietly.

'How?' she queried scornfully.

'By loving your mother all these years.'

Sara gasped. 'But he said—'

'Yes?' Dominic quirked one eyebrow. 'Your father never at any time this afternoon said he didn't love your mother. They had a momentary setback because like a lot of young people they wonder how they're going to manage to live when they start a family. It's often a time of great strain. Your mother coped with it by involving herself in plans for the birth of her baby, your father coped with it—'

'By having an affair!'

'By being with a woman who maybe listened to his anxieties—'

'Among other things!'

Dominic sighed. 'I accept that it wasn't a very sensible thing to do, but then human beings aren't infallible. When it was too late to save the marriage or revive your mother's love for him, he realized how much he really loved her. And he's continued to love her. Finding out she's dead hit him very badly.'

Sara turned away, wishing she could feel compassion for her father, but still feeling only resentment. 'How do you know all this?' she finally asked him. 'About him still loving my mother.'

He shrugged. 'Michael's never made any secret of it. Maybe now that she really is dead... Well, maybe now he'll start to forget. And forgive.'

'My mother—'

'Not your mother, Sara,' he interrupted patiently. 'Himself.'

'Himself...?'

'It can't have been easy living with himself all this time. Maybe you should try to forgive, too.'

'And maybe you should mind your own damned business,' she snapped. 'You may be going to marry my sister, but that doesn't mean you have any say in how I live my life.'

His expression was harsh. 'You can live your life any damn way you please, but when it involves Marie then I have a say in it. She's very fond of you already, and I—I like her to have things that make her happy. *You* make her happy.'

Sara knew that they were engaged, but she hadn't figured on Dominic being that besotted with Marie. He didn't seem the sort of man who would ever allow his emotions to rule his head. He must love Marie very much. And somehow Sara didn't like that idea.

She brought her thoughts up with a start. Somewhere along the line, probably when she had appealed to him for his support, she had become more than a little attracted to Dominic Thorne. Now wouldn't that be ironic, twins in love with the same man! She certainly couldn't allow that to happen.

'Where are you taking me?' she asked sharply, already too confused to delve into what she now felt towards Dominic Thorne. If she felt anything at all!

He shrugged. 'I was just driving around. Until you calmed down.'

'I'm calm now. And I'd like to go home.'

He turned the car in the direction of her home. 'Michael's going to want to see you again—you know that, don't you?'

Her mouth set stubbornly. 'Then he can wait—forever.'

'Sara—'

'I'm grateful for your support, Mr. Thorne, but that's all I am. I won't be seeing Michael Lindlay again.'

'And Marie?' he asked hardly.

She swallowed hard. 'Marie is—well, that's different. I—I said I would call her, and I will.'

'Thank you,' he said softly.

Her aunt was out when Sara let herself into the house, so she was able to collect her thoughts together in private. She hadn't asked Dominic in, and he didn't seem to mind her abrupt departure.

She wasn't an orphan after all! She had a father and a sister, a sister she already loved. It would be impossible not to love someone who looked so much like her, and her affection seemed to be returned.

'You're looking pale, love,' her aunt told her when she returned from the shops loaded down with groceries.

Sara helped her put the food away. She had thought long and hard about mentioning her meeting with her father and Marie to her aunt, and she still didn't know what to do about it. Obviously her aunt and uncle must have known about Marie and herself, which also now explained away her aunt's flustered behaviour when she had broken the cup. It hadn't been the smashed cup that had upset her at all, it had been the mention of Marie's name.

'Sara?' Her aunt was frowning at her now.

She blinked, biting her bottom lip. She hadn't made her mind up what to do about her father, and to talk it over with her aunt was not something she felt like doing at the moment. No matter how kind her aunt and uncle had been to her during this visit, they had also helped to deceive her about the past.

'I—er—I have a headache,' she lied.

'Now that's a shame, I think Eddie wanted to take you out tonight.' Her aunt seemed satisfied with her explanation. 'He said he wanted to see you before you leave.'

'But I'm not going for several more days.'

'You know Eddie,' her aunt teased. 'He's become very fond of you.'

And Sara was fond of him too, in a brotherly sort of way, which was why she accepted his invitation. He took her to the pub they had visited on their first evening together, cheering her up in a way that no one else could have done.

'That's better.' He smiled as she laughed at one of his jokes. 'I was beginning to wonder if I would ever get a smile out of you tonight!'

'Sorry,' she said ruefully, realizing that this couldn't be a very pleasant evening for him.

'Aunt Susan said something about a headache when I rang. Do you still have it?' he asked sympathetically.

They were sitting in one of the booths in the lounge bar, having decided not to join in the darts match this evening. Sara felt relaxed with Eddie, her discovery of earlier today not seeming quite so traumatic now she was with him. But the problem of it had only been pushed to the back of her mind. She knew that tomorrow, or even later today, she would have to think about it once again.

She shook her head in answer to his query. 'No, it's gone. And I'm sorry if I've been a dampener on the evening.'

'Upset about leaving, are you?'

'Oh, yes,' she didn't hesitate with her answer. 'England seems like—home.' Even more so now! Her life in Florida seemed like a dream, and England now seemed like reality. Which was pretty stupid when she had lived in Florida virtually all her life.

'Are you thinking of staying on?' Eddie asked interestedly.

She shrugged. 'I—I don't think so. I have to go back for a while anyway. But I—I may come back. I'm not sure.'

He put his hand over hers. 'I'd like you to.'

Alarm flared in her deep brown eyes. 'Eddie—'

'In a purely sisterly sense.' He grinned at her.

She smiled. 'Do you always hold your sister's hand in this way?'

'I don't know. I've never had a sister.'

She burst out laughing. Eddie always managed to reduce things to normality, making her panic this afternoon seem stupid. She wasn't the first person to suddenly discover she had a family, after all, and at least she liked Marie. Her feelings towards her father were harder to define. Her mother had brought her up to love his memory, hence the photograph she always carried with her, and yet when presented with the flesh and blood man, a man still alive, she had recoiled from such a relationship.

And she still recoiled from it! Richard was her father and always would be.

Both her aunt and uncle were still up when Eddie brought her home, so she made coffee for all of them. Eddie seemed to find their determination not to leave them alone very amusing, and finally got up to take his leave.

'They're getting worse than parents,' he joked at the front door.

'Don't say that.' Sara grimaced. 'I've had my fill of parents today.'

'Really?'

'Forget I said that, Eddie,' she advised hastily, realizing she was revealing too much. No one must know about Marie and her father until she was ready to accept it herself. 'I've been a bit down the last couple of days. Delayed reaction, I think.'

He gently touched her cheek. 'Never mind, love. Just remember you have Aunt Susan and Uncle Arthur. And there's always me.'

'Thank you.' She gave a quavery smile. 'You don't know how comforting that is. Really!' she insisted at his sceptical look.

'Only I could end up with a beautiful girl like you wanting to be my *friend*,' he said with disgust. 'Or my sister, which is worse,' he groaned. 'Just my luck!'

Sara reached up and kissed him warmly on the cheek. 'Thank you for being here.'

Eddie frowned. 'When you needed me, hmm?'

'Yes,' she admitted huskily.

''Night, love.' He bent to kiss her on the mouth, grinning at her gasp of surprise. 'Brotherly privilege.'

'I'll bet,' she said with a laugh.

Her aunt and uncle were still in the lounge when she returned, and she frowned at their grave expressions. Something was wrong here, very wrong.

'We had a visitor this evening,' her aunt told her softly, her gaze searching Sara's pale features.

'Oh, yes?' They often had visitors, being a very popular couple, so she knew there had to be something special about this particular visitor or else they wouldn't have mentioned it.

'A Mr. Dominic Thorne,' her uncle told her, one eyebrow raised questioningly.

Sara drew an angry breath. 'He came here!' she gasped.

Her uncle nodded. 'He seemed concerned about you, wanted to make sure you were all right.'

Her hands clenched into fists at her sides. 'What did he think I was going to do?' she rasped. 'Commit suicide?'

'Now then, Sara,' her uncle chided. 'That isn't the way to be. Susan and I much appreciated his visit.'

'He's told you, hasn't he?' she accused angrily. 'Why couldn't he mind his own damned business?' Her American accent was very strong in her fury.

'He seemed to feel it was his business,' her aunt put in softly.

Her eyes flashed. 'He knew it wasn't—I told him it wasn't.'

'Sara—'

'He had no right to come here,' she stormed, overriding her aunt. 'No right!' she repeated vehemently. 'This is my problem—'

'It was never just your problem,' her aunt told her firmly. 'Both families are involved as well, and Mr. Thorne is engaged to your sister.' She shook her head. 'I just couldn't believe it when people started taking you for Marie, not just once but a couple of times. We'd seen photographs of her, of course, the Lindlay family are often in the society columns, but even so we had no idea the similarity was so extreme. Mr. Thorne says it's almost impossible to tell you apart.'

Sara's mouth twisted. 'Only almost?' she taunted. 'He seems to have trouble knowing the difference.'

'Really?' Her aunt gave her a sharp look.

'Only my fath—only Michael Lindlay,' she amended quickly, 'could tell the difference. He knew on sight that I wasn't Marie.' She wondered *how* he had known.

'How is Michael?' her uncle asked.

'A bit dazed at the moment,' she revealed huskily. 'I'm afraid I walked out on him this afternoon.'

Her aunt nodded. 'Mr. Thorne told us that.'

Sara's mouth tightened. 'What else did he tell you?'

Aunt Susan shrugged. 'Just that you knew about Marie and your father. He thought we should know.'

Dominic Thorne took too much upon himself. She didn't like having her life taken out of her hands in this way. And if he thought he had got away with it then he was in for a surprise!

She sighed. 'I'm not going to ask you for reasons, I'm sure you're as incapable of giving them as Mr. Lindlay is.'

'Probably,' her aunt nodded. 'But I can tell you that your mother regretted what happened all her life.'

'I don't believe that! She was happy with Richard, they—'

'Not that part,' Aunt Susan interrupted gently. 'Rachel always regretted taking you away from your sister. I think in the end she would rather have given you up completely than risk the pain you're going through now.'

'No!' Sara cried chokingly. 'No, she loved me. She—'

'Of course she loved you. It was because she loved you, and Marie, that she knew she'd done the wrong thing in separating you. It's strange, really,' her voice broke emotionally, 'but your mother was actually going to tell you about Marie, was going to bring you over here next month on your birthday and introduce the two of you. But fate decided it wouldn't work out that way.'

Sara frowned. 'My mother was really going to do that?'

'Oh, yes.' Her aunt nodded. 'I can show you the letter if you like.'

'No, no, that won't be necessary. I—I think I'll go to bed now.' She turned blindly out of the room.

'Sara—'

'Leave her, Susan.' She could hear her uncle's firm voice. 'Leave her on her own, she needs time to adjust.'

Time. Everyone seemed to think that with time she would be able to accept this situation. And maybe she would.

She spent a restless night, eating an almost silent breakfast before leaving the house. Her aunt and uncle were still respecting her wish to be left alone, and she felt grateful to them.

The woman behind the desk was the capable middle-aged woman Sara had expected to be Dominic Thorne's secretary.

'Miss Lindlay,' she greeted with a smile. She was a woman of possibly forty-five, her appearance smart, very attractive in a mature sort of way, her ringless hands evidence of her single state. 'Shall I tell Mr. Thorne you are here?'

Why not? 'Please do.' Sara's voice was distinctly English.

There was a short conversation on the intercom before the secretary told her to go in.

'Thank you.' Sara smiled.

The inner office was even more impressive, wood-paneled walls, thickly carpeted floor, drinks cabinet and easy chairs, and most impressive of all, Dominic Thorne seated behind the huge mahogany desk.

He looked up as she entered the room, putting down the gold pen he was working with, his smile welcoming. 'Mar—' his eyes narrowed and he frowned. 'But it isn't, is it? Hello, Sara,' he greeted huskily, standing up.

Her irritation was impossible to hide. 'How did you know?' She used her own voice when talking to him.

Dominic shrugged. 'I'm learning, that's all.'

'You mean there is a difference?'

He gave her a considering look, bringing a blush to her cheeks. 'Yes, there's a difference.'

'What is it?' She frowned.

He held back a smile. 'I'm too much of a gentleman to tell you.'

Her eyes flashed. 'You aren't a gentleman at all, which is why I'm here.'

Dominic sighed, moving around the desk to lean back against it. 'I had no idea you wouldn't have told your aunt and uncle everything, the parts they didn't already know anyway.'

'I needed time to think.'

'And have you now thought?' he mocked.

'Not completely.' Sara turned to look at the rows of books in the bookcase along one wall. They were all on engineering, something she knew nothing about.

'What do you need to think about?' he asked from behind her. 'They're your family.'

'Yes,' she agreed dully, turning. 'But it isn't easy accepting that.'

'Why are you here, Sara?' His eyes narrowed. 'Really here, I mean.'

'I told you—'

'The real reason,' he persisted, his blue eyes intent on her pale features.

She flushed, resentful of his perception. 'I came to tell you I didn't appreciate your visit to my aunt and uncle,' she mumbled.

'No,' Dominic shook his head, 'that isn't the real reason, Sara.'

Her head went back in challenge. 'Then what is?'

His face was suddenly harsh. 'Would you like me to tell you—or show you?'

'Sh-show me?' she repeated with a gulp.

His burning gaze on her mouth was almost like a caress, his masculinity at once overwhelming, his sensuality a tangible thing. 'Yes, show you,' he said throatily.

'I—No.' She broke away from the spell he was weaving about her senses, once again looking at the books, but still dangerously aware of him standing a few feet away from her.

'You're right.' He drew in a controlling breath. 'Michael wants to see you.'

'No!' She turned round, and at once wished she hadn't, his gaze burning her at a glance as he seemed to be holding some fierce emotion in check. Sara looked away again, thrown into confusion by—she didn't know by what! She only knew it frightened her, but not in a terrifying way, in a—a *moral* way. This man was engaged to her sister, and yet—and yet—

'Sara!' he groaned achingly.

She swallowed hard. 'I don't want to see Michael Lindlay,' she answered his statement of a few minutes ago, although they had both passed beyond that, and a wild emotion was building up between them, an emotion that threatened to spiral out of control. And that must not be allowed to happen!

Dominic received her silent plea, at once the cool businessman, almost as if Sara had imagined that momentary lapse. But she knew she hadn't imagined it, the wild beating of her heart told her she hadn't.

'He doesn't just want to see you, Sara,' Dominic told her calmly, his raw passion of a moment ago completely erased. 'He wants you to go and live with him, with him and Marie.'

CHAPTER FIVE

'IS HE MAD?' she cried scornfully.

'No, just a father who wants to get to know his daughter.'

'I surely don't have to go and live with him for that,' she dismissed scathingly.

'It's surely the best way?'

'Not for me! I'm going back to the States in two days' time. I intend resuming my career.'

'You aren't well enough for that.' His voice was sharp. 'Your legs—'

'Are healed.'

'Beautifully,' he nodded. 'As far as it goes. But they aren't strong enough for the arduous job of a model.'

'I'm strong enough to do what I damn well please,' Sara snapped, resenting his bossy behaviour.

'I forbid you—I *ask* you not to do it,' Dominic amended with a shake of his head. 'I'm sorry, I think the last few days have gotten to me too. You have no need to work, Sara. As Michael's daughter—'

'Will you stop saying that!'

'All right, then,' he barked angrily, 'as Marie's *sister*, won't you do this?'

Her mouth twisted. 'Because you like to see Marie happy?' she taunted.

'Partly,' he admitted grimly.

'And the other part?'

'For you. I'm sure you can't feel happy about turning your back on your own sister.'

She wasn't. He knew she wasn't. This man knew her, knew everything about her, and it wasn't just because he was close to Marie. 'You aren't being fair,' she spluttered. 'I don't owe Michael Lindlay anything, least of all loyalty.'

'But you think he owes you something.'

'Yes! No—I don't know,' she said miserably.

'Well, he doesn't. You were happy with your mother, weren't you?'

'Very.' She nodded, frowning.

'Then Michael gave you all he owed you when he let you go. He did, Sara,' Dominic insisted as she went to protest. 'Just think for a moment. Your mother left your father to be with her lover. She shouldn't really have been allowed to take either of her children, and yet Michael let her have you. Why did she never have any other children?' he asked shrewdly.

'Richard wasn't able to have any,' she revealed slowly.

He raised his eyebrows. 'Then Michael did her more of a favor than she first realized. I would have been less charitable.'

'Charitable!' she echoed furiously. 'When he'd been having an affair himself?'

Dominic sighed. 'I can see there's no reasoning with you.'

'None at all,' she confirmed. 'I—'

'Dominic.' For the second time in two days Michael Lindlay walked unannounced into the room containing Dominic and Sara. He came up with a start. 'Sara!' he gasped.

He had aged overnight, even she could see that; there was a drawn look to his handsome face, a bleak look in his eyes. His expression was agonized as he looked at her, seemingly undecided about whether to enter the room or simply leave again.

'Come in, Michael,' Dominic made the decision for him. 'Perhaps you can talk some sense into Sara.'

'I don't think so,' she denied tightly, turning away.

A few seconds later she heard the door close. She didn't know whether she was relieved or saddened that her father had so calmly accepted her refusal to speak to him. She had no doubts that Dominic would never accept such a decision himself. Maybe that was the reason she felt she could rely on him. Even after the way they had reached out to each other just now? She couldn't begin to work out what had happened between them a few minutes ago, except to think that Dominic had momentarily confused her with Marie. That would be the obvious explanation.

'Sara.'

She spun round. Dominic hadn't been the one to remain in the office after all; her father had. She swallowed hard, biting her top lip. 'How is it you were able to tell Marie and myself apart from the start?' she asked shyly.

Some of the tension seemed to leave him, although he still eyed her warily. 'I know my girls,' he said huskily.

She flushed. 'Both of us?'

'Oh, yes,' he nodded.

'How?' Her head went back in challenge.

'Photographs of you. And I have Marie with me.'

Sara frowned. 'You have photographs of me?'

He nodded. 'Sent to me by your mother. With Richard's consent, of course.'

'You've corresponded with my mother?' she gasped.

'Occasionally.' He nodded again. 'Although perhaps corresponded is too strong a word. Once a year, sometimes twice, your mother would send me a photograph of you, and I would do the same thing with Marie. I doubt we've written more than a dozen words to each other in twenty years, but the photographs became a ritual.'

'So you've known exactly how I looked all the time?' Sara was having some trouble taking all this in.

He smiled. 'Every step of the way.'

'Did you know that this year you weren't to receive a photograph?' Her voice was bitter. 'That my mother and I were actually going to visit you here in England?'

'No.' Her father looked startled. 'I had no idea.'

'Apparently my mother considered it time Marie and I were made aware of each other. I think we should have been told a damn sight sooner than this.'

'I realize you're angry, Sara—'

'Angry?' she repeated tautly. 'I'm furious!' Her eyes sparkled with anger. 'Marie might be able to take all this calmly, but I'm afraid I can't.'

Her father gave a rueful smile. 'Marie didn't accept it calmly either—she gave me hell once you'd left yesterday.'

'Good.' Sara felt some of the anger leaving her. 'I like Marie,' she admitted huskily.

'She likes you too.' There was a shimmer of tears in his deep brown eyes so like her own. 'But not as much as I do. Sara—'

'How about inviting me back for lunch?' she broke in on what she felt could only be an emotional speech. And until she had decided what the future held for her she wanted to keep emotion out of this situation for as long as possible. Even her own anger and resentment must be dampened down for the moment.

'You mean that?' he asked eagerly.

'Why not?' she gave a casual shrug. 'Although I'll have to let my aunt and uncle know where I am.'

'Susan and Arthur? We can call in there on the drive back if you like.'

'I'm not sure—'

'We've remained on quite good terms, if that's what you're concerned about,' her father cut in.

'It seems to have been palsy-walsy all round,' Sara said bitterly.

'I—'

'I'm sorry.' Her movements were jerky as she picked up her handbag from the desk top. 'Shall we go now?'

'I just have some papers to collect from my office first. Would you like to come with me or wait here?'

'I'll wait here. You won't be long, will you?'

'Two minutes,' he promised, his eagerness almost embarrassing.

Dominic returned to his office a few seconds later, obviously having been waiting outside. 'There goes a happy man,' he drawled.

'It's only lunch,' Sara snapped awkwardly.

He shook his head. 'Not to Michael it isn't.'

Her eyes flashed at his taunting tone. 'You don't sound as if you approve.'

'Oh, I approve, for Michael's sake.'

'And Marie's!'

'Yes.' The word came out as a hiss. 'But not for my own. And you know why, don't you?' he added harshly.

'No...' The awareness was back, only stronger, and once again it frightened her.

Dominic slowly closed the door behind him, his gaze locked on her parted lips. 'Yes, Sara. God, yes...!' he groaned, pulling her into his arms. 'I've been wanting this since—since—Oh, God!' His lips ground down on hers.

There was no thought of denial, her mouth opened to accept the probing intimacy of his, her body arched against him. She had never been kissed so intimately, so thoroughly, each touch of Dominic's lips was more drugging than the last.

The situation was spiralling out of control, Dominic's hands probing the curve of her back, sending shivers of delight down her spine, his mouth now caressing the hollow below her ear.

But she was a substitute, Marie's double. It wasn't her he was kissing at all. This realization made her spin away from him, the fierce desire in his face reaching out hungrily to her, their breathing ragged.

'I have to go,' she said jerkily. 'I—I'll wait for my father outside.'

Dominic made no move to touch her, standing pale and dazed as she quietly left the room.

Sara smiled nervously at the secretary, pushing her long hair back from her pale face. What had happened in there? It had been like a minor explosion, their bodies fusing together in a tide of sensual abandon. Dominic, a man she had believed to be in control at all times, had definitely been out of control for a few brief minutes, had wanted her with every fiber of his body. And she had wanted him too.

But she hadn't been Sara Hamille to him, she had been Marie Lindlay! He seemed to have trouble separating them, and until he could she would have to stay out of his way. If only she weren't so attracted to him!

'Sara!' Her father appeared at her side, a briefcase in his hand. 'Sorry I was longer than anticipated. I just called Marie to make sure she would be at home.'

After what had just taken place between herself and Dominic Sara wasn't sure she would even be able to face Marie.

Luckily she had to visit her aunt and uncle first, which helped to banish Dominic from her mind somewhat. It seemed her father was right about there being no resentment, because Aunt Susan and Uncle Arthur greeted him politely enough.

'Now that we're here I think I'll change, if you don't mind,' she spoke to her father.

'Go ahead.' He seemed quite at ease. 'I'm sure Susan and Arthur will keep me company in your absence.'

Sara hurried to her room, changing from the denims and T-shirt she had hastily donned that morning and putting on a silky summer dress with a halter neckline and shaped in at the waist. Its tan color suited her golden skin, making her look cool and composed. At least now she looked more in keeping with a guest of Michael Lindlay.

She hurried downstairs, intending to rescue her aunt and uncle from what could only be an embarrassing meeting, even though they appeared to be putting a brave face on it.

'Sara doesn't know about this, does she?' she heard her aunt say, halting her entrance at these puzzling words. What else didn't she know?

Michael Lindlay sighed. 'It isn't something I find easy to tell anyone, but especially Sara.'

'It's unbelievable,' her uncle said emotionally. 'Poor Sara, I don't think she'll be able to take it. First her mother and stepfather, and now—'

'Ssh, Arthur!' his wife told him. 'I think I heard Sara.'

Sara sighed her frustration. What had her uncle been about to say? First her mother and stepfather, and now—? Now was her *father* going to die too? Oh, God, surely not! But what other explanation could there be?

She forced a bright smile to her lips as she breezily entered the room. 'I'm ready,' she announced generally, looking at her father with new eyes. If he was dying, and there could surely be no other explanation, then of what was he dying? He was only in his forties, what could strike a man dead at that young age? A weak heart, a terminal disease? The list was endless. And it made her continued resentment of him seem childish and cruel.

Her father stood up. 'And looking very nice too.' He turned to her aunt and uncle. 'Can I persuade you to join us?'

'Perhaps another time,' her aunt refused.

Sara studied her father on the drive to his home. He didn't look ill, a little strained perhaps, but not ill. Still, some illnesses were like that, the person looking completely normal until it was too late.

Unless she had it all wrong. But what else could have been meant by that conversation?

'Sara!' Marie ran out of the house to greet her as soon as the car drew up outside. She pulled Sara's car door open, tugging her out onto the gravel driveway. 'I couldn't believe it when Daddy rang to say you were coming to lunch.' She hugged her tight. 'After yesterday I didn't think you would ever want to see us again.'

Sara gave a tearful smile. Marie's pleasure was completely genuine. 'Not want to see my own sister?' she choked.

'Oh, Sara!' Marie hugged her all the tighter. 'Isn't it fantastic?' She put her arm through the crook of Sara's. 'We're going to have such fun together,' she told her, taking her into the house.

'Hmm-hmm?'

They both turned at the rather pointed cough. Marie grinned at her father's pained expression. 'Okay, Daddy, you can come too,' she permitted graciously.

'You're so kind.' He grimaced, a lithe, attractive man who didn't look old enough to have twenty-year-old daughters.

Lunch was a lighthearted affair, with Marie and her father doing their best to make Sara feel at home. And to a certain degree they succeeded, all of them greatly enjoying the staff's amazement at there seemingly being two Maries. It took a bit of explaining, but everyone was very welcoming once they knew who Sara was.

'I have to go back to work this afternoon,' their father said regretfully. 'Will you be here when I get back?' He looked hopefully at Sara.

'Well, I—'

'Oh, do stay, Sara,' Marie cut in on her refusal. 'Then after dinner we can—'

'Dinner?' she laughed. 'I only came over for lunch.'

'I want you to stay,' her father told her huskily.

She shrugged. 'All right—dinner.'

He shook his head. 'Not just to dinner, Sara. I want—we *both* want, Marie and I,' he seemed to be having trouble articulating. 'We want you to stay here with us.'

Sara bit her lip. 'Dominic said something about that. I have to go home—'

'This could be your home,' her father cut in. 'With Marie and me.'

'Surely Marie will be getting married soon?' Her voice was shrill at the thought of Dominic marrying Marie. She might have only been a replacement for Marie this morning, but as far as she was concerned Dominic had been Dominic, the man she and Marie both loved. Yes, *loved*. She had fallen in love with a man who wasn't just engaged to any woman, he was going to marry her own *sister*, a girl she couldn't possibly dislike or fight.

'All the more reason for you to come and live with Daddy,' Marie said smilingly. 'Then he won't be lonely when I've gone.'

There was no bitchiness intended in that remark, Marie just didn't have it in her, and yet Sara realized that once again she was being used as a replacement. She had never felt second-best in her life before, but she did so now. Marie was a lovely, friendly girl, well liked by everyone, and Sara felt that she was being compared to her and found wanting. Marie was placid where she was fiery tempered, accepted without demur the wishes of the people around her, namely their father and Dominic, whereas she rebelled at restrictions being put on her. Her independent upbringing was possibly responsible for that.

'I want you to come and live with us for yourself.' His father perhaps sensed her bitterness. 'After all this time I would just like us all to be together.'

'I—I'll think about it,' she told him jerkily.

'You go back to work, Daddy,' Marie cut in on the tension. 'Sara and I will go for a swim this afternoon, and I promise you she'll still be here when you get home tonight.'

'Okay.' He bent to kiss her on the cheek. 'I think your persuasive powers are a lot stronger than mine.' He hesitated in front of Sara. 'May I?' he asked huskily.

She raised her cheek in acceptance, watching as he left the room with long strides. He was a man any girl would be proud to have as a father, and she was fast coming round to thinking that way. After all, what had happened twenty years ago had been a joint decision, and she had loved her mother very much, so why shouldn't she eventually come to love her father! Eventually? The way he had been talking earlier to her aunt and uncle, there might not be time for 'eventually.'

'Poor Daddy,' Marie giggled. 'All this has put him in a terrible state. He hasn't rested since he found out.'

Sara frowned. 'I don't understand how you can accept it all so easily.'

Marie shrugged. 'Life is too short to make an issue out of something like this. Oh, I know you think Daddy treated you badly, but your mother—*our* mother, treated me just as badly, and I don't resent her. After all, she did leave me behind. New angle?' She quirked a teasing eyebrow.

Sara laughed, nodding. 'New angle.'

Her sister became serious. 'What was she like? Was she beautiful? I mean, we must have got our looks from someone.'

'Conceited!' Sara's eyes twinkled merrily.

'Well, I have to be something to have captured Dominic. Everyone thought he was a confirmed bachelor before he asked me to marry him. I would have been a fool to refuse. Don't you think he's just gorgeous?'

Sara was puzzled. If Marie thought he was so wonderful, and she obviously did, then why did she go out with other men, men Dominic knew about, even though it angered him? Marie didn't seem the sort to try and deceive Dominic, she seemed to love him very much, and yet she had these other men. And she didn't know Marie well enough yet to ask her why she did!

'Sara?' Marie prompted at her continued silence.

'He's very nice.' Her manner was rather stilted, her love for the man a feeling she had never before experienced. 'You'll have to excuse me if I'm a bit reserved about him,' she gave a nervy smile. 'After all, the first time I met him he verbally attacked me, the second time he accused me of all kinds of things.'

'Oh, yes,' Marie giggled, 'I can sympathize. You should have heard what he said to me the next day! He's so protective. I think he must be the best friend I ever had. Shall

we go for a swim?' she suggested. 'You can wear one of my
bikinis, it's sure to fit you. You still haven't told me what
our mother was like. Oh, dear,' she gave a rueful smile,
'I'm chattering again! Dan—Dominic always says I talk
nonsense. And I suppose I do. But I do hate silence, don't
you? I never like to be alone.' She grimaced. 'I really hate
that.'

Sara was aware that her sister was now chattering not for
the sake of it but to cover something up. She hadn't been
going to say Dominic at all, she had mentioned someone
called Dan and then tried to act as if she hadn't. Who was
Dan?

There were so many questions unanswered about the
family she now had. Dominic was just as much of a mystery. Why kiss her when he was engaged to Marie?

She mentally shook her head. Each and every one of
these people was a complex personality, and she certainly
wouldn't be able to analyze them on a few days' acquaintance.

'Our mother was very beautiful, very intelligent. She
had a bubbly personality, loved to entertain, and she was
very happy with Richard, my stepfather.' Sara shrugged.
'I liked her. And I'm not just saying that because she was
my mother.'

'I'm sure you aren't,' Marie agreed readily. 'It isn't always possible to like a parent, even though you love them.
I like Daddy too. I think you will when you get to know
him better. He really wants you to stay, Sara,' she added
wistfully. 'We all do.'

Dominic didn't. He wanted her to go back to the States,
and she wasn't sure that wasn't the right thing to do.
Wouldn't she just be bringing heartache to herself to stay
here, tormenting herself with what she couldn't have?

'I've said I'll think about it,' she told Marie firmly, 'and that's what I'm going to do.'

'Without any pressure from me,' Marie said ruefully. 'Okay, let's go and have that swim.'

The pool was deliciously cool in the heat of the day, situated at the far end of the acre or so of land that surrounded the house, shielded from the house by a high hedgerow. As Marie had thought, her bikini fitted Sara perfectly, its scantiness only just decent.

Sara telephoned her aunt later in the day, and they encouraged her to stay to dinner, saying they had no plans for the evening anyway.

'I think maybe I'm a bit underdressed for dinner.' She looked down at her halter-necked dress.

'You look lovely,' Marie assured her. She frowned. 'Or is that being conceited, too?' She shrugged. 'Oh, well, it can't be helped—you do look nice. But if you want to wear something of mine then you're welcome.'

Sara pulled a face. 'I'm beginning to feel like Little Orphan Annie!'

'How can you be Little Orphan Annie when I'm sure you have lots of clothes at home?' Marie dismissed that idea. 'It must be fun being a model.'

'Hard work,' Sara corrected.

'Mmm, I suppose so. I bet if Mummy and Daddy had stuck together I would have been allowed to work, too.' Marie flung open the doors to her wardrobe that took up one wall of the bedroom. 'Take your pick,' she invited.

Sara had never seen one person own so many clothes before, and all of them beautiful, the fashion designers' labels showing how expensive they were. She shook her head. 'I'd be afraid of spilling something on them.'

'Don't be silly,' her sister tutted. 'They're only dresses.'

Sara finally allowed herself to be persuaded into wearing a blue velvet dress, the material sensuous against her bare skin. It, too, was halter-necked, although it revealed a larger expanse of her breasts, and was long and straight to the floor in style.

When Dominic arrived with their father she wished she had turned down this dinner invitation. She hadn't been expecting him, and color flooded her cheeks as she vividly remembered being in his arms earlier, being kissed by him. She wrenched her gaze away as it seemed to lock with his, glad that she had seconds later as she heard Marie greeting him.

'Darling,' she said softly, the next few moments of silence telling their own story, a painful one to Sara.

She looked up just in time to see Marie moving out of Dominic's arms, her lipstick slightly smudged.

'Sara,' Dominic greeted her abruptly.

'Mr. Thorne,' she acknowledged just as abruptly.

'You can't call my fiancé Mr. Thorne,' Marie dismissed with a laugh, her hand resting in the crook of his arm. 'Can she, darling?'

'No,' he agreed curtly.

Sara tried not to call him anything through dinner, concentrating most of her conversation on her father. He was intelligent, amusing, and altogether a charming companion. She was coming to like both members of her family, but falling in love with Dominic made it impossible for her to stay in England.

'Sara?'

She looked up to find her father looking at her enquiringly. 'Sorry?' She blinked her puzzlement.

He laughed. 'It's all right, it wasn't anything important anyway. Did I remember to tell you how beautiful you look this evening? I like the dress.'

She laughed. 'You should—you paid for it!'

He looked startled. 'I did?'

'It's one of mine, Daddy.' Marie grinned. 'Although it never looked that good on me, it must be all that training to be a model.'

Sara blushed at the compliment, studiously avoiding Dominic's piercing blue eyes. He was watching her, she knew he was; he always seemed to be watching her. She just wished she knew why.

'I—er—I think I should be going now,' she suggested brightly.

'I'll drive you,' Dominic offered instantly, almost as if he had been waiting for just such a suggestion.

'No,' she refused sharply, not trusting herself to be alone with this man. 'What I mean,' she added hastily, 'is that I can get a cab—taxi. There's no need to take Dom—Dominic away from Marie this early.'

'You won't be taking me away early,' he drawled. 'I can easily come back.'

'Yes . . .' Sara bit her lip. If he came back he would no doubt spend time giving Marie a prolonged goodbye. Jealousy ripped through her as a physical pain. And then she cursed herself for being a fool. Marie and Dominic could even be sleeping together for all she knew, it was very common in this day and age, and the idea of that was even more unpalatable to her. She couldn't let Dominic drive her home knowing he would be coming back to Marie. 'But I really would rather get a taxi, there's no point in breaking up everyone's evening.'

'You won't be doing that,' Dominic assured her smoothly, standing up to look down at her expectantly.

'Aren't you coming with us, Marie?' she asked her sister almost desperately. 'For the ride?'

'I don't think so.' Marie shook her head regretfully. 'You see, when I've had one of my migraines I usually go to bed early for a few nights.' She grimaced. 'Doctor's orders. I wouldn't do it otherwise.'

'We know that,' her father teased. 'Actually, it's after ten now, so perhaps you ought to go to bed as soon as Sara and Dominic leave.'

Sara and Dominic. Sara repressed the shiver of pleasure that she felt at hearing her name coupled with Dominic's. 'I'd really rather get a taxi, especially as Dominic wouldn't be coming back here.'

Dominic shrugged. 'I have to leave now anyway, so if you want a lift I have an empty car.'

'Of course she'd like a lift,' her father smiled. 'Sara was just being tactful, wanted to leave you two alone.'

'Oh, you don't need to do that,' Marie declared. 'I'll just take Dominic outside now and then you won't need to feel in the least guilty. Come along, darling,' and she took her fiancé's hand and led him out of the room.

'You mustn't mind Marie,' her father excused as the door closed after them. 'She's very forthright.'

'Yes.' Sara's cheeks were fiery red as her imagination played overtime. 'I—I like that. My mother—' she broke off, biting her lip.

'Yes?' he prompted. 'Don't stop talking about her because it's me,' he said huskily. 'It's been so long since I heard news of Rachel that I would love to hear about your life with her.'

'I'm sorry,' she said with genuine compassion, realizing Dominic had been right about her father's love for her mother. 'My mother brought me up to be completely honest too,' she finished her previous statement.

'We always did have similar views on bringing up children,' he said. 'I don't think either of us did a bad job of it.'

At that moment Marie and Dominic rejoined them, Marie's mouth pointedly bare of lipstick. Sara winced, turning away, making her expression blank as she sensed Dominic's gaze on her once again. Marie looked thoroughly, glowingly kissed, and Dominic was looking at *her*.

Why? Did he expect her to act jealous? Was he one of those men who liked to have more than one woman interested in him? Most of all, did he like having *twins* interested in him?

'The dress!' she suddenly exclaimed as they were leaving. 'I still have your dress on, Marie.'

'Well, that's all right.' Her sister giggled. 'I'm sure I'll see you again soon.'

'Oh, yes, yes, of course.' She gave a jerky smile.

The silence in the car was uncomfortable, Sara not knowing what to say to Dominic now that they were alone.

'You didn't—'

'I hope I—' Both of them began talking at the same time, both of them breaking off at the same time. Sara gave a nervous laugh. 'Go ahead,' she invited.

'It wasn't important,' he said dismissively.

She sighed. 'Neither was what I had to say.'

'You don't like being with me, do you?' he guessed bluntly.

'Not much,' she answered with the honesty she had told her father her mother had instilled in her.

'Because I kissed you?'

She blushed in the darkness. 'No,' she answered tautly.

'Liar!' His voice was harsh.

'No lie.' She shook her head. 'You weren't kissing *me*, you were kissing Marie.'

Dominic's laugh was bitter. 'If I kissed Marie like that I'd frighten the hell out of her! I was kissing *you*, Sara. Fool that I am.'

Now he had thrown her into even more confusion. Could her surmise be correct, was he a man who liked more than one string to his bow? And yet he seemed to love Marie very much. Maybe he did love her, but that certainly didn't prevent him being attracted to someone else!

'Then I would appreciate it if you didn't do it again,' she told him tightly.

'I'm trying, Sara,' he revealed grimly. 'I really am trying.'

'Then try a little harder. It's bad enough for me here without having to fight off passes from my sister's boyfriend!'

Dominic's mouth tightened with suppressed anger. And she wasn't surprised. It must be years since anyone had called him a 'boy.' He was thirty-five, all man, and no one could mistake him for anything else. But Sara knew that her only weapon was verbal attack. She was powerless against him physically.

'It wasn't a pass,' he rasped. 'I—I couldn't stop myself.' He obviously hated admitting the weakness. 'But if you'll stay in England I promise it won't happen again.''

''If I go back home it won't happen again either!''

He gave her a sideways glance. 'I could always follow you.'

Sara gasped. 'That wouldn't be very practical,' she warned.

'For once in my life I would like to act *un*practical!' He was gripping the steering wheel so tightly his knuckles showed white.

'When *is* the wedding?' Sara asked with pointed sarcasm.

Dominic drew a shaky breath. 'No date has been set yet.'

'Then perhaps it should be. Maybe if you had a wife to keep you busy you wouldn't chase other women.' Her eyes sparkled angrily. 'Marie would be very distressed if she knew about the way you've been acting with me. I believe my father would be too.' There was a threat in her voice, and she knew it had gone home.

A white ring of tension appeared about Dominic's mouth. 'I would prefer you not to tell them.'

'I bet you would!' she flung at him.

'Not for the reason you're thinking,' he snapped. 'There's something—a reason you don't understand. If you tell them what happened between us then you'll be causing more damage than you realize. And Marie, and of course your father, are going to need you in the very near future.'

That feeling of foreboding again! Wasn't Dominic just confirming what she already guessed—her father was dying?

'And what about me?' she asked shrilly. 'Who's going to help me?'

His hand moved to grip hers in the darkness, strong and sure, and wholly dependable. 'I'll always be around to help you, you can be sure of that.'

She knew that; hadn't he already become the one person in this whole crazy situation that she knew she could rely on? And yet he was the one she feared the most emotionally, the man who could destroy her at a glance.

'I know,' Dominic said suddenly, huskily, seeming to read her tortuous thoughts. 'And it isn't going to be easy for me, either.' He sighed. 'But I swear to you that from now on I'll just be your friend. Stay, Sara,' he pleaded softly. 'Stay, and I'll take care of you.'

She looked up to meet the dazzling passion in his eyes, knowing that she couldn't go back to Florida now even if she wanted to. The man she loved was here, and she had to be where he was.

She nodded. 'I'll stay,' she agreed in a choked voice.

The tension left him in a sigh, and he lifted her hand up to his mouth, kissing the palm with intimate intensity. 'Thank you, Sara! You'll never regret your decision.'

Strange, she already regretted it!

CHAPTER SIX

MARIE WAS OVERJOYED by her decision, when she turned up at their aunt and uncle's house halfway through the next morning.

'But how did you know?' Sara frowned, hardly awake yet, having spent a very restless night.

'Dominic rang me this morning.' Marie grinned. 'He rings me every morning.'

Ever the doting fiancé! If it wasn't for the remembered delight of his lips on hers, and the way she quivered with pleasure every time he looked at her, she might have been convinced of his single-minded devotion to Marie. But her own memories were too strong for her to accept that, although she in no way doubted his love for her sister. If only she didn't love him too!

'He said you've decided to stay,' Marie continued excitedly.

After a little 'friendly' persuasion from him! He had half seduced her into making that decision, and she resented him for it.

'I have,' she confirmed. 'But—'

'Move in today!' Marie interrupted eagerly. 'Now! Let's give Daddy a surprise when he comes home.'

Sara looked at her aunt for help. There had been a tearful meeting between aunt and niece, and now Aunt Susan was watching them both indulgently from her usual chair by the window, her knitting in her hand. 'Aunt Susan?' she prompted desperately.

Her aunt shrugged. 'It seems like a good idea to me.'

'But—'

'Your place is with your father and Marie now,' her aunt said firmly.

Of course her aunt knew of her father's illness. And of course, she was right, her place was with them. 'It doesn't seem very polite to just walk out on you and Uncle Arthur in this way.' Still she hesitated about committing herself. Staying in the country was one thing, staying where she would have to constantly see Dominic was another.

'Your uncle and I don't mind in the least,' her aunt dismissed that problem. 'You can always come over and visit us. And we would be happier knowing you're still in England, rather than letting you go back to Florida alone.'

Sara could see the sense of that, and knew herself beaten. 'Okay,' she gave in. 'Although I think you should let your—our father know I'm going to be there. I don't want to give him a shock.' Especially as she had no idea what was actually wrong with him.

'Daddy won't be shocked,' her sister assured her. 'He'll be delighted.'

'Maybe Dominic will have told him.'

Marie grinned. 'I asked him not to. Dominic knows how I love to play tricks on people. I used to do it to him all the time. We practically grew up together.'

'He seems a nice man,' Aunt Susan remarked absently.

'Oh, he is,' Marie agreed. 'A bit intense, but very nice. Listen to me!' She giggled. 'Of course *I* think he's nice, I'm going to marry him. Do you like him, Sara?'

Sara hated the evasion she knew must be in her expression, but she could do nothing about it. 'Yes, I like him.

Now, shall we get my things together?' she asked briskly. 'I don't have much, so it shouldn't take long to pack.'

Marie seemed to have enthusiasm even for such mundane tasks as packing suitcases. 'Daddy's going to be so pleased,' she said as she stowed Sara's suitcase in the back of her red sports car, having already taken their leave of Aunt Susan, Sara having promised to visit as often as she could. She had a feeling she was going to need her aunt and uncle's down-to-earth attitude every now and again.

'I hope you're right.' She got in beside her sister.

'I am,' Marie said with certainty. 'Hey, we could have a party, introduce you to all our friends.'

Sara shied away from such a suggestion. 'I don't think so, Marie, not for a while anyway. Let me just get used to being with you and Dad first.'

'Don't be silly.' Her sister dismissed the idea. 'You don't need to get used to us, we're your family. And I want to show you off to all our friends.'

Sara didn't put up any more arguments, it was useless against Marie's determination anyway. Her sister was used to having her own way, and she did it in such a goodnatured way that it was hard to deny her. Even Dominic, a man Sara felt sure could be very ruthless, both in business and his social life, even he gave in to Marie's slightest whim.

Dominic again! Why couldn't she just put him out of her mind, forget about him? Or at least stop thinking of him every minute of the day and night!

Marie showed her into the bedroom next to her own. 'I knew I could persuade you.' She gave a rueful smile, putting Sara's case down on the bed. 'So I had Edith make up your room for you. Do you like it? If you don't you could always have one of the others. There are six other bedrooms, besides Daddy's and mine, so you can take your pick.'

Sara was sure that none of them could be more comfortable than this, the furniture white and delicate-looking, the carpet a deep brown, the bedspread gold with a dark brown velvet headboard, restful paintings hanging on the brown and gold flower-print wallpaper, the curtains a brown velvet.

'This will be fine. But are you sure your father—'

'*Our* father,' Marie corrected firmly. 'And he won't mind at all. Just wait until you see how pleased he is!'

Sara was in her room when her father arrived home, but she had looked out of the window as soon as she heard the car—*cars*. Once again her father hadn't come home alone, there was the familiar blue Rolls-Royce parked behind her father's Mercedes. Dominic was to be here for dinner again this evening! Oh, well, she was going to have to get used to him being around all the time.

She heard her father go to his room to change, and decided that this was the best time to make her presence known.

'Hello, darling,' he answered her knock on his door, for the first time confusing her with Marie. Not that she was surprised, he would hardly expect her to be entering his bedroom. 'Did you see Sara today?' he asked eagerly.

Sara felt a lump rise in her throat at the love he already felt for her. 'Yes,' she said huskily.

'I thought she might be here to dinner.' His eyes were shadowed with his unhappiness.

She smiled, holding out her hands to him. 'I am,' she told him softly. 'I'm here to stay,' she added reassuringly.

'Sara?' He shook his head wonderingly.

She bit her bottom lip to stop it quivering. 'Yes.'

She was at once pulled into a bear hug; her father's body was shaking as he held her to him. When he finally moved back enough to look down at her there was a bright shimmer of tears in his eyes.

'You don't know how happy you've made me,' he said chokingly.

'I think I do.'

He gave a triumphant shout of laughter. 'Yes, I suppose you do.' His arm remained about her shoulders. 'Now, which bedroom are you in?' She told him. 'Next to Marie,' he murmured almost to himself. 'Oh, well,' he shrugged, 'it can't be helped.'

Sara frowned. 'If you would rather I slept somewhere else . . .'

'No,' he reassured her. 'No, I didn't mean that. It's just that sometimes Marie—well, she walks in her sleep.'

'Is that all?' she smiled her relief. 'I can cope with that. Mummy used to do it all the time. Oh, I'm sorry! I didn't mean—'

'Talk about your mother all you want, Sara,' he cut in firmly. 'So Rachel didn't grow out of the habit of sleep-walking?'

'No.' She relaxed a little. 'We used to find her wandering about all over the place.'

Her father nodded. 'Marie started doing it about six months ago. The first time it happened she fell down the stairs.'

'Oh, no!' The horror in her face was echoed in her voice. 'Was she hurt?' she asked worriedly.

'Just a bump on the head.' He turned away to put on his tie. 'She had a black eye for several days afterwards.'

'I bet that pleased her!'

'It did,' her father agreed ruefully, pulling on his jacket.

Sara suddenly frowned. 'Six months ago, you said,' she repeated slowly.

He nodded. 'About five-thirty one morning. I wondered what on earth was going on when I heard all the noise.' He grimaced. 'You've no idea how much noise a person falling downstairs can make.'

'This is only a guess,' Sara continued slowly, 'but did Marie fall down the stairs some time in December?'

'I'm not sure. It was—Yes! Yes, it would have been December. I remember now, Marie had a bandaged ankle for Christmas.'

Sara frowned. 'Bandaged ankle?'

'Mmm, she sprained her ankle as well as bumping her head.'

'And I bruised my head as well as breaking both my legs—on the twentieth of December,' she added pointedly. 'At twelve-thirty at night.'

Her father was suddenly still. 'What are you saying, Sara?'

'Well, six months ago *I* was involved in an accident, so was Marie, and we both received similar injuries. It just seems too much of a coincidence to me.'

'I suppose so. But as you said, it must just be coincidence.'

Sara shook her head. 'I don't think so. You don't remember the exact date of Marie's fall?'

'Not offhand, no.'

'Then I'll ask Marie, she's sure to remember.'

'Remember what?' Marie appeared in the doorway, spectacularly beautiful in a silver dress that flowed about her as she walked. She grimaced as she saw Sara's surprised expression. 'I have to go to a party at Dominic's mother's this evening. It was too late to get out of it.'

They all walked down the stairs together, Sara's purple dress much more subdued than Marie's but no less attractive, clinging revealingly to the slender curves of her body.

'There's no reason why you should,' she told her sister as they entered the lounge together.

She looked up reluctantly at Dominic, seeing the narrowing of his eyes as he looked at them. He looked magnificent, dressed as he had been the first time Sara had seen him, the black evening suit and snowy white shirt impeccable. Not that Dominic needed these trappings to stand out in any company. He was a man apart, a man who commanded and received attention.

'Which one do I kiss?' he drawled mockingly.

'Guess!' Marie smiled impishly.

Dominic pretended to consider them, although Sara knew he had guessed their identity as soon as they entered the room. After those first few occasions Dominic never confused them. And yet he was pretending to now, bringing Sara out in a hot flush, her breathing shallow as she waited for him to decide.

Her heart stopped beating altogether as he seemed to walk in her direction, changing his mind at the last moment and kissing Marie lightly on the mouth.

He turned to look at Sara. 'Did I have you worried?' he taunted.

'Hardly worried, Dominic,' Marie tapped him lightly on the arm. 'No girl would feel *worried* about being kissed by you.'

'If you say so,' he drawled.

'I do. I was just explaining to Sara that this evening with your mother can't be put off.'

'And I was just saying that it isn't necessary,' Sara said hastily.

'But it's your first night here with us,' Marie protested.

Sara shrugged. 'There'll be plenty of other nights.'

'Why don't you change your mind and come to the party, Michael?' Dominic suggested smoothly. 'My mother was very disappointed that you weren't coming. She's already looking forward to meeting Sara.'

Marie pouted. 'But I wanted to give a party and introduce Sara to everyone.'

Her father smiled indulgently. 'You can still have your party, there'll still be plenty of people for Sara to meet. I doubt your mother has invited all of London, has she, Dominic?'

'Not quite,' the other man smiled at him, joining in his teasing of Marie.

'There you are, then,' their father grinned. 'You'll still have hundreds of people to invite, Marie.'

'I don't want to intrude on your evening,' Sara told her sister. 'And I can surely meet your mother some other time, Dominic,' she added stiltedly.

'Then why not tonight?' he asked, his eyes narrowed.

'Because—well, because—'

'She's a little shy.' Her father put his arm about her shoulders. 'Diane will make you very welcome, Sara. And I did originally have an invitation. I turned it down because of my worry over you. But now that you're here with us I think we should all go. I'm sure the party isn't to be a big one, is it, Dominic?'

'About thirty people.'

Thirty people at the moment seemed like the whole world, but she raised no more arguments. She was just embarrassing herself and everyone else. Besides, what was one evening?

'You were going to ask me something earlier, Sara,' Marie reminded her partway through dinner. 'Something you said I was sure to remember.'

She felt a little foolish about her idea now, especially in front of Dominic, feeling sure he would just ridicule her. Dominic was a man who dealt in facts, a man of logic, and what she was suggesting certainly wasn't logical.

She looked down at her succulently cooked chicken, wishing she had an appetite for it. 'I just wondered what the date was when you fell down the stairs,' she shrugged dismissively. 'It isn't important. I'm sure you don't even remember it.'

All humour had left Marie, leaving her face haunted. 'I remember exactly,' she said hollowly. 'It was the twentieth of December.'

Once again Sara's interest flared. 'The same day!' she told her father excitedly. 'Don't you see, it's the same day!' She clutched his arm.

'But a different time,' he shook his head. 'It has to be a coincidence.'

'You've forgotten the time difference, Dad.' She didn't even notice she had called him that in the excitement of the discovery, but the other occupants of the dining room table did. Her father flushed with pleasure, Marie and Dominic smiled approvingly. 'It was five-thirty here,' she explained, 'but twelve-thirty in Florida.'

'The same day as your accident,' Dominic suddenly realized.

'Yes!' She looked at him, her eyes glowing. Then she frowned. 'But how did you know that?'

'The file,' he reminded her.

'Oh, yes,' she nodded absently. 'Don't you think it's weird?'

'Extremely so.' He surprised her by agreeing.

Over the next few minutes they discovered that these similarities had occurred several times during the last twenty years, a case of them both having measles at the same time, both having their tonsils out within days of each other. The list was endless once they started comparing notes, and each new discovery added to their amazement.

'Maybe we'll both fall in love with the same man,' Marie said mischievously, not knowing how near the truth she was, or Sara felt sure she wouldn't have said it. Marie wasn't in the least vindictive or cruel, and the remark would have been both those things if she had known of Sara's feelings. 'How would you like that, darling?' she teased her fiancé.

His expression was grim, his mouth a thin taut line. 'I wouldn't like it at all,' he said curtly.

'I was only joking, Dominic,' Marie was instantly contrite. 'I'm sure Sara already has a boyfriend in America.'

Dominic looked at Sara with sharp eyes. 'Do you?' he demanded abruptly.

She thought of Barry and then dismissed him. 'Not in America, no,' she replied slowly. 'But I have a—friend here. His name is Eddie.' And she hoped Eddie would forgive her for using him in this way. But she needed some form of defence, was afraid to let Dominic know just how deeply she had become interested in him.

'You work fast,' he snapped. 'After all, you've only been here a little under two weeks.'

She gave him a brittle smile. 'Sometimes it takes only a glance to feel you know someone, like them.'

'Love them?' he prompted tautly.

She gave what she hoped was a light laugh. 'It's a little too soon to tell.'

'You'll have to invite Eddie over one evening,' her father suggested. 'I'd like to meet him.'

Sara shrugged. 'Maybe the night of the party.'

'Then we must have the party very soon,' Marie said eagerly. 'How about Saturday?'

'That's a little too soon for me,' Sara refused laughingly. 'Maybe next week, hmm?'

'All right,' her sister accepted reluctantly, looking at her wristwatch. 'I think we should be leaving now.'

At once the nervousness returned to Sara. She didn't want to meet Dominic's mother, to know about his family, his home life. Somehow that would bring her even closer to him, make it all the harder for her to accept his marriage to her sister.

She travelled with her father in his car, Marie and Dominic in the Rolls. At least she had been given this respite, time to collect together the poise and control she had been taught during her career, something that seemed to have deserted her the last few days, along with her carefree nature.

'Relax,' her father seemed to sense her tension. 'I can assure you that Diane is a most gracious hostess.'

'I'm sure she is. It's just—well—'

His hand moved to clasp hers. 'You'll be fine, Marie and I will see to that.'

Diane Thorne's house was just what Sara had expected, a detached house set in its own grounds, a butler to show them in and take their wraps, a maid to show them into the gracious lounge where a dozen or so people were already chatting around the room in groups of twos and threes.

The entrance of Marie and herself caused just as much of a sensation as she had known it would. It had been this attention that she had been dreading, and when she felt her father's arm go protectively about her waist she leaned gratefully back against him.

'Come and meet my mother,' Dominic murmured against her earlobe.

Sara turned with a start, quickly moving out of the arc of his arm. 'I didn't realize—I thought you were my father!' she accused.

'I told him I would take care of you—Marie has taken him to get a drink. Now come and meet my mother,' he repeated firmly.

She nodded, licking her lips nervously; Dominic's touch had completely unnerved her.

Dominic put a guiding hand under her elbow. 'I'm sorry about earlier,' he said huskily. 'It was—a stupid thing to do.'

'I'm sorry?' She shook her head, determinedly not looking at him, knowing that people were watching them as they moved across the room. 'I don't know what you mean.'

His hand tightened. 'I was almost tempted to kiss you and not Marie,' he revealed gruffly. 'It was an utterly stupid move on my part. Who is Eddie?' he demanded tautly.

She shrugged. 'A friend—I told you.'

Dominic turned her to face him, his expression fierce. 'How much of a friend?' he wanted to know.

'Really, Dominic.' Her tone was deliberately taunting. 'My friendship with Eddie is none of your business.'

His eyes turned almost black, his gaze compelling. 'You know damn well it is! Sara—'

'Dominic!' A small woman with gray-black hair appeared at his side, a beautiful woman, her make-up and figure impeccable for her age, which must have been at least fifty. Looking at her closely, Sara could see certain resemblances to Dominic, the same deep blue eyes, the same determined chin, so she guessed this to be his mother, which meant she was well over fifty. The woman turned to Sara, a warm smile on her lips. 'You must be Sara,' she held out her hand.

She blushed, taking that hand. 'It's nice to meet you, Mrs. Thorne,' she said shyly.

The other woman shook her head. 'Your likeness to Marie is incredible!'

Sara smiled. 'And yet you knew the difference.'

Diane Thorne glanced at her son. 'Go and get Sara and me a drink, darling.'

For a moment Dominic looked like ignoring that imperious demand, then with an angry glare at his mother he turned and walked in the direction of the bar.

Both women watched him go, Sara with relief, and his mother with—Sara couldn't tell the other woman's feelings, deliberately so, she felt.

'My father and Marie—'

'Are talking to my other son,' Diane Thorne nodded.

Sara's eyes widened. 'I didn't realize you had another son.'

'And a daughter too. I'll introduce you to them both later, and to Samantha's husband Brett. They're expecting their first child soon, my first grandchild.' She smiled. 'I'm not sure I'll like being a grandmother, it's very ageing.' She grimaced.

Sara laughed at her rueful expression. 'My mother always said you're only as old as you feel.'

'A good saying.' Blue eyes twinkled merrily. 'As long as you don't feel a hundred at the time!'

Sara spluttered with laughter. 'I know that feeling.'

'Dominic tells me you're a model,' Mrs. Thorne said interestedly.

She frowned at the mention of Dominic. 'I was. I'm not sure what I am any more.' She shrugged. 'My father doesn't appear to approve of women working for a living.'

'You mean Marie?'

'Mmm.' Sara nodded.

Diane Thorne shrugged. 'I'm sure your father will respect your wish for independence. Marie is different, she likes acting as hostess. She's going to make Dominic a wonderful wife.'

'Yes,' Sara agreed hollowly, watching Dominic as he strode across the room towards them, the requested drinks in his capable hands.

His mother gently touched her arm. 'Don't,' she pleaded huskily.

Sara looked stricken. 'Don't what, Mrs. Thorne?'

The other woman's eyes were filled with compassion. 'Don't love my son, Sara.'

'I—'

'Here we are.' Dominic handed his mother her drink, frowning as he looked at Sara's pale face. 'Sara?' he queried sharply. 'Sara, what's wrong?'

'Nothing. Nothing is wrong! I—Excuse me.' She pushed past him, heading for the open doors that led to the moonlit garden. She trembled in the warmth of the evening, wondering how Diane Thorne had guessed her feelings so quickly.

'Sara!' Dominic spun her round to face him, forcing her chin up. 'What did my mother say to you?' he rasped.

'I—Nothing.' She looked down at her feet. 'I—I just felt faint for a moment.' She forced a smile to her numb lips. 'I'm all right now. Shall we go back inside?' She made a move towards the door.

'No!' Dominic stopped her, a fevered look in his eyes. 'I want to know what my mother said.'

'She—she—Oh, what does it matter?' She dismissed the idea impatiently, her gaze locked on the strength of his face, the sensuousness of his firm mouth, and she couldn't break free of the spell he was casting on her. 'Dominic!' she groaned, swaying into his arms.

He needed no further encouragement, but devoured her lips with his own, his arms like steel bands about her. Their hearts beat as one, their desire flamed as one, their mouths joined even if their bodies couldn't be.

'Oh, God, Sara,' Dominic moaned into her throat, his mouth sending liquid fire through her veins. 'I want you so damned much!' he agonized, his lips touching the firm curve of her breasts.

She feverishly unbuttoned his shirt, her hands moving inside to caress the hard strength of his back and chest. She had never touched a man this intimately, loving the silky texture of his skin, the ripple of muscles as he quivered beneath her touch. He felt so good, so sensually warm and exciting that Sara just wanted to lose herself against him, and she knew he felt the same way, could feel the throbbing hardness of his thighs, his ragged breathing as her fingertips caressed lower to his waist.

Neither of them had the strength to stop this explosion of emotions between them, their hands roaming freely over each other's bodies, straining for a much closer contact.

'I want to possess you!' Dominic shuddered against her as he fought for control. 'I want to feel you naked against me, to know every inch of your body, every quivering nerve. Am I frightening you?' he groaned as she trembled.

'You're exciting me.' She instantly denied fear. 'I want that too, Dominic. I want you so badly!' She blushed at her own admission.

'When, my darling?' he moaned, caressing her breast through the material of her dress. 'When will you be mine?'

'Whenever you want me,' she told him breathlessly, aiding his entry down the low cleavage of her dress, her breath catching in her throat as his hand closed possessively over her bare breast.

'*Now,*' he groaned. 'I want you now!'

Sara gasped as her nipple hardened and rose to the touch of his fingertips, feeling herself swell into his waiting hand, raw desire ripping through her body. 'Oh, God, Dominic!' She swayed against him, almost fainting with her need of him.

'Dominic? Dominic!'

Panic washed over Sara as she realized that was Dominic's mother calling to him. God, she thought, what must the other woman be thinking; they had been out here ages!

'It's your mother,' she told him in a choked whisper. 'I—She—You have to go in, Dominic.'

If anything his hold tightened about her. 'And leave you here all alone?' He shook his head. 'I can't do that. I never want you to be alone again, Sara. I want to take care of you, but not as a friend, I want you as a—'

'Lover?' she queried shakily. 'It wouldn't do, Dominic. No man could bed two sisters, in all decency.'

He closed his eyes as if to shut out the pain. 'At this moment I don't feel decent. I feel—'

'Dominic!' His mother's call was an angry whisper now. 'Dominic, we have guests!' She was obviously very agitated.

He gave an angry sigh, reluctantly buttoning his shirt. 'I have to go in, Sara. I don't want my mother coming out here.'

Neither did she; her senses were still very much attuned to Dominic's caresses. 'Yes—go. I—I want to stay here for a while. If anyone asks, my father or Marie, tell them I have a headache I'm trying to clear.'

His shaking fingers gently touched her cheek. 'You won't be long?'

'No.' Just long enough to calm down from the excitement he had caused in her body.

'Oh, Sara, I wish—God, I wish—'

'Please go in, Dominic,' she begged shakily. 'Please!'

With great reluctance he turned to go, stopping suddenly to turn and look at her. 'I won't forget about tonight, Sara, so don't ask me to.' His eyes were still alight with his own passion. 'And whatever my mother said to you—'

'She said for the best,' she cut in firmly. 'Now go. But first...' she reached up and wiped all traces of her lip gloss from his mouth.

His answer was to once again bend his head and crush her lips with his own, this time wiping his mouth himself, not angrily or roughly, but sensuously soft, as if feeling the taste of her lips against his fingertips. With one last telling glance he was gone, and Sara felt her body relax from the tension she had been under.

She was mad, insane, and yet if she were insane then so was Dominic. He had lost all control, didn't seem to care that someone could have walked out here at any moment and caught them in what could be called a compromising situation. But perhaps his mother had made sure that didn't happen, had somehow prevented anyone from coming out here.

Where would it all end? How could such a situation have an *end*? She wanted and loved Dominic, Dominic obviously wanted her, and yet he loved Marie. Sara loved Marie, too, could never hurt her in any way, and yet that love didn't seem to matter when confronted with her wild longing for Dominic. How could he want both of them? How could he do that to either of them? At least Marie didn't know he was cheating her, at least she was being spared that pain. But Sara knew all about his duplicity, was in fact the 'other woman' in this affair. Once again she asked herself where it would all end.

She stepped back into the shadows of the garden as someone else came out onto the balcony, still not feeling up to seeing anyone just yet. The shadow of another person approached, and the first person let out a gasp of dismay.

'Go away, Danny!' Marie could be heard saying.

Danny? Sara instantly became alert. The other day Marie had been about to say Dan—something. Could this be the Danny she had been talking about?

'Marie—'

'Leave me alone!' She pushed him away from her. 'You know you shouldn't be out here with me.'

'You knew I'd follow you,' the man protested, his voice strangely familiar to Sara.

But why was it familiar? She didn't know anyone called Danny in England.

'Marie, we have to talk,' he went on. 'This marriage to Nick just isn't on.'

Nick, this man called *Dominic* Nick! She had met only one person who did that, the man she had met in Soho. That must be the reason his voice was so familiar.

'You're wrong, Danny,' Marie told him firmly. 'My marriage to Dominic is very much on. In fact, he's the only man I would marry.'

'Last year you wanted to marry me,' the man reminded fiercely.

'I made a mistake. Every girl is entitled to make one,' Marie said lightly. 'You were mine. But I'm over that now, and I'm going to marry Dominic.'

'I won't let you!' Danny pulled her into his arms. 'I love you, Marie, and you love me.'

Sara was embarrassed at being a witness to this conversation, but it was too late to move now.

Marie emerged from Danny's suffocating kiss. 'Let me go, Danny,' she ordered coldly. 'My sister's out here somewhere. She's the reason I'm out here at all—I came to look for her.'

At the mention of her Sara's foot accidentally knocked against one of the flowerpots standing along the verandah, and she moved back into the shadows.

'I heard someone,' Marie whispered, pushing Danny away from her. 'Please, you have to go. That could be Sara, and I don't want her to see me with you. Please, Danny!' she pleaded as he still didn't move.

'All right!' he accepted angrily. 'But this isn't the end of it. I won't let you marry Nick.'

Even from this distance Sara could see Marie's eyes flash, her chin thrust out in challenge. 'Try and stop me,' she hissed. 'Just try it, Danny. I'll never come back to you. Never!'

'We'll see!' he snapped before turning around and going back into the house.

Sara heard her sister's ragged sigh, giving her a few minutes to collect herself before making her presence known. Even in the gloom she could clearly see Marie's paleness, her wide distressed eyes.

But all this was quickly masked as she saw Sara, her smile on the shaky side. 'How are you feeling now?' she asked concernedly.

'A lot better,' Sara replied, remembering the headache she was supposed to have. 'I—Shall we go back inside?' She wished she could show Marie that she knew of her distress, but without revealing her eavesdropping she couldn't very well do that.

They rejoined their father and Dominic, and Marie was the one who looked ill. Dominic's arm came about her protectively.

'I think it's time we went,' he said softly. 'You're looking tired, Marie.'

'I—I think maybe I am,' she agreed hesitantly. 'It must be the—the heat.'

Or her rather heated meeting with the young man called Danny! Sara was in utter confusion about her newly acquired family. So many secrets, past and present, that she just didn't have access to.

CHAPTER SEVEN

MARIE THREW HERSELF wholeheartedly into the preparations for their own party, or perhaps wholeheartedly was the wrong description; mindlessly fitted better. She was like a butterfly, flitting from one arrangement to another, never seeming to stop long enough to think, let alone plan anything.

And then mid-week she fell prone to one of her migraine attacks. Sara heard her moving restlessly about her room in the middle of the night, and at first she stayed awake in case Marie began sleepwalking. Then she realized that the frenzied walking was due to something else. Marie was in pain of some sort, whether physical or mental she didn't know, she only knew her twin was in pain.

Marie was sitting on the bed when she went in, bent double, her head cradled in her hands. 'Oh, God, make it stop,' she groaned. 'Make it stop!'

'Marie!' Sara ran to her, holding her against her shoulder. 'Marie, what is it?'

'My head!' her sister choked. 'Oh, God, make the pains stop!' Tears streamed down her face.

'What sort of pains, Marie?'

'Sharp, *digging* pains.' She quivered. 'I can't stand it, Sara. I just can't stand it!' she repeated hysterically.

'It's all right now, honey,' Sara soothed. 'I'm with you. Now we're going to make the pains go away. You and I together are going to make them stop. Now lie back,

Marie. Come on, back on the bed.' All the time she was talking she was easing her sister back on the pillows. 'That's the way,' she cooed once Marie was finally lying down. 'Now I'm going to turn out the lights—'

'No! No, don't leave me in the dark!' Marie struggled to sit up.

'I'm not going to leave you at all,' Sara reassured her, holding her firmly against her. 'I'm going to stay right here with you.'

'Please don't turn off the light,' her sister trembled. 'I don't like the dark. It—it makes me think of death.' She swallowed hard. 'Do you think when you die that it's all darkness, that you're alone in the dark forever?'

Sara frowned, smoothing Marie's heated brow, feeling the tension starting to recede. 'I don't think so,' she comforted.

'Don't you really?' Marie asked hopefully.

'I really don't.'

Right now she would give anything to know how long Marie's headaches had been occurring. She would take a bet on its being since she had found out about their father's illness. These migraine attacks were brought on through fear of her father's death. Marie was one of those people petrified of death and all it entailed. It held such a fear for her that she had nightmares, sleepwalked, and had these terrible tension headaches, headaches that caused actual physical pains.

'All right.' Marie sighed against her. 'You can turn out the main light now. But leave on the bedside lamp!' she pleaded.

'I will,' Sara reassured her. 'But I'm sure a dim light will help your head.' She rejoined her sister on the bed, putting her arms about her and holding her tight. 'I'm here now, Marie,' she murmured. 'You can go to sleep, you aren't alone any more.'

'Thank you.' Marie sighed. 'I—I feel better now.' She closed her eyes, starting to relax. 'I'm sorry to be such a baby,' she murmured.

'You aren't a baby.' Sara smoothed her sister's hair. 'You're in pain, and you're naturally upset.'

'The pain's going now.'

Of course it was; Marie had been comforted and reassured, and now the headache was fading. As the pain receded sleep took over, and it wasn't long before Sara knew her sister to be asleep. But still she didn't leave her, feeling that Marie needed her close, could sense she was there even though she was now fast asleep.

Someone ought to be told the reason for Marie's migraine attacks. They were very serious, their father's worried return from his business trip had been evidence of that, and yet they could all be stopped if Marie were able to discuss her father's illness with someone. At the moment she was obviously afraid to, and as Sara wasn't even supposed to know about the illness she couldn't really introduce the subject. The trouble was she didn't yet know her father or sister well enough to interfere in this situation. That left only Dominic.

But she couldn't talk to Dominic either, had avoided even looking at him the last couple of days; the memory of their behaviour out in his mother's garden was still too vivid in her mind for her to think of it without blushing. She had behaved shamelessly, had given in to a passion that she had never known before, a desire to be possessed by Dominic, her own sister's intended husband.

Dominic hadn't accepted her cool behaviour of the last few days without demur, but there was little he could do in front of Marie and her father. Any attempts by him to get her alone she had so far managed to rebuff, and yesterday when she had received a telephone call from a man who wouldn't give his name she had refused to take the call, guessing it to be Dominic. They had to stay away from each other, and if Dominic wasn't strong enough to see that they did then she would have to be the one who did.

Sometime towards morning she must have fallen asleep herself, because the sun was filtering through the curtains when next she opened her eyes. A quick look at the bed-side clock showed her it was almost eight o'clock. Marie would be all right now, now it was daylight, and as she was still asleep, Sara moved gingerly from her side and made her way back to her own room.

She met her father out in the corridor, his dark pin-striped suit evidence of his having just prepared to go to work.

He frowned as he saw her softly close Marie's bedroom door. 'Has she been ill?' he asked worriedly.

'Just one of her headaches,' Sara shrugged. 'I think she's all right now.'

'I'll go in to her.' His hand moved out to the door han-dle.

'No,' Sara stopped him. 'She's asleep. I should leave her.'

He looked taken aback. 'She actually managed to fall asleep? Usually when she has one of these attacks some-one has to sit up with her all night.'

This made Sara wonder how many times Dominic had been the one to sit through the night with Marie. After all, their father had been out of the country when she had had her last attack.

She pushed these thoughts to the back of her mind, knowing that Dominic's relationship with Marie, the closeness of it, was none of her business. 'She's asleep this time!' Her voice was sharper than she intended with the intimacy of her thoughts.

'What did you do?' Her father was still obviously amazed by this unusual occurrence.

'Sat with her, talked with her. Then I just held her while she went to sleep. She doesn't like the dark,' Sara added tautly, wishing she could tell him *why* she didn't.

He looked away. 'I know,' he admittedly grimly.

'I think Marie should see a doctor,' she insisted firmly. Maybe if Marie could tell her fears to a doctor he could pass them on to their father.

'She's seen one, more than one.'

'And?' Sara prompted.

'Just tension headaches,' he said, dismissing it with a shrug. 'Probably due to her engagement to Dominic and the excitement of getting married. They tell me a lot of engaged girls get them.'

'That bad?' she asked.

'Sometimes,' he nodded, and glanced down at his wristwatch. 'I have to go down now, I just have time for breakfast before my early appointment.' He bent to give her a preoccupied kiss on the forehead. 'I'll see you later, darling. I should leave Marie, she usually sleeps all day after one of these attacks.'

'I doubt she will today, not when she's slept most of the night.'

'Maybe not. I should get some rest yourself, Sara. It must have been a long night for you.'

Sleep was out of the question now, now that she had thought of Dominic. 'I think I would rather dress and have breakfast.' She smiled at her father.

He nodded. 'Then I'll wait downstairs for you.'

It didn't take her long to shower and dress in her usual denims and casual top, this time a short-sleeved checked shirt, the top two buttons left undone for coolness. She checked on Marie before she went downstairs, and found her sister still fast asleep.

She joined her father at the breakfast table, pouring them both out a cup of coffee. 'These migraines of Marie's,' she persisted, 'does she always have so many? I mean, it isn't long since the last one.'

'They have become a little more—frequent lately,' her father admitted, 'But I'm sure it's nothing to worry about.'

'When did she last see a doctor?'

'A couple of weeks ago. Please don't worry about it, Sara.' He smiled. 'Marie will be over it by tomorrow.'

She frowned. 'Not today?'

'Not usually.' He looked thoughtful. 'I think she was supposed to be acting as Dominic's hostess this evening, too.'

'Surely he can put it off?'

Her father shook his head. 'These clients are only in town for this evening. Oh, well, I'm sure Dominic will think of something.'

He did; he asked Sara to take Marie's place. He arrived shortly before lunch to visit his fiancée, spending some time alone with Marie in her bedroom.

Sara began to tremble as he joined her in the lounge, and put down the book she had been pretending to read since he had arrived, pretending because she couldn't concentrate knowing Dominic was in the house.

'How is she?' she asked for something to say, knowing how Marie was, because she had been in to see her herself only half an hour earlier.

'Fine,' Dominic confirmed her earlier findings. 'How have you been?' he asked huskily.

'Me?' she said brightly. 'Oh, I'm very well. It's Marie I'm worried about. My father doesn't seem all that concerned—'

'Then I'm sure he knows best,' Dominic interrupted.

'Are you?' she probed. 'Aren't you in the least concerned about her either?'

Dominic's mouth tightened, his eyes narrowing. 'What are you implying?' he demanded tautly.

Sara moved impatiently, standing up to pace the room. 'It seems to me that no one takes these attacks of Marie's seriously. It isn't natural—'

His hand came out to grab her arm, his fingers biting painfully into her wrist. 'Don't interfere in things you don't understand. You haven't been here long enough to realize—'

She pulled out of his grasp. 'To realize what?' she asked furiously, her eyes sparkling dangerously. 'That neither my father or you seem to give a damn about Marie, that you even make passes at me behind her back?'

'Passes!' Dominic ground out fiercely, his handsome face alight with anger. 'You think they're *passes?*' he asked incredulously.

Her stance was challenging. 'What else could they be?'

He sighed, his anger fading. 'If you only knew . . .'

'Something else I shouldn't know?' Sara snapped tautly. 'Something else I haven't been in this family long enough to be privileged to hear? Your own words, Dominic.' She frowned at his darkening expression. 'I haven't been here long enough to understand!' she repeated in a choked voice, turning to run out of the room and up the stairs.

She knew that Dominic followed her, could hear the pounding of his feet on the stairs, could hear him panting not far behind her. But she hoped to reach her bedroom and lock the door before Dominic caught up with her, knowing he would never dare cause a scene outside her bedroom door, not with Marie so close.

What she hadn't taken into account was the fact that there was no lock on her door. Dominic crashed into the room after her, closing the door behind him, moving towards her with determined strides.

'No, Dominic!' She cowered back against the far wall.

There was a strange expression in his eyes, a glazed look that showed her he hadn't really heard her protest. 'You made me come up here,' he muttered, 'made me follow you to your bedroom. Sara . . . !'

He loomed over her like a dark shadow, and Sara knew he was right. She *had* made him follow her, whether intentionally or subconsciously she didn't know. But he was here now, and the outcome of this was as inevitable as the setting of the sun.

She moved forward to meet him, their bodies moulding together like two parts of a broken sculpture. Sara felt truly at home for the first time in days, knew this was where she belonged, where she wanted to be. But with her sister in the next room—!

Dominic seemed to sense her withdrawal and let her go with great reluctance, a rueful expression on his face as he looked down at her. 'I just can't keep my hands off you,' he groaned, running his hands through the thickness of his hair. 'But this isn't the place, hmm?'

Her gaze went unwillingly in the direction of Marie's bedroom. 'Nowhere is the right place for us. You've got to leave me alone, Dominic,' she pleaded. 'I can't say no to you—'

'For God's sake never say no!' he agonized, his handsome face flushed with wanting her. 'I need you, Sara. I need your presence here.'

She swallowed hard. 'A few days ago you wanted me to leave England and never come back.'

'You know why.' His gaze was heated. 'And I've been proved right. Every time we meet I—' he broke off, biting his lip. 'My mother liked you.'

'Did she?' Sara blushed, knowing what had sparked that comment. His mother must have guessed what had been happening out in the garden, especially after guessing how she felt about Dominic.

'Very much,' he nodded. 'She would like to meet you again.'

'She will.' She put a nervous hand up to her hair, thinking what a strange conversation this was to be having in her bedroom. 'At the party, on Saturday,' she reminded him.

Dominic smiled. 'I meant somewhere less public.'

Sara bit into her bottom lip, uncaring of the pain she caused. Physical pain was nothing compared to the emotional hunger of loving Dominic. 'Dominic... Your mother, she—she knows,' she revealed hesitantly.

His eyes narrowed and he stopped his pacing of the room to look at her. 'Knows what?'

She licked her lips, unaware of how provocative she was being, but suddenly noticing Dominic's gaze fixed on her mouth. She blushed fiery red. 'At the party she—she warned me, your mother. She doesn't approve of—of—'

'You?' he asked furiously, his eyes blazing.

In that moment he looked more like the man she had first met, the self-assured arrogant man who wouldn't suffer fools gladly. 'No, not me exactly,' she hastened to assure him, not wishing to bring this anger down on his mother. 'Just this—this situation.'

'It isn't a situation,' he dismissed disgustedly. 'It's a bloody mess!'

Her mouth quirked into a derisive smile. 'Yes,' she agreed shakily. 'Could we go back downstairs?' she suggested nervously. 'I'm not sure how thick these walls are, and Marie—well, she could hear all this.'

'Yes.' He sighed. 'We should go back downstairs. God, it's so good to talk to you again, Sara. I know you've been avoiding me, and I also know the reason for it, but if I promise—'

'No, Dominic!' she warned. 'No more promises.'

His expression was rueful. 'I made a poor job of keeping this last one, didn't I?'

'Yes.'

'Sara—'

'Please, let's go downstairs!' Her voice was shrill.

'Oh, yes, yes, of course.'

All the time she was walking down the stairs she was aware of his gaze burning into her back. Normally he seemed such a self-controlled, arrogant person, and yet whenever he was near her this veneer seemed to fall away and he became a passionately demanding man. She had no doubt that he loved Marie, and yet that love was nothing like the consuming fire that flared up between *them* every time they met, a fire that threatened to flame out of control.

'What are you thinking?'

She looked up to find Dominic watching her with narrowed eyes. 'I was just wondering about you and—and Marie.'

He stiffened. 'What about us?'

Sara took her courage in both hands, lifting her head high to meet his watchful blue eyes unflinchingly. 'Do you sleep with her?'

'No!' The denial exploded out of him.

'There's no need to be so vehement,' she huffed, relief washing over her. 'You seem to want to sleep with me.'

'That's different,' he snapped.

'Really?' she taunted. 'Why is it?'

'Because—well, because—Do you sleep with Eddie?' he attacked in a vicious voice.

'Eddie?' she frowned. 'No, of course not. And talking of Eddie,' she gave a hurried look at her wristwatch. 'I'm meeting him for lunch. If I don't leave now I shall be late.'

'Sara!' Dominic's call stopped her at the door. 'Don't go,' he requested huskily.

'I have to.'

'Why?' he groaned.

'Because I never let my friends down.'

'Do I count as a friend?'

'Hardly!' she declared.

'How about Marie?' he asked softly.

Sara flinched. 'You bastard!' she glared at him. 'You almost attack me every time we meet, and you have the nerve to remind *me* of my loyalty to Marie!'

He closed his eyes. 'I wasn't doing that, I was just asking you if you would let Marie down.'

'I already have,' she said bitterly, 'and I'm not proud of the fact.'

'Neither am I!'

'You could have fooled me!'

His mouth tightened into an angry line. 'You either infuriate me or inflame me, and at the moment I can't cope with either emotion.'

'What do you think you do to me?' she groaned. 'Oh, God, I can't stand any more of this—I'm going out!'

'Marie wants you to stand in for her tonight,' Dominic revealed in a rush.

Sara frowned. 'At your dinner party?'

'How did you know about that?'

'My father mentioned it.'

'I see. Yes, that's it. Marie wondered whether you could take her place.' He eyed her questioningly.

'At the table, or in your bed?'

'Please, Sara,' he groaned, 'don't!'

'That's what your mother said,' she remembered bitterly.

Dominic frowned. 'Don't what?'

She shrugged. 'Don't become involved with you.' She couldn't reveal that his mother had guessed at her love for him!

'Are you involved?'

'You're going to marry my sister,' she stated the obvious involvement.

'Yes,' he sighed heavily. 'Will you act as my hostess tonight?'

'Why can't your mother do it? You live with her, don't you?'

'Hardly,' he gave a half smile. 'None of us live with her, we all fled the nest long ago. I have a penthouse apartment in town.'

Her eyes widened. 'And that's where I would be expected to act as your hostess?'

'Yes.'

Sara shook her head in alarm. 'I can't. You know I can't!' she groaned.

He made no move to touch her, and yet his eyes caressed wherever they looked. 'It would make Marie happy,' he told her huskily.

Sara sighed defeatedly. 'And you like her to be happy,' once again this was made plain to her. 'All right, I'll do it. On condition,' she added coldly, 'that you stay away from me.'

'I'll try.'

'You'd better do a damn sight more than that,' she warned. 'Or I'm likely to embarrass you in front of your guests. And you can believe I mean that, Dominic. I never make idle threats.'

'I believe you,' he accepted dully.

'You'd better!' came her parting shot.

As it was she was ten minutes late for her date with Eddie, although he assured her he had only just arrived himself.

'Very flattering!' She grimaced, seating herself opposite him.

He laughed. 'Would you rather I'd sat here waiting for you?'

'No,' she smiled ruefully.

'Don't look now,' he said, sitting forward to whisper, 'but I think we're being watched.'

'Watched?' she frowned in puzzlement.

'Mmm, by your future brother-in-law.'

Dominic! 'Where is he?' she asked tautly.

'A few tables back, to your left.'

They were sitting in a quietly exclusive restaurant, but nevertheless Sara knew it wasn't the sort of place Dominic usually frequented. He had followed her here! The waiter was just approaching him for his order, so Sara got hastily to her feet. 'I won't be a minute,' she muttered to Eddie before making her way purposefully over to Dominic.

He waved the waiter away as soon as he saw her approaching him, looking up at her expectantly.

'What the hell do you think you're doing, following me this way?' Sara lashed out furiously.

'Following you?' he repeated guardedly, curiously pale.

Sara's anger melted at the haggard look of him. 'Go away, Dominic,' she pleaded raggedly. 'I'll see you tonight.'

'You won't let me down?'

'No,' she sighed.

'All right,' he stood up, 'I'll call for you at seven o'clock.' He turned to glance at Eddie. 'I'm glad you didn't kiss him when you arrived,' he said grimly. 'I would probably have punched his face in.'

'Dominic!' she gasped.

He bent to kiss her lightly on the cheek, a gesture perfectly in keeping with her sister's fiancé—if he hadn't unobtrusively caressed the corner of her mouth with the tip of his tongue! His eyes were tortured as he looked down at her. 'Until tonight,' he murmured throatily.

Her eyes flashed deeply brown. 'When there'll be no more of that.'

'No.'

But he didn't sound very convincing. Sara watched him leave the restaurant, half smiling at the arrogant nod he gave Eddie as he walked past their table.

'What's the matter?' Eddie asked as she sat down again. 'Doesn't the high and mighty Dominic Thorne approve of you seeing a mere garage owner?' he mocked.

Sara laughed, her tension leaving her. 'It's nothing like that. He wasn't watching us at all, it was just coincidence that he was here.'

'Oh, yes?' he said scornfully. 'When his office is on the other side of London?'

She flushed. 'He's just been to see Marie,' she defended.

'Is he bothering you?' Eddie asked shrewdly.

'Don't be ridiculous!' she snapped, blushing fiery red.

His eyes were narrowed in suspicion. 'Am I being?'

'Very,' she said tightly.

'Okay,' he shrugged. 'Let's order. But if he ever does bother you just let me know and I'll bruise his handsome face a little.'

'Strange,' she drawled with amusement. 'He said the same thing about you,' she explained with a smile.

'Did he now?' His eyebrows rose. 'Maybe I like him after all.'

Sara laughed at the respect in his voice, then changed the subject without being too pointed about it. She had met Eddie a couple of times since her move to live with her father and sister, and usually they went back to her aunt and uncle's house. Today was no exception. She told her aunt of her concern for Marie's headaches.

'Well, I'm sure your father knows best,' her aunt consoled as they made tea and cakes for the two men.

'That's what Dominic says,' Sara sighed.

'Then you must listen to them, dear.'

That was easier said than done, especially when she saw Marie's pale face later that evening. She was dressed to go out with Dominic, and had gone in to see her sister until he arrived.

Marie sat up while she rearranged her pillows for her, her face chalky white, her eyes shadowed. 'I hope I didn't make too much of a fool of myself last night,' she said ruefully.

Sara gently pushed her back against the coolness of the pillows. 'You didn't make a fool of yourself at all,' she reassured her.

'I'm so grateful to you for taking over from me tonight.' Marie put her hand up weakly to her forehead. 'I always feel so washed out after one of these headaches.'

Their father appeared in the doorway. 'I've come to keep you company,' he told Marie. 'Dominic is downstairs, Sara.'

'No, I'm not.' He appeared in the doorway behind their father. 'How are you this evening?' He looked directly at Marie.

'I'm fine.' She patted the bed invitingly beside her.

'I'll wait downstairs,' Sara mumbled, hurriedly kissing her sister on the cheek before rushing out of the room, her head down. She collided with Dominic in the doorway, and his strong hands came out to steady her. There was pain in her eyes as she looked up at him, pain that she quickly hid. 'Excuse me,' she said gruffly.

He instantly released her. 'I'll be down in a moment.'

'Take your time.' She forced a lightness into her voice that she didn't feel, very much aware of her father and Marie. 'I'm in no hurry,' she added, almost running down the stairs.

She was trembling by the time she reached the lounge, knowing that Dominic was probably kissing Marie right at this moment. She was going to be ill herself if she wasn't careful, her appetite having completely deserted her, her nights spent restlessly tossing and turning. And it was all because of this hunger for Dominic!

She had dressed with extra care this evening, had dressed with Dominic in mind if she were honest with herself, and she had to be that, she was deceiving everyone else! She knew perfectly well this evening wouldn't end innocently, knew that before she returned here tonight that she would have spent time in Dominic's arms. And she wasn't able to do a thing about it. He was like a drug in her veins, an addiction she couldn't fight.

Her dress was knee-length, Japanese in style, made of a silky blue material, its very demureness making it very sexy, with its provocative split up the side of her left leg, the narrow styling showing off her pert uptilted breasts and narrow waist, fitting neatly over her bottom and thighs. Her hair was secured loosely on top of her head, her only jewellery the pair of gold stud earrings her mother and Richard had given her for Christmas two years ago.

She looked up guiltily as her father entered the room, blushing under his searching gaze. Oh, God, she thought, don't let him guess I love Dominic, don't let him guess!

"I hope we haven't ruined any of your own plans for this evening,' he said.

Sara almost laughed with relief. Her father had put her behaviour down to an altogether different reason than her love for Dominic and her jealousy of Marie. 'Not at all,' she answered smoothly.

'Oh, good,' he seemed relieved. 'Only you seemed a little—upset.'

'No,' she shook her head, 'just nervous. I know how important this dinner party is to you and Dominic.'

'Not that important that you have to worry yourself about it.' He put his arm about her shoulders. 'Just be yourself, Sara. You'll like Martha and Jim, they're a nice couple.'

Sara frowned. 'Will they be the only people there?'

'Mmm. Jim's thinking of giving us a contract to supply equipment to all his British offices. One look at you and he won't hesitate to offer us that contract.' He smiled down at her affectionately.

'Do I look all right?' she asked worriedly. She had dressed with a party in mind, albeit a dinner party, but a quiet evening for four was another matter.

'You look beautiful, doesn't she, Dominic?' he asked the other man as he came into the room.

'Very lovely,' Dominic confirmed, the intensity of his gaze making her blush. 'We should be going,' he said abruptly.

'Have a nice time, darling.' Her father bent to kiss her. 'Don't keep her too late, Dominic. I've noticed she's looking a little pale lately.'

Sara bit her lip, as she led the way out to Dominic's car parked in the driveway. So her father had noticed her pallor too. He mustn't ever be allowed to guess that it was because of her helpless love for Dominic. Plus there was this added worry of her father, of the illness that everyone knew about but no one discussed. Maybe if they had talked about it Marie wouldn't be in this emotional mess.

There was a man getting out of the car parked next to Dominic's, and he turned to acknowledge them. 'Good evening, Dominic. Marie?' he frowned. 'But I thought—'

'This is Sara, Simon.' Dominic held firmly on to her elbow, opening the car door for her.

The man nodded, a man of possibly forty-five, very tall and distinguished-looking. 'Nice to meet you, Miss Hamille.'

Sara gave him a friendly smile, wondering why Dominic was pushing her into the car and not introducing her to the other man as he should have done. 'Who was that?' she asked once they were on their way.

Dominic shrugged. 'A friend of your father's.'

'What's his name?'

'Simon.'

She frowned. 'I know that, I heard you call him it. But Simon What?'

'Forrester,' he revealed in a stilted voice.

'Should I know him?' The name did sound vaguely familiar.

'No,' Dominic denied abruptly.

'Then why do I feel as if I should?'

'I have no idea.'

'Dominic?' She gave him a searching look. 'Dominic, what are you hiding from me?'

His expression lightened. 'I'm not hiding anything,' he smiled. 'Simon is a friend of your father's, there's nothing to add to that.'

'Isn't there?' she persisted.

'Not a thing.'

Sara didn't know why, but she didn't believe him. He was being deliberately casual, and in the light of their meeting this morning she knew he had to be acting. Simon Forrester was a friend of her father; could that possibly make him a doctor, was that the reason Dominic was being so close-mouthed about him? It seemed to be the logical explanation, so she knew it was no good pursuing the subject of Simon Forrester; everyone, including Dominic, clammed up whenever she tried to approach the subject of her father's illness.

Dominic's apartment covered the whole of the top floor of a huge block of flats, the luxurious fittings of the reception area alone showing her that his apartment was going to be quite something.

When they stepped out of the lift it was to be confronted by the man Sara knew to be Danny, the man who had been kissing Marie the last time she saw him.

He pushed away from his leaning position against the wall, his expression one of aggression as he approached Dominic. 'How dare you keep something like that from me?' he attacked. 'You had no right, Nick. No right—'

'Danny!' The use of the other man's name was a warning. 'I'm not alone,' Dominic reminded him.

'I know that.' The other man's mouth twisted as he looked at Sara. 'You're Marie's sister Sara, aren't you?'

'Yes,' she acknowledged quietly.

Dominic unlocked his apartment door. 'Wait for me inside, Sara,' he instructed abruptly. 'I won't be long,' he added as she hesitated.

'I wouldn't count on that,' Danny snarled.

'You have five minutes, Danny,' Dominic told him firmly. 'After that I'll have you thrown out.'

'Typical! What I have to say could take longer than five minutes,' the other man snapped. 'Telling you what I think of you could take all damned night.'

'All night you don't have, five minutes you do,' Dominic told him grimly.

'I—'

'Sara.' Dominic pointedly held the door open for her.

She took his hint, and heard the door firmly close behind her. She could hear their raised voices outside, Dominic's controlled, Danny's very heated, and she wondered what on earth Dominic could have done to have so angered the younger man.

Not that she was particularly worried about Dominic's welfare; he was perfectly capable of taking care of himself, both verbally and physically. But Danny had been angry, extremely so. Dominic might have been just as angry if he had known the other man was in the habit of kissing his fiancée.

The apartment was as she had imagined it to be, luxurious, expensive and totally male. It was a typical bachelor home, clean, uncluttered, and obviously kept that way by a daily woman or housekeeper. It turned out to be the latter, a small busty woman setting the table in the dining room.

Sara ducked back into the lounge before the woman saw her. Marie would obviously have visited Dominic here, and she didn't feel up to explaining to the housekeeper that she wasn't Marie.

She was sitting in one of the armchairs when Dominic entered the apartment, and instantly stood to look him over for damage. He didn't appear to be hurt, as he moved to the array of drinks displayed on the side table and poured himself out a large shot of brandy.

He turned to her after swallowing most of the fiery liquid. 'Would you like anything to drink?' he asked grimly.

'No, thanks. Has he gone?'

'Yes.' Dominic's eyes were narrowed, his expression stern. 'Yes,' he said with a sigh, finishing the brandy in his glass, 'he's gone.'

Sara frowned. 'What did he want?'

He seemed to withdraw from her. 'Nothing important.'

'Nothing important!' she scorned. 'I thought he was going to kill you!'

His mouth twisted. 'Nothing so melodramatic. I'll admit Danny was a little annoyed with me—'

'Annoyed? He was furious!' she persisted.

Dominic shrugged. 'My brother is always furious about something, he always has been.'

Sara paled. 'Your—your brother?'

'Yes,' he bit out grimly. 'Danny is my younger brother, didn't you know that?'

No, she hadn't known that. What she did know was that Dominic's own brother was in love with Marie.

CHAPTER EIGHT

'I—ER—I didn't know.' She licked her lips. 'We didn't get to meet at your mother's the other evening.'

'You didn't miss much,' Dominic dismissed scathingly.

'I'm sure that when he isn't angry he can be very nice,' she said primly.

His eyes blazed. 'Yes, Danny can be charming when he wants to be. Were you attracted to him?' he demanded tautly.

Sara gasped. 'Of course not!'

'Why not?' He slammed his empty glass down on the table top. 'He's young, presentable—and free!'

'Ah, yes, he's free,' she taunted him, seeing the rigid anger in his body. 'Perhaps you could introduce me to him some time, when he isn't quite so angry. Hmm?'

Dominic went white. 'No, I damn well can't!' he exploded, pulling her towards him. 'You aren't going out with Danny, Sara. Over my dead body will you go out with him!'

Once again she had woken the sleeping tiger; Dominic was now shaking with fury. He didn't like the idea that she might date his brother, and his jealousy gave her a warm glow.

'Only joking, Dominic,' she murmured huskily. 'I was only joking.' She smiled, gently touching his rigid cheek.

He clasped her hand in his, taking it to his mouth to feverishly kiss her palm. 'Don't tease, Sara,' he groaned.

'Not about something like that. As far as you're concerned I have a very low pain level.' The doorbell rang. 'Hell!' Dominic muttered. 'That will be Jim and Martha.'

Sara moved deftly away from him as she heard the housekeeper coming to answer the door. 'I'm not interested in your brother, Dominic,' she assured him softly. 'Although I'm willing to like him simply because he's your brother.'

His tension started to ease. 'Not too much,' he advised huskily. 'He had a thing for Marie last year, he might consider you a suitable replacement.'

She flinched away from him. 'Like you do?' she said bitterly.

'Sara—'

'Your guests, Dominic.' She turned as the middle-aged couple were shown into the room.

On the whole the evening was a success, although Dominic's brooding attention to her wasn't conducive to helping business along. She eventually suggested showing Martha Jarvis the view from the balcony as a means of leaving Dominic alone with Jim.

It was a magnificent view, the whole of London spread before them like a huge lighted carpet, beautiful and dreamlike.

'It always looks so different like this,' Martha smiled, a still attractive woman of about fifty. She and her husband came from the North of England, and they obviously missed their daughter and grandson whenever they travelled on business, talking of them constantly.

'Even likeable?' Sara teased, knowing that the other couple believed there was nowhere as nice as their beloved North.

Martha goodnaturedly accepted her teasing. 'I like the shops, but that's about all I can say in London's favor.' She wrinkled her nose. 'It's a big, dirty place, where people don't have time for each other.'

Considering that Sara had heard that Northerners were among the most dour people of England she found this comment amazing. Still, who was she to question its validity, having lived in America most of her life?

'I like it,' she said shrugging.

Martha touched her arm. 'You'll have to get Dominic to bring you up to visit us some time. You'll see, the North's best.'

'You forget,' Sara said stiffly, 'it's my sister who is marrying Dominic.'

'So it is,' the other woman tutted at her stupidity. 'Still, that's no reason why you shouldn't come with them. I have a son who would be just right for you,' she added conspiratorially.

Sara opened the balcony doors for them to go back inside, laughing at Martha's matchmaking. 'Maybe,' she grinned. 'But would I be right for him?'

'For who?' Dominic asked sharply as they entered the lounge.

'For my son,' Martha told him as she sat down. 'I've been trying to persuade Sara to come and visit us and meet my son John,' she explained lightly.

Sara held her breath at Dominic's darkening expression. 'I doubt I'll have the time,' she put in hastily. 'Although I thank you for the offer,' she smiled at the other couple.

Jim looked at his watch. 'Time we were going, Mother.' He stood up, holding out his hand to a now standing Dominic. 'We've had a grand time, lad. I'll be in touch with you about that contract.'

Sara stood beside Dominic as they made their good-byes, smiling to herself as she turned back into his apartment.

Dominic followed her, scowling heavily. 'What's so funny?'

She was laughing openly now. 'I just wondered how long it is since you were called "lad".'

He returned her smile ruefully. 'At thirty-five I'm a little old for that, hmm?'

She sat down, curling her legs up beneath her on the sofa. 'Not to a man of fifty-five,' she grinned.

Dominic joined her on the sofa, his long legs stretched out in front of him. 'We got the contract, by the way.'

'I gathered.'

'What was that about the Jarvises' son?'

'Just a mother's usual interest in her son's love life,' she dismissed. 'No threat to you, Dominic, I can assure you.'

His eyes were deeply blue as he looked at her. 'What does that mean, Sara?' he asked softly.

She drew a ragged breath. 'What do you think it means?'

He swallowed hard, a pulse beating rapidly at his jaw-line, his hands clenched into fists. 'I—I'm afraid to think,' he groaned.

'Try,' she encouraged throatily.

'God, I love you!' he burst out, straining her to him.

Sara froze. 'Wh—what did you say?' she gasped, not believing her own hearing, wanting to be sure she wasn't hallucinating—could you get high on one glass of wine?

'I love you.' His lips were at her earlobe, nibbling along the sensitive cord in her throat. 'God, how I love you!' He claimed her lips in a fiery kiss.

Love—Dominic *loved* her! She kissed him back with all the love there was inside her, losing herself in the sensation of loving and being loved in return. Her mouth opened to his, their lips moving over each other's as if starved.

'Tell me,' he groaned feverishly. 'Tell me you love me!'

How could she deny the truth? 'I love you,' she breathed against his mouth. 'I love you very much.'

'Then that's all that matters, all that can matter.' He stood up to gather her in his arms and stride through to his bedroom. 'I want you, Sara,' he told her deeply.

Her head rested on his shoulder. 'Yes.'

'Yes—what?' He seemed almost afraid to breathe.

'Thank you?' She quirked one eyebrow, trembling.

The tension between them didn't lessen at her levity, more it seemed to deepen, as Dominic gently laid her down on the bed to look down at her almost reverently. 'What do you want, Sara?' The pulse at his jaw was beating even more rapidly as he waited for her answer.

'You,' she told him simply.

He closed his eyes, shuddering as he fought for control. 'Are you sure?' he asked almost inaudibly.

She raised her hand to smooth the hair at his temple, saddened at the extra gray hair she found there. 'I'm very sure, Dominic.' She met his gaze unflinchingly.

'Then so be it!' He sank down on the bed beside her, ravishing her mouth with his, probing her lips farther apart with the sensuous tip of his tongue, running it along the sensitive area of her inner lip.

Sara was trembling with excitement, her hands tangled in the dark length of his hair, massaging his scalp when she found he liked it, groaned with the pleasure of it. Over the next heated few minutes she discovered several other places of pleasure that excited him, her teeth nibbling his neck and causing him to shake.

'Undress me, Sara.' He lay back invitingly.

She needed no second bidding, and knelt beside him to slowly unbutton his shirt, having already discarded his jacket. His chest was tautly muscled, liberally sprinkled with dark hair, soft and silky to her touch.

She gasped as she felt Dominic's lips on her thigh, the slit up the side of her dress giving him easy access to her silky skin. Her hands travelled over the tautness of his back, her nails digging painfully into his muscled flesh as his hands caressed her inner thigh.

'I can't do anything when you do that,' she collapsed on his chest.

Dominic pulled her on top of him, a hand either side of her face as he gazed deeply into her eyes. 'I go wild just looking at you,' he told her huskily. 'I want to take this slowly, love you as you deserve to be loved, but I'm not sure I'll be able to control this,' he admitted shakily.

Sara knew what this admission cost him, and it only made her love him all the more. She hugged him, her face buried in his throat as she cried for joy. 'Let's get undressed sensibly,' she murmured against his warm skin, 'or else I'm likely to rip your clothes off you.'

Her teasing eased the heated tension between them, and Dominic shook with laughter. He gently moved her up from him. 'Okay—you first,' he requested, his eyes warm on her flushed cheeks.

'I meant together!' she gasped her dismay.

'I know what you meant, but it's more fun this way.'

'I wouldn't know,' she said in a stilted voice, and moved to unzip her dress, all the time wondering how many other women had stripped for him in this very same way. Hundreds, no doubt. And how many of them had he told that he loved them? a traitorous voice asked. Hundreds, no doubt. None of them, she told herself firmly, as she stepped out of her dress, wearing only a pair of minute briefs, ironically with 'LOVE' embroidered across them! She hadn't dreamt when she had dressed this evening that Dominic would see her like this.

'Sara?' He knelt on the bed in front of her, bare to the waist himself, his silky hair growing down his chest, over his navel, and provocatively lower. 'Sara, will this be the first time for you?' He held her firmly in front of him.

She licked her lips nervously. No man liked inexperience in this day and age. She gave a casual shrug of her shoulders. 'Of course not,' she lied lightly.

'Sara!' He shook her gently. 'I'll be able to tell, you know.'

Not if she stopped herself from crying out he wouldn't! 'I'm sorry if you're disappointed, Dominic,' she was deliberately nonchalant, 'but you'll be far from the first.'

'I'm glad,' he gathered her into his arms. 'Loving you is one thing, taking your innocence from you is something I just couldn't do.'

Thank God she had lied! She couldn't be denied knowing his full possession now, as she removed her last article of clothing to stand before him naked. She was well above average height, her breasts proudly erect, her nipples a deep rose pink, her waist slender, her hips perfectly shaped, her legs long and supple. She watched Dominic shyly from beneath lowered lashes, doing her best to gauge his reaction, wondering if she compared favorably with the other women he had made love to.

He said nothing for several long painful minutes. 'You're the most beautiful, desirable woman I've ever seen in my life,' he told her in awe.

She began to breathe again, throwing herself into his arms. 'That was exactly the right thing to say,' she told him tearfully.

He smoothed her tears away with his thumb-tips. 'The truth often is,' he said huskily. 'You are beautiful, all of you.'

'So are you,' she told him shyly.

'You haven't seen all of me yet.' He firmly sat her down on the bed, his hand going to his belted waist. 'But you will.'

Sara felt that she stopped breathing as he stepped out of his trousers, a pair of navy blue briefs now his only clothing, his thighs powerfully muscled. At the last moment her courage deserted her and she turned away to climb beneath the covering of the sheets, their coolness soothing against her heated flesh.

'Do you want the light on or off?'

She looked up, then quickly looked away again, her face fiery red, that one brief glimpse of Dominic's naked flesh showing her what a truly magnificent body he had, strong and powerful, clearly wanting her as badly as she wanted him. 'Off, please,' she croaked, hoping she wouldn't prove a disappointment to him.

The room was instantly put into darkness, temporarily blinding Sara, and making Dominic a mere shadow. The bedclothes were thrown back as he joined her on the bed, his mouth instantly claiming hers. She relaxed against the hard demand of him, gasping as his hand moved to claim her breast, caressing the nipple to hardness with the tip of his thumb, moving slowly down her body to claim her other breast with his pleasure-giving lips and tongue.

Excitement such as Sara had never known existed coursed through her body, as Dominic's leg moved over hers to trap her to the bed as she would have struggled against that pleasure. It was too much, driving her into ecstasies, making her gasp, cry out as it became unbearable.

Dominic raised his head, his expression one of puzzlement. 'It's all right, darling,' he soothed, sweeping her hair back from her face. 'Calm down, sweetheart.'

She swallowed hard, the tension easing as he gently caressed her. 'I—I'm sorry, Dominic,' she bit her lip. 'I'm just—It's—'

'You're a virgin, aren't you!' he realized tautly.

'It's obvious, is it?' she asked with dread.

His answer was to get off the bed, pulling on a towelling robe before switching on the light. 'Yes, it's obvious,' he confirmed abruptly.

'It matters, doesn't it?' She held the sheet up over her breasts, still throbbing from the touch of his lips.

'Of course it matters!' The lover of minutes ago was completely erased.

'But why?' she cried out her puzzlement. 'When we're married—'

'Married!' he repeated harshly. 'We aren't getting married, Sara.'

'We—we aren't?'

'I'm engaged to Marie!'

'Yes, but—'

'And I'm going to stay that way,' he told her coldly.

'But you said you loved me!'

'And I do,' he groaned.

She blinked dazedly, as she felt her world collapsing about her. 'But you're still going to marry Marie?'

'Yes!' he hissed. 'I wish I could make you understand—'

'You can't,' she muttered, getting out of bed to dress hurriedly. 'I've been a fool. I thought loving me meant you wanted to be with me, for all time. But I guess Eddie was right about you from the first,' she added bitterly, leaving her hair loose in her hurry to leave.

Dominic's eyes were glacial. 'Eddie?' he echoed sharply.

'Yes.' Her head went back challengingly. 'That first evening we met, when you thought I was Marie, I asked Eddie about you. He told me then exactly what sort of man you are.'

'Considering he's never met me that's quite something!'

Her look was contemptuous. 'People like you don't need to be known. He told me then that one day you intended owning all the business, and that by marrying Marie you would have it. And now you've proved that. You say you love me—if you even know what that word means—and yet you still intend to marry Marie, my father's heiress.'

Dominic had gone white beneath his tan, his eyes blazing. 'You're forgetting something,' he snapped harshly. 'Your father now has two daughters.'

'And you've been trying to bed both of them! You're a bastard, Dominic Thorne, and you can forget what I ever said about loving you! Right now I loathe and despise you, and I doubt that opinion will ever change!' She flounced out of the bedroom, and continued on out of the apartment, hiring a taxi to take her home.

The drive to her father's house seemed never-ending as she sat in hunched-up misery on the back seat of the taxi, her love and belief in Dominic in ruins about her feet. He had been using her, making her a pawn in his ugly game—and how easily she had fallen for it!

But never again, never again would she listen to his words of love or passion. If he could betray her father and Marie after having known them for the past ten years, then he would have no compunction about exploiting her own attraction to him. It must have been obvious to him from the first, and how useful it could have been to him. But she had ruined his plan, hadn't been besotted enough with him to still want to sleep with him after she had found out he still intended marrying Marie. Admittedly he hadn't been corrupt enough to pursue his seduction once he realized her innocence, but she had no doubt he would have overcome those *scruples* given time. He had wanted her completely and utterly in love with him, agreeable to his every whim. What a pity for him that he had failed!

It made her wonder what he could have done to Danny, his own brother, to make him want to attack him in that way. Danny had accused him of something; could it possibly be that he had finally found the courage to stand up to his brother about his engagement to Marie, to tell Dominic of his own love for her? To think that Dominic had gone that far, dazzled and captured Marie from his own brother merely for his own mercenary ends. The thought disgusted her. And what disgusted her more was that she had almost been a victim of his lethal charm herself.

To her dismay she wasn't to be allowed to escape to the privacy of her bedroom to wallow in her misery. Marie's bedroom light was on, and she called Sara in to speak to her.

'You should be asleep,' Sara scolded, sitting down on the side of the bed.

'Ssh!' Marie smiled mischievously. 'Daddy doesn't know I'm still awake.'

'You're feeling better.'

'I was feeling better this afternoon,' her sister admitted with a grin, 'but I hate these business dinners of Dominic's.'

'I wish I'd known earlier,' Sara groaned. 'Headache or no headache, you would have gone.'

'Was it ghastly?'

'Yes! No.' She shrugged. 'Not really.' Only the latter part of it!

'I promise I won't land you in it again.' Marie giggled. 'I just didn't feel like being entertaining this evening.'

'I'll let you off this time.' Sara frowned, remembering something that had been troubling her. 'Marie, tonight when—when Dominic and I were leaving a man was just arriving. I think Dominic said his name was Simon Forrester.'

'Simon?' Marie's voice was sharp.

'Yes,' Sara watched her closely. 'Dominic said he was a friend of Dad's.'

'That's right, he is,' her sister answered with obvious relief.

Sara bit her lip, deciding to take a shot in the dark and see if it paid off. 'He also said he was a doctor.' She watched Marie's reaction, seeing her blanch.

'Yes, he is,' Marie's tone was brittle. 'Does it matter?'

'Not really,' Sara replied casually. 'I just wondered whether he was here professionally or socially.'

Marie began to pleat the sheet between nervous fingers. 'Why on earth should he be here professionally?'

'I thought perhaps because of your headaches . . .' She had thought no such thing. If Simon Forrester had been here professionally then it had been to see her father, and conveniently when she was out of the house.

'No,' Marie denied instantly. 'I'm feeling rather tired, Sara, perhaps I should go to sleep now.'

'Yes, of course.' She stood up. 'I'll see you in the morning.' She bent to kiss her sister goodnight.

But she didn't sleep once she reached her bedroom, too disturbed by the evening's events to be able to relax enough for that. She had been stupid tonight, more stupid than she had ever been before in her life. She was ashamed of her-

self for being taken in so easily. But the reason she had
been taken in still existed—she still loved Dominic!

How could she love such a despicable man, a man who
was marrying her own sister for mercenary reasons?
Maybe he did love Marie, maybe he loved her too, but it
made no difference to his plans to be the sole owner of the
business he and her father now ran jointly.

And tomorrow, or the day after, she was going to have
to face Dominic again, put on a show so that he wouldn't
guess how much he had hurt her. After what she had said
to him she doubted she would have to fight any attempts
on his part to kiss or touch her.

She didn't give him the chance the next day, spending the
whole day with her aunt, telephoning Eddie and going out
with him that evening. He was the uncomplicated companion she needed at the moment.

There was no sign of Dominic when she finally arrived
home, so she entered the house with a light heart. After
crying herself to sleep the night before she had spent the
day pushing Dominic firmly to the back of her mind, and
the last thing she wanted was to run into him now. Eddie
had given her her confidence back in herself with his
lighthearted flirting, receiving a casual kiss good-night to
his surprise. Purely sisterly, she had assured him with a
laugh.

The butler came to remove her coat once she got in. 'Mr.
Thorne has been calling you all day, Miss Sara,' he informed her.

She stiffened, frowning. 'Did he leave a message?' She
did her best to remain calm.

'No, Miss Sara, although I think he wanted to talk to
you quite urgently. He's gone away on business for several days, but he said he would call you again as soon as he
could.'

'I didn't realize he was going away. Wasn't he here this evening, Granger?'

For a moment he looked puzzled. 'I think you may have misunderstood me, Miss Sara. I didn't mean Mr. Dominic Thorne, I meant Mr. Daniel Thorne.'

'Danny?' she echoed sharply. What on earth could Danny want with her?

'That's right,' the butler nodded.

'Are you sure he wanted me, Granger?'

'Very sure, Miss Sara.'

'Did he mention where he was going?'

'Germany,' he supplied. 'And he wasn't sure when he would be returning.'

'Thank you,' she said absently. 'I—If he calls again, let me know immediately, won't you?'

'Of course, Miss Sara.'

Why would Danny want to see her? They had met briefly last night for the first time, very briefly, and he hadn't seemed that desperate to talk to her then.

He didn't call again, his business in Germany was probably keeping him fully occupied. And she didn't see or hear from Dominic either, although she knew he and Marie met most evenings. Perhaps her message had gone home, whatever the reason he left her alone.

'We're going shopping,' Marie announced on Saturday morning as the two of them breakfasted together.

'We are?' Sara asked tolerantly.

'Yes,' her sister nodded. 'Well, it isn't shopping exactly,' she added a little guiltily. 'I know where we're going, and I've already bought the—whatever it is we want. We just have to pick them—it up.'

'Marie...?' Sara eyed her suspiciously. 'What have you been up to?'

'Nothing. It's a surprise. For you!' She could hardly contain her excitement. 'Have you finished?' she tried to hurry Sara's breakfast along.

'No, I haven't.' Sara refused to be rushed, slowly sipping her coffee.

'Yes, you have.' Marie took the cup out of her hand, standing up expectantly.

Sara didn't move. 'What about the party tonight? Shouldn't we be doing something towards that this morning?'

'It's all arranged. Everything will be arriving this afternoon. Anyway, Granger is perfectly capable of dealing with any hitches that may arise.'

'He wasn't yesterday when you couldn't be spared to help me tidy Dad's study,' Sara reminded her ruefully.

Marie grinned. 'I've been doing it for years, simply because Daddy won't let the staff go in there. I thought it was time you took a turn.'

'And you were very conveniently busy with other things,' Sara said dryly.

'Very conveniently,' Marie grinned.

The dress salon wasn't exactly a surprise to Sara, she had half expected it. Marie hadn't been out and bought a new dress for the party yet, so it followed that today she was going to get one. Only she had gone one step further, she had had identical dresses designed!

'Aren't they lovely!' she cried ecstatically as they were brought out for their approval.

They were indeed lovely, but *identical!*

'At the time you ordered two dresses the same,' the saleswoman gushed. 'I admit to being rather puzzled. But now...' she waved her arms in their direction pointedly, 'now I understand.'

Sara wished she did. 'No one will be able to tell us apart,' she complained.

'That's the whole idea!' Marie was flushed with pleasure at her idea. 'Let's fit them on.'

'Marie—'

'Come on, Sara!' She dragged her towards the changing rooms.

The dress fitted her as if it had been made for her, but then it should, it had been modelled on Marie! It was black chiffon, a color she didn't usually wear, very simple in design, its very simplicity its main attraction, strapless, held above the breasts only by their pertness, fitted over the bust to be caught in at the waist, flowing out in several layers of chiffon to her feet. It was beautiful, gave her added maturity and sophistication, and she could see it did the same for Marie when they met minutes later.

'My goodness!' the saleswoman gasped. 'You look like mirror images!'

'Don't we! Don't we, Sara?' Marie pleaded for her approval.

Sara sighed. 'Yes, we do. But we're going to cause a lot of confusion at this party tonight.'

Marie smiled her glee. 'That's the whole idea.'

The first person to fall foul of their little trick was their father, who stared at them in utter confusion when they joined him in the lounge before their guests arrived.

'Clever,' he smiled, putting an arm around each of them and holding them to his sides. 'Sara,' he turned to kiss her. 'Marie,' he turned to kiss her.

Marie pouted her disappointment. 'You guessed!'

He laughed. 'I cheated. I can tell by the perfumes you wear,' he explained.

Marie brightened. 'You couldn't tell otherwise.'

'No,' he answered solemnly.

'Sure?'

'Sure,' he nodded.

Dominic was the first to arrive, and his eyes narrowed as he looked at them both. 'I seem to have played this scene before,' he murmured. 'I'm supposed to guess which one to kiss. Right?'

Marie nodded, having extreme difficulty not speaking and so giving away her identity.

It was the first time Sara had seen him since the night at his apartment, and she noticed that he looked drawn and tired, despite his forced smile. Perhaps his conscience had been bothering him; she hoped so.

This time he didn't even hesitate, but walked straight over to Marie and kissed her confidently on the lips.

This didn't please her at all, and she glared up at him. 'You weren't supposed to guess!'

He raised his eyebrows. 'You would rather I kissed Sara?'

'Yes—I mean no.' She sighed. 'How did you know which one was me?'

'Shouldn't I know the girl I'm going to marry?'

'I suppose so,' she accepted ruefully. 'But I bet Sara's disappointed that you guessed right.'

Sara gasped, turning fiery red. Could Marie possibly have guessed that she had been kissed by Dominic many times before?

Dominic turned glacial blue eyes on her. 'Are you?' he asked coldly.

Her head went back, her mouth tight. 'Not at all. I have my own boyfriend arriving shortly. I'm sure he'll be only too pleased to supply as many kisses as I want.'

'Eddie?' he rasped tautly.

'Of course.' She made her tone appear light, aware of her father and Marie even if Dominic wasn't.

His mouth twisted. 'Of course.' He turned away.

Once the guests began to arrive, exclaiming over how alike the two girls were—as if they wouldn't be when they were identical twins!—she was able to push Dominic to the back of her subconscious, vaguely aware of his being in the room, even feeling his gaze on her on occasion, but making no effort to return it.

Eddie was enjoying himself immensely, his arm loosely about her waist in casual possession. 'Is he rising to the bait yet?' he bent to whisper in her ear.

Sara frowned up at him. 'What are you talking about?'

'Not what, who. And it's Dominic Thorne.' He grinned. 'He's been glaring at me for the last ten minutes.'

An involuntary movement had her facing in Dominic's direction, to find herself looking straight into his narrowed blue eyes. Yes, he was staring at them, not just looking, but staring straight at them, and making no effort to look as if he were doing anything else. Her answer was to stand on tiptoe and kiss Eddie firmly on the mouth. When she glanced back at Dominic he was no longer looking their way, although he was slightly pale under his tan, his mouth set in a rigid line.

'I liked that,' Eddie murmured. 'But not the reason behind it.' He gave her a reproachful look.

Sara blinked hard. 'I don't know what you mean.'

His fingers pinched in at her waist. 'Liar,' he whispered close to her ear. 'But I'll forgive you this time. Just stop putting the poor man through the hoops.'

'Eddie—'

'I know,' he interrupted her warning tone. 'Mind my own business. The way he keeps looking at me it could become my business any moment now. He looks ready to hit me!'

Her eyes sparkled angrily. 'He has no right!'

'That isn't what your pulse rate is telling me,' Eddie taunted.

She glared up at him. 'That's just anger.'

He laughed softly. 'Of course it is,' he mocked. 'Who on earth is that woman talking to Aunt Susan?'

Sara followed his line of vision, and her mouth quirked into a smile. 'That's Cynthia Robotham-James,' she said with humour. 'The woman who gave the party Pete took me to,' she explained.

'Pete's still interested in photographing you, you know. He would love to work with you.'

'Well, he's going to be disappointed. I think we should go and save Aunt Susan,' she grimaced. 'Cynthia tends to be a bit overwhelming. On second thoughts,' she saw Danny Thorne just arriving, 'you go and rescue her, there's someone over there I have to talk to.'

'I see.' Eddie saw her looking at Danny. 'In that case I'll go and console myself with Cynthia.'

Sara spluttered with laughter. 'Good luck!'

'I'll need it, she could probably eat me for breakfast.'

'And not even know it!' she taunted.

'Cheeky! Just because you don't fancy me it doesn't mean I'm unattractive to women.' He straightened his cuff. 'I'll go over there and captivate her with my charm.'

The last Sara saw of him he wasn't doing a bad job of it, Aunt Susan smiling with obvious relief as Eddie drew Cynthia's attention away from her.

Danny was searching the crowds of people at the party, stopping when he saw her walking towards him.

'It's Sara,' she told him before she could be an unwilling witness to any embarrassing declarations of love on his part.

'I know,' he nodded. 'I have to talk to you.'

She didn't question his knowing her identity. If he loved Marie he was probably able to tell she wasn't her as well as Dominic had. 'Perhaps my father's study...?' she suggested.

'That will do.' He seemed charged with a nervous energy, sparing not a glance for the other people at the party as he led the way out of the room.

Sara shut the study door after them, instantly shutting out the noise. 'Now what did you want to talk to me about?'

'Marie,' Danny said heavily, his eyes dark with pain.

He was going to try and enlist her help in getting Marie for himself! She shook her head. 'There's nothing I can do.'

His expression became fiercer. 'There must be something someone can do! I can't just sit back and let Marie die!'

Sara looked at him dazedly, clutching on to the back of the chair for support. 'Wh—what did—' she swallowed hard. 'What did you say?' she asked shakily.

Danny avidly searched her face, shaking his head. 'My God,' he groaned, closing his eyes, 'you didn't know, did you? No one told you Marie is dying!'

CHAPTER NINE

'I DON'T believe you!' Sara choked. 'You're lying!' Her voice rose hysterically and her legs began to shake, finally giving out on her as she collapsed to the floor, her eyes huge in her white face. 'Tell me you're lying,' she pleaded tearfully, numb with shock.

Danny came down on the floor beside her, pulling her into his arms. 'I'm not lying, Sara,' he murmured into her hair.

She shook against him. 'But why? How?'

'I would have thought the "why" was obvious,' a steely voice interrupted them. 'The "how" should be equally obvious,' Dominic added contemptuously.

Danny turned to look at his brother. 'Shut your filthy mouth!' he snapped.

Dominic raised his eyebrows. 'Perhaps if you both got up off the floor I just might be able to do that.'

Danny sprang to his feet, his expression fierce. 'What the hell are you saying now?'

His brother closed the study door and came farther into the room. 'If the two of you have to sneak off together at least choose somewhere a little more private—and comfortable—for your lovemaking.'

'No, Danny!' Sara screamed as he flew at Dominic, his fist landing on his brother's chin.

Dominic's face darkened with an anger even fiercer than Danny's. 'You'll never know how glad I am that you did that,' he muttered through bared teeth. 'I only needed the excuse to hit you . . .'

Sara closed her eyes to shut out the sight of Dominic beating his brother to a pulp. The furniture was flying everywhere as first one man and then the other fell across the desk or against the chair. Sara couldn't make a move to stop them, although she did manage to pull herself to the corner of the room out of harm's way.

'That's enough.' Danny leaned against the side of the desk, trying in vain to staunch the flow of blood from his nose.

'More than enough,' Dominic agreed grimly, a trickle of blood escaping from the cut on his mouth. 'Get out of here. And don't come near Sara again,' he added threateningly.

Danny looked stricken as he turned towards her, seeing her sitting wide-eyed and shocked in the corner of the room, and went down on his haunches to her, helping her to her feet. 'Stop it, Dominic,' he warned as the other man made a savage movement towards him. 'Can't you see the state she's in?' He sat her down in a chair, rubbing her chilled hands.

If anything Dominic's expression darkened even more. 'Were you forcing yourself on her?' he demanded tautly. 'Because if you were—'

'Shut up, Dominic.' Danny sighed, all the time dabbing at his bleeding nose. 'Sara has just received the biggest shock of her life.'

His eyes narrowed sharply. 'My God, you didn't—'

'Yes!' Danny hissed. 'Someone should have told me that even Marie's sister didn't know.'

'You stupid—! My God, you're going to answer to me later for this!' Dominic exploded. 'In the meantime you'd better get to a hospital and get something done about your nose.'

'But Sara—'

'Will be perfectly safe with me,' he interrupted grimly. 'Just get the hell out of here, Danny. I think you've caused enough trouble for one day.'

'How was I supposed to know Sara hadn't been told? I naturally assumed—'

'We would hardly come out and baldly tell her something like that. In time—'

'In time!' Sara repeated shrilly, suddenly coming to life, looking up at Dominic with accusing eyes. '*In time* you and my father were going to tell me Marie is dying, that having found my twin I'm now going to lose her again! And how much *time* was it going to take for you to tell me—on her deathbed, perhaps?' Her voice broke emotionally.

Dominic looked at his brother. 'My God, you did a good job of this!'

'Don't blame him,' Sara snapped. 'Maybe his method wasn't very tactful, but at least he considered me adult enough to *be* told.'

'Would you please leave us, Danny?' Dominic said tautly.

'Sara?'

She looked at Dominic's set, rigid features. 'Yes, go, Danny. You really should get your nose seen to.' It was still bleeding.

He grimaced. 'I think it's broken,' he muttered as he left.

'Sara—'

She shook off Dominic's hand, standing up and moving away from him. 'Don't touch me!' she spat the words at him. 'Don't ever touch me again. Just tell me, tell me what's wrong with Marie.'

He licked the blood from his lip. 'Perhaps your father—'

'No, *you!*' she told him heatedly. 'I want you to tell me.'

He sighed. 'Then perhaps we should sit down. This could take some time, and you've already received enough of a shock.'

Sara sat. 'I'm waiting,' she said in a cold voice.

'You know that Marie fell down the stairs about six months ago,' he began.

She nodded. 'The same day I had my accident.'

'Yes. Well, that fall did more than cause a bump on the head and a twisted ankle.'

'What else?' she asked dully.

'Shortly after falling Marie began to have excruciating pains in the head, so severe that she would cry out with the agony of them.'

'She still gets them,' Sara recalled tightly.

Dominic frowned. 'That bad?'

'Yes.'

He shook his head. 'She said they were getting better.'

Her mouth twisted. 'Perhaps she didn't want to worry you.'

'She eventually went to see a specialist,' Dominic ignored her bitter dig at him. 'Simon Forrester is that specialist.'

God, what a fool she was! All this time she had been blinded by her belief that it was her father who was ill, when all the pointers had really been to its being Marie. Marie was the one with the headaches, the one kept in bed by her illness. She should have realized that Marie was the one her father had told her aunt and uncle was dying, instead she had jumped completely to the wrong conclusion. Was it more painful to lose her sister than her father, could one gauge a loss like that? She couldn't, and she wouldn't even try.

'Why can't Simon Forrester do anything for her?' she demanded to know.

Dominic shrugged. 'Clever as he is he just can't perform miracles. Simon discovered a minute fracture of the skull that wasn't apparent at the time of the accident. That fracture of bone could move at any time and kill her.'

'Can't it be removed?' Sara cried.

'No,' he replied grimly.

'But surely—'

'No!' he repeated tautly. 'It can't.'

'This is absurd! She's young, beautiful, a wonderful person. God couldn't be cruel enough to take her life. Besides, she doesn't look ill,' she added foolishly.

'Believe me, she is.'

'Then why are you marrying her?' Sara turned on him angrily. 'You must have known she was dying when you asked her to marry you—you've only been engaged a few months.'

Dominic's expression was remote, unapproachable. 'My reasons for marrying Marie are my own.'

'And your reason for making love to me?' she asked shrilly. 'Could it be that you decided to have a standby, just in case you didn't get to marry Marie before she dies? After all, one Michael Lindlay daughter is as good as another!' Her head flew back with the force of Dominic's palm against her cheek. She didn't move, looking up at him with lifeless eyes, too numb to even feel the pain he had just inflicted. 'I wouldn't marry you if you got down on your knees and crawled to me across broken glass,' she told him with cold vehemence. 'Just the thought of being in the same room with you makes me feel nauseated!'

Dominic was gray, harsh lines etched into his face. 'Goodbye, Sara,' and he quietly left the room.

As soon as he had left Eddie came in, frowning his concern as his sharp gaze took in her white shocked face, her dishevelled appearance. 'What the hell is going on in here?' he asked concernedly. 'World War Three? The two

Thorne men have just walked out of here looking as if they've been in battle, one with a bleeding nose, Dominic Thorne looking as if he would like to hit someone.'

'Me,' Sara acknowledged dully. 'He—he's a bastard, Eddie. A cold, heartless, mercenary bastard.' She began to shiver, even though the room was very warm. 'Get me out of here, Eddie,' she cried her desperation. 'Get me away from here.'

'All right, love.' His arm came protectively about her shoulders.

'Out through the French doors. Don't make me see anyone.' She couldn't face all those people in the other room.

He took her to his flat over his garage, a comfortable two-bedroom flat. He poured her out a glass of whisky, watching while she drank it all down.

'Now,' he sat down, holding her hands in his, 'tell me about it.'

'I—I can't!' She collapsed sobbingly against his chest, knowing she couldn't discuss Marie with him, not until she had spoken to her father and sister. 'I just can't, Eddie!' She looked up at him appealingly.

'All right, love.' He smoothed her hair back with gentle fingers. 'Just sit here with me and don't worry about a thing. No one can touch you here, I won't let them.'

She knew that he wouldn't, felt confident of his ability to protect her. She certainly wasn't able to protect or help herself, her thoughts were all on Marie and the injury that was going to take her from them.

And then there were the terrible things she had said to Dominic, the awful damning things said in the heat of the moment. She couldn't really believe the things she had said to him, had hit out at him because he happened to be there, not because she really *meant* those things.

But he wouldn't know that, and she doubted he would give her the chance to tell him. Besides, she might not believe *that* about him, but he had still made love to her while intending to marry Marie.

When she woke up all was silent about her, the only light in the room from the electric fire Eddie must have switched on while she slept. Her head was resting on the slow rise and fall of his chest, his relaxed pose telling her of his own slumbers.

She moved gingerly, stretched her cramped limbs. 'Sorry,' she said ruefully as Eddie's eyes instantly opened. 'I didn't mean to wake you.'

'You didn't.' He sat up too. 'I wasn't really asleep, just resting.' He looked at her searchingly. 'How do you feel now?'

'Stiff.' She grimaced. 'What time is it?'

'Almost three o'clock,' he supplied.

'Oh, God!' she groaned, putting a hand up to her temple. 'They'll be wondering where I am.'

'No, they won't,' Eddie said quietly. 'I telephoned your father and told him you were with me. He told me everything, Sara,' he added softly.

She at once looked stricken, as the memory of the evening just past came painfully back to her. 'Everything?' she croaked.

He nodded. 'Yes. I told him I would take you home when you're ready.'

Sara shivered. 'I'll never be ready to go back and accept that!'

Eddie's hand covered hers. 'You can't make it go away by ignoring it.'

'She's too young, Eddie,' Sara groaned.

He nodded, compassion in his eyes. 'And she has everything to live for, a father and a sister who love her, and a fiancé who would sacrifice his own happiness to make her happy.'

Sara gave him a sharp look. 'You mean Dominic?'

'Of course.'

'What do you mean?'

He shrugged. 'I mean he likes Marie to be—happy.'

Yes, she knew that! Something else that should have told her it was Marie she was in danger of losing. Dominic was obsessed with seeing that Marie had everything she possibly could to make her happy.

'We all do,' she said huskily.

'But not like he does.'

'Possibly not.' Although it hadn't stopped him trying—no, succeeding, in getting her into bed with him. 'I'd better go, Eddie. My father is probably expecting me.'

He nodded. 'He said he would wait up.'

The light was on in the lounge when she arrived home, despite the lateness of the hour. She hesitated at the front door, looking uncertainly at Eddie.

'You would rather go in alone, hmm?' he guessed shrewdly.

She smiled her relief. 'Thanks, Eddie.' He had been so kind to her she hadn't wanted to tell him she wanted to see her father in private. She reached up and kissed him on the mouth. 'I think I love you,' she whispered huskily.

He touched her gently on the cheek. 'That's what honorary brothers are for. 'Night, love.' He bent and kissed her.

Her father was alone, and stood up as soon as she entered the room. He looked old, defeated and old.

'Oh, Dad!' She launched herself tearfully into his arms, her body shaking with deep racking sobs.

'I know, child. I know.' He stroked her hair, cradling her to him.

'I don't think I can bear it!' she choked.

'We have to, Sara. And we have to be strong, for Marie's sake.'

'I know,' she sniffed, wiping the tears away with the back of her hand. 'Why didn't you tell me, Dad? All this time I thought it was you, and I couldn't understand why you hadn't told me about it.'

'Me?' he frowned. 'Why on earth should you think a thing like that?'

She explained overhearing part of his conversation with her aunt and uncle. 'I'm afraid I jumped to conclusions,' she admitted ruefully. 'It's just that Marie is so young—' she broke off emotionally. 'I'm sorry, this must be worse for you than it is for me.'

'No. I've seen how close the two of you have become the last few weeks, almost as if you've been together all your lives. I'm grateful for that, Sara.' He ran his hand tiredly over his eyes. 'It's made it a little easier for her.'

Sara swallowed hard. 'She—she knows?' remembering the conversation they had had about death she thought she must do.

'Oh, yes,' he sighed. 'Not at first. But when the headaches continued,' he said with a shrug, ' she guessed. She went wild for a few weeks, although that stopped once she became engaged to Dominic.'

But had it? Dominic hadn't seemed surprised when he had thought she was Marie out with another man. He had been angry, but not surprised. Maybe it had happened before. But wouldn't she feel the same way in Marie's place, wouldn't she want to break out too, hit out at the world for taking her young life from her? She knew she would, although their father obviously had no idea of it.

'I'm very grateful to Dominic,' her father continued. 'And sorry for him too. It must be very hard for him knowing the woman he loves is going to die.'

So hard that he occasionally wanted to hold a living, breathing replica of Marie, to make love to her double knowing that she wasn't going to die? She knew with sickening clarity that this was the reason Dominic made love to her, told her he loved her—he had wanted her to be Marie, a Marie who would live.

She licked her dry lips. 'Will they—will they marry—before—'

'I have no idea,' her father revealed heavily. 'I haven't interfered in their plans in any way, either the engagement or wedding plans. If they want to marry they will.'

'But is that fair on Dominic?' It was already obviously tearing him apart now, but if Marie became his wife...!

'No.' Her father sighed. 'But Dominic has a definite mind of his own.'

She knew that, but at the moment Dominic's mind didn't seem to be functioning rationally. Marie's illness was filling him with a desperation that made him turn to Sara. God, the things she had said to him earlier, how he must hate her for that! No more than she hated herself!

She took a deep breath. 'Is Marie asleep now?'

'Mmm.' Her father nodded. 'She wanted to wait up with me, but I wouldn't let her. The party was strain enough for her.'

'I'm sorry to be such a worry to you.' Sara bit her lip.

He put his arm about her shoulders. 'You aren't a worry, Sara, you're part of this family. Maybe we're at fault for not telling you, but that was the way Marie wanted it.'

She frowned. 'Marie didn't want me told?' Somehow that hurt.

'Only because she wanted your reaction to her to be that of any sister towards another. Very few people know of her illness, only myself, Dominic, his mother—and his brother, too, now.' His mouth twisted.

'I think Danny is in love with her,' Sara revealed huskily.

'I know,' her father acknowledged heavily. 'But it won't do him any good, Marie just isn't interested.'

'No.' Dominic was Marie's love, but Sara felt pity for Danny, knowing such an unwanted love herself, for Dominic. It seemed that both of them had lost out, that they had loved tragically.

She went to bed, but she didn't sleep, and Marie seemed very restless, too, tossing and turning in her bed. She went in to look at her once, just to make sure she wasn't awake and in pain. Marie was asleep, but muttering constantly, actually crying out a couple of times. She looked so young and vulnerable lying there, the bright bubbly personality she showed to other people stripped from her, leaving her looking like a lost little girl.

Marie slept in late the next morning. Sara didn't sleep at all, finally giving up to go and sit downstairs. It seemed her father was sleeping late, too, and when the maid announced Dominic's arrival she had no other choice but to receive him, her embarrassment acute as she sat up from her lying position on the sofa.

Dominic looked no more pleased to see her than she was him; his expression was forbidding. 'Marie and your father are still resting?' he asked stiffly, looking very tall and attractive in navy blue trousers and a matching fitted shirt, the sleeves of the latter turned back to just below his elbows.

'Yes,' she answered gruffly.

'But you didn't feel the same need?' There was bitter mockery in his voice.

'I—I couldn't sleep.'

'Couldn't, or wasn't allowed to?' Dominic scorned.

Sara was very pale, her brown eyes shadowed. 'What do you mean?'

'You spent the night with your lover, didn't you?' he derided harshly.

She blushed. 'I spent part of the night with Eddie, yes,' she confirmed in a stilted voice. 'But not all of it.'

'At least your father was spared that humiliation.' Dominic's mouth twisted. 'Explaining away your sudden absence wasn't very easy, worrying about what you were doing was even harder on him.'

'What I was doing . . . ?' Sara echoed in a choked voice.

'Yes,' he snapped tautly. 'Spending the night with your lover wasn't supposed to be conducive to his peace of mind, was it?'

'Eddie wasn't my lover—'

'Wasn't?' Dominic cut in sharply. 'Does that mean he is now?' He grasped her arms and shook her. 'Does it, Sara?'

'And if he were?' Her eyes blazed with anger. She was exhausted from her sleepless night, crying with the pain of her sister's illness, and aching with the love she felt towards Dominic. Just to have him touch her, even in anger like this, was an agony of pleasure almost too much to bear. She shook out of his grasp, anger her only form of defence against his overwhelming attraction. 'What does it have to do with you?' she asked him defiantly.

He thrust her even farther away from him. 'Not a lot, apparently. What time did you get home? And don't ask what that has to do with me, I just wanted to know what time Marie got to bed.'

There was silent condemnation in his glacial blue eyes, and all fight left her. 'She was already in bed when I got home just after three,' she told him dully.

His mouth tightened. 'Why him, Sara?' he ground out fiercely.

'Why him—? He isn't my lover, Dominic,' she admitted softly. 'I just cried on his shoulder a little.'

'You found his preferable to mine?'

She swallowed hard. 'After what I said to you last night I doubted you would ever talk to me again. Dominic—'

'No more recriminations, Sara,' he advised grimly.

'I wasn't going to accuse, I was going to apologize! What I said to you was unforgivable. You obviously love Marie very much, and I—I'm only sorry I can't be her.' She looked down at her kneading hands.

He drew a ragged breath. 'Sara—'

The lounge door opened noisily to admit Marie. 'Good morning, everyone.' She smiled. 'Dominic!' She reached up and kissed him. 'Sara,' she said more softly, gently kissing her on the cheek. 'All right?' She held Sara's hands.

Tears filled Sara's eyes at her sister's concern, concern for *her*, when she was the one who was dangerously ill. 'I—I'm fine,' she stumbled. 'I—Oh, God!' she collapsed into Marie's waiting arms, sobbing out her distress. 'I'm sorry,' she moved back seconds later, wiping away her tears. 'This is the last thing you need.'

'I don't mind,' Marie assured her. 'I realize it was a shock for you.'

Sara gave the ghost of a smile. 'Not as much as it must have been for you.'

Her sister shrugged. 'I've got used to it. You will too, in time.'

'Never!' Sara vowed vehemently.

'I hate to interrupt,' Dominic said quietly, 'but my mother is expecting us, Marie.'

'Of course.' She nodded, smiling.

'You—you're going out?' Sara asked dazedly.

Marie moved to Dominic's side. 'I'm not being trite, but life has to go on. I'm lunching with Dominic's mother.'

She nodded. 'Of course. I—I'll see you later, shall I?'

She knew Marie was right, life did have to go on, but for her life was limited—and it didn't seem fair. There had to be something they could do, something *she* could do. She wouldn't let all the life and vitality in Marie die without a fight.

Her father was still asleep, and she didn't want to disturb him. But she wanted Simon Forrester's address, wanted to talk to him about Marie, find out if there really was nothing that could be done for her.

She did something in that moment that she had never done before, she deliberately violated someone else's privacy, looking through the address book on her father's desk in his study, sure that Simon Forrester's address would be in there, it was sure to be somewhere it could be found at all times.

The telephone number was there, but no address, so she called him instead. He might not even be in, it was a Sunday after all, and like most busy men he probably liked to relax on his day off.

The telephone rang only twice before it was picked up. 'Forrester here' was barked down the telephone.

Oh, dear, he didn't sound very happy! 'It's Sara Hamille, Mr Forrester,' she began tentatively.

'Ah, yes.' His voice mellowed somewhat. 'You want to see me, hmm?'

'Yes,' she answered dazedly. 'But how did you know?'

'I could say telepathy,' he said in an amused voice. 'But if I did I would be lying. Your father telephoned me last night, so I knew I would hear from you today. Come over, my dear, and we'll have a little chat about your sister.'

'You're sure I won't be causing you any inconvenience?'

'Not at all,' he said warmly. 'Come over now and we'll have lunch together. I'll expect you in a few minutes.'

She obtained his address and rang off. She hadn't expected him to agree to see her so soon, but she felt grateful that he could, leaving a message with Granger that she would be out to lunch, knowing her father would worry about her when he found her gone.

Simon Forrester's house was impressive, and surely much too big for one man. He probably had a wife and family, although he hadn't given that impression on the telephone.

He had neither wife nor family, and lived in this big house alone. Although he didn't look as if he spent much of his time alone; there was a roguish smile on his lips as he appraised her from head to foot.

'Let's go into the drawing room,' he suggested with a smile, very casually dressed in denims and a light blue shirt, looking nothing like the famous surgeon he undoubtedly was. 'Now, what would you like to know?' he asked once they were both seated.

A direct man himself, Simon Forrester expected her to be equally direct. 'I want to know what you can do to save my sister,' she told him simply.

He raised dark eyebrows. 'And what makes you think I can do anything?'

Her hands wrung together as she sat on the edge of her seat. 'I just know that you can,' she told him with feeling. 'Don't tell me how I know, I just do.'

Simon Forrester nodded. 'Your father told me about this affinity you have with Marie.'

'You don't think it's stupid?'

'Not at all. It often happens with identical twins. You found several similar illnesses that occurred during your childhood, I believe, and yet I'm sure that if you really went into this deeply you would find other similarities. You and Marie are incredibly alike.'

Even down to loving the same man! 'Then there is something you can do for her,' she persisted. 'I just know there is.'

'There is a chance—'

'I knew it!' Her eyes glowed, there was an air of excitement about her.

'A chance neither your father nor Marie is willing to take,' he finished.

Sara frowned. 'I don't understand. Surely any chance is better than none at all?'

Simon Forrester was deadly serious now, his flirtatious air completely gone. 'Not when there's a chance you could be dead, or as good as.'

She went white. 'You mean—'

He stood up to pace the room, as if impatient with his own inability to bring a happy ending to Marie's suffering. 'The brain is the most sensitive organ in the body, the slightest mistake with that and—well, any number of things could happen, and do.'

'You mean she could be paralyzed?'

'Or have permanent brain damage,' he affirmed.

'Oh, God!' She felt sick. Hope had been given to her only to be taken away again.

'Yes.' He sighed. 'It isn't much of a choice, is it?'

'No.' She swallowed hard, and stood up. 'I think I should be on my way now. I—Thank you for giving me your time.' She couldn't even begin to think about eating lunch now, and she knew Simon Forrester sensed that, as he did not press her at all.

His expression was full of compassion. 'I wish there were some sort of guarantee I could give you that I could bring Marie through an operation of this kind, but unfortunately that isn't possible. Marie claims she would rather die than be imperfect in that way. In a way I can understand that—brain damage, of any kind, isn't like losing an arm or a leg.'

Sara was very depressed when she arrived home, although she did her best to put on a brave face for her father.

When Dominic suddenly arrived home with Marie, a Marie obviously in agony, both Sara and her father helped to get her to her room.

'Oh, God! Oh, God!' she kept groaning.

'What happened?' their father asked Dominic anxiously once they had got Marie into bed in her darkened room, leaving her as she seemed to drift off into a restless sleep.

Dominic paced up and down the lounge. 'Apparently the pain started in the night—'

'I thought so.' Sara sighed. 'She was very restless,' she explained. 'I—I went in and sat with her for a while.'

'She didn't tell anyone because she didn't want us to worry,' Dominic continued harshly. 'She finally half collapsed with the pain just after lunch.'

'This can't go on.' Sara's father shook his head. 'Just lately the headaches have become worse, more frequent, with much more pain. 'I—Oh, God, I'm afraid we're going to lose her!'

'No!' Sara denied shrilly. 'There's the operation.'

Dominic sighed heavily. 'Marie says no.'

'But we can't just let her die!'

He put a hand up to his temple. 'I've tried to talk her into having the operation, but she won't even listen to me.'

'Then maybe she'll listen to me,' Sara told him fiercely. 'I won't let her die without putting up a fight!'

'Marie isn't you, Sara,' Dominic said softly. 'You would fight, Marie would rather die than risk being paralyzed or retarded.'

'That isn't true,' she denied harshly. 'Do you know how terrified she is of dying? Death petrifies her, gives her nightmares. In fact, I'm sure it's this fear that triggers off half of her headaches.'

'She told you about—about this fear?' her father rasped.

'Yes.'

'Then I want you to try and persuade her to have the operation. I think if anyone can do it you can.'

She hesitated. 'Dominic?'

He looked at her with tormented eyes. 'I agree with your father, you're the only person who might be able to do it.'

'Then I'll try.'

'Thank you.' He squeezed her hand.

She had to try and save her sister, even if it meant losing any chance of ever being able to have Dominic herself. There could never be any happiness for her with Dominic anyway; she could always only ever be Marie's substitute.

Marie was moving about restlessly when she entered the room, wide awake. 'Is the doctor coming?' she groaned.

'Yes.' Sara soothed her brow as she had the night she had stayed with her. 'And when he arrives I want you to agree to have this operation.'

'No!' Marie shuddered. 'Never! I don't want to be a vegetable in a wheelchair, unloved and unable to love.'

Sara held her tightly to her. 'You must know Dominic will always love you, no matter what happens.'

Marie looked up at her with wild frightened eyes. 'No man could love me if I were like that.'

'Dominic would,' Sara said with certainty.

'No. No, he wouldn't. He would hate me—'

'You know that isn't true. Marie, you're my sister, a part of myself.' She gripped her arms tightly. 'Wouldn't you rather die fighting?'

'I don't want to die at all!'

'I know that, darling, I know. But we all have to die sometime. I know which way I would prefer.'

Marie shook her head. 'You're different from me.'

She knew that, Dominic had just told her so, and there was no question about which one of them he preferred. And if it were humanly possible she was going to bring Marie through this for him.

'I may be different from you, Marie,' she said with determination. 'But if I had someone in love with me, someone who wanted to marry me, to be with me for ever and ever, then I'd want to fight this thing.'

Marie's eyes were huge. 'You would?'

'Of course.' Sara's voice became less heated as she realized Marie was actually listening to her now. 'You can't just sit back and let life deal you a blow like this. You have to have this operation, for yourself, for Dad, and most of all for Dominic.'

'And for you too?'

'Yes, for me too.' Sara blinked back the tears, wishing she could stop being so emotional. She couldn't be helping the situation.

Marie was calming. 'You would stay with me all the time?'

'As much as they would let me,' Sara agreed eagerly.

Marie bit her lip. 'I'm not sure...'

'Just think of the future, Marie.'

'The future?' She sighed. 'There hasn't been one to think of lately.'

'Well, think of it now. Think of being with the man you love for all time, of having his children.'

'Oh, yes,' Marie gave a dreamy smile, 'I would like that, Sara.'

'Then take the one chance you've got. Please!' she added pleadingly as Marie still seemed to hesitate. 'Children, Marie,' she repeated, although the thought of Marie being the mother of Dominic's children caused her actual physical pain. 'Children who look just like their father,' she said softly, achingly.

Marie drew a ragged breath. 'I—I'll do it,' she said after long troubled minutes.

Sara swallowed hard. 'You—you will?'

'Yes.' Her sister nodded.

'You won't change your mind?'

Marie licked her dry lips. 'No.'

Sara hugged and kissed her, both of them laughing and crying at the same time, Marie's headache apparently forgotten.

A knock sounded on the door before Dominic entered the room. 'The doctor's here, Marie.' He frowned as they both beamed at him. 'What's happened?'

Sara stood up. 'I'll leave you two alone.' She moved to the door, unintentionally brushing past Dominic as she went out, her breath catching in her throat at the warm vitality of him. 'I—er—I'll send the doctor up in a minute.' She hastily closed the door and fled down the stairs.

When Dominic came down a few minutes later he was somewhat dazed. 'How did you do it?' he asked Sara softly.

She didn't even pretend to misunderstand him. 'I pointed out what a lovely future she had as your wife,' she said, looking down, biting her bottom lip, 'as the mother of your children.'

'And that caused this change of heart?'

Her head went back. 'Yes.'

'Well, of course it would,' her father said excitedly. 'We should have thought of it before, Dominic, should have talked about the future instead of the present. God, I don't care how it came about, I'm just glad she's agreed at last.'

His arm went about Sara's shoulders. 'I don't know how to thank you.'

'I don't want or need thanks. I just hope that Mr. Forrester can operate now, before Marie has time to have second thoughts.'

Dominic frowned. 'Do you think she might?'

She swallowed hard. 'Not if I keep reminding her of her future as your wife.'

'Sara—'

'I think I can hear Mr. Forrester,' she interrupted brightly, turning towards the door, swallowing down the raw emotion she felt at Dominic's husky exclamation. Why couldn't he leave her alone now? Couldn't he see how the thought of him and Marie as husband and wife was breaking her up?

Simon Forrester looked very pleased when he came into the room. 'If I could just use your telephone, Michael? I want to get Marie to hospital as soon as possible.'

'You're going to do it now?' Sara's father asked. 'To-day?'

The doctor nodded. 'I don't think we have any time to lose.'

After that things moved very fast. The hospital room was arranged, the ambulance sent for. Sara herself went in the ambulance with her sister, Dominic and her father following behind in Dominic's car.

'She's already sedated,' the doctor warned Sara as she joined Marie in the ambulance. 'So don't expect a great deal of conversation from her,' he smiled, patting her hand comfortingly.

For the first part of the journey Marie seemed to be asleep, but Sara sat and held her hand anyway, sure that her sister could feel her presence beside her, could even draw on some of her strength to help her get through this.

It felt weird to be travelling through London in an ambulance, the siren wailing to warn the other traffic of the seriousness of the patient inside.

'Sara? Sara!' Marie opened bleary eyes; their journey was almost over.

'I'm here,' Sara reassured her, bending forward into Marie's vision.

'Tell him I love him, Sara. No matter what happens I want you to tell him I love him.'

'He already knows,' Sara said huskily.

'No,' Marie shook her head, her voice slurred from the sedation. 'No, he doesn't know. Tell—tell Danny I love him.'

'Danny?' Sara repeated sharply, frowning heavily. 'Surely you mean Dominic? Marie, it's Dominic you love, Dominic you're going to marry.'

'Tell—tell Danny I love him,' Marie repeated, dozing back into a drugged sleep.

Sara frowned. Tell *Danny* she loved him?

CHAPTER TEN

IT WAS A LONG night, not least because of Sara's utter confusion about Marie's emotions. Had she really meant for her to tell Danny, Dominic's brother, that she loved him? It didn't seem very likely. Marie had probably been confused by the sedative, had gone back into the past, to last summer when she and Danny were dating. Consequently, Sara didn't make that call to Danny, sure that there had been some sort of mistake.

Dominic looked ghastly, pacing the waiting room they had been shown into like a caged lion. There were lines of tension beside his mouth, a grayness beneath his tan, and the last thing he needed to be told right now was that Marie had talked of another man before falling asleep.

The operation seemed to have been going on for hours, and the strain of it all was beginning to tell on their father. He looked haggard, dark shadows beneath his eyes, a weary droop to his shoulders.

'How the hell much longer are they going to be?' Dominic muttered, but received no answer as he continued to talk to himself in that low angry tone.

Sara stood up. 'Would either of you like a cup of coffee?'

Her father gave a wry smile. 'I think it's starting to run out of my ears already.'

'Oh.' She sat down again.

'I'll have one,' Dominic requested huskily.

She stood up again. 'Black?'

'Please,' he nodded.

He didn't really want the coffee, he knew it and so did she, but Dominic had sensed her need to do something, to feel useful at a time when they were all powerless to do what they really wanted to do, and that was to save Marie.

She was out in the corridor, putting money into the coffee machine, when Danny walked into the hospital, a plaster across the bridge of his nose.

'How is she?' he immediately demanded to know. 'How's Marie?'

'We don't know yet.' Sara shrugged. 'She's still in theater.'

He drew a ragged breath. 'I came as soon as I found out. Do you have any idea how long they'll be?'

'None,' she told him gently, aware that if her father and Dominic looked ill, Danny looked ten times worse.

'Where's Dominic?' he scowled.

'With my father.'

Danny sighed, gingerly touching his nose. 'Do you think he would mind if I waited with them?'

'I'm sure he wouldn't,' she assured him warmly. 'I doubt he even remembers your fight, Danny.'

'Probably not,' he acknowledged heavily.

'Come on!' She took hold of his arm.

Her father gave Danny an absentminded nod as he recognised him, while Dominic scowled heavily when he saw his brother, evidence that he hadn't forgotten their last meeting at all.

'Your coffee.' She left Danny to cross the room to Dominic, holding out the plastic cup to him.

'Thanks.' His expression was brooding as he took it. 'What's he doing here?' His eyes were narrowed on his brother.

She put her hand on his arm. 'He heard about Marie,' she explained softly. 'He's concerned, Dominic.'

'Yes.' He sighed. 'Yes, I suppose he is.'

'Go and talk to him,' she encouraged.

'Mmm, I suppose I should apologize for breaking his nose.'

Her eyes widened. 'It really is broken?'

Dominic nodded. 'So my mother informed me. She wasn't very happy with the situation. Danny and I used to argue when we were younger, but not lately.'

'It was my fault, I'm sorry.' Sara sighed. 'I should have explained what had happened, but I was just so shocked.'

'Of course you were.' He squeezed her hand. 'I just—I jumped to conclusions.'

'As you have about Eddie too,' she put in softly.

Dominic frowned, his eyes narrowed as he looked at her searchingly. 'Is that the truth?'

She met his gaze unflinchingly. 'Yes.'

'Thank you for that,' he again squeezed her hand. 'I'd better go and reassure Danny that I don't intend turning violent on him again. He looks as if he could do with some reassuring about something.'

'It's Marie. He—Danny—'

'I know,' Dominic cut in harshly. 'I'm well aware of my brother's feelings towards Marie. He loves her, he's always loved her.'

Sara's eyes widened. 'Knowing that you still asked Marie to marry you, even though you must have realized how hurt your brother would be?'

'Danny's feelings were considered—'

'And discarded,' she said scornfully, turning away. 'As mine were. Go and talk to Danny by all means, although whether or not he wants to speak to you is another matter entirely.'

'Sara—'

She shook off his hand. 'Just go, Dominic,' she told him vehemently.

'I'll go, for now. But we'll talk again, Sara. There are some things I have to tell you.'

Her head went back. 'There's nothing I want to hear from you. Please go and talk to Danny, I have to go to my father.' She walked away before he could make any further move to stop her.

Her father looked even worse now, and Sara made him sit down, holding his hand tightly as the door opened and Simon Forrester came in, still in his gown from operating.

The surgeon looked very tired. 'Surgically I've done everything I could,' he told them. 'Now we'll just have to wait and see.'

They took it in turns to sit with Marie through the night and most of the next day, and her father and Dominic were both with her when she woke up.

Sara had been sent home to rest, but she knew by her father's face when he arrived home that Marie had come through the operation with no harm to herself. She instantly started to cry, the strain of the last few days finally taking over.

'Hey!' her father chided, his relief obvious. 'You're supposed to be happy, not burst into tears!'

'I am happy,' she wailed. 'Is she really all right, Dad? Is it really all over?' She blinked back further tears.

'Really.' He crushed her to him. 'She asked for you.'

'Then I'll go to her. I—'

'Calm down, Sara!' He laughed, looking younger now that the tension was finally over. 'She's resting now, you can see her later.'

That first meeting with her sister was an emotional one, and during the next few weeks they became closer than ever, Sara spending most of her time at the hospital—when Dominic wasn't there. Dominic she avoided at all costs.

The bandage was finally removed from Marie's head, revealing that it would be a long time before the two of

them were again confused with each other. Marie's hair
was now a blond downy thatch only half an inch long. But
she was alive and out of danger, and that was the important thing.

'I feel ridiculous!' She put up a self-conscious hand to
her hair.

Sara smiled. 'You look beautiful.'

'That's what Dominic said,' Marie told her ruefully.

Sara's smile became brittle. 'Well, he should know.'

Dominic was the one to drive Marie home when the time
came for her discharge, his arm about her waist to support her into the house. At the first sight of him in several
weeks all Sara's love towards him came bounding back, her
lashes instantly lowering over her revealing eyes.

It was agony to watch his solicitous concern for Marie,
so she made her escape as quickly as she could, using a visit
to Eddie as her reason for excusing herself.

'Sounds serious,' Marie teased. 'Doesn't it, Dominic?'

'I don't know.' His gaze was intent on Sara. 'Is it?'

She daren't look at him, daren't risk giving herself away.
'I don't know that myself, yet,' she said lightly, knowing
that she was lying. Eddie and she were friends, and that
was all they would ever be. 'I'll let you know if it is.'

'Before the wedding, I hope,' Dominic said tautly.

'We mustn't tease her.' Marie laughed.

Sara made good her escape, wondering how Marie had
ever gained the impression that Dominic was teasing. He
had been deadly serious, his expression grim.

When she arrived home later that evening Marie called
her into her bedroom, patting the side of the bed for her to
sit down beside her.

Sara did so. 'Shouldn't you be asleep?'

'Yes,' Marie grinned. 'But I wanted to talk to you.
How's Eddie? I like Eddie.'

'He's well,' Sara replied guardedly.

Her sister laughed. 'I really was only teasing earlier about you and Eddie being serious.'

'I hope so,' she grimaced. 'Eddie is in no more of a hurry to get married than I am.'

'Dominic is.'

Sara looked up sharply. 'Dominic is what?'

Marie sighed. 'In a hurry to get married.'

Sara licked her suddenly dry lips. 'Is he?' she said brightly. 'Well, you've been engaged for some time, and now that you're well I suppose—'

'He doesn't want to marry me, Sara,' Marie interrupted.

'Don't be silly!' Sara's smile seemed to be fixed on her lips, a bright meaningless smile. 'Of course he wants to marry you—'

'No,' Marie insisted softly. 'And I don't want to marry him. You remember what I said to you the night of my operation?'

'A-about loving Danny?' It hadn't been mentioned since!

'Yes.' She nodded. 'Well, I do. I always have.'

Sara gasped. 'But—but Dominic!' This didn't seem to be making sense at all.

Marie sighed. 'It's a little complicated.'

'A little?' Sara scorned. 'I can't make any sense of it!'

'You will, I'll explain it to you. You see, Danny and I argued last summer, I can't even remember why now. Anyway, Dominic took me out for a while to try and cheer me up. Then I fell down the stairs.' She sighed. 'Danny came rushing round to see how I was, but—well, even then I think I must have sensed there was more wrong with me than they first realized, and I turned Danny away. But he kept coming back, and then when I found out about my injury I knew I had to stop him.'

She swallowed hard. 'With Dominic?'

Marie nodded. 'But it was with Dominic's consent. We never intended getting married, I just couldn't agree to marry Danny knowing I was going to die. So Dominic and I became engaged, and Danny finally left me alone. You do see, don't you, Sara? Danny would be hurt less that way?'

'Maybe. But I think he should have been given the choice.'

'No.' Marie shook her head. 'He would only have been noble, insisted on marrying me anyway.'

Sara frowned, trying her best to understand. 'Where did Dominic stand in all this?'

Marie smiled. 'Dominic is the best friend I ever had.'

'Friend? But you haven't been behaving as if you were just *friends*.'

'All acting.' Her sister grinned. 'Enjoyable acting, I'll admit, but acting just the same. Then tonight he started discussing weddings for real.' She frowned. 'I couldn't understand it.'

'He loves you—'

'No, he doesn't.' Marie laughed at the thought of it.

'But—'

'He really doesn't love me, Sara, he just thought *I* wanted to marry *him*.'

'He did?'

'Yes, and that was your fault. Yes, it was,' Marie insisted as Sara went to protest. 'You told Dominic it was the thought of being his wife and having his children that had encouraged me to face the operation. What you said to me was that I had to think of being with the man I loved for ever and ever. And I did that—I thought of Danny.'

'*Danny?*' Sara gasped.

'Yes,' her sister smiled happily. 'I'm going to marry Danny. And you love Dominic, don't you?'

'I—'

'Don't you?' Marie quirked an eyebrow.

Sara licked her lips. 'Yes.'

Marie nodded. 'I told him you did.'

'You did *what*?'

'Don't look so annoyed.' Marie smiled. 'He didn't believe me.'

'Thank God for that! Don't you realize—'

'He loves you too, Sara.'

She paled. 'He—he what?'

'He loves you,' Marie repeated happily. 'I had my suspicions, the way you kept avoiding each other and everything, but tonight I knew for sure.'

'H-how did you know?'

'He told me,' Marie announced calmly.

Sara was beginning to wonder if she were hallucinating. Marie had only got engaged to Dominic so that Danny wouldn't get hurt, the man she really loved, and Dominic had aided her in this plan. And now Marie was going to marry Danny after all, and Dominic had admitted to Marie that he loved her, Sara. None of it sounded very plausible, and yet Marie seemed very confident.

'See?' Marie held up her bare left hand. 'No engagement ring. Danny is going to buy me one tomorrow.'

'Oh, he does know about this, then?' Sara mocked dazedly.

'Silly!' Her sister giggled. 'Of course he knows about it, although he was furious with Dominic and I when he found out what I had done.'

'I'm surprised he understood it!'

Marie eyed her teasingly. 'Don't you want to know more about Dominic loving you?'

Sara blushed and stood up to turn away. 'I don't believe he does. Oh, I know he's attracted to me, but only because I look like you. I think you're wrong about him not loving you, Marie. He must be very upset about your marrying his brother.'

'Not at all. He went and got Danny himself once I'd explained the misunderstanding to him.'

She shrugged. 'Just a cover-up to his real feelings—'

'What does it take to convince you?' Marie said impatiently. 'The man loves you, he wants to marry you.'

'M—Marry me?'

'That got your attention, hmm?' her sister teased. 'Of course Dominic wants to marry you, but he says you don't want him.'

'But he knows I do—I mean—well—' Sara blushed scarlet. 'I do,' she said lamely.

Marie's eyes twinkled mischievously. 'I won't ask how he knows. The thing is he doesn't,' she sobered. 'He says you despise him.'

She had only said that in the heat of the moment, surely he realized that. But it seemed not. She was almost afraid to believe what Marie was telling her, and yet her sister seemed so confident.

'I've never seen him like this before,' Marie continued at her silence. 'Dominic's always been like an older brother to me, always confident and in command—that's why I turned to him for help. But he's as uncertain as a schoolboy about you. I'm not sure I like to see him like that.'

'So you intend putting him out of his misery?' Sara was beginning to hope, to believe what Marie was telling her. Could Dominic have really meant it that night he had told her he loved her? Oh, God, she hoped so!

'No, I want you to do that. Tonight.'

'Now?' she exclaimed.

'Why not?' Marie shrugged.

'Because it's after twelve o'clock at night!'

Marie grinned. 'I'll make your excuses to Daddy in the morning.'

'In the—! Even if I did go and see Dominic now I'd be back tonight,' Sara claimed indignantly.

'Of course you would.'

'I would!'

'I just agreed, didn't I?' Marie gave her a look of exaggerated innocence.

'It was the way you agreed.'

Marie smiled. 'I know Dominic.'

'Do you indeed?' Sara's eyes flashed jealously.

'Not like that.' Her sister laughed. 'There was never anything like that between us. Now with you it's different, he goes all tense and white about the mouth when he talks about you—so much so that once he gets you alone I know he won't let you out of his sight.'

'Okay.' Sara sighed. 'You convinced me. I'll go and see him.'

'Take my car.' Marie searched through her handbag for her keys. 'Daddy was going to buy you a car, but now that you're getting married I suppose Dominic will buy you one.' She held out the keys with a mischievous smile.

'Don't jump ahead,' Sara warned. 'No one said I was getting married.'

'You will be. Poor Daddy will be totally confused!'

Sara only wished she felt as confident about Dominic's feelings as Marie seemed to be. Could it really be true, had Dominic just been pretending with Marie, could it really be that she was the one he loved? Only he could tell her that.

He answered the door to her himself. 'Marie called me,' he revealed deeply.

Sara gave an angry sigh. 'I know she's my sister, and I love her dearly, but she's an interfering busybody.'

'She just called to tell me to expect you, Sara, nothing else.'

'Oh.' She bit her lip nervously. 'Can I come in?'

'Of course.' He opened the door wide. 'Although if you do,' he added huskily, 'I doubt I'll be able to let you out again.'

So Marie was right, she had to be. Sara looked up at Dominic with steady brown eyes. 'I don't want you to,' she said softly. 'I don't ever want to leave you again.'

Dominic swallowed hard, seeming to sway where he stood. 'God, I love you!' he groaned achingly.

She fell into his arms, holding him so tightly her arms ached. 'I love you, too,' she choked, any last doubts dispelled.

He pressed featherlight kisses down her throat, his lips warm and fevered. 'Marie told you everything?'

'Everything,' she nodded, raising her mouth invitingly. 'I'm so sorry I ever doubted you.'

'It was my fault for not telling you the truth. I wanted to—God, how I wanted to, but I couldn't break a confidence like that, not even for the woman I love. And you are the woman I love, Sara.' His mouth lowered to hers.

He was like a thirsty man in a desert, devouring her with his love and passion, his caresses heated, and he carried her over to the sofa. They lay close together, murmuring words of love between caresses, hours passing as if minutes, lost to each other as they frantically tried to convince each other of their love.

Dominic lay against her breasts, his arms possessive. 'The first time I saw you I knew you were the most beautiful thing I'd ever seen.'

'You thought I was Marie!'

He shook his head. 'I don't think I did, not even then. I was excited just looking at you, and that had never happened with Marie.'

'She assures me you're only friends,' Sara taunted, smoothing the darkness of his hair.

'We are. Marie has always been like a kid sister to me, you were something else completely, right from the first. I become aroused just looking at you.'

'Dominic!' She blushed her confusion.

'But I do. I want to love you, darling.' He kissed her bare breast.'

'Yes.'

'You said that once before, in exactly the same way—'

'And you turned me down,' she remembered with pain.

'Because of your innocence! I was tied to Marie, by loyalty if nothing else, and it wasn't fair to involve you when I couldn't marry you.' He caressed the soft curve of her breast with his tongue.

'Did you want to marry me even then?'

'I did, and I do. Will you marry me, Sara?'

'Yes! Yes to marriage, and yes to—'

He put silencing fingers over her lips. 'I can wait until after we're married.'

'Well, I can't.' She looked at him with love-drugged eyes. 'I want to stay with you tonight, Dominic. Tonight and every other night.'

He gave a rueful smile. 'Tonight I might get away with, then I think we'll have to wait until after the wedding. Otherwise your father might take a shotgun to me.'

Sara held him fiercely to her. 'I'm so glad I came to England, so glad I found my father and Marie, and so very, very glad I found you. I love you so, Dominic.'

'And I love you too.' He picked her up and took her into the bedroom, to the first night of a lifetime of nights together.

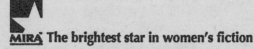

UNLOCK THE DOOR TO GREAT ROMANCE AT BRIDE'S BAY RESORT

Join Harlequin's new across-the-lines series, set in an exclusive hotel on an island off the coast of South Carolina.

Seven of your favorite authors will bring you exciting stories about fascinating heroes and heroines discovering love at Bride's Bay Resort.

Look for these fabulous stories coming to a store near you beginning in January 1996.

Harlequin American Romance #613 in January
Matchmaking Baby by Cathy Gillen Thacker

Harlequin Presents #1794 in February
Indiscretions by Robyn Donald

Harlequin Intrigue #362 in March
Love and Lies by Dawn Stewardson

Harlequin Romance #3404 in April
Make Believe Engagement by Day Leclaire

Harlequin Temptation #588 in May
Stranger in the Night by Roseanne Williams

Harlequin Superromance #695 in June
Married to a Stranger by Connie Bennett

Harlequin Historicals #324 in July
Dulcie's Gift by Ruth Langan

Visit Bride's Bay Resort each month wherever
Harlequin books are sold.

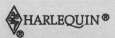

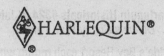

Bestselling authors

ELAINE COFFMAN
RUTH LANGAN

and

MARY McBRIDE

Together in one fabulous collection!

OUTLAW Brides

Available in June wherever Harlequin
books are sold.

HARLEQUIN ®